THE PERFUME GARDEN

THE
PERFUME
GARDEN

KATE LORD BROWN

THOMAS
DUNNE
BOOKS

ST. MARTIN'S GRIFFIN

New York

THOMAS DUNNE BOOKS.
An imprint of St. Martin's Press.

THE PERFUME GARDEN. Copyright © 2015 by Kate Lord Brown. All rights reserved. Printed in the United States of America. For information, address St. Martin's Press, 175 Fifth Avenue, New York, N.Y. 10010.

www.thomasdunnebooks.com
www.stmartins.com

"Walking Away" by Cecil Day-Lewis (from *The Gate and Other Poems*, published in 1962) is used with the kind permission of the Cecil Day-Lewis Estate.

The Library of Congress has cataloged the hardcover edition as follows:

Brown, Kate Lord.
    The perfume garden / Kate Lord Brown.
        p. cm.
    ISBN 978-1-250-04827-1 (hardcover)
    ISBN 978-1-4668-4893-1 (e-book)
    ISBN 978-1-250-07515-4 (Canadian edition)
    I. Title.
    PR6102.R6912P43 2015
    823'.92—dc23

                                        2014040688

    ISBN 978-1-250-09140-6 (trade paperback)

Our books may be purchased in bulk for promotional, educational, or business use. Please contact your local bookseller or the Macmillan Corporate and Premium Sales Department at 1-800-221-7945, extension 5442, or by e-mail at MacmillanSpecialMarkets@macmillan.com.

A different version of this book was published in the United Kingdom in 2013 by Corvus.

First St. Martin's Griffin Edition: May 2016

10 9 8 7 6 5 4 3 2 1

For VL and KL,

PB and DB

I have had worse partings, but none that so
Gnaws at my mind still. Perhaps it is roughly
Saying what God alone could perfectly show—
How selfhood begins with a walking away,
And love is proved in the letting go.

—CECIL DAY-LEWIS, *"Walking Away"*

You can go proudly. You are history. You are legend.

—*La Pasionaria's Final Speech*
to the International Brigades,
Barcelona, October 1938

THE PERFUME GARDEN

ONE

You see, Em, the trouble is they—the doctors that is—said it will give me "closure" (what a ghastly word), to leave a letter for you. I said, "Do you really think I can distill a lifetime's worth of experience into a single letter? Can I say everything I want to my daughter on a few sheets of paper?" I cannot. You know me, I never did stop rabbiting on, did I, darling?

An image of Liberty came to Emma then—her mother sitting on the kitchen table in her grandmother Freya's house. It must have been the late 1970s, because, against the morning sun, Liberty's hair was a chestnut halo of Kate Bush crimping, and Blondie was on the radio. She was flapping her arms as she talked, and Freya was doubled over laughing. Emma was curled up in the dog basket by the stove, eating toast as she cuddled Charles's new pug puppy. That's what she remembered—the certain smell of home, of coffee percolating, fresh toast, the dry biscuit smell of the dog as he pawed at the green enamel "Head Girl" badge pinned to her woolen sweater. Some people's memories lie in images or songs, but for Emma it was always fragrance. Liberty had taught her well, and even as a child she instinctively detected the harmonious notes of the scent accord that to her conjured "home."

"Emma, do get up, darling," Freya had said. "Look at you, your school uniform is covered with hair." Emma remembered the warmth of the dog, the delicious fawn belly wriggling in her small hands. She remembered how Liberty had tickled her until they were both on the floor giggling, the puppy leaping around them. As her mother hugged her, Emma breathed in the scent of her perfume. Roses—Liberty always smelled like a rose garden in full bloom to her: warm, sunlit, a pure *soliflore*.

As you'll see, I got a bit carried away. I've left you a whole box of letters, one for every occasion I can think of. And I've enclosed my last notebook. I like to think of you picking up where I left off, Em. Promise me you'll carry on. Use it. Fill it with wonderful things.

Emma leaned her elbow on the suitcase at her side. She had been traveling for months, but as the number 22 Routemaster bus lurched through the lunchtime traffic along the King's Road, she felt the days fall away. It was a typical cool, gray London morning, a light autumn breeze scurrying leaves along the pavements. Nothing had changed, except her. The nausea that had dogged her for months welled up again, and she rummaged through her pocket for a mint. The lining had torn, and as she read Liberty's note, she wriggled her index finger down to the hem, searching in vain.

She had turned to the last page in her mother's notebook a hundred times, pen poised, and frozen, unable to pick up where Liberty had left off. Nothing seemed wonderful enough. Emma scanned the note one last time. It was the only one she had taken with her on her travels, and she had read it so many times the paper was falling apart along the folds. The letters were waiting for her, unopened, in a black lacquer box in Liberty's studio.

After her mother's will had been read, and Joe had left, Emma had sat looking at the box for hours as dawn light filtered through the sloping glass roof. She had placed it in the middle of Liberty's desk—a specially built perfumer's "organ" surrounded by tiered shelves of bottles, each one containing a note of fragrance. That was how Liberty had taught her their craft—to think of each essence as a musical note, each bottle on the organ as a key. This was where Liberty had composed all of her masterpieces, where Emma had played as a child. It was the place she still felt her mother's presence most.

The sound of milk bottles being delivered on the street below had roused her finally, and she had lifted off the lid of the box. She wasn't quite sure what she was expecting from Liberty—an explosion of confetti, a coiled paper snake to leap out. She laughed with relief when she saw her mother had simply painted the interior bright orange—her favorite color. Her hand trembled as she lifted the loose sheet of paper on top. Beneath was a parcel of letters tied with cerise velvet ribbon, and the small black notebook. The first envelope was marked "On Family." As Emma read her mother's accompanying note, tears filled her eyes.

I love you, Em. I am so terribly proud of the woman you have become. I can't bear the thought of leaving you, but know my love goes with you, will always be with you. I know that love lives on.

Mum x

She had been tempted to rip open all the envelopes that morning, to gorge hungrily on Liberty's words. Just reading the note over and over brought her closer. But she waited. When she told Freya she had decided to leave the letters in London while she traveled, Freya had laughed.

"It's up to you, Em," she said. "You always did save your treats, even as a child. I've never known anyone who could make a bar of chocolate last so long."

Emma took a deep breath, and gazed out of the bus window. It was almost her stop. *Perhaps it's time to stop saving the best till last,* she thought. She folded the note and slipped it into her mother's Moleskine notebook on her lap, flicking on through the pages illuminated with Liberty's flamboyant handwriting. Words leaped out at her—"neroli," "*duende,*" "passion." Her mother had pasted in cuttings alongside the notes and formulas for the new perfume she had been working on—pictures of orange groves, searing blue skies, a yellowed newspaper advert for a Robert Capa exhibition. It was the famous "falling soldier" picture. Emma traced her finger over the soldier's face, wondered what he was thinking at the moment when death caught him running down that hill. She wondered what he saw as he fell. As she touched the paper, she felt the contours of something beneath. She flipped to the next page and laid her hand on the smallest envelope Liberty had left in the box with the letters. On it, her mother had written an address: Villa del Valle, La Pobla, Valencia, Spain. Inside, there was just an old key. *I must ask Freya if she knows anything about this,* she thought. Emma had lain awake the night she opened that envelope, turning the key over in her hand, her mind full of possibilities. *Typical Mum,* she thought, remembering all the magical mystery tours Liberty had taken her on as a child, the trails of clues she had laid for Emma to follow to hidden presents. The chase, the anticipation, was always more fun than the present itself.

Emma turned the pages, glimpsed the melancholy, serene face of a Madonna, a photo of a whitewashed wall with flaming bougainvillea spilling over it. The notes became sparser, the hand less sure toward the end. She sensed Liberty had been looking back, as well as forward. Next to a pasted label from Chérie Farouche, the perfume Liberty had created for Emma on her eighteenth birthday, she had written: "Some perfumes are, like children, innocent, as sweet as oboes, green as meadow sward—Baudelaire." It was still Emma's signature scent. On her it smelled like rain in a garden at first, fresh and intoxicating; then as the green top notes evaporated Emma always thought of the earth, of picking flowers in a forest with her mother. The heart note of lily of the valley and jasmine melded perfectly with the base of sandalwood and musk. Liberty always said the scent was like her— shy but surprisingly fierce. A photograph of Liberty with Emma as a baby was tucked into that page. She flicked on, unbearable longing piercing her as she looked at her mother's beautiful, open smile. Emma paused at her mother's final sketch of a new Liberty Temple perfume bottle, her hurried scrawl: *"Jasmine? Orange blossom, yes!"*

Then came the poignant empty spaces. The blank pages her mother had left her to fill. Emma blinked quickly as she touched the gold filigree locket around her neck. She hadn't expected to feel so upset returning home. For months, she had convinced herself that she was coping as she sleepwalked through endless meetings. Countries and hotel rooms kaleidoscoped in her mind. Her hand instinctively fell to the gentle swell of her stomach. *Something wonderful,* she thought. She pulled a pen from her bag, smoothed her hand over the first clean page, then wrote: "Spain."

TWO

SPAIN, SEPTEMBER 1936

Freya huddled in the back of the truck as it bumped along the road toward Madrid, a purple dressing gown tied over her head against the wind.

"Damn," she said under her breath as they hit another pothole and her pen skittered across the page. She hunched over her dog-eared copy of *Gone with the Wind*, the pages flapping in the breeze.

Spain is quite beautiful as you know, Charles, she wrote to her brother on the blank back page.

You simply must come. Thank you for the fruitcake by the way. It is a boost to get your letters. It seems like a lifetime since people showered us with flowers at Victoria Station as we left—was it only last month? The drive down from the Spanish border was exhilarating. We had the truck loaded up with toffees and liquorice for the children. At every village we passed, they would come running to us. Women pressed oranges and melons on us—Charles you would not believe the bliss of cold melon when your throat is tight and dry from hours on the road.

We are desperately short of everything in the hospitals. The nurses are exhausted and hungry all the time, and the winter will be worse, but we mustn't grumble. You would not believe how brave and marvelous the people I am working with are. This poor country. I cannot bear it that this civil war is tearing it in two.

Come, as soon as you can. For the first time, there is only one choice for us. We cannot let the fascists crush democracy here. This is our war too, dear brother—every freedom we hold dear is in peril, and we cannot look away for today the fight is in Spain, but tomorrow it could be on our own doorstep.

The truck shuddered to a halt at the first checkpoint outside the city, and Freya looked up. Vehicles streamed past, and she heard a babble of voices, a phone ringing nonstop in the guardhouse. Freya signed the note quickly and tore out the page, stuffing it in an envelope she had ready to send. She untied the arms of the dressing gown from under her chin, and shook out her bobbed blond hair.

"*Salud, compañero!*" she called to one of the guards. "The post?"

"He comes soon." The soldier motioned for her to pass him the letter. As the truck pulled away, she thrust it into his outstretched hand.

"*Gracias!*"

"*De nada.* You're welcome."

Freya sat back among the other nurses, and looked toward Madrid as they drove on toward the city. She had heard that fifty churches had been set ablaze, and acrid smoke still hung in the sky, dark and sulphurous. *This is it,* she thought, suddenly aware that they were driving right into the heart of the battle. Freya glanced at the pale faces of the nurses around her and saw her fear reflected there. *Pull yourself together,* she told herself. Her eyes smarted with the dusty wind buffeting her face. Freya's guts coiled with adrenaline as beyond the crashing noise of the trucks she heard in the distance the first thunderous boom and explosion of war.

In Cambridge, the last punts of the year drifted along the Backs on the River Cam, autumn leaves swirling in their wake. Charles tucked the letter from his sister Freya into the breast pocket of his tweed jacket, and settled back, his hands laced behind his head.

"How is she?" the fair-haired boy at the stern asked, heaving down on the pole.

"Freya? It sounds ghastly in Spain, to be honest."

"Shall we go or not?"

Charles thought of the copy of *Vu* he had seen the night before, of Robert Capa's photographs of the war. One of the students from King's had stood on a chair in the pub, thrust the magazine into the air, shouting above the noise of the bar that anyone in their right mind had to join the International Brigades and fight fascism in Spain. Charles was haunted by the photograph of the falling soldier he had seen, could almost feel the impact of the bullet, the thud of the body as it hit the ground.

"Charles!"

"Sorry, Hugo. I was just thinking."

"Thinking?" Hugo laughed. "A student of lepidoptery thinking instead of wasting time chasing butterflies, whatever next?"

Charles dipped his hand into the river and splashed water at him. "Hugo, you are my dearest friend, but I'd rather spend my days hunting butterflies than mucking around with those modernist daubs you call paintings—"

"Come on, Charles!" Hugo interrupted. "This matters—we can make a real difference in Spain. I heard there's a chap in Paris sneaking people down on the railway, or over the Pyrenees. I have an address on the Rue Lafayette that we can go to. There's a train of volunteers leaving in a couple of days from the Gare d'Austerlitz. Your friend Cornford said we could be at the training camp in Albacete in a few days."

Charles thought of the Movietone News headline he had seen the night before as the fug of cigarette smoke in the cinema joined the leaping black-and-white flames on the screen: *Civil War follows fascist revolt in unhappy country. All is turmoil.* Ever since General Franco's rebel Nationalist forces had staged a coup against the democratically elected Republican government in Spain in July, the students had talked of little else but joining the International Brigades to fight the rebels. *This is just the beginning,* he had thought, watching the scenes of carnage in the cinema. *If they take Spain, fascism will spread across Europe, perhaps the world.*

"Charles, let's go tomorrow—"

"I haven't squared everything with Crozier at the *Manchester Guardian* yet. If there's no job for us . . ."

"Then we shall just be common soldiers like the rest of them," Hugo said, laughing. "It would serve you right for spending your savings on that ridiculously expensive camera. You could have bought a car, Charles. Personally I shall just be taking a pencil and notebook."

"Photography is the future, Hugo. If people see a photo, or a film, they believe it, mark my words." He paused. "Still, perhaps it was a bit rash. If we don't get this job I can't afford my ticket down."

"You could always take wedding portraits if you don't make it as a photojournalist."

Charles scowled at him as he stood and took the pole. "Shut up, Hugo. For goodness sake, sit down. You'll tip the ruddy thing over." Clouds scudded across the sky, reflected in the windows of King's Chapel like a bridal train sweeping by. Rain began to pepper the smooth surface of the river.

"At least in Spain we might make a difference. Look at what is going on in my country, what Hitler is doing." Hugo's face fell for a moment. "I can't just hide away here in an ivory tower, much as it would please my parents. It's the first chance we've had to fight back. If we don't, Hitler, Mussolini, Franco . . . well, they'll take the whole of Europe." He lit a cigarette, flicked the match into the river. "Besides, it's a beautiful country. I can't bear to think of it being torn to pieces."

"I told you we came back too soon," Charles said. As the rain pattered down on his face, Charles remembered the shimmering June heat of the southern Spanish hillsides near his friend's old house in Yegen, the swish of the dry long grass against his legs, the scent of rosemary and lavender crushed underfoot as he hunted down butterflies. He thought of the snow on the Sierra Nevada, the stars that seemed to glow with unusual brilliance there. "Do you remember how beautiful it is? I can't believe the country is eating itself alive."

"Well, that's civil war." Hugo exhaled a plume of smoke. "The Spanish are a bloodthirsty lot. Bullfights and flamenco, peasants on mules—it's like the Middle Ages still."

"Perhaps it's better than all this," Charles said, idly watching a woman in a beige gabardine mackintosh who was walking a wheezing Labrador along the bank. "There's still passion. They look death square in the eye, see it as the ultimate, culminating moment of existence." He leaned toward Hugo. "The cemetery is the *tierra de la verdad*, their moment of truth. To the Spanish, all life is an illusion."

"I still say they are backward."

"No, they are in touch with the earth. They still believe in *hechiceras*, white witches, you know. They think they fly in the moonlight and meet on the threshing room floors. You have to watch out for the *brujas*, though, the black witches . . ."

"Don't be ridiculous," Hugo said, laughing. "You are a romantic,

Charles—perhaps the last of a dying breed." He held out his hand to his friend. "So, we shall go. Agreed? The world hardly needs another second-rate German artist, and for you there will always be butterflies if we return."

"When. When we return." Charles shook Hugo's hand, then stood back and laid his fingertips against the rough wool of his jacket, felt Freya's letter crinkle in his pocket. "It's our chance to stop this. Freya's right. If we don't fight the fascists on the roads to Madrid, we'll be fighting them on the King's Road next thing you know."

THREE

Emma leaped down onto the pavement from the bus, rose petals and golden ash leaves drifting at the steps of Chelsea Registry Office like hearts and bones. Her black coat swirled around her as she strode through the crowd, the heels of her polished tan boots clicking as she dragged her silver suitcase behind her, airline tags fluttering. She paused, looked up at the newly married couple embracing in the doorway. As their friends cheered, she walked on. *It could have been us,* she thought, searching through her bag as her phone rang.

"Hello. Emma Temple," she said, crooking the mobile against her shoulder as she turned into Flood Street.

"Thank God. I've been worried sick. Are you home yet?" Freya asked.

"Just." She smiled as she stopped outside Chelsea Manor Studios. A group of young Dutch tourists was taking photographs by the entrance. They stepped aside to let her pass, and one of the boys heaved her suitcase up to the door. "Thank you," she said.

"Is *Sergeant Pepper,* yes?" the boy said. "The Beatles?"

"Yes, that's right. They took the cover photo in my mum's studio." Emma was dizzy with jet lag, her eyes red and raw. All she wanted to do was collapse into bed, but their young faces touched her. "Here, let me." She beckoned for him to hand over the camera, and took a picture of the teenagers.

As they walked away she leaned against the doorway and shifted the phone. "Sorry. I've just arrived home. The flight was delayed."

"We've moved all your things in. It's a bit of a mess I'm afraid, but then the studio always was, even when your mother was alive." Freya paused. "I haven't unpacked the boxes. I thought you might want to clear out some of Liberty's things before you settle in?"

"There's no hurry. Thanks for taking care of everything. I couldn't bear to go back to the house." She frowned. "So she's moved in, then?"

"Delilah?" Freya's voice hardened. "Yes. Our Ms. Stafford didn't waste any time, though I wouldn't be surprised if she forced Joe to sell up and move to the States—"

"How is he?" Emma interrupted.

"Fine, he's fine. It's you I'm worried about. Have you seen the doctor yet?"

"Freya . . ."

"Don't worry, there's nobody here. They're all at lunch. I haven't told a soul, I promise."

"Let's keep it that way, at least until I speak to Joe."

"What a bloody mess," Freya said. "I could kill her, honestly. Delilah always was a cuckoo in the nest. I haven't spoken a word to her for weeks, not since you left. The atmosphere in the office has been hideous."

"I can imagine. I'm sorry everyone is caught up in this."

"What are you apologizing for? None of this is your fault, Emma. As I'm always telling you, you are too damn nice. When I think what she has done to you. That woman pushed her way into the company, and then . . ."

"She didn't force him to choose her, you know. It was Joe's decision."

"I know it's un-Christian of me, but I can't wait to see the look on her face when she finds out you are carrying his child."

Emma perched on her suitcase, rested her head wearily against the wall. "I'm thrilled about the baby, of course, but I can't say I feel proud about it. We had already separated when we . . ." Emma thought back to the day her mother's will was read.

"Only just. It's perfectly understandable that you needed each other. I hope— Well, let's hope he sees sense."

"It's too late, Freya. I thought, when he came to me that night he'd chosen me." Emma paused. "That's why I had to get away. I feel like a complete fool."

"No. You're far from that. Oh, it breaks my heart. You two were practically children when you met."

"Maybe it would have made a difference if I'd agreed to marry him."

"Nonsense."

"Joe's always been more traditional than us."

"No, Delilah has been after him for years." Freya clicked her tongue in annoyance. "You know, she had the nerve to say to me that you took him from her!"

"I hope she hasn't been giving you a hard time while I've been away?"

"Don't worry about me, darling. I can handle Ms. Stafford—my cat has more attitude than her."

"Anyway, they were just friends when I met them at Columbia." Emma frowned. She had always wondered if that was true. "You know what he said, last time I saw him? He was confused. He said he loves us both."

Freya muttered something under her breath, and said, "Joe's not cut out for complicated affairs of the heart. He doesn't know what he's doing, he's still upset about your mother."

Emma rubbed the bridge of her nose. "He was as devastated as us when Mum finally died."

"They were very close. In some ways I'm glad Liberty's not here to see all this, though she would have loved being a grandmother. I feel positively ancient at the thought of being a great-grandmother . . ." Freya's voice became muffled as she covered the receiver to speak to someone. "Listen, the office is filling up again. Are you coming over?"

"In a while. I'm going to grab a shower." She paused. "I guess I should call Joe."

"He's in New York. *They* are in New York."

"Delilah went with him?"

"Of course," Freya said. "She couldn't risk the deal folding, could she? Not now that she can smell the money. I hope you're not rushing into this. You don't have to sell the company, you know."

Emma sighed. "Yes I do. There's nothing here for me now. We've spent years building the business, but the American offer is too good to pass up. It's a clean break."

"Your mother would hate it. She always wanted it to be a family business, for the three of you to carry on. She would never, never have split the company between you all in her will if she had known what Delilah was up to."

"What can I do? It seemed best she didn't know about their affair." Emma closed her eyes. "I'm glad she didn't know. Anyway, now Joe and Delilah have a controlling interest together. There's nothing we can do. Once we've sold, I can move on."

"Do you think so? You know the Americans will want you to stay—Liberty groomed you to be the face of the company."

"I was just window dressing. We all built the brand together." Her face fell as she glanced along the street. A line of five-year-olds from Hill House walked past. How many times had she and Liberty walked that route from school? *All those precious, unremarked moments, gone.* Emma's throat tightened, tears pricked her eyes. No matter how hard she was working, Liberty was always there to pick her up—often late, but she always came. It was their time, after school and in the early mornings, the only times Emma ever had her mother to herself. *Backward and forward, hundreds of times, and I can only remember a handful of moments.*

"It just seems a damn shame, after everything we've worked for."

"Hm? No, it's time for a new start. Hey—you can retire at last," Emma teased as she riffled through her beaten-up tan Mulberry handbag for her keys.

"Me?" Freya let out a short, deep laugh. "That's what Charles said. It will never happen. Work keeps me going. If I wasn't pottering around the office getting under everyone's feet, what would I do?"

Emma smiled. Liberty had never had the heart to force Freya to retire. "How is Charles?"

"Same as ever."

"I am sorry I missed your birthday last month."

"I'd rather forget I am eighty-four, darling. Why don't you come over and have a bite with us?"

"Thanks, but I'll grab a sandwich from the café. I just want to sort everything out here as quickly as possible, and head off to Spain."

"Yes," Freya said, drawing out the word. "We really need to talk about that."

"Please don't start. I know you hate the idea, but it's just what I need. I had no idea Mum had bought a house down there."

"Darling, it's not at all what you think. I know you—you're picturing some divine little finca, a whitewashed farmhouse with jasmine spilling over the walls."

"I am not." She was, of course.

"Spain . . ." Freya paused. "Well, I was surprised when your mother told me she had bought the house."

"Why don't you come with me? It's about time you took a break."

"No," Freya said firmly. "Charles and I swore we'd never set foot in Spain again."

"What happened there? Neither of you have ever talked—"

"It doesn't matter now," Freya interrupted. "It's a lifetime ago."

"Do you have any idea why Mum picked Valencia, though? That is where you were nursing, wasn't it?"

"Valencia, Madrid . . ." Freya cleared her throat. "We moved around a lot, wherever we were needed."

"Well it sounds beautiful. I've been reading about it online. You know, they call it the Spanish Eden." Emma's thoughts filled with neroli-scented orange groves, gardens rich with jasmine, and cool churches infused with heady incense.

"Of course I know," Freya snapped. "It's a ridiculous idea. I don't know what Liberty was thinking of. From what she said, no one has done a thing to the house for decades. It's probably a death trap, and you will have your hands full with the baby. You're mad! You have no idea the amount of work a child is. You need family around you."

"I need—" Emma paused. "To do this." She heard Freya take a deep breath.

"You're as willful as your mother."

"I know I can make a go of it. I've worked my whole life, and thanks to Mum I've always saved. I can afford to take a few months off, get help to sort out the house, maybe even someone to help with the baby."

"I know, I know. You're a sensible girl, you always were."

"I promise I'll be back and forth. I'm just going to use it for holidays, so it's not like I'm taking your grandchild away from you."

Freya fell silent. "Of course. Look, I don't want to argue the moment you're home. Come over once you've settled in."

"I will."

"Love you, Em," Freya said.

"You too, Gammy." Emma twisted the gold locket at her neck, winding the chain around her finger. "I couldn't have got through all this without you, but what I need now is a new beginning."

FOUR

MADRID, SEPTEMBER 1936

Q*ué pasa?* How was the meeting?" Rosa strolled up to the café, her hand on the gun at her belt. She was dressed like a Republican militia, but her movements had the rhythm and precision of a dancer, and her tightly belted *mono* revealed a waist as tiny as a child's. She glanced down the cobbled alleyway to the barricades, saw three men crouched over a single plate of food as the red, yellow, and purple Republican flag fluttered overhead. The walls of the street were lined with bright revolutionary posters. DEFENDEOS CONTRA FASCISMO! one cried beneath bones in the shape of a swastika. Rosa adjusted her beret, smoothed her cropped black hair against the nape of her neck. Jordi sat on the hood of the old bus, waiting in the sunshine for her. He was watching a flock of sheep being herded through the city, escaping the battlefields and heading for Valencia. He turned at the sound of her voice, his dark brilliantined hair gleaming. When he saw her, he leaped down and raised his fist in greeting.

"*Señorita Montez. Mi compañera.*" He grinned, pulled her into his arms. "*Mi amor,*" he murmured, and kissed her. "You didn't miss much. Some anarchist from Valencia has annoyed the Communists," he said as his lips grazed her neck. "He doesn't want the Russians involved—Spanish affairs concern only the Spanish, that's what he said in his speech." Jordi shook his head. "Tell that to Hitler and Mussolini. They are arming Franco's troops—without the Russians, what hope do we Republicans have?"

They walked down stone steps into the shade of the basement café, and behind the bar, a record played: "... *the music goes round and round and it comes out here* ..." Jordi slipped his hand over her eyes.

"What are you doing?" she asked, smiling.

"I have something for you." From his pocket, Jordi pulled a long gold chain and clasped it around her throat. "Happy Birthday." He kissed the soft curls at the nape of her neck.

"I thought you had forgotten!" Rosa looked down at the gold necklace and gasped. "Oh, Jordi, it's beautiful. How could you afford this?"

"It was my mother's. I took it last summer in Valencia when Vicente wasn't looking. Oof ..." He doubled over as she punched him on the arm. "He won't notice! All my brother cares about is money—if he had seen it he would have sold it. Mamá always thought it was too good to wear." He carefully opened the oval filigree of entwined leaves and roses. "I think people used it for perfume in the old days."

"It's a pomander?" Rosa inhaled, caught the ghost of a fragrance.

"But I put our photographs inside."

Rosa recognized the studio portraits that had been taken a few months ago, carefully trimmed to fit the gold frame. "I love it." She kissed him, lingering, tasted the hot salt on his lips, his skin.

"Promise you'll wear it always," he said quietly. "Whatever happens, we will be together forever."

"Nothing can keep us apart, Jordi."

"No," he said, his hand falling to her stomach. "I won't have you fighting with us anymore. Just as soon as I can I am taking you to Valencia. Vicente will take care of you." He took one of the last of the wild roses from a jam jar on the bar, and threaded it through the buttonhole of her suit.

"I won't go." Rosa dug her hands into the pockets of her *mono*. "I can still fight. We are together. That is enough."

Jordi turned to embrace his friend Marco, who was standing near the bar. Rosa listened to the snatches of conversation drifting from the packed lunchtime tables, watched as the waitress twisted skillfully through the sea of soldiers' hopeful, lonely hands.

"Valencia is safe for now," one of the soldiers was saying. "The city is full of dockers loyal to the CNT trade union, and the Huerta is full of rich peasants who will keep their heads down and quietly continue to grow rice and oranges in their smallholdings."

"Rice and oranges!" Marco laughed, nudged Jordi. "You should know all about that."

"I am not a farmer! I am a *recortadore.*" Jordi leaped with the grace of a cat onto the bar, and the people at the tables nearby cheered and clapped. "I am the greatest bull leaper in all of Spain!" Rosa tugged him down, laughing. Jordi swept the hair from his eyes. "It is my father who was the farmer." He put his arm around Rosa. "He was a landowner who lost his land. He poured his dissatisfaction down his throat with his cognac, and spoiled my brother for life. Vicente is a failed matador, an unhappy butcher who thinks he should be an aristocrat. He drinks in the café till three or four, sleeps a few hours, serves the women of the village with pork bellies—"

"And more, from what I hear," Marco murmured.

"You want me to stay with this man?" Rosa laughed awkwardly.

Jordi shrugged. "It will be safer than here. Vicente is no *político*—he is firmly on the fence. But he is my brother, and I love him. Me, I was a little surprise for my parents—they thought after what my mother went through with Vicente's birth she couldn't have more children. To me, growing up, he was a god." Jordi turned to her. "You should see him. Yes, he is bald now, and his beard and chest hair are gray, but when he goes down to the lake each day to swim after siesta, and takes off his pink dressing gown, there is still something of the arena, the roar of the crowd . . ."

Rosa giggled. "You're teasing me!"

"No! You wait till you see him. Vicente stands like this . . ." Jordi puffed his chest out, planted his thighs firmly apart, put his hands on his hips and looked slowly from left to right. "All the women adore him. He keeps them mesmerized with his stories of the *toros.* The way he drops his dressing gown like a silk cape . . ." Jordi mimed tossing it aside. "When he sniffs the air like a bull, he is still Vicente the Magnificent."

"It is true," Marco said. "He has had half the women in the village."

"Why hasn't he been shot by an angry husband?" Rosa asked.

"The men are either afraid of him, or admire him." Marco sipped his drink. "I think the mark of Vicente's gold incisors on your wife's body is like a brand of quality to some men!" As the old friends swapped stories about Jordi's elder brother, Rosa frowned and tuned in to the conversations around them again.

"At least now they will not advance on Madrid from the east," a soldier said. Rosa thought of the west, the noise of the battle. The blood still rang in her ears, a shrill whine, the aftershock of the explosions.

"We shall hold them back on the other fronts, and the Valencia road is clear."

"They are evacuating the pictures from the Prado, you know."

"You know what Franco's Nationalists are saying? They claim the Republicans are raping nuns . . ."

"Well, what about General Queipo de Llano's broadcasts from Seville, eh? Did you not hear he offered up the women of Madrid to his Nationalist troops as a reward if they seize the city from us?"

Always the women and children who suffer. Rosa's gaze fell to the polished wood of the bar as the conversations overlapped. She leaned against it as Jordi ordered three more goblets of sherry. The tiles were wet in the café, freshly washed, and Rosa breathed in the tang of wine-soaked wood, the salt air clinging to the shellfish. The display was pitiful, she thought, her stomach grumbling for the days when crabs and oysters spilled across the crushed ice.

"Queipo de Llano said for every man we kill, he will kill at least ten."

Jordi spun around to interrupt their conversation. "This is why we cannot let them win, *compañero*. Yes, there are atrocities on both sides—this is war—but Franco will destroy half of Spain if he has to. They are throwing entire villages from cliff faces."

"I heard the Falangists are organizing peasant hunts on horseback," someone called over to Jordi.

"That I can believe," he said. "All I hear is reports of those fascists 'clearing up' towns after the troops have passed through, careering around in their parents' cars, with their girlfriends, firing pistols like it is some game."

The game of life, Rosa thought. She remembered the early days in the summer after the rebel Nationalist uprising. She rode out to Toledo with her Republican friends armed with guns, tortillas, and bottles of wine—then went home to sleep and make love. There was singing everywhere then, she remembered; she had never heard so much singing. She remembered the excitement when the grand hotels threw open their doors—where aristocrats had dined, ordinary men and women now ate on bone china in the new workingmen's clubs. All was equal—but already things had changed. There had been so much loss, so quickly, so violently. Prisons were emptied, criminals avenged themselves. It was the criminals responsible for the worst of the atrocities, not the Republicans, she was sure. The war was suddenly too close to home.

"It isn't a game!" she cried. "Let them come, but fight me face-to-face on level ground."

As the café erupted in cheers, Rosa turned away. She felt Jordi watching her. "Jordi, I can't bear the cruelty," she said. "What kind of a world are we bringing a child into?"

He took her face in his hands. "A good world. We will make a free Spain, a better Spain for our child. Don't be afraid. The Nationalists have to terrify the workers—that is the only way they will win, through fear. This is why they display corpses, why they allow people to set up snack bars at the site of executions. To them it is a holy crusade and they want to put the fear of God into us. But they are only men, and we will win."

Rosa glanced up as a group of men jogged down the stairs, greeted by cheers and fists shooting into the air. The first man raised his arm, silhouetted against the light.

"Viva la República! Viva la Libertad!" Robert Capa shouted.

"Eh, Capa!" Jordi called, embracing him when he walked over. "Congratulations! Everyone is talking about the photograph of the falling soldier. Now the world will sit up and take notice of Spain."

Capa shrugged. "It was a lucky shot."

"Have you met my girl? This is Rosa." Jordi turned to the barman. "Drinks for my friends."

"No, let me." Capa threw a roll of money onto the bar.

"Who are these people?" Rosa whispered to Jordi.

"Photographers, journalists," Jordi said. "Capa took photos of me a while ago. They are going to tell the world the truth about Spain."

"Damn right we are," Capa said. He turned to Rosa, kissed her hand, raised his gaze to hers. "You are a lucky man, Jordi. I would like to photograph your girl."

"No, I don't think so," she said.

"Why, are you afraid I might steal your soul?"

"I don't think it is my soul you are interested in."

Capa's laugh reminded her of a cat purring. He winked at Jordi. "Like I said, you are a lucky man."

"I am." Jordi put his arm around Rosa. "And right now, Capa, we need all the luck we can get."

FIVE

The door of the Picasso Café swung closed behind her, and Emma pulled the collar of her coat up. A few locals lingered over a late lunch at the pavement tables, and one of the market traders from Antiquarius called over to her in greeting. She waved back, sipped at her Styrofoam cup of tea as she waited for a break in the traffic. A taxi slowed to let her cross; she nodded in thanks and ran across toward the cinema.

Every cracked flagstone was familiar to her, every face it seemed. The crisp autumn air, the smells of exhaust fumes and coffee—she knew and loved them all. Sometimes she daydreamed about creating fragrances that captured cities in a bottle. *London would be coal fires, tea, petrol,* she thought. This was her home, her corner of the world, and yet it would never be the same again. She had taken one look at the silent studio piled high with packing crates, showered, and left. The lacquer box had been exactly where she'd left it months before, surrounded by the fragrances on Liberty's desk like a conductor at the heart of an orchestra.

Emma skirted the side of Habitat and strode toward St. Luke's. The church gardens were almost empty, the office workers returned to their desks. A few mothers were pushing children in buggies toward the playground as Emma walked toward what she had always thought of as their bench, hers and Liberty's. She had come here with Freya, Charles, and Joe after the funeral, and scattered Liberty's ashes on the rose border. The thought of the flowers to come in the summer reminded her of one of the first trips her mother had taken her on, to their suppliers in Turkey. Men had stood waist deep in roses, and Emma had plunged her small hand into a sack of petals, silken and perfumed. The fragrance was so intense, it seemed to have a texture to her, a powdery voluptuousness. Emma had missed these roses' single flowering. Now the earth stood bare again, the bushes cut back for the winter.

"Hello, Mum," she said quietly as she sat down. In her mind, as she looked at the garden, she played out their conversation, told her mother how she missed her, how she was going to be a grandmother at last. *"Roots and wings, Em,"* she remembered her mother saying. *"That's what you give your children."*

Emma's face fell as a bus trundled by emblazoned with an advertisement for the new Liberty Temple fragrance. The marketing department had gone into overdrive to prepare for the launch, introducing Emma as Liberty's successor. Emma thought back to the final interview with *ES Magazine,* how Joe had shown the journalist around their new house, pointing out all the toys he had installed—the home cinema, the statement artworks by Hirst, the furnishings that read like a Design Museum catalog. The photographer, meanwhile, had asked Emma to sniff the orchids on the mantelpiece.

"But they have no scent," she said.

"Well, stroke them, lovey. Look inspired." He circled his hand in the air without bothering to look up from his viewfinder.

While she played along, caressing the orchids, Joe's mobile had beeped in the kitchen. They were waiting for news from Liberty at the hospital, so she decided to check the message. A hundred times she wondered what would have happened if she hadn't. *"Miss you,"* it said. *"Tonight x."* Emma heard Joe's footsteps echoing down the new wenge staircase. She quickly turned the phone upside down as she had found it, and poured a glass of champagne for everyone.

"This place is fabulous!" the journalist said, settling onto a stool beside the gleaming Corian countertop. "How long have you been here?"

"Not long," Emma said. She was trying to think clearly. "It's all Joe's hard work, really."

"Nonsense!" Joe settled back on the Eames lounger by the fireplace, and put his hands behind his head. "I took care of the bricks-and-mortar stuff, but Em has a great eye. She was e-mailing me orders from all over the place."

"I travel a lot for work." The pieces began to fall into place. "Our biggest markets are Japan and the U.S."

"Em's mum ran a cosmetics company for years, but then in the late eighties we got involved, and the Liberty Temple perfume brand just exploded. Emma is the creative brains now—the nose—aren't you?"

"Sorry?" She glanced at him, his familiar face suddenly strange to her. Was that a new shirt from Pink he was wearing? He was immaculate as always. Though he hadn't followed his father into the American armed forces, there was something military in his bearing and precision. His hair had been freshly trimmed at Trumpers that morning, his nails buffed. Emma looked down at her hands—she hadn't had time for a manicure for weeks. She forced herself to concentrate, and began the story she had recounted a thousand times at different press conferences, how a family business started on a kitchen table had grown to become one of the world's leading independent perfumers.

"My mother always wore Calèche," the journalist said. "You know, sometimes I pass a woman in the street wearing it, and I think it's her."

"Exactly. I love the emotions fragrance evokes in us." There was a tight knot in Emma's throat. "I'd love to make a classic fragrance like Chanel No. 5."

"Yeah, I'm sure the accountants would be over the moon too," Joe said, laughing.

Emma's hand was shaking as she put down her glass. "Did you know, in some parts of the world the word 'kiss' means 'smell.' Isn't that amazing, the link between scent and sensuality." She was staring hard at Joe.

"Maybe that's my title," the journalist mused. " 'Scent and Sensuality,' you know, like *Sense and Sensibility*. Everyone loves Jane Austen."

Emma settled back on the bench. For a moment, she allowed herself to imagine a perfect life where she and Joe were still together. Longing spread through her. It would never be the same, she was old enough to realize that. The simple, open trust had gone, but she had loved Joe too long for her feelings to simply disappear. Emma glanced at her watch, turned the heavy-duty, man's Patek Philippe over. It was nearly two.

Emma walked on toward Chelsea Green, took a deep breath as she pulled out her phone, and speed-dialed 1.

"Em?" He answered instantly. "I've been trying to call you for weeks."

"Hey, Joe," she said, just like always. She blinked slowly as she remembered him looking up from his MBA books in the Columbia University library, his blond bangs falling over his indigo eyes. *Hey, Joe.* Rolling over toward her in the dawn light of their curtainless first flat together in Battersea. *Hey, Joe.*

"Where have you been? You just dropped off the radar after Tokyo."

"I stopped off in Vancouver to see Dad."

"Your dad?" Joe sounded surprised. "You haven't seen him for years."

"It felt like it was about time. I just wanted . . . I don't know what I was hoping . . ." She took a deep breath.

"Sure, I understand, after your mum . . ." His voice trailed off. "Are you in London?"

"Just back." She hoped she sounded calm, offhand. She recalled the last time she had seen him, when he'd left with tears of regret, and loss in his eyes. *Hey, Joe.*

"Well done. The guys in Japan were over the moon." He paused. "I've been worried about you. You OK?"

"Sure. You sound tired." *You sound guilty*, she thought.

"Yeah, hell . . ." She heard him exhale. "You know what it's like."

What what's like? She kicked angrily at a Coke can in the gutter. *The business? Being with Delilah?* Just the sound of his voice, his easy East Coast accent killed her. The night she confronted him, they had held each other in the gleaming kitchen of their new house, weeping like children for everything that was broken and lost. It was like something she had carried within her tore free. *Love?* Now, that space was a wound, a hole that ached for him, for them, for everything they had been. She thought of the e-mail Charles had sent her at her lowest point: *"What breaks us makes us stronger. Hold on to that, Em. It will get better."* She cleared her throat. "So, is it good to be home?"

"New York? Yeah, it's always good to be back."

"Are you going to stay?"

"Maybe. Listen, did you get the papers?"

Emma glanced left and right as she crossed the road. "Aha."

"Sign them, Em. It's what we've worked for."

"To sell out?"

"No, to make a fortune, to do what we want with our future."

"What future, Joe? We have no future." She hesitated. "Oh God, you mean with her, don't you?"

"I don't know what I mean." She imagined him raking his hand through his hair. "You're the one who left."

"What was I supposed to do? You were sleeping with my friend, our friend—" A businessman glanced up at her as she walked past. She turned away, cupped the phone. "It's such a cliché, Joe. I would have thought you'd have more imagination."

"You were away so much . . ."

"I was working for *us*! For *our* future." She hesitated, almost told him then.

"Anyway, we had to go ahead with the winter launch without you. Lila stood in for you at the press conferences."

"She's obviously very good at standing in for me."

"Don't, Em. She was useless, too full on. We've argued. Emma, I need to see you. I've made a dumb mistake. I don't know what I'm doing anymore."

"You're right, Joe," she said. "Let's quit on a high. We've all put years into Liberty Temple."

"I'm not talking about the business."

"Lila wants the money, Joe—that's all she's ever been interested in."

"*She's* nagging me to sell, you disappeared, Freya's telling me we should hang on to the company. Between all of you I just feel like disappearing too."

"Well why don't you then?" she snapped. "I didn't disappear. I've been on the road for months making sure the brand survives."

"I miss you."

"Don't say that." She stopped walking, closed her eyes. "You have no right."

"It's not too late. We can work this out."

"I have to go."

"OK, OK. We'll speak later." She heard him whistle for a cab, pictured him standing on the curb beneath the skyscrapers of New York, traffic streaming toward him. "I've got to get across to the World Trade Center. I'm meeting the guys at Windows on the World for breakfast."

Eggs Benedict, she thought. *Double espresso, two sugars.*

"I'm not going to leave here until we get everything hammered out. Will you fax the papers over once you're in the office?"

Emma scowled. "Yes." She strode on, rounding the corner into Pond Place.

"Thanks for everything. Em . . ." He paused. "I'm sorry. I'm an idiot. I love you. You know I'll always love you."

"Right."

"Tell me you still love me."

"No."

"Give me a chance. I can make it right."

"No," she said again, angry this time. "Nothing is ever going to be the same."

"I'll call you."

"You do that." As she stopped by the Liberty Temple offices, Emma punched in a final text message. *Love? Show me. We're having a baby.*

Instead of going into the office, she went next door and knocked on the bright red door. As she waited, she imagined Freya walking stiffly through the cottage, her silver-topped ebony cane tapping on the creaking boards. Emma heard the chain slide back, and as the door opened an Ella Fitzgerald tune drifted out.

"Oh no you don't, Ming," Freya muttered, blocking the path of a Siamese cat with her cane. She glanced up. "Em!"

Emma hugged her grandmother. She seemed thinner, her bones more angular beneath the soft black cashmere roll-neck she was wearing. "I've missed you," she said, her words muffled.

"Let me look at you." Freya held her at arm's length. "Love what you've done."

"Thanks." Emma ran her hand through her dark, shoulder-length hair. "I had it chopped in Tokyo. Thought I'd go back to my natural color."

"Just as well. No hair dye for a few months now for you," Freya whispered, squeezing Emma's hand.

"So, do I pass?"

Freya pursed her lips. "You look a bit peaky, but I'm not going to start nagging you the moment you get home. Come on, come in," she said, ushering her inside. "Charles is in the conservatory."

"It is good to see you," Emma said, taking her arm as they walked through the cottage. *At least nothing has changed here,* she thought, comforted by the familiar chaos of Freya and Charles's home. The yellow living room lined with books and bright abstract paintings fronted the street, and a constant stream of pedestrians and cars passed in front of the sash windows. Worn kilims flanked the sagging sofas, and a large tuberose candle on the ottoman perfumed the air. A fire glowed in the hearth, and from upstairs the sound of vacuuming drifted down. In the small kitchen, a Welsh dresser piled with blue-and-white crockery and old postcards leaned companionably by a scrubbed table, and Ming lolled on an old red armchair in the sunlight, turquoise eyes watching the women.

"Charles!" Freya called, shuffling into the conservatory, her cane tapping on the terra-cotta floor. Among the plants the wings of iridescent blue butterflies beat slowly in the hot, liquid air, tongues unfurled to nectar. Condensation dripped from leaves, and a swallowtail settled, unnoticed, on Emma's hair. "Charles!" Freya shook her head. "He must be in his study." She swept aside a curtain of fine chains, opened the back door, and leaned against Emma as she negotiated the low step to the garden. Freya walked gingerly along the uneven paving stones to a sky-blue shed, and pushed open the door. They found Charles bent over his roll-topped desk, pinning a fritillary onto a corkboard.

Emma smiled. She had spent hours in here with Charles as a child, helping her great-uncle catalog his specimens. The walls were lined with cases of butterflies, a Technicolor mural of wings. A grizzled pug snored softly at his feet while a longcase Mora clock ticked away the minutes. "Hello . . ."

"He won't hear you." Freya nudged his back with the cane. "Charles! We have a visitor."

"What the ruddy hell?" He spun around, pushed his half-moon glasses back on his mane of thick white hair. His empty left sleeve, pinned at the elbow, swung against his side. "Do you want to give me a heart attack?" He smiled, shuffled forward as he noticed Emma. "Em!" He embraced her with his right arm, and she kissed his dry, smooth cheek.

"Turn it on." Freya motioned to him.

Charles flicked on his hearing aid. "Only way a chap can get a moment's peace in this madhouse, people coming and going all day," he grumbled to Emma.

"Stop moaning," Freya said. "You'll miss them when they're gone."

"It is good to see you. You look well," Emma said.

"Do I? At our age you're just glad to be alive. All our friends are dropping like flies." He sighed. "Every year there are a few less of us at the Brigades' commemoration in Jubilee Gardens."

"You know what he's like." Freya folded her arms. "Always turns to the obituaries first to see if he knows anyone."

"I do not. Ah, you have a passenger, Em." Charles caught the butterfly on her hair in a small net box and closed the lid.

Face-to-face, Emma thought the similarity between the siblings was unmistakeable even in age—both had tall, slender bodies, rather stooped now, the same high cheekbones, aquiline noses. Whereas Freya was a picture of understated, monochrome chic, Charles's umber cords were flecked with scorch marks from years of log fires and cigarettes, and hung loose from his hips. As he turned to the desk and slid a sheet of glass into the frame, Freya sighed.

"Look at the state of you, Charles." She brushed some dog hair from his sleeve. "I do wish you'd let me buy you some new clothes."

"Stop fussing, woman." He dug his hands into the stretched pockets of his navy cardigan and pulled out a tobacco tin. "What do I need with new clothes?" he muttered as he lit a roll-up.

Freya smoothed down her immaculate gray bob and turned to Emma. "Everyone is dying to see you. Shall we go through?"

From the chaotic mews house that had been the family home for nearly seventy years, Freya, Charles, and Emma stepped onto the pavement, and through the door into the adjoining house. The Liberty Temple office was bustling. As Emma pushed the front door open the breeze made the orchids on the white reception desk dance. The open-plan back offices were buzzing with elegant young women and languid men; snatches of French, English, Japanese and the scent of roses drifted on the air.

"Welcome home, Em," the receptionist said.

"Thank you," she replied as she strode through. "Hello, everyone."

Freya and Charles waited in reception as the team crowded around to greet Emma. "I hope she's doing the right thing," Freya said quietly. "This is the closest thing she has to a family right now. Once the company is sold . . ."

"Are you talking about Emma, or yourself?"

Freya dug him in the ribs.

"Ow, not so ruddy hard," he winced.

"I'll be fine, don't you worry." Freya tucked her chin down into her black polo neck and crossed her arms over her narrow rib cage. "I've spent my life looking after Liberty, and Emma, and the company . . ."

"Exactly. The girls have kept you young."

"Unlike you."

Charles pulled a face at her. "I shall choose to ignore that remark." He glanced at her out of the corner of his eye. "Will you move to the Cornish house permanently?"

Freya shook her head. "You won't get rid of me that easily."

"You do love it down there, and there will be no need for—" Charles's breath caught in his throat as he glanced over at the flat-screen television above the fireplace. He shuffled over and turned up the volume. "Be quiet!" he shouted, the newsreel footage on the BBC glimmering in his glasses.

"What's going on?" Freya was the first at his side. She gazed in horror as smoke plumed from the World Trade Center. "Oh God, no!" Her hands flew to her mouth as another plane plowed into the second tower.

Emma ran over. "I don't understand. What's happening?" She put her arm around Freya. "Joe's there," she said, her voice catching. "I just spoke to him half an hour ago. He's in the North Tower."

SIX

MADRID, NOVEMBER 1936

Hugo!" Charles called, and jogged to catch up. The Eleventh International Brigade marched along Gran Via, and Charles fell in with the British machine gunners and Germans of the Edgar André Battalion. Neon signs, vivid in the winter light, flickered along the road as the *madrileños* cheered them on.

Hugo turned his pale, tired face to Charles. "Did you get any photos this morning?"

Charles shook his head. "I thought perhaps the paper might like a few shots of ordinary men and women . . ."

"Couldn't find any?"

"Very droll. What's the latest?"

"The Nationalists are advancing into the university."

"Just as well the Brigades are here then," Charles said, shifting the old Soviet rifle slung over his shoulder. "The Eleventh should drive them out." Nearby he could hear the sound of marching feet, shouting, singing, the noise of motor horns. But beyond that was the sound of battle—rifles, machine guns, mortars. For the first time they were getting closer and closer to the front.

Charles thought back to their arrival in Spain. Comrade Marty's voice had drifted over the crowd of new recruits packed into the Albacete parade ground like candles in a box. The woolen cap Charles had been given was itching, and his boots were bad. They had already worn blisters on his heels during drills that morning, but when he looked around at the eccentric rags worn by many of the soldiers, he realized he had been lucky. Some were dressed in World War I surplus, some in pantomime costume it seemed. The commander, however, wore a black leather jacket and a dark beret, and on his Sam Browne belt hung a 9 mm automatic pistol.

"These ruddy lice are driving me insane," Charles whispered to Hugo, scratching at his thigh.

"It's the rats you have to watch out for," Hugo said. "Haven't you heard the song? 'There are rats, rats, rats as big as cats . . .'"

"You will be sent from here to the training center at Madrigueras," the commander shouted above the murmurs of the crowd.

"How come he gets a pistol?" Charles said.

"He's the boss," Hugo whispered. "Broom handles are fine for the rest of us. It looks to me like those sentries are handling rifles for the first time." He looked across at a boy leaning against the wall. "For God's sake stop smoking, man!" he hissed, and pointed at the boxes of dynamite stacked beside the boy.

"I'm not sure about this," Charles said. "You'd have thought they'd have enough guns to go round."

"Yes, it would have been nice."

"I know what we are fighting for, but I'm not quite sure how."

"It's too late to back out now, Charles," Hugo said. "They took our passports at Figueras."

Marty raised his voice. "Who can drive a truck?" A few men put up their hands. "Right, line up over there. Who can ride a motorcycle? Anyone with medical training?" As the last men shuffled away, he looked out across those who remained. "The rest of you are infantry. You will make history."

"Even maps would be nice," Charles said under his breath. He gazed around the ragged group of dockers, miners, and dreamy undergraduates. "Surely someone must have a Michelin map at least, somewhere?"

"No maps, no compasses," Hugo said cheerfully. "It will be chaos. I have a feeling we should be getting more than ten pesetas a day."

"You! Temple!" Marty pointed at him. "You are reporters, yes?"

"We are with the *Manchester Guardian*, sir." Charles stood to attention. "But we wish to fight alongside the Brigades, sir, if we can."

"Good. There are too many reporters and photographers along for the ride."

Marty sorted through a file. "Make Madrid your base. Report to Brigade headquarters there." He scribbled his signature on a piece of paper. "Here is a safe conduct pass for you both. I want you to report from all over the country. Show the world what is going on here."

The columns of men marched on into battle. It seemed to Charles the whole city was blazing, light flaring into the sky. They worked their way through smoke-filled streets where splinters of rafters snagged the sky like broken ribs. His hair was thick with dust as he ran his hand through it, his ears ringing from the continual, deafening bombardment. *Show the world,* he thought, watching a covered stretcher being carried away, a man's arm swinging free from the bloodstained sheet.

"Wait," he said to Hugo. Charles shouldered his way out of the lines of marching men. He lifted his camera and focused on the vacant, masklike faces of a dead mother and child laid out side by side on the edge of the road.

"What are you doing?" A Spanish militiaman shoved him away. "You vulture! You make me sick, you newsmen." He spat on him.

Charles raised his fist, but Hugo grabbed his arm and dragged him onward. "My job," Charles shouted back above the deafening explosions. "You'll see. I'm going to show the world."

SEVEN

"Open your eyes." Emma remembered Joe's voice, full of laughter, the warmth of his breath against her ear. She had felt the weight of his hip against hers, their thighs touching.

"I can't!" Emma had frozen to the spot, stretched out across the cool glass of the World Trade Center observation deck window, unable to move. She jammed the soles of her Converse high-tops against the ledge, tried to inch backward.

Joe squeezed her hand. "Trust me. Open your eyes."

She opened one eye, flinching.

"Look at it." He laughed. "It's beautiful." They turned their faces toward the earth, gazed out across New York. "I feel like we're flying." Beneath them, the city was dazzling, spring sunlight dancing across the water, illuminating thousands of windows, warming the fresh green of Central Park.

Emma had felt the world spin as vertigo swept over her, and her mouth dried. All she could think of was what would happen if the glass gave way. She inched backward, turned to Joe. "Are you happy now? I accepted the dare."

"Look at you, you're shaking like a leaf!" He pulled her to her feet, laughing. "I've got you now and I'll never let you go."

Emma buried her head against his chest, slipped her arms beneath his

Puffa vest. The feel of him was still intoxicating then. That morning they had kissed for hours. When they were together it felt as though they were one, not two, their bodies lean and hungry, new.

"Hey," he said. "You weren't kidding, were you? Are you OK?"

"I told you I hate heights." Emma punched him gently in the stomach. "Let that be a lesson for you. Never dare a Temple woman. You owe me lunch."

He grinned, an even, white smile breaking across his tanned face. "You've got a deal." He slung his arm over Emma's shoulders as they walked to the lift. "Anyway, we'd better get a move on, Delilah's waiting for us."

"Again? When am I ever going to get you alone?"

"Now *that* I like the sound of," he said as they squeezed into the lift. "Lila's my friend, honey. Her nose is kind of out of joint since we got together— you don't mind if she tags along, do you? She's still getting used to the idea that some beautiful Brit has swept me off my feet." As the lift plummeted, he slipped his hand around Emma's waist, searching for the band of her Levi's 501s. She felt his fingertips, warm and firm, tracing the indentation of her spine. The lift doors opened, and he kissed the top of her head. "We can be together later, I promise. I've got a late tutorial, but I'll pick you up around seven, OK?"

"Sure," she said, forcing a bright smile as they walked through the lobby. *"Smile, Emma."* She thought of her mother's advice. *"I think it's charming if his best friend is a girl—shows he has a sensitive side. Delilah is part of the package, and you're just going to have to get used to it. Befriend her. Boys hate it if you're clingy and jealous. If Delilah is upsetting you, smile, darling. She'll soon get bored and give up."* Emma spotted Delilah immediately, sitting in the plaza waiting for them, her blond hair shining in the sunlight and her seemingly endless legs stretched out across the bench. *Right, Mum! She doesn't look as if she's ever given up on anything in her life.* As they walked toward her, Delilah unfurled herself. The light glinted on the large gold hoops in her ears.

"Hello, children," Delilah drawled. She stood with the easy grace of a girl who has taken dance lessons her whole life, and the shoulder pads of her linen jacket accentuated her tiny waist. Emma felt awkward as she looked down at her jeans and sneakers.

Joe slung his free arm over Delilah's shoulder. "Hey, Lila, how was the class?"

"Dull, dull, dull. But I aced that final paper," she said.

"Don't you mean 'we' aced it?" Joe laughed.

"Whatever. I've helped you out enough over the years."

Emma flinched. It felt like Delilah was constantly reminding her how well she knew Joe, how long they had been friends. She glanced uncertainly at them.

"At least we graduate in a week; then it's so long to all the textbooks and hello expense account." Delilah tossed her hair.

"What will you do?" Emma asked.

"I have a few options."

"I wanted to talk to you both about that," Joe said as he guided them toward the crossing. "I had an interesting conversation with Liberty yesterday. Let me take my two favorite girls to lunch, and we can discuss it."

As Emma looked at the Twin Towers on television now, she recalled every detail of that day over ten years before. She had forced herself to look calm, smile warmly, as Joe talked about the three of them working together with her mother to expand the company. Liberty had loved Joe the moment they met—Emma always thought he was the son she had never had. Naturally, where Joe went, Delilah went too, and as Liberty Temple took shape they became the business and marketing brute force that Liberty needed to push the new company forward. Emma was the creative brain, Liberty's successor, the "nose" who would shape the future. Liberty had insisted that Emma do a short business course at Columbia after studying perfumery in Grasse, hoped a spell in New York would toughen her up. Emma remembered the late nights sitting around Freya's kitchen table as Liberty paced, talking endlessly about how she worried her daughter was too cloistered, too unworldly to cope with running a business alone.

"You're an artist, darling, like me," she had said. "An artist of fragrance. You're too fragile to cope with the business side of things. It's a different world from when I started out making soap and face cream on this kitchen table while you played with your blocks underneath. You need help." That was how Joe and Delilah came to join them in London.

Emma's head swirled now, and she reached out to steady herself. She couldn't grasp that the images on the screen were real. "I spoke to him, just a few minutes ago," she said, fumbling for her bag. She dialed his number. The line was engaged.

Three missed calls and a voice mail flashed up from Joe: "Em! You're kidding! A baby?" She heard him laugh. "My God, you always were good at surprising me. I don't know what to do . . . I've done something really stupid. Listen, I'm going to make this right. Em, I've got to go in now. I'll call you after the meeting. Love you."

"Oh God," she cried. "He can't be in there . . ."

Freya put her arm around her, gripped her shoulder. They watched in stunned silence as the headlines scrolled: *"Breaking News. Plane has crashed into the World Trade Center Tower in New York."*

"It's not possible," Emma whispered, her gaze fixed on the top of the tower. She imagined him sitting at the table across from the buyers, a fresh white shirt, his lucky blue tie that brought out the color of his eyes. She heard the chink of china, of cutlery, the hiss of the coffee machine, the swift, efficient steps of the waiters. And then the impact. Emma gasped for breath. All the anger and pain she had felt fell away. "Joe, oh God, Joe . . ." She saw the smoke billowing upward, knew he would be fighting for a way out, taking charge, getting people together. That's what Joe did. That's what he always did. She imagined him looking out across that terrible, beautiful clear sky.

"He'll get out," Freya said quietly. "If anyone can get out, Joe will."

The shrill sound of the telephone cut through the air. The receptionist ran to the desk. "Good morning, Liberty Temple," she said automatically. "Yes, Ms. Stafford—"

"Is that Delilah?" Freya called. "Put her on the conference phone." The sound of sirens crackled from the speakers as everyone crowded to the meeting room table. "Delilah. It's Freya. Are you all right?"

"Freya?"

"Where are you?"

"I'm on the street, near the South Tower. Oh God, Freya, what's happening?"

Emma leaned toward the speaker. "Is Joe with you?"

"Emma? Christ, I don't know! I—"

"Where is he, damn it?"

"Both of you, calm down!" Freya snapped. "We need to think clearly. Delilah, where is Joe?"

"He was at the meeting. I was meant to be with him, but the heel broke on my shoe and I had to stop off."

In the background, they heard a woman shrieking, "People are falling! God, save their souls! They're jumping, oh please God!"

Delilah's voice was choked, it sounded like she was running. "They're telling us to clear the area . . ." She gasped. "There are people falling, falling . . ." The line cut out.

Freya turned to the receptionist. "Keep trying their phones, Joe's and Delilah's." In silence, they gathered once more in front of the television.

EIGHT

Rudolph Valentino's profile flickered on the white sheet hung in the village market square, the light of the projector cutting through the darkness, moths casting shadows as they danced in its beams. Rosa looked up at the clear night sky, at the blanket of stars above them, and curled up closer to Jordi, her feet resting in his lap. He pulled his coat around them, held her warm in his arms.

"You don't like the film?" he whispered. The villagers were watching *Blood and Sand* in rapt attention, only the whir of the projector breaking the silence, distant dogs barking. At the side of the square, children were playing. A small boy—feet close together, chest out, buttocks in, chin lowered—raised his arms. "Ha-da!" he cried, and stamped his foot. The other boy lowered his horns, charged.

"No, the film is fine," she said, frowning. "It is this place I don't like."

"You've only been here a day. Give it a chance." Jordi stood, and took her hand. People behind them grumbled, craned their necks to see the film. Jordi ushered her away to the side of the square. "Rosa, we have talked about this. I grew up in La Pobla, you will be safe here." He checked his watch. "Vicente will have finished work by now. Come, I said we would meet him in the bar; then I must get back to Madrid."

Vicente, she thought. Their first meeting had not been a success. Jordi had parked the car beside a whitewashed wall on the outskirts of the village, and taken her hand as they walked. "This is the Villa del Valle, our family home," he said, pointing at the closed metal gates, "and this is Vicente's shop." The smell of cold blood on the air turned her stomach. Jordi pushed open the door, and a bell chimed.

"Vicente!" Jordi cried. Rosa's eyes adjusted to the dim light. In profile, Jordi's elder brother was handsome. But then he turned, and smiled. Rosa fought hard not to recoil. His top lip was scarred, his teeth gleamed gold. Jordi put his arm around her, steered her forward. "This is my girl, Rosa." He leaned down to her ear. "Don't let Vicente scare you. He lost an argument with a bull once."

Vicente laughed, wiped his hands on a cloth streaked with blood. "But now people are eating the fighting bulls, so maybe I win the argument after all." He stepped forward, inspected Rosa with a practiced eye. "Very beautiful. Congratulations, little brother." He held Rosa's gaze. "Jordi tells me you are a dancer."

"Rosa is many things," Jordi said proudly. "Her ancestors are from Sacromonte—they are dancers, healers."

"So, a little gypsy, eh?" He stepped closer, his eyes black pools. "Jordi tells me you knew Lorca. Too bad they took him for a ride."

Dar un paseo. Rosa flinched as she remembered him. Such an innocent phrase before all this. *How many more will be forced to "take a ride" and dig their own grave?* "I still don't understand why they are killing poets," she had said to Jordi one night as they lay in bed. "He wasn't a politician, or a soldier."

"Lorca wounded them more with his pen than he could have with a gun, that is why," he said. "He stood for everything they hate—love, freedom, justice, compassion. This is why our poets are being shot at the cemetery walls."

Rosa had drifted into sleep, thinking of Lorca's beautiful "Sleepwalking Ballad," the most famous of his *Gypsy Ballads*. It always made her feel like she was floating in clear emerald water, or flying through whispering green leaves. She always felt he wrote those lines about the little gypsy girl for her. The first time she met Lorca, she was just a child, pulling water from the well in Granada.

She remembered how Lorca's verse about two friends climbing into the rafters of a house came to her in a dream, and how she had jerked awake. With dazzling clarity she saw Jordi and Marco climbing, higher and higher, trailing blood. Rosa had tried to shake the image that flashed into her mind. She had seen these visions before, trusted them. Jordi turned now and smiled at her. She hoped she was wrong.

"My brother, the poetry lover?" Jordi laughed.

Rosa stared Vicente down. "Yes, I knew Lorca. I danced for him," she said proudly. "I inspired him, the great poet. We met at the Concurso de Cante Jondo, the flamenco festival. I heard Caracol and Pavon sing, I danced with them."

"You must have been a child!" Jordi said.

"I was."

"Maybe, one day, you will dance for me, eh?" Vicente turned away. "Meanwhile, you can help in the house, with the cleaning . . ."

"I'm going to work," she said clearly. "If they won't let the women fight anymore, I can help in the hospitals in town, at least until the baby is born."

"How old are you?"

"Nineteen." She raised her chin defiantly. "Old enough."

"Are you going to marry her?" he asked Jordi.

Jordi held up his hands. "I've asked her, believe me."

Vicente shrugged. "As long as you pull your weight here, I don't care what you do."

"Take me with you," she begged Jordi. "I can't stay here. It makes me sick to see the shops full of hams and cakes, people taking their evening *paseo* like there is no war. Don't they care what is happening in Madrid? Have they forgotten what happened in the summer? There is no distant front now against the fascist assault—Madrid *is* the front." She buried her head in his chest. "I should be there, fighting beside you."

"No," he said. "I will not hear of it. If you love me, and you love our child, stay here. I will come back to you, I promise."

"But what if . . . ?"

"Rosa." He took her face in his hands. "No fascist bullet can keep me from you. I will come back. I swear." He glanced over at the boys play-fighting. "See? That little boy has it in him too. To fight the bull, you must have the courage to stand still. You must not run—you must conquer your fear."

"That's what you want me to do? Stand still?" Rosa's dark, kohled eyes flashed as she looked up at him.

"Not stand still, be still." He kissed her hairline. "Rest, eat well. Make sure our son is strong."

"Son?" Rosa laughed. "What if it is a girl?"

"Then she will be as beautiful and stubborn as her mother."

Jordi slung his arm over her shoulder, and she slipped hers around his waist as they walked. She wanted the air between them to disappear. Ever since the night they had first met, at a bar in Madrid where Rosa was dancing, she'd felt a hunger for him, an ache in the pit of her stomach. She looked down at their feet, walking in unison along the moonlit street. From the moment he had taken her in his arms, she had been unable to resist the rhythm their bodies created—when they danced, when they walked, they moved as one. She wanted him now, wanted to feel his body with hers one last time before he left. Rosa looked up at him, and he knew, without a word. He led her by the hand down a dark alleyway, to the sanctuary of a hidden doorway. She pressed her lips, her tongue to his. Music drifted from an open window far above, a guitar, the liquid notes, the rhythm of drumming fingertips on the soundboard. She felt his fingers trace the darkness, reaching for her. The air between them felt phosphorescent, electrified, fresh against the warm skin of her thighs. She closed her eyes, heard the music, castanets clicking like oil-blue scarab beetles, the metallic clink of his belt.

"*Mi amor*," he whispered in the crook of her neck, his hand at the base of her spine, lifting her to him. Rosa felt fresh longing rise in her like sap in a pine tree, rising up from the earth. As he touched her in the darkness, she felt his fingerprints mark her body like tracery, she felt the light break out in her like a sun-warmed fruit splitting open.

"*Te amo,*" she whispered, "*te quiero*. I love you, I want you . . ."

"Always," he said, the breath catching in his throat. "Always."

NINE

Just before three, Charles stepped out onto the empty street, and lit a cigarette. Freya joined him, reached across and took it from him.

"You haven't smoked for years," he said.

"I can't believe it," she said, exhaling. "Not war, again."

"This isn't war. This is terrorism. At least when we were at war you could see the face of your opponent. You knew where to hit back."

"We *are* at war, don't you see?" Freya said, her voice breaking. "Oh God, will no one ever learn?" Her face was pale as she looked at him. "This is just the beginning. This is our war, just as much as the Americans'." She turned to the office as she heard a collective gasp of "No!"

Charles tossed the cigarette into the gutter, and they pushed their way inside through the people crowded in front of the television. "What's happened?"

"The South Tower has collapsed," Emma said, her face drained of color. They all watched as vast clouds of dust powered through the streets of New York.

"There's still a chance," Freya said. "They may have time to evacuate the North Tower."

Emma shook her head. "He's trapped. If he was in the restaurant, Joe's trapped." She hugged herself, hooking her hands tightly around her elbows.

"Joe," she whispered. *Hey, Joe.* Her Joe. Joe and Emma. And he was alone in there. She blinked back tears. "Get out, Joe," she murmured. She remembered him on the observation deck: *"I feel like I'm flying . . ."*

In silence, they stood transfixed as minute by minute half an hour ticked away. "I feel so helpless," Charles said hoarsely.

"We all do," Freya said. "There's nothing—" She gasped, her hand flew to her face. "No, no . . ." Her head shook in disbelief as the North Tower crumpled, and fell.

Emma stepped forward, touched the television screen. "Joe," she said under her breath as tears trickled down her cheeks. "Oh God, Joe."

"Go home, everyone," Charles said quietly. "Go home and be with your families."

They stayed up late into the night, switching between CNN and the BBC, the light from the television and the fire in Freya's living room flickering. Gold light from the streetlamps spilled through windows where they had not bothered to draw the curtains. Emma fell into exhausted sleep, curled up beside Freya on the old sofa.

"Terrorist attacks can shake the foundations of our biggest buildings, but they cannot touch the foundation of America," they heard George W. Bush saying. "These acts shatter steel, but they cannot dent the steel of American resolve . . ."

Freya reached up absentmindedly to stroke Ming where he lay, draped across her shoulders. "What kind of world is this?"

"Same as it ever was," Charles said as he heaved himself out of his armchair. He shuffled across the room and stoked the fire. "Don't you remember, when the fascists used the bombers at Guernica, and in Madrid and Valencia for the first time, we said the same?"

"This is different," Freya said angrily. "This is cowardly. My heart breaks when I think of the thousands of men and women, the children whose parents aren't coming home tonight." When she closed her eyes, she saw the image of the falling man.

"Why is it different? Just because it is a different sort of war?"

"The people who died weren't soldiers, Charles. They were ordinary, like Joe, just going about their day."

"You're forgetting," Charles said, his face hard. "They weren't soldiers in Spain, not most of them. Remember the women, the children?"

"Of course I do. You don't need to remind me of what we saw."

"They were innocents, just like our girl here." He stroked Emma's hair as she slept. "There's not a damn thing we can do about it. Joe's gone. Emma has to think about herself now, herself and her child." He offered Freya his hand, and they draped a blanket over Emma before going upstairs to their rooms.

Emma woke at dawn, curled up on Freya's sofa, the gray embers of the fire smoldering beside her. A muffled ringing forced her completely awake now, and she pushed back the blanket, searched for her bag. "Hello," she mumbled as she flicked open her phone. She rubbed her red, swollen eyes.

"Em? Emma? It's me." The line crackled.

"Lila? Where are you?" Emma hesitated as she heard Freya's bedroom door open upstairs.

"Oh, God, Em . . ." Her voice was choked with sobs.

Emma stood, the blanket tumbling to the floor. "Have you found him? Have you heard anything about Joe?"

"No. Nothing. I thought you might have heard something at the office?"

"No one's called. We haven't heard a thing."

"He's just . . . They've all just disappeared. All those people. I . . . I can't believe it," Delilah said, weeping. "He can't be gone. He can't be. It's not fair, I can't live without him. What am I going to do?"

"Where are you?" She heard Delilah trying to compose herself, her breath catching.

"I'm back at the Paramount."

"Why aren't you looking for him?" Emma cried out.

"I have been! I've been out for hours trying to find out if anyone has seen Joe. People are keeping vigil at Union Square Park. Everyone is wandering around with photographs of all the missing people . . ."

Emma looked up as Freya's slim feet appeared at the top of the staircase, a silver kimono wrapping around them. "I'm going to come out."

Delilah paused. Her voice was cold, suddenly. "Why? There's no need. Besides, all the flights are grounded."

"I have to come out. I have to find Joe." Emma followed Freya with her gaze as she walked downstairs, her pale bony hand gripping the banister.

"That's not necessary. I'm here now." She could hear the defensive tone in Delilah's voice. "I should have been with him. I can't . . . I can't be without him. If he's dead . . . I wish I'd died with him."

"It's not finished, Lila," Emma said, her voice cracking. "I spoke to Joe, just before the meeting . . ." Freya walked toward her, shaking her head, her expression filled with compassion. "He told me he'd made a mistake. He told me he loved me."

"That's rubbish."

"He said he'd always love me."

"Yeah, but not like *that* anymore." Delilah laughed, her throaty, sexy laugh that Emma had seen reduce grown men to stammering fools. "You lost, Emma. He chose me."

"We were going to get back together."

"That's what you think." Delilah paused. "So I guess Joe didn't tell you?"

Emma's heart clenched in her chest. "Tell me what?"

"I think he wanted to tell you face-to-face."

"Tell me what?"

"We got married, Em. Last month."

"No." Emma felt a wave of nausea rise in her stomach. "You're lying. He *married* you?" Emma could tell from Freya's stricken face that she had no idea either.

"You walked out on him. I love Joe, I always loved him. We would have been together years ago if it hadn't been for you."

"He was having an affair with you, for God's sake! What was I supposed to do?" Emma ran her hand through her hair. "So you just swooped in and pushed him to marry you the minute I was gone?"

"You know how much Joe wanted to get married and have a family. You turned him down enough times."

"A family is one thing you could never give him, isn't it?" Emma curled her arm protectively across her stomach.

"That's low."

"How many abortions did you have over the years, Lila?"

"We were going to adopt."

"How lovely. A ready-made family, to go with the ready-made home I built with Joe."

"It was Joe who made that house happen, while you were off traveling."

"Building the business!" Emma shook her head in disbelief. "How could you? How could Joe?"

"Anyway, we weren't coming back," Delilah said. "I'd found a place out here, near his parents. We were going to sell up in London. Don't worry, you'll get your cut."

"As if I give a damn about the money!" Emma wiped angrily at her eyes with the heel of her hand. "When I think you'd been sneaking around for months—"

"We couldn't tell you when Liberty was dying!"

"I found out anyway, didn't I?" She rummaged under the sofa, pulled on her old pair of Uggs.

"We never wanted to hurt you."

"You have, and you did." Emma slung her bag on her shoulder. "Well it's all yours now, Lila. If Joe's dead, it's yours—the house, two-thirds of the company. You're rich. I hope it makes you happy. It's all you ever wanted."

"No . . . Maybe once. All I want is Joe."

Emma backed away as Freya reached out to her, flung open the front door. "That's all we ever wanted, wasn't it?" she said before she hung up, and ran down the street.

"Emma!" Freya stumbled as she followed her onto the pavement. "Come back!"

Charles padded down the stairs behind her, and pulled her gently indoors. "Let her go. Em's a big girl now. We can't fight her battles for her. She knows we're here if she needs us."

"But . . ."

"But nothing. You were always the same with Liberty. You can't protect them forever, Frey."

"I know." Freya's face was etched with grief. "That poor girl. What will she do now?"

"She'll go off, lick her wounds. It's what she always does." Charles kissed the top of Freya's head and sighed. "Let her go."

TEN

Charles staggered along the corridor of the Hotel Florida toward the bar. The doors of the rooms stood open, and as he glanced through he saw men hunched over typewriters, writing their reports to cable home. One, a cigarette clamped in the corner of his mouth, smoke swirling about his fingers as they flew along the keys, swore quietly under his breath. "Those bastards," he muttered. "They're still denying the Nazis are down here. If they're not, then what the hell has been bombing the crap out of us for the last three days, hey? You watch, I'm going to tell them what I saw, Junkers of the Condor Legion filling the sky. I bet you it won't make it to press . . ."

"Over here!" Hugo called across the crowded bar to Charles. As he pushed his way through, Charles felt like he was swimming through the noise of a multitude of languages, the fug of smoke and the smell of the battlefield, sweat and cheap cologne. "Have you met Capa?"

A man in his early twenties with thick dark hair looked up from under strong brows. He was leaning against the bar, smoking. Charles noticed his hands—strong, long fingers, strangely feminine. Charles knew Capa's work—he had seen *Falling Soldier* in *Vu,* and he'd been dying to meet him, to talk about photography.

"Ah! The Englishman?" Capa put his arm around Charles's shoulders. "I hear it was your first battle. Feeling any better?"

"A little."

"Hugo—a drink for our friend. Today, he has lost his virginity."

The whiskey burned Charles's throat, and his hand shook as he leaned against the bar to steady himself.

"It gets easier." Capa offered him a cigarette. "You came here with Hugo, didn't you? Are you press too?"

"Yes, I'm meant to be reporting for the *Manchester Guardian*. I take . . . well, I'm learning to take photographs."

"What do you use?"

"A Contax."

Capa let out a slow whistle. "Nice camera. I use a Leica myself." He raised his glass. "Welcome on board. We're quite a motley crew as you can see." Capa leaned against the bar and sipped his drink as he scanned the room, and signaled to a bespectacled man playing chess. "That's Chim."

Chim wandered over and held out his hand to Charles. "Pleased to meet you."

"Hey, Capa, there's a call for you," the barman shouted.

Capa switched his cigarette to his other hand, and hooked the phone under his jaw. "To whom am I speaking?" His face creased into a flirtatious smile as he listened. "I'm sorry. You'll have to remind me. Taro? Have we met?" He grinned, took a drag of his cigarette. "Tell me, are you a brunette? Tall? Shapely legs?" He winked at Chim, and laughed. "Ah, that Miss Taro. The little fox."

God, I wish I could talk to girls like that, Charles thought. He turned to Chim. "How long have you all been here?"

"A while. I've been photographing behind the scenes. I leave the dangerous stuff to him and Gerda," he said, tilting his head toward Capa.

"Gerda?"

Chim smiled. "You'll meet her. Everyone is crazy about Gerda."

"Is she with Capa?"

"Yes. More's the pity for a lot of men."

"I think I'm in love with you, Miss Gerda Taro." Capa went to hang up the phone. "Come soon. It hurts."

As he rejoined them, Chim raised his glass. "When's she coming?"

"Soon."

"Is this your girl?" Charles tried to sound casual, worldly.

"We're going to marry when this is over," Capa said.

"Congratulations."

"Ah, love . . ." Hugo staggered as he reached for the barstool and sat down, his whiskey slopping in the glass. "You know, the bishops are saying this war has been called by the Sacred Heart, and God's love has given power to Franco's soldiers." His face contorted with anger. "What kind of love is that? That is not my God."

"Nor mine." Charles's jaw set. "But no one wants to know the truth."

"Then we shall make them see, my friends." Capa hooked his arms over their shoulders. "Come on. Who's up for cards? Couldn't help noticing you had a bottle of schnapps upstairs, Hugo. Shall we?"

ELEVEN

Emma closed her eyes, raised her face to the clear sky, where gulls wheeled overhead. A cold wind blew in from the sea, and Bamaluz Beach was deserted. This had always been her favorite beach as a child—most of the visitors to St. Ives didn't even know it existed, following the crowds instead to Porthmeor or Porthminster. Liberty had always brought her here. At this time of year, when all the emmets—as the locals called the tourists—had deserted Cornwall, Emma had the beach to herself. The tide was high, and the waves crashed beneath her as her footsteps crunched along the shoreline. The beach was a short walk from the old fisherman's cottage Charles and Freya had bought decades ago, before St. Ives became fashionable. This beach had been her mother's playground, growing up, and to Emma it always meant summer holidays, surfing, sunkissed skin. It always made her feel safe.

She had driven nonstop to Cornwall the morning she left Freya's, pausing only to pick up her suitcase and Liberty's box of letters from the studio. By the time she arrived in St. Ives, night was falling. She parked outside the cottage, listened to the hot engine ticking in the silence. The street was deserted, lamplight spilling onto the pavement from the pub, the muffled sound of someone's television drifting from over the road. Emma glanced across. Illuminated in a golden window she saw a family sitting down to their evening meal, the husband pecking his wife on the cheek as he sat at the head of the table. She had never felt so alone.

Her breath caught in her throat as she walked to the beach, her footsteps echoing. *Joe,* she thought, the same images playing again and again in her mind. She thought of the night she first guessed there was something wrong. It was Millennium Eve, a party in London. Familiar faces at the party had gone through the motions like a performance chess match, each living up to their usual role, and Emma was Emma, good old reliable Emma, as always.

"Will there be wedding bells this year then, Em?" the host had asked as she helped him clean up afterward. "It's about time Joe made an honest woman of you."

"What's the point?" She had laughed. "We're happy as we are."

They were happy. She had answered that question with the same words so many times she felt like an automaton, but this time something did not ring true. Like a muffled bell, the words were dead on her lips. Happiness tasted of dust, of pressed flowers and yellowed photographs now. Nothing had changed on the surface, but something had sucked the life from their love.

No one would have known to look at them. Two pipers at the party led the procession down to the riverside at midnight, piping aside the crowds, clearing a path through the gardens. Although Emma began the walk arm in arm with Joe, by the time Big Ben began to strike, she found herself alone, holding back a friend's hair as she vomited in a flower bed. She missed the fireworks, the river of fire, in the crush, supporting the girl as her body heaved. Perhaps if she hadn't been walking so slowly, practically carrying the girl back to the party, she wouldn't have seen Joe. He didn't see her, she knew that. As the departing crowds drifted around them, she saw him in a doorway halfway down Lord North Street. He was talking to someone on his mobile. She didn't have to hear what he was saying to know that this was the beginning of the end. The sight of him was enough. He was talking how he used to talk to her when they were first together.

When he found her at the party later, Emma pretended nothing had happened. He had been looking for her, he said. They walked home at sunrise to their half-finished house on Old Church Street, and made love. Joe proclaimed a new beginning while Emma sensed a last good-bye. It took some time, more than a year. Joe was very careful. And then Liberty's cancer returned. Emma had been too young to know what was happening the first time, but now there was no mistaking that this was the end. Between work and caring for her mother, Emma felt herself pulled away from him, just when she needed him the most. She would wake at night in a hotel in Hong Kong or Sydney, tangled in the sheets, her chest heaving as she caught her breath from a dream that had scared her witless. She was always falling, a spiral staircase that went on and on, plunging down, gathering speed, calling for Joe to help her, but he was never there.

After ten years together there was no wedding dress to weep over, no children, not even cats to fight for custody of. She waited for the formality of hard evidence because she knew he would deny it without proof. In her heart, she hoped that she would be proved wrong. Finally, he relaxed too much, left the key to his filing cabinet behind one day when he went to play squash. There it was, a neat paper trail of restaurant and hotel receipts, of one familiar number punctuating his phone bills too often. Emma told herself perhaps there was an innocent explanation—Joe often traveled for business too, and of course he had to call her for work. Then she saw Delilah's text.

Emma moved out, went to Liberty. Her mother was the one person she wanted to pour her heart out to, but couldn't. How could she destroy her mother's love and trust in Joe, now that she was so close to the end? Emma said that Joe was being very understanding, that she wanted to be with her mother constantly, for whatever time they had left. *Which was true,* Emma thought as she walked on the beach. During the last weeks, as Liberty grew frailer, they kept up the pretense. Delilah came one last time to say goodbye, unable to look at Emma until the moment she left—when she shot her a single, triumphant glare.

After the funeral, Emma left Joe's life as she had arrived, with a single case, the years between them slipping away like sand between the cracks. He had denied everything at first, as she had expected, but eventually he caved in under her calm fury. She was not a vindictive woman. She toyed with the idea of slashing suits, or destroying future pleasure in his wine by turning up the heating. But she knew that for him to have to return to their life and find it complete, except for her, would be the best revenge. Joe hated change. He loved their life. He told her Delilah had caught him at a weak time—they could start again. He said their new home was a testament to their years of love. The ashtray on his desk was there because they had picked it out together in a little shop in Hamburg; every painting on their walls had been discussed and hunted out in tandem on their Sunday trips to Christie's in South Kensington.

Emma thought of the night Liberty's will was read, how they drowned their grief in the familiar comfort of each other's arms. He did not want her to go, he told her that much in their final conversation, his voice thick with regretful tears. It was insane, he loved her, this was just a fling. When he returned from New York, he said, they would start again. She mustn't do anything rash. He would break it off with Delilah. She remembered how her heart stood still.

"You mean you're still seeing her?" Emma had pushed him away, pulled the sheet protectively around her. "Get out! How could you . . . ?"

"Emma, I love you," he said.

"Get out!" She had thrown his clothes at him, bolted the door behind him as he stood in the hallway begging her to forgive him.

When Joe returned a week later, he found their house as clean, as perfect-looking as a blown egg. He congratulated himself, thinking Emma had seen sense. He ignored Delilah's frantic messages and cooked dinner for Emma—oysters and roast chicken, their favorite—and uncorked a bottle of Sancerre. As the night grew darker, Joe waited by candlelight for her to come home. He called her phone—it was switched off. The oysters grew dull, the chicken dry and burned. Finally, he searched the house. He found only a few things had gone. Her favorite perfume—the others left half used on her dressing table. Her best knickers, old jeans and boots, the leather jacket they had both worn on and off, though it looked a hundred times more at home on her than on him. He glanced at her bedside table. She had left behind the photograph of the two of them at the party on the night when they had first become lovers but taken the one of her as a baby, in her mother's arms. A small rectangle of dark mahogany shone in the silvery dust. She had taken the best of her life and gone. She was traveling light.

The week in Cornwall had done her good. Emma felt more herself, she thought, as she scrambled up onto what she had always thought of as "her" rock and looked out to sea. Beams of sunlight between the clouds illuminated the surf. The pain was less keen already, she realized, as she tucked the leather jacket around her. She felt the baby kick, push against her hand. She rubbed her stomach, thinking of the night she had arrived. That first night on the beach she had cried Joe's name into the wind again and again, her body convulsed with sobs as she let him go. The salt air had lashed her face, mingled with her tears. "Why?" she cried out. "Why me? Why him? Why take Joe from me?" She had stumbled back to the cottage, searched for the key Freya left hidden beneath a stone beside the back door. On the step she found a pint of milk and a pot of soup, still warm. Through her tears, she laughed. Freya had obviously called the neighbors and told them to keep an eye out for her.

Am I that predictable? she wondered now. She buried her face in her soft pink scarf, inhaled the warm, white floral scent of Chérie Farouche. From her pocket, Emma pulled one of Liberty's letters. She had been saving this for her last morning. When she'd arrived at the cottage she had laid the letters out on the old kitchen table, and sat looking at the titles, choosing which to open first. The seventh was marked "In Case of Emergency" and her hand had hovered over it. *No. Better save that one.* She had smiled to herself and picked this one instead. Her mother's handwriting looped across the envelope: "On Family." Emma turned it over in her hands, and tore it open.

Em, if I know you, you will have kept these letters unopened for some time. You always did prefer the anticipation of wrapped presents, always savored every gift. You're not quite as bad as Freya, who still saves every sheet of wrapping paper to reuse, but I think she taught you the value of enjoying every moment, something I understood too late.

   Do you remember that time when you were about seven years old, and you released a load of Charles's butterflies? I think you thought you were doing them a favor, giving them their freedom, but of course they were tropical and Charles lost his temper with you. You weren't a naughty child at all. In fact I remember being rather relieved that you had done something so uncharacteristically spontaneous. I said to you to learn from your mistake. I told you that you have to discover life's lessons yourself; no one can teach you. You said, "That's not fair, Mum. What are the lessons?" I still think you have to experience them for yourself, but as I won't be around to guide you, I'll try in these letters to tell you the lessons I've learned.

   I rather hope you might read this listening to Sister Sledge. "We Are Family . . ."—do you remember, we used to dance to that all the time? We are a family of women—and Charles, of course. I've always regretted that your father chose 2.4 kids, a station wagon, and a woman who wore drip-dry nylon over you and me, but what could I do? Trust me to choose the most traditional hippie on the West Coast of America. My relationships were a disaster, but we made the best of it, I think, you and I, we made our family.

I wonder if Freya has talked to you about me, now that I have gone? I have had suspicions for years, but Freya always refuted them. I think she was trying to protect me, in some misguided way. I never quite felt like I belonged, Em, never really felt at home. It's like I was missing something that I had never known. Perhaps she will tell you more. Perhaps you will be able to solve the mystery of our family. I have run out of time. Maybe that's the first lesson—I suspect in life the families you create are not always tied by blood. I hope that you will discover the truth about ours. I love you.

Mum x

TWELVE

The surgeons in the field station near the Jarama front worked bare-chested, their legs wrapped in white aprons and their feet in white boots. A rickety metal scaffold supported a weak spotlight above the patient.

"What have we got coming in?" one of the surgeons called.

"Six abdominals and a couple of heads, Doctor," Freya said.

"How is the last man doing?"

"He's stable, Doctor. The transfusion is helping."

"Good. Scalpel."

Freya groped around in the darkness behind her for the right instrument, candlelight flickering over the silver scalpels on the tray.

"How many bottles of blood have we left?" he asked.

"We just used the last one," a nurse near the refrigerator replied.

"Damn. The delivery is late." He wiped the sweat from his brow with the back of his hand. "Get a message to the blood bank to send us everything they can." He leaned wearily against the edge of the operating table. "Right, we'll have to give this chap a direct transfusion. Who is type O?"

Freya raised her hand.

"When did you last give blood?"

"A couple of months ago."

"That'll do."

In a side room, Freya lay down on a cold, damp camp bed next to the wounded man and closed her eyes. She tried desperately not to think about the apparatus she could hear being set up at her side. Instead, she forced her mind to linger on the handsome old *palacio* in Madrid where she'd been billeted for a couple of nights on her way to the front, with its beautiful stone staircase, clipped hedges, and palm trees. It had been abandoned by a Nationalist supporter at the start of the war, and now nurses and ambulance drivers played billiards in the grand rooms with their silk drapes, and flicked through magazines in the library. Each night they ate their bread and chickpeas from the gilded dinner service. It seemed unreal that they were in such peace and luxury only a few miles from the front.

"Right," a male voice said. "You'll just feel a little scratch."

Freya tensed. "That was very good. I didn't feel a thing."

"Good. Let's just get you hooked up to this guy's vein."

"If it's all the same to you, I'd rather not have a blow-by-blow description." She opened her eyes and looked at the doctor gazing down at her. She could tell from the crinkles at the corners of his eyes he was smiling behind his mask.

"You had your eyes screwed so tight anyone would think you're afraid."

"I am. I can't stand needles, at least when they are anywhere near me."

"That's a bit tricky for a nurse, surely?" He glanced over at the wounded soldier. "I'm sure this guy is going to appreciate it." The doctor settled her arm, checked the blood was flowing to the patient at her side. "There, well done. You're kind of busy in here today."

"Aren't we always?" Freya said. "At least when this place is crammed full, there's a bit of warmth from all the bodies. We have over two hundred at the moment, even though this unit is designed to cope with only fifty. The men are three to a bed, lying on the floor, everywhere . . ." She felt she was talking too much, forced a smile as she flexed her hand. It still ached from the cold. That morning she had helped some of the Spanish nurses wash sheets in the freezing water of a stream that flowed into the Jarama river, scrubbing them clean on the rocks. The air smelled of the battle, but also of thyme, the herbs crushed beneath the boots of thousands of men.

"I love you Brits"—he laughed—"always looking on the bright side. I'm Tom Henderson by the way."

"Pleased to meet you, Dr. Henderson."

"Call me Tom."

Freya looked up at his kind blue eyes. "I'm Freya."

"Well, Freya, I reckon after this you've earned yourself a cup of tea," he said, mimicking an English accent.

"Tea? I wish. I'm not sure the tea *is* tea anymore," Freya said. "You're too kind. I must get on. The casualties are pouring in."

"You know what they are calling this battle?"

"I believe they are calling it Suicide Hill." Freya sighed. "I heard the Fifteenth Battalion are doing their best, but we've lost virtually every officer, and over half the British men."

Tom checked the patient. "Good, his color's getting better." He sat on the edge of Freya's bed and pulled down his mask. "I think the Abraham Lincoln Battalion lost even more. Those poor, brave American guys marched right into the Nationalist lines without any artillery cover. They were cut to shreds."

Freya shook her head and sighed. "At least we've stopped them cutting off Madrid."

"'They shall not pass'?" Tom looked at her. "When you see these boys in here, I wonder at what cost." He smiled sadly. "Say, when was the last time you had a proper meal?"

"Why? Do I look ghastly?"

"No. A little pale."

"They gave us some stew last night." Freya's teeth began chattering. "Every time I get something with small bones, I tell myself it's rabbit not cat."

"Me too." Tom stood and checked the patient. "I reckon you're about done," he said. "A few more minutes." He settled back beside her. "Would you like me to hold your hand? You seem a little shaky."

"Would you mind awfully?"

"Jeez, you're freezing," he said, rubbing warmth into her fingers.

"I'm fine. I think I'm just rather tired. We've been working nonstop for the last few days. I've only had a couple of hours' sleep." Freya fixed her gaze on his, tried to fight the wooziness she felt.

"Here, give me your other hand."

"Thank you." Freya looked at his lowered head, his dark hair falling forward over his brow. "How long have you been down here?"

"The Canadian Blood Transfusion Service has been going since last November, but I came across in January to join Dr. Bethune's unit. We traveled over with a group of Americans from New York. I'm with the Mackenzie-Papineau Battalion."

"Oh, I assumed . . ."

"No, I'm Canadian." Tom glanced up, grinned at her, dimples forming in his stubble-covered cheeks. "Toronto born and bred." He checked his watch. "It wasn't a great journey—third class all the way across the Atlantic, four bunked up in each cabin and everyone sick as a dog. I spent most of the voyage on deck."

"Did you stop in Paris?"

"Yeah, what a swell place. I'd love to go back there someday."

"So would I." Freya was already imagining strolling arm in arm with him along the cobbled streets of Montmartre.

"Then we hopped a train to Marseilles and a truck to Perpignan, and made it over the Pyrenees. How about you?"

"Our first base was on the Aragon front, near Huesca. Some of us went on to other field stations from there. Eventually I ended up in Madrid, then came here with the Medical Aid ambulances—"

"Did you?" Tom interrupted. "You mean some lucky guy had you alone in his ambulance all the way here? I'm going to change the way I travel."

Freya blushed. She wasn't used to someone being so bold. "It's a beautiful country, don't you think?"

"It's getting better with every moment."

"The orange trees, the dusty roads . . ."

"Maybe you'd like to take a walk later?" Tom stood and stretched, his white T-shirt pulling taught over his hard stomach.

"That would be . . ." Freya glanced up at him. "I'd like that very much."

He leaned down to remove the needle, and Freya turned her head away. "Listen," he said. "They've got us holed up in some swanky house back in Madrid. Apparently it's safer—the fascists won't bomb the wealthy districts. I saw the way you worked today. If you're happy to take your chances with Bethune's temper, we need a new nurse for the unit—one of ours had to go home with typhoid. Would you consider transferring?"

Freya didn't hesitate. "I'd love to."

"It's tough work, you'll be out on the front line a lot. Delivering blood, administering it to dying men." Tom pressed some gauze against the inside of her elbow. "There you go. Just keep the pressure on this for a moment or two."

She rolled her head toward him, and winced. "As long as you don't ask me to do another direct transfusion for a while, I think I can handle it. Sometimes I wish I could do more. It's chaos. There are so many wounded men everywhere, the awful noise of them crying out . . ." Her voice trailed off as she thought of the neat, clean wards she had been used to working in at the Nightingale Training School back in London.

As the orderlies lifted the wounded man's stretcher, Tom offered Freya his hand. "If they are crying out *'Enfermera, curandera, ven aquí!* Nurse! Come here!' they stand a chance. It is the silent ones like this guy you have to watch." Tom checked the patient's papers, and tucked them under the man's blanket. "Jordi del Valle. I went against my gut instinct trying to save him, but he's so young."

"Will he make it?"

"Who knows? Amputations are tough. He almost gave up on the table." Tom sighed. "There are too many for us to treat, and we're short on resources." He gazed down at her. "Look at us, we're working by candlelight half the time."

"It's rather romantic, if you look at it in the right way."

"There you go again, looking on the bright side." Tom checked the dressing on her arm. "Does it ever bother you, when some of the guys get amorous? I've seen the way they carry on."

"Not at all. They're like children, most of them. They're lonely. The ones who aren't, well . . ." Freya pulled a pistol from the pocket of her apron.

Tom held his hands up, laughing. "Thanks for the warning."

"I didn't mean . . ." She fell silent as they heard shouting outside. An explosion shook the room. Freya felt the ground tremble beneath her feet. The blood in her ears sang. Tom pulled her into his arms, shielding her, crouching against the wall as plaster dust rained down.

"I thought we were safe here." The bed where Freya had been lying was littered with plaster. Instinctively they both looked at the ceiling, waiting for more explosions.

"Maybe he got lucky, maybe he had lousy aim. Are you OK?" Tom shifted back a little, his arm still encircling her waist. They could hear shouting, footsteps running along the corridor.

"I'm fine. Funny, isn't it? How your reflexes kick in." Freya looked at him, brushed the dust from his nose. Her heart was beating fast, coursing with adrenaline and the closeness of him. He leaned in to kiss her then, his lips brushing hers. "Do you kiss all your donors, Dr. Henderson?"

"Only the cute ones." He smiled, glanced up as they heard car horns blaring from outside. "I've got to get back to Madrid, but I'd like to get you that cup of tea sometime."

Freya held his gaze. "I'd like that."

"I'll talk to Beth about getting you out of here too," Tom said as he stood. "See you soon." He paused in the doorway and turned to her. "Happy Valentine's Day, Freya."

THIRTEEN

I am glad you're back," Freya said to Emma. "I was worried when we couldn't get through to you."

"I'm afraid I threw my mobile in the sea." Emma scuffed through a pile of golden leaves on the path. She had listened to Joe's final message one last time: *"I've done something really stupid. Listen, I'm going to make this right."* It was unbearable to her. It was too late.

"You're making rather a habit of this," Charles said as he walked stiffly beside them along the Serpentine. "Disappearing."

"Liberty always taught me that you can't rely on anyone except yourself. I just needed some time alone." A brisk wind chopped at the water as a small boy sent a red sailing boat skimming across the surface.

"Nonsense. You know you can always rely on us." Charles turned up the collar of his black wool coat. "We were both worried. You can't cope with all this by yourself, Em."

Freya shook her head. "I hate seeing you like this. You look just how you looked when you were a child, determined not to cry when you'd fallen over."

"I'm fine." Emma's throat was tight.

"There's been no news of Joe," Freya said quietly.

"I know." Emma walked on. "I asked his mother to let me know if they heard anything."

"They'll be pleased about the baby . . ." Freya's voice trailed off.

"I'll tell them, in time. Not yet." Emma flinched. "I mean, they have a proper daughter-in-law now."

"Delilah's on her way home."

Emma spun around to face her. "Please don't say anything to her."

"She'll have to know eventually."

She shook her head. "I'm not ready to tell her yet. This baby is the one good thing I have in my life right now, and I'm not going to let her spoil that too." Emma realized what she had said. "One of three good things." She looped her arms with Freya and Charles and they walked on. "Has the deal gone through? I signed the papers."

"Yes, I saw you'd dropped them into the office last night." Freya pointed to a bench. "Shall we sit down?" Charles dusted off the seat and offered Freya his hand as she sat. "The thing is, the American buyers have pulled out. Frankly, I had a feeling they might."

"Because of 9/11?" Emma took a deep breath, gazed across the lake. "So now what happens? I can't possibly work with Lila. Not now that Joe's gone."

"The package is all there. Delilah thinks she can find another buyer."

"Let her, then."

"Are you sure, Emma?" Charles said. "You don't have to rush into anything. She should be the one to go."

Emma shook her head. "I can't possibly buy her out, not with her and Joe's stake. She holds all the cards as his wife. She's won. Delilah has all the money she ever wanted. I mean, Joe was always so organized. I bet he changed his will right after the wedding?"

Freya nodded. "Delilah faxed me a copy, as if I needed proof. It's so unfair." Freya poked angrily at a crumpled crisp packet with her stick. "Why should you lose everything?"

Emma looked at her. "No one said life is fair. Look at Mum."

"What will you do? There's the studio, of course. You could start again . . ."

"No." Emma shook her head. "I'm going to sell it."

"Where will you live? You're welcome to come to us, but there's only two bedrooms."

Emma paused. "You know, I sat on the beach one night and thought 'I can go anywhere.' I have you and Charles, and I'll always be there for you, but I have no ties anywhere now, not really. It's amazing how quickly everything that feels solid can fall apart. Joe, Mum, my home, my job, they've all gone."

"Oh, Em, darling." Freya took her hand.

"I'm not feeling sorry for myself," she said. "I'm just . . ." Emma raked her hand through her hair. "I went through Mum's will again while I was away. I've decided to move to Valencia permanently."

"You've what?" Freya's eyes opened wide. "Using the place as a holiday home is one thing, but why move there?"

"Why not? I want to bring my child up away from here, away from all this. I want to start again."

"But Liberty said no one has lived in the house for decades, Emma." Charles dug an old coin out of his pocket, rubbed the face of it with his thumb. "It's probably falling to pieces."

"I don't care if it is. I'm going to take the money from selling the studio to do it up. I'm going to make a new life. Of course, I hope you'll come and visit, come and stay as long as you want."

"No, I don't think so." Charles looked away.

"Why not? You loved Spain."

"The country I loved did not survive, nor did many people I loved. Everything has changed." Charles's fingers worked nervously, turning the coin over and over.

"But surely after all this time? Valencia sounds wonderful."

"It is." Freya paused. "It always was heaven on earth. 'The land of flowers, light and love.'"

"Really?"

"Oh, that was an old song." Freya stared out across the lake. "The mountains, those wonderful blue domes, *Blood and Sand* . . ." She sensed Emma's confusion. "Tyrone Power and Rita Hayworth, darling. It's magical. Did you know the Holy Grail is in the cathedral?"

"You're kidding?" Emma smiled, but it felt strange to her, the muscles of her face unused to it. "You must come with me."

"No. No, I don't think so. You must discover the country for yourself. Our memories of the civil war . . . Well, a lot of idealists saw their beliefs broken and destroyed when Franco won." Freya glanced at Charles. "If you've made up your mind to go, I don't want our experiences to color your time there."

Charles cleared his throat. "What's that lovely old Majorcan saying?"

"'It was and it was not so,'" Freya said. "That sums it all up, doesn't it? Two sides to every story. Light and shade," she murmured. "I still maintain that there were remarkable acts of individual courage and mercy—they got you through the worst. But the killing was brutal. Who was that ghastly man who said 'Death to intelligence, long live death'?"

"Millán Astray." Charles grimaced. "He founded the Spanish Foreign Legion. They were nasty when you came up against them, I can tell you. Very fond of their knife work."

Freya nodded. "War is always bloody, civil war more than most."

"Brother turned against brother," Charles said, shooting a glance at Freya. "There was such suspicion everywhere. The Republicans tried to rout out the secret Francoists—they called them the 'Fifth Column,' the enemy within."

"But they didn't get all of them," Freya said quietly. "Frankly the politics were irrelevant to many of us. People like Charles and I went to Spain because it felt like the only decent, human thing to do."

"The British government was scared, so were conservatives everywhere," Charles said. "All they saw were headlines about Reds raping nuns, massacring priests and landowners. I tell you I never met such a decent crowd as the men and women I fought with in the Brigades. They were just ordinary workers, dockers, and miners many of them, who saw that people like them were suffering and democracy was at stake. Now, people think the International Brigades were full of poets with flowers in their caps."

"Or butterflies," Freya shot back.

"You were just starting your Ph.D. when you went, weren't you, Uncle Charles?" Emma said "You had a scholarship, didn't you?"

"Hm—oh yes, I was a grammar school boy. Our parents rather left us in the lurch when they were killed. I managed to scrape together enough to buy the cottages—Chelsea was terribly run-down and boho in those days, and St. Ives was a little fishing village. Do you remember, Frey, we had damp running down the walls? We had to hide behind the sofa from the milkman on many an occasion."

"Is that why you didn't finish your studies?"

"Well, you didn't need to in those days, to teach of course. In some ways it was almost looked down upon—a bit ungentlemanly. Look at Nabokov—one of the finest lepidopterists there ever was, and a complete amateur."

"You had a correspondence with him for a while, didn't you?" Freya tucked a strand of hair behind her ear, pulled her black beret down. "Charles was quite the catch in those days," she said mischievously. "He was one of the terribly fashionable set. It was such an interesting time. A lot of his contemporaries became quite notorious."

"I was rather naive, to say the least." He paused. "About a lot of things."

"Did you join the Apostles in the end?" Freya said. She leaned toward Emma and whispered, "I've never been able to get a straight answer out of him."

"Hm? No." Charles crossed his legs. "I did get an invitation through my pigeonhole, but I thought it was for some happy-clappy church group, and tossed it out."

"Poppycock, I don't believe that for a moment!" Freya laughed. "It was a secret society," she said to Emma. "Chaps from Trinity and King's would meet on a Saturday evening to debate. There was a lifelong bond: people like Lytton Strachey, Rupert Brooke, Burgess and Blunt belonged over the years. Was Cornford ever a member?"

"John? No, he was far too self-effacing," Charles said.

"Of course by Charles's time they were recruiting for looks rather than intellect."

"Oh, shut up, Frey. You're talking about things you know nothing about."

"I've never understood why he didn't go back to King's after Spain, he loved it so there. It was almost like he was punishing himself," she said to Emma.

"Punishing myself? Do you think so? Perhaps there were too many memories." Charles frowned. "I was happy enough at Downing. I went back after 1945 when Wigglesworth took over from Imms. He specialized in butterflies and moths, you see. Marvelous family man, very warm—though you wouldn't think so from Updike's poem about him. It was an exciting time. We really revolutionized the way people looked at insects with the work we did in Cambridge. I was looking into scent scales on butterfly wings at first—you know they release chemicals, pheromones, to attract females?"

Charles had explained his theories a hundred times, but Emma humored him. "It sounds fascinating, Uncle Charles."

"Not bad for little creatures who weigh the same as two rose petals and only live for a matter of days."

"Did many of your friends go to Spain?"

"Oh yes. There was me, Hugo, John Cornford . . ."

"He was a poet, wasn't he?"

"Yes," Charles said. "He came back in '36 to persuade us to join the International Brigades. Of course, he was dead a few months later. I saw him, briefly, in Madrid." Charles smiled sadly at the memory. "He looked like Byron, terribly dark and romantic with a bandage around his head. They left by train for the Andújar front on Christmas Eve. We lost Ralph Fox, and John, the day after his twenty-first birthday." He sighed, and looked at Emma. "If you're really interested in all those old stories, I have a going-away present for you. Come and see me in Cambridge before you leave."

"Thank you. I will. I hope you'll change your mind about Valencia. There's no hurry. It will take a few months to get the place straight." She waited, hopefully. "I'm sure you'll want to come out and see the baby?"

"We'll see." Freya smiled thinly. "I hope you know what you're doing."

"How will you support yourself?" Charles asked.

"I'll think of something. Perfume, cosmetics, it all seems so pointless after 9/11."

"You're wrong," Freya said. Emma caught the sudden hardness in her voice. "People need things like perfume and poetry, music and art, more than ever during times like this. People need to remember the simple joys in life. If you forget, if life loses its color then they have won. Those cowardly, heartless bastards have won."

"Frey," Charles said.

"I'm sorry. It's talking about the past, it always . . . Well . . ." She blinked, lowered her gaze. "We can't let them win."

Emma realized suddenly that she had never seen Freya cry, not once, not even when Liberty died. She had wanted to ask her about Liberty's letter, but this didn't seem like the time. Freya looked tired suddenly.

"I just hope you know what you're doing," Freya said.

"Don't listen to her," Charles said. "She's always been overcautious . . ." Freya scowled at him. "Nonsense. I've had my moments."

Charles patted Emma's hand. "Good luck to you, Em. If this is what you need to do, then do it." He looked out across the lake. "It all goes by so fast. We have to enjoy what can be enjoyed."

FOURTEEN

Freya worked with a couple of the Spanish nurses until almost sunset, clearing debris from some of the ruined rooms in the abandoned farmhouse, scrubbing the uneven floors, and setting up more beds for the field station to use. She was exhausted, her hands rubbed raw from moving bricks and rocks, her shins bruised and scraped from tripping over metal camp beds. All she wanted now was a stiff drink and to relax with Tom back in Madrid. She longed for a hot bath, for her bed. She felt like a princess waking there in the mornings, surrounded by the luxury of the Nationalists' abandoned home where the Canadian blood transfusion unit had established its headquarters. The contrasts of her life amazed her, the vividness of her days, that in so much horror she had found happiness. She had found Tom. She leaned against her mop and lifted up the tin can of olive oil, its wick sputtering as she surveyed the low-ceilinged, windowless room, the closest they would come to a proper ward.

"Well done, girls," she said. "At least now you will be ready for the morning."

"There you are!" a male voice said.

"Tom?" She spun around. She caught the curious look one of the other nurses shot her. "This room is ready, Dr. Henderson."

"Good. You didn't have to help out with this, Nurse Temple. You're work-ing hard enough with the transfusion unit as it is."

"I wanted to," she said, hand on hip.

"Very well. Are you ready to head back to Madrid?" he asked, looking up from the notes he had been reading. He waited for the Spanish nurses to leave, and tossed the clipboard onto the bed. He took Freya in his arms, kissed her then, his fingers arcing across the small of her back, pulling her to him. "So this is where you've been hiding. I missed you today," he said, kissing her neck. They fell back against the wall together, Freya's fingers tan-gled in his thick, dark hair. "Christ, I've never wanted anyone so much in my life as you."

"Tom." She whispered his name, her lips against his ear. Her head was swimming with tiredness and desire. At the sound of footsteps in the cor-ridor, they both froze, and then broke apart. Freya waited, staring at the ruined doorway, her chest rising and falling with her quick breaths.

"Come on." Tom led her outside once the orderlies had passed with a swaying stretcher. "We have a little time before the ambulance leaves."

They walked away from the farmhouse, cut across the fields along a mule track. The sun was low in the sky. It felt to Freya like she was looking at the land through amber, clear golden light spilling around them. Once they were out of sight, Tom took her hand.

Freya pulled the red scarf from her hair and shook out her blond bob. Her body ached with exertion, but as they walked side by side, she felt it quicken with desire. The warm wind carried the clean scent of him, of cotton, fresh sweat, cologne. She felt the heat rising in her cheeks. In the distance they could hear the boom of the guns on the front line. Freya leaned in to him, their shoulders touching.

"Moments like this, it seems impossible that we're at war," she said.

Tom slung his arm over her shoulder, and she embraced his waist, felt the lean hard muscles of his back working as they climbed away from the field station, away from the war. He pressed his lips to the top of her head. "This is beautiful. I bet this place is full of poppies in the summertime." The hillside blushed rose around them, the earth salmon pink, umber, peach, dotted with sage green and silver trees, dusted with white powder like the cheek of a courtesan. "We could be any young couple, out enjoying the sun-set, each other's company . . ." He broke off as a sniper bullet zipped past them and embedded itself in a tree. "Jesus! Get down!" Tom pulled her to the ground, shielded her with his body in the long grass.

"What was that?" Freya shuddered as a second bullet hit the tree in front of them, splintering the bark.

"We must have drifted too close to the lines." Tom rolled onto his side, looked around. He pointed to a small copse of trees they had passed not far down the hill, and a tumbled-down wall of stones. "You go first, stay low on your stomach and head for that wall. That guy's a long way off but we don't want to take any chances."

"Tom, I'm scared."

"I'll be right behind you." He kissed her quickly. "If he's going to get to you, he'll have to go through me first."

Freya pushed through the grass on her stomach, panting, rocks and dry earth cutting at her elbows, her knees. The stalks of grass danced above her, dark against the sunset. After what felt like an age, the wall loomed ahead, and she scrambled around, sat with her back against the warm stones, catching her breath. Tom was right behind her, his boots scattering earth and pebbles as he joined her. They looked at each other, and burst out laughing. Tom reached into his pocket and shook out two cigarettes from a crumpled packet. He lit them, and passed one to her.

"This is going to make dates at the cinema seem kind of dull in comparison," he said, laughing.

Freya exhaled a curl of smoke, and smiled. "It will take some beating."

"Still," Tom said, wiping some dirt from her cheek with his thumb, "it will be something to tell the grandkids about."

Freya felt the space between them contract and shift. "Or perhaps not," she said quietly. The moment, the possibility was there. "I want you," she whispered, her lips fluttering across his cheek, his neck, like the slow-beating wings of a butterfly. He reached over, stubbed out the cigarettes and pulled her into his arms. They fell back against the earth, tangled in each other's arms, in the swaying grass.

Freya stared up at the sky, pinprick stars illuminating one by one. "I wish we could stay like this forever," she murmured. Tom raised his head from her stomach, kissed the arc of her rib cage, her breast. He rolled onto his back and took Freya in his arms. She felt the warmth of his chest against her cheek, heard the steady beat of his heart.

"We should be careful," he said.

"I don't think anyone knows we're seeing each other."

"I don't mean that. I don't give a damn who knows we're together. I meant that I want to take care of you." He smoothed her hair back from her brow. "Maybe we want a little time together alone before . . ."

"Oh! You mean . . ." Freya blushed. "I wouldn't worry. I haven't had . . . I mean, my . . ."

"You know, for a nurse you can be awfully prim," he said, laughing.

Freya dug him in the ribs. "They've stopped, anyway. I haven't had one for months so it's very unlikely I'd get pregnant. And if I did . . ."

"It would be wonderful," he said, holding her tight. "Stay with me tonight," he said. "Do you love me, Freya? Could you?"

"Of course." She sat up, held his dear face in her hands, smiled as she looked at him. "Of course I love you, Tom."

He reached up to her. "Marry me."

She turned her cheek, kissed the palm of his hand. "You're crazy. You hardly know me."

"I know you," he said, holding her gaze. "I've never been more sure of anything in my life. Marry me, Freya."

FIFTEEN

Emma raced along the platform and waved her arm at the guard. Just as the last doors were closing, she jumped onto the packed train. By the time she found her seat in the buffet car, the carriage lurched, and they pulled out of Atocha Station, sunlight blinding her as they clattered along the line. A businessman sitting opposite helped her place her suitcase on the rack, and Emma settled back for the journey to Valencia. She pulled the blind down slightly, and closed her eyes. She had spent the morning exploring the museums in Madrid, and the image of Picasso's *Guernica* danced in her mind as she dozed.

The aroma of lunch cooking in the train kitchen drifted to her—she picked out the scents of garlic and onion, the rich, dull fragrance of saffron. In Spain, Emma felt like she was coming out of hibernation. The night before, she had walked miles, exploring the city streets, stopping for tapas in pavement cafés and watching the elegant natives taking their evening *paseo*. The smells of the city were intoxicating to her—black tobacco, steaming coffee, drains, fresh tomato frying—each one helped her senses come back to life. She had paused outside the door of an old *perfumería*, transfixed by the gilded, colored bottles in the window. She closed her eyes, and inhaled as the door swung open. *Roses,* she thought. *Mum's perfume.* It was then she was sure she had done the right thing in coming to Spain.

The train clattered out of the city, and Emma took a book from her bag.
She ran her fingers over the embossed title on the linen cover—*Butterflies
of Andalusia* by Charles St. John Temple—flicked it open, and smiled at
the studio portrait of Charles. Thick fair hair swept over a smooth brow, a
flamboyant tie knotted loosely at the collar of his white shirt. His familiar
blue eyes gazed into the distance. *This must have been taken before the war,*
Emma thought. *He's never looked that unguarded in all the time I've known
him.* She turned the pages:

"Spain. The greatest misery and greatest happiness of my life." Emma
raised an eyebrow as she read the first line. She had never heard Charles talk
in such passionate terms.

I felt the wind of change blowing from the south. I walked the dusty roads,
brown as a prophet, bitten by more than the bugs in the roadside inns. I
traveled through days of searing light and heat. My Spain was one where
chickens pecked the floors and swallows roosted in the eaves of an old
dance hall strung with carnations. Where black-eyed girls danced, savage,
controlled, terrifying in their beauty, to a boy singing with the lovely lam-
entations of Islam in his voice. My Spain was a land where men who were
vigorous, independent, undisciplined called you "hombre." It was a land
that drew you into the heart of its large, warm families—and yet I have
never felt more alone than in deserted villages shuttered by shadows, or in
vast fields where suddenly a thousand white butterflies rose like a melody
on the wind.

Emma blew a slow whistle under her breath, and shook her head. This
was not the Charles she knew. Just as she always did, she then flicked to the
last page:

Some said that Spain was an emotional luxury for a bunch of wet-behind-
the-ears idealists, but any man or woman who loved and fought for the
country would disagree. Spain is Europe in miniature. The Civil War was
an explosion in an armory, a force that had been building for centuries. I
fought for this country, and, like many, I paid the price. My Spain, the
land of moonlit walks in the Albaicin and Alhambra, of the chink of
mules' hooves on loose stone paths, of ocher earth and crushed mint, of
dark parchment faces aged too early, has gone. Life is a puff of air compared to the moment of truth, the Spaniards say—and in this beautiful,

benighted country I have seen too many face that moment when we are
all entirely alone.

Emma riffled through the pages, searching for the photographs. She had
expected the book to be a dry catalog of the butterflies Charles had seen in
Andalusia, but drawings and notes of these were juxtaposed with images
and recollections of the war. *He took all these? I didn't know Charles was a
professional photographer too.* She paused at a photo of a slight, fair woman
resting her head against the broken column of a bombed-out building. She
read the title: *Gerda.* Gerda had a smile on her lips, but she was looking
away from the camera, as if she was trying not to laugh. Emma imagined
Charles then, pacing the ruined building, his camera trained on the woman.
Gerda, she thought. *Gerda Taro, she was Robert Capa's partner.* Emma sensed
the intensity of Charles's eye. She checked the date—*Cordoba Front, June
1937.* It was a few weeks before the battle at Brunete.

As the train sped along, Emma looked out at the ocher hills sweeping
past beneath the watchful gaze of a huge, iconic black Osborne bull bill-
board. *Poor Charles,* she thought.

Emma flicked on through image after image of the war: soldiers' solemn,
defiant faces, broken bodies on the barricades, children with the knowing,
exhausted look of old men and women. *The things you and Freya saw.* At
the final photograph, she paused, and turned the book sideways. It was a
nude—a young woman, modestly draped with a white sheet, a black fan
obscuring her features. *Charles!* Emma smiled. *Well I never, you old devil.*
She scanned the final paragraph, opposite:

If this poor, beleaguered country rises from the ashes it will be because
of her women. What man fails to appreciate is that societies can move
backward as well as forward. We believed in victory, it was not possible
that we would lose. Yet, we lost. We fought with our women at our side,
and yet Spain returned to the past. Spanish women have in them all
that is good in Spain. It is alive in their hearts and their devotion. In
Spain I met the most beautiful women of my life, luminous and fragile,
fleeting and lovely as any butterfly. If Spain rises, free again, it will be
because of them.

Charles had blushed when he'd given her the book. "It's terribly dated,
of course," he'd said as she unwrapped the brown paper parcel after their

tea together at Fitzbillies, near his Cambridge rooms. "At the time it was eclipsed by Lee's book, and Orwell's. I'm a bit like that chap on the Yellow Pages advert. Whenever I pass a secondhand bookshop, I feel compelled to ask, 'Do you have a copy of *Butterflies of Andalusia* by Charles St. John Temple?'" Charles laughed. "The prose leaves something to be desired, but perhaps the photographs have stood the test of time."

Emma flicked through foxed pages that smelled of mildew. "You're being modest. They are marvelous! Why did you stop taking pictures?" She could see how proud he was of the little book.

He dabbed at his lips with his napkin. "I had my moment. There was a little show, at the club. They still have one of my photos, you know. But, well . . ." His gaze fell as he nodded at his injured arm. "This was something of a handicap. Frankly, we needed a steady income when your mother was a child. Freya went back to nursing once Liberty was at school, but when she was a baby we had to make ends meet on my salary."

Emma took his hand. "Thank you, I'll treasure it."

"I can't believe you're going to Spain," he said quietly.

"You'd visited before the war, hadn't you?"

"Me? Oh, yes. I'd been fannying around chasing butterflies in Andalusia just before war broke out. Hugo and I stayed at Gerald Brenan's old place near Yegen. He was very in with the Bloomsbury Group, you know. Lovely chap, taught me so much about Spanish history." Charles cleared his throat. "They have the most marvelous blues down there, and the fritillaries . . . oh they are lovely. It's a wonderful place—I remember seeing swarms of ladybirds that turned the rivers bloodred." He paused, leaned against the table as he rose, stiffly. At the door, he passed Emma her coat and retrieved his trilby and scarf.

"Thank you," she said, and they stepped out onto the cold pavement. Rush-hour traffic swept by in the night, and streetlights gleamed through the bare-branched trees. A crowd of students heading back to their digs drifted past them as Charles and Emma walked slowly, arm in arm.

They paused at the gate of his college, and Charles put his arm around Emma's shoulders and hugged her.

"Take care, Uncle Charles," Emma said, hugging him tightly. She breathed in his familiar scent—Acqua di Parma, mothballs, Drum tobacco. "I hope you're not doing too much."

"Me?" he said. "I retired officially ages ago, but they're good enough to let me pootle around the place. I'm amazed they haven't stuffed me and put me in a glass case along with the other relics." He winked at her. "It's just good to get out of London to be honest. Frey doesn't need me under her feet all the time. I've spent sixty-odd years at the university on and off. I belong here." He tipped his hat to her. "Take care of yourself, Em. You know we are always here if you need us."

Emma thought of Liberty's letter: *In Case of Emergency.* "Same here. You know where I'll be if you need me."

"The land of flowers, light and love . . . ?"

SIXTEEN

When they weren't reporting from the front line, Charles and Hugo helped out at a battlefield school for the Republican soldiers. The men were being taught to read and write and instructed in the virtues of being faithful to one's wife, of teetotalism, vegetarianism. The earnest study of the uneducated men had moved them both, and as Charles taught them the basics about flora and fauna, Hugo created wonderful illustrations of poppies, butterflies, and insects on the old chipped blackboard.

After the class that morning, as they walked among the troops, Charles had seen their students lining up for the mobile *peluquería,* where men were getting shaves and haircuts. The sight of their vulnerable necks, pale skin exposed by the clippers, struck him. He felt at that moment such fraternity with the men he was fighting with, so proud of them, that he felt tears prick his eyes. He knew, suddenly, what it was they were fighting for. If the Nationalists won, everything would go back to the way it had been. These people would be crushed, denied knowledge, beaten back again. He settled down on a warm patch of grass, near a group of new recruits being taught how to strip down and reassemble rifles, and watched their sunworn peasant faces. In the field, village boys were being drilled, marching backward and forward with broomsticks on their shoulders. Charles felt for the first time in his life that he was exactly where he needed to be.

Gunfire had suddenly broken the silence, and Charles scrambled to his feet, looking for his rifle, his camera. Hugo jogged over, and handed him a pair of binoculars. Charles trained them on the figures running toward the hill. He caught sight of a small redheaded woman up ahead, racing across open ground. "Who is that? She's mad!" Even as he said it, Charles knew who she was. The girl everyone was talking about.

"Haven't you met Gerda yet?" Hugo had laughed. "She's Capa's girl, fearless, just like him. They're gamblers, Charles, gamblers with life. They are like two children in love with each other, and life."

Charles watched as Gerda's head disappeared below the line of a foxhole, the sunlight gleaming on her red-blond hair. He remembered seeing a fox at home, disappearing into the long grass, lithe and bright, vanishing like an extinguished flame.

Charles finally met Gerda the next morning. He was striding through the corridor of the Casa de Alianza on the way to the cars, talking to one of the secretaries.

"Can you get this over to the press office in the Telefónica Building immediately, please?" Charles said. He made a quick amendment to his report, his pen tearing the thin, translucent paper. "Damn. This stuff is hopeless."

The secretary laughed. "At least you still have paper. I know some girls who are typing on Izal loo roll."

"Hey! Are you Charles?"

Charles looked up from the draft of his report, and through an open bedroom door saw a dark-haired man, typing on a Royal typewriter. "Thanks," he said, handing the report to the secretary. He hoped it would get the all-important stamp of approval from the censors. Charles ran his hand through his fair hair and walked over to Ted.

"Charles Temple. I'm with the *Manchester Guardian*."

"Ted Allan. Good to meet you. I saw you at lunch yesterday. Capa said there was a little Englishman kicking around the place." He stood and offered Charles his hand. "I was having dinner with Dr. Bethune last night and your sister asked me to give you this." He handed Charles a board wrapped in tissue paper.

"Thank you." Charles unwrapped the board, and turned over a detailed painting of an orange grove, luminous purple mountains in the distance.

"She's quite the artist, young Freya." He tilted his head. "Beth loves art. He's trying to get her to loosen up a bit."

I bet he is, Charles thought as he glanced into Ted's room. *Little Englishman indeed.* He was easily the same height as this American. Charles froze as he noticed Gerda sitting cross-legged on the bed, her head bent over a camera as she threaded fresh film onto the spool. As she looked up, her close-cropped red-gold hair was a luminous halo in the morning sun. She reminded him of statues of goddesses he had seen in books about the East—self-contained, golden, radiant. Cool eyes observed him from beneath sweeping arched brows—he felt her look at him and through him, like a cat.

"Have you met Gerda?" Ted said.

"No, I'm delighted to meet you." Charles strode over and offered her his hand. "You're a photographer as well?"

"Yes. What about you?"

"I'm still learning."

"Aren't we all."

"Capa told me it's not enough to have talent—you also have to be Hungarian. I may as well give up."

Gerda laughed. "Sounds like him." She stood and looked up at Charles. He guessed she was all of five feet tall. "You know, a camera is only as good as the man—or woman—who uses it." Her green eyes shone with amusement as she gently placed her fingers on his chest. "It's an extension of this . . ." She touched his heart. "And this," she said, touching his forehead, as if in blessing. "The pictures are there, waiting for you."

"Oh, I . . ." The words hung on Charles's lips. He felt the heat rise in his cheeks.

"Are you coming out to Guadalajara today?"

"I . . . Yes. I've just got to send this report through."

"We'll wait for you. There's room in our car."

The three young reporters settled into their car as it swung out toward Plaza de Cibeles. Gerda pulled the collar of her coat up around her ears.

"Are you cold?" Ted put his arm around her, held her close.

Charles watched them out of the corner of his eye as he cleaned the lens of his camera.

"How do you like the Contax?" Gerda asked.

"It's good. What do you work with?"

"Rollei," she said, turning to face the two men, her back against the window of the car. Charles couldn't help noticing the familiar way she tucked her toes under Ted's leg. "The Contax is too expensive for me. I'm thinking of changing to a Leica though."

"Gerda's stepping out from the considerable shadow of our Mr. Capa," Ted said.

Charles didn't like the tone of his voice. "When's Bob due back from Paris?"

"I'm joining him there in a few days," Gerda said.

"You do get around, you two."

"You've got to chase the work." She flashed him a smile. "We'll be back. Have you seen the shots of the refugees from Málaga I took with him in February?" she asked Charles, pushing her hair behind her ear. "I've never seen anything like it. It's like a biblical exodus—there has got to have been a hundred and fifty thousand refugees on the road to Almería. Those bastards just kept coming at them. I saw the planes machine-gunning women, children, the elderly . . ." She held Charles's gaze. "Marvelous, powerful images, of course."

SEVENTEEN

Emma strolled through Plaza del Ayuntamiento in Valencia, and checked the address of the agent again. She was early, so she decided to explore. There was a voluptuousness to the city, a softness in the light that had entranced her immediately. A little farther up the street she saw a young woman sluicing the pavement with a tin bucket of water outside a café as a man set out tables and chairs ready for the morning rush. Emma wandered along the square, taking in the baroque architecture and the virile bushy palms. She paused outside a religious icons shop. Serried ranks of identical madonnas gazed out at her, eyes full of melancholic understanding.

The Santa Catalina Café looked warm and welcoming, and she settled at the bar. The mirrored walls reflected several Emmas above the ceramic checkerboard floor as she chatted to the barman.

"Have you tried the *horchata*?" he asked her.

"What's that?"

"*Chufas*—tiger-nut milk. Or perhaps the hot chocolate is good for you?"

"When is chocolate ever not good?" Emma cupped her chin in her hand. White bowls were stacked behind the bar, beneath a gilt-framed print of the Valencian Madonna of the Dispossessed, a football trophy, and old advertising posters curling at the edges. Doe-eyed flamenco dancers in red-spotted dresses and fringed shawls enticed her to buy Hilo de Oro olive oil, just as they had for decades.

"Are you on holiday?" the barman asked as he placed a dish of *buñuelos* fritters at her side.

"No, this is my home," she said, testing it out.

Just after nine, Emma pushed open the steel-framed double-glazed door to the estate agent's. The heels of her boots tapped on the ceramic tile floor.

"Buenos días." A receptionist glanced up listlessly from behind an old manual typewriter. Her long lank hair fell over a nylon frilled shirt, and she looked as enthusiastic as the dusty plastic flowers sitting on a doily at her side.

"Buenos días, Señorita," Emma said carefully. "I am sorry, my Spanish is a little rusty."

The girl shrugged. "So is my English."

"My name is Emma Temple. My assistant said she would call you . . ."

From an office next door, Emma heard the sound of metal chair legs scraping on the tiles.

"Fidel! Eh! Fidel!" the girl called. A plume of smoke announced his entrance. A plump man in a home-knitted sweater with a black cigarette clamped between his teeth emerged, sausage fingers extended toward her. Thick gray hair fell over his eyes. Emma guessed he was around her mother's age.

"Encantado. Fidel Pons Garcia. Will your husband be joining us?"

"My husband?"

"Eh, none of my business, right?" He glanced at the girl, who was following the conversation agog. "Maria!" He clapped his hands, and she began to type. From a cupboard he pulled a large hoop of keys.

Emma stepped out onto the pavement. "It's beautiful here. Do you live in the city?"

"Me? No, I live in my parents' old house in La Pobla, not far from the Villa del Valle." He ushered her around to a side street. "My car is over here. You know, I work with my five brothers and our sister. We live in a house on top of one another, work together . . ." He tossed his cigarette into the gutter as they turned the corner.

"You're lucky," Emma said. "To have a large family is wonderful." Someone shouted from a car, and Fidel stepped out into the traffic. He leaned down to the driver's window and chatted amicably for a minute as traffic backed up behind them. No one honked. As the conversation finished, Fidel waved magnanimously at the queue and everyone drove on.

"You're going to live alone in the house?" he said, taking short bouncing steps along the pavement. He stopped by a small, dented Renault and unlocked the door.

"Yes."

He shrugged as he opened the door for her. "You're brave. Half the village thinks it is haunted." He swept a pile of papers into the footwell. As Emma settled into the car, the fetid smell of damp dog embraced her. The engine caught on the second turn.

"Really?"

"The other half thinks it's cursed."

They drove out of the city and were soon among orange groves and fields of onions. He pulled off the main road toward a small village, skirting the terra-cotta-tiled houses on a back road. Emma wound down the window, sniffed the air. She smelled moist earth, the clean green scent of the water cascading down the irrigation ditches. A flock of brown sheep huddled under an old olive tree by the cemetery. Fidel pointed up the hill to a tall pair of iron gates in a solid whitewashed wall. Above them, Emma could just see a four-square bell tower with a Moorish arch.

"There it is," he said, bringing the car to a sudden stop in a cloud of dust. "Take your time, I will unlock the gates."

By the time she caught up with him, Fidel was in the middle of an argument with a Moroccan man who was selling rugs and roses in front of the main gates. Gesticulating, he told the young man to get out of the way.

"No, really, it's OK," Emma said. She ran her fingers over a chipped ceramic sign: VILLA DEL VALLE.

"This is your house now. You don't want this."

"But the flowers are beautiful." She held out her hand. "Hello. I'm Emma."

"Aziz."

Close up, she could see how young he was. She guessed maybe fifteen, sixteen. "You can stay, it's fine. This is my house." Nodding, he offered her a single dusky pink, full-blown rose.

"Thank you," Emma said. She smiled, thinking of Liberty.

"Be careful." The agent scowled at him. "People like that take advantage."

"Do you think so? I've always found if you treat people with respect they tend to live up to it." She leaned against the wall, shielding her eyes from the morning sun. An old woman, seeing the gates open for the first time in years, crossed herself and scurried to the other side of the road.

Fidel gave the rusted gates a final shove and steered her inside. Once the gates closed behind them, the noise of traffic, the village, faded away. Emma found herself in a walled garden. She turned around slowly, a smile breaking out on her lips. *Oh, Mum,* she thought. *It's beautiful.* Thorny bougainvillea with scarlet flowers consumed the walls, and a grove of orange trees filled the lawns. As she walked along the untended path, long grass caressed her bare legs. Insects hummed like paper on a comb. "I'll need a gardener," she said.

"You'll need more than that." Fidel led her toward a side door. She was mesmerized by the tall stucco walls, the shaded terrace at the base of the bell tower. All she could see was potential.

"There's no electricity, the water is from the well—and that may be dry— the plumbing hasn't been looked at since the thirties . . . I told your mother she was crazy, but she insisted."

"You met my mother?"

"I . . . We helped her with the paperwork." He pulled the keys from his jacket pocket, searching now for the door key.

"Wait," Emma said, and fished out the box of letters from her bag. She flicked through the envelopes until she found the one marked "Villa del Valle," and she tipped the key onto Fidel's palm.

"*Gracias,*" he said, and unlocked the door. "Once, all the fields at the back belonged to the villa, all the orange groves as far as you can see. Now all there is is this." He waved his hand dismissively at the tangled mass of the garden.

"It's perfect." The door's blue paint was peeling. The houses on either side were more modern—smart villas with shiny tiles and metal shutters, but the Villa del Valle was clearly far older. The windows were tightly closed behind wooden shutters, the heavy wooden doors at the base of the tower bolted shut. Emma looked up at the ornate parapet on the roof and the three wrought iron balconies on the first floor. "It's like something from a fairy tale."

The agent raised an eyebrow as he tried the door handle. "As I said, there's no power, so I don't know how much you'll be able to see." Emma looked at the black cables snaking over the house next door and thought starting from scratch would probably be a good thing. *"Joder!"* Fidel swore under his breath. He shouldered the swollen door open with a triumphant *"Vamos!"*

A tabby cat appeared from the long grass, and eyed them warily. "Ha! You are the same," the agent said, miming a swollen stomach. He handed her the key, and some papers. "All the contracts are there."

"Thank you," Emma said.

Fidel looked doubtfully into the dark house. "Are you sure you want to stay here?"

Emma smiled. "I've never been more sure of anything."

"Listen, I'll tell my daughter to send up a box of fruit and vegetables for you. She runs the greengrocer's in the market square. If you need anything, ask her, or call me in town. Good luck."

Once they were alone, Emma squatted down and held her hand out to the cat. "Hello," she said. It backed away from her, hissing, slunk along the wall into the shadows of the house. "Not feeling friendly?" She straightened up and watched the cat disappear into the dark hallway, hips swinging, tail high. "What do you think? Can we be happy here?"

She stepped from room to silent room of shuttered, whitewashed space, her footsteps leaving traces on the dusty terra-cotta floors. She threw open the windows and light poured in. There was little to see. The last inhabitant had left only old yellowed newspapers, empty bottles of cognac, petrified soap on the basins. The only piece of furniture was a big wooden table in the kitchen. She guessed it had been built in the kitchen, and had been too big to remove, too much effort to saw up and use for firewood. Emma took the bottle of water from her bag, and tucked the rose into it, placing it at the heart of the table.

She stepped out into the back garden and wandered through the knee-high grass. Among the tangled weeds, she found mint, rosemary, and lavender growing wild and untended. Emma crushed a stalk of rosemary in her fingers and inhaled. She realized she was looking at the remains of an herb garden. As she paced around the perimeter walls, she plotted out the old raised beds in her mother's notebook. She had always dreamed of creating a scented garden, and had spent hours with Liberty walking the aisles of the Chelsea Gardener, planning the plants that they would choose. She knew instinctively what she wanted to do here, sketched out the planting and new water channels, a small pool at the back of the house. As she stood at the front gate and looked across to the villa, she imagined a tiled fountain, and a low channel of water in the path leading to the house. She would bring the garden back to life. *Maybe,* she thought, *it will do the same for me.* She had no idea how or why Liberty had found this house, but this, she realized, was her last gift to her. "Thank you, Mum," she said under her breath.

Emma slept on the kitchen floor of her new home that night, the shutters wide open to the stars. She had bought an inflatable mattress, two blankets, and a pillow from the village market, and a cooked chicken from the *pollos asados* store. She decided to risk lighting a fire in the hearth, and sat on her bed, eating with her fingers in the firelight. After brushing her teeth with a bottle of Evian, she flung herself down, and bounced straight off the mattress. As she lay in a tangle of blankets, she began to laugh in spite of herself. *So much for the dream,* she thought.

Emma flicked on the torch, reached for her washbag, and pulled out a bottle of almond oil. She sorted through the dark bottles of essential oils and picked out two. Then she measured out a couple of drops of chamomile and lavender into the carrier oil, and warmed a small amount in her hands, rubbing them together, inhaling the relaxing scent. She placed her palms on her stomach and massaged gently, felt her baby's answering kick. "Hey you," she said, smiling. "Well, we're here." She looked uncertainly around the dark shadows of the kitchen. "Tomorrow we'd better find out about doctors and hospitals." It all suddenly felt overwhelming.

She gingerly lay down, and reached for her mother's box of letters. By torchlight, she flicked through them, and selected one. "On Perfume," she read aloud to her baby. "Let's see what your grandmother had to say about that." She tore open the envelope and unfolded the paper. Pressed rose petals cascaded out onto the bed, and Emma laughed.

> We are a family of perfumers. It's in our blood, Em, that I'm sure of. Freya says as soon as I could walk I was always picking flowers in the park, making concoctions for her, and you were the same. Perfumers, apothecaries, healers—we all make people feel better.

Emma thought back to Freya's words, her anger by the lake in London: "People need things like perfume more than ever during times like this."

> Perfume is the key to our memories. Someone like Kipling said it makes our heartstrings crack. An unexpected smell pulls back the years and lets

you glimpse other places, lovers, countries, times. Who doesn't remember the fragrance that their first love wore, or the smell of their mother's dressing room? I always wanted to make perfumes that made people feel how they do when they smell newly cut grass, the scent of a freshly bathed baby's head. Perfume tells us we are here, we are alive.

I remember a Bahraini princess I dined with one night. She carried round a crystal bottle of sandalwood oil and anointed the wrists of her guests. That is what I wanted to do—give perfume as a gift, a blessing. Perfume is sacred—think of the garden in the Song of Songs.

Emma remembered Liberty reading to her as a child, curled up beside her beneath a tree: *"His cheeks are as a bed of spices, as sweet flowers; his lips like lilies, dropping sweet-smelling myrrh."* It was always Liberty's favorite.

Maybe you've wondered why I always stuck faithfully with rose as my perfume. You know, in the midst of holy war, soldiers returning from the Crusades carried damask roses home with them. I loved that. I like to think they were bringing them to the women they had loved and left behind. You know, perfume is love. Cleopatra drenched the sails of her golden barge in the fragrance of roses, and when she visited Rome, the perfume lingered in the streets long afterward. Perfume is romance—that is why I fell for the rose.

I traveled for years, as you know, a hunter of fragrances. I loved them all: frangipani in the tropics, coiled incense in the East, roasting coffee and petrol in America. It was never more fun than when I traveled with you—do you remember? I showed you where sandalwood comes from in Mysore, and the iris fields in Tuscany. That's how I learned my craft, on the road, seeking suppliers in Turkey and Bulgaria, India and Syria, and of course France. Everything I learned, I passed on to you, Emma, and you have surpassed me. You are an artist of fragrance, the heir of healers, alchemists, apothecaries—you are a magician! Never forget that. It takes time to create a great fragrance, there is no hurry. It took me eight years to create Chérie Farouche for you, but then it took eighteen years for you to become the remarkable woman I made that perfume for. Good things come, with time.

Follow your heart, Emma, follow your nose—listen to the quiet voice inside you. Make people's heartstrings crack. Make perfumes that remind people how wonderful it is to be alive. Because it is, Em, to be alive is glorious, and people need to remember that, and to stop and smell the flowers.

Love, Mum x

That night as Emma slept, her dreams inhabited the house, filling it with treasures, secrets, the scents of linen chests and spices, the hushed breath of words once spoken. At daybreak on the first morning in her new home, in the slow dawn of consciousness, she tried to locate herself. Her back ached, and her feet were freezing. She was on the floor. Whose floor? As her eyes adjusted, making out the slim, brilliant cruciform of light breaking through the shutters, she remembered.

She was in Spain. This was her floor, her house, her home. It was a moment she had imagined a thousand times, waking in a new life, in a new country.

Now all she could hear was a buzzing. She wondered at first if it was an alarm clock somewhere else in the house. Joe had an alarm clock like that when she first met him. She hated it so much that he had thrown it out of the window the first morning she woke alongside him. *What is that?* she thought, rubbing her eyes, her fingers blackening with the kohl she had not been able to remove the night before. Her eyes flickered open.

"Oh. My. God," she said aloud. Emma wasn't the kind of person given to hysterics, but even she realized how lucky she had been. A few feet above her head, dangling from the beamed roof, was the largest wasps' nest she had ever seen—gray, silvery, like some seething ghost of summers past. Slowly, ever so slowly, Emma crept out of the blankets and closed the door on the room, swatting away a curious wasp that followed her into the hall.

She leaned against the wall, breathing deeply, one hand protectively clasped around her stomach. She had hated wasps ever since Freya had told the apocryphal tale of an aunt who had swallowed one in a bottle of lemonade during a family picnic and promptly died among the scones and jam from asphyxiation. Few things bothered Emma these days. She had traveled around the world alone, but her morbid fear of wasps had endured.

Glancing out of the window, she saw Aziz setting up outside the gates. She called to him, waving him to come inside.

"Are you all right?" He ran toward her.

"Wasps . . . Or hornets?" Her eyes were wide. "In there." She pointed at the kitchen door, pulled her robe around her.

"Do you have any petrol?"

"Maybe. I saw a jerry can in the workshop."

"Good." He ran outside, and Emma heard him dragging the can into the garden. He returned armed with a broom. "Stay here." He disappeared into the kitchen, and she heard muffled curses as he knocked down the nest and flung it outside, where he set fire to it.

"Did they get you?" she asked when he reappeared.

"A little. But most of them were dead already, as it's nearly winter." He sucked at the stings.

"Thank you," she said. "Come, let me help you." In the kitchen she searched through the bag of groceries she had bought and found some vinegar. She sloshed some onto a clean cloth, and dabbed at the welts on his arm.

"You can't live like this," he said, looking at the tangled mess of her bed. "You're crazy."

Emma shrugged. "Maybe. It's what I want, right now."

"Crazy woman." He laughed. "Stubborn like my mother, my sisters. My mother, she is dead now."

"Mine too." Emma looked closely at him. She trusted her instincts. "How about some coffee? I have a proposal for you."

The sun cast long shadows on the ocher walls of the Casa de Cultura. It had taken some time for Emma to sort out the paperwork in the village, but finally with Fidel's reluctant help and all the council's stamps in place, she was ready to let Aziz know the good news. He had jumped at her idea to open a proper flower stall in the old shop that fronted the street in the wall of the Villa del Valle. As they had waited for the permits to be stamped, he had told her his story. It turned out he lived with his little sisters on the edge of the village in a run-down chalet. Their parents had died, and at sixteen he was the man of the family, responsible for feeding and clothing everyone.

"Look," Emma said that morning as she unlocked the street doors of the old shop. Someone had evidently been using it as a garage, but the original shelves were there still. She gazed uneasily up at the sharp hooks hanging from the ceiling. "What do you think?"

"I think it is a big mess," he said. "Like the rest of this place."

Emma ran her hand across the wooden countertop. "We could have a till here. If we unblock the windows at the back, there will be natural light, and the double doors at the front will give us a good street display."

"A till?" He picked up on her excitement.

"A shop, Aziz. We could make a little flower shop here."

His face clouded. "But I could never afford . . ."

"Listen, this shop is sitting empty, and it would make me happy to help you. I'll pay you the going wage, and a percentage of the profits. What do you think?" She held her hand out to him.

He grinned as he shook her hand. "How can I ever thank you?" Aziz helped Emma work loose the rusted bolts on the back door leading to the garden. Light flooded the shop from front and back now, and he squinted as they stepped out into the villa's garden. "I know!" He gestured at the tangled grass and weeds. "I will make this good for you. Besides, it is bad for business if the garden is a mess."

Emma laughed. "It's a deal."

"I don't know what to say. Why me?"

"I like you. I see how hard you work. You have regular customers already." She laughed. "And if I'm going to have the builders in for the next couple of months, I need to use the main gates!"

Aziz looked back into the shop. "There's a lot to do."

"So get cracking!" She glanced up at the ceiling again. "The first thing that can go are those horrible hooks."

"I talked to one of the old women, she told me this was a butcher's shop."

"Ah, that explains it." Emma folded her arms. "I still don't like the feel of it. But we can make it better. We'll need a sign, and some whitewash." She looked around. "Some buckets and things too. I'll ask Fidel where to go for them."

"What shall we call it?"

"We need a good name." The words in Liberty's letter came into her mind. "We'll call it the Perfume Garden."

EIGHTEEN

Nurse Temple, where have you been?" Dr. Jolly's assistant said, without looking up from his notes. "You're late."

"I'm sorry," Freya said. "The planes were firing at us as the ambulances drove back from the station."

He shook his head. "I think those animals think the red crosses are targets, not symbols of humanitarian work."

The same thought had crossed Freya's mind as she cowered in a ditch at the side of the road with the precious bottles of blood the men had dragged from the ambulances. Machine-gun bullets strafed the earth a few feet from her face. She could still taste the dust.

"Well, get to work please. I think the battle is only just beginning here. We have five hundred wounded men to cope with tonight." He glanced up at Freya, concerned. "Are you all right?"

Freya touched the side of her face, felt the nerve ticking in her eye. "Yes, of course," she said. She liked the little Frenchman—he always reminded her more of a pirate than a doctor, with his dark beard and sparkling eyes. She picked up a fresh apron from the nurses' station and smoothed her hair. "Thank you."

"Oh, Nurse Temple," he called after her. "Dr. Henderson was looking for you."

Freya picked her way through the lines of men lying on the floor of the hospital. A spectral bandaged man staggered on crutches ahead of her, stumbling. They had been so busy doing transfusions on the front line, Freya had volunteered to stay at the hospital for now. She hadn't seen Tom for over a week, and the thought of him now comforted her.

Every floor, every room of the hospital was filled with wounded and dying men. Freya trod gently around the bodies that clogged the dimly lit hall. A doctor was going from man to man with Mimi, one of the French nurses, to see which ones they could help.

In the station in Madrid, as they were seeing off the wounded on a hospital train on its way to the convalescent homes on the coast, a second train had pulled in to the platform, full of fresh, shining faces, red scarves gleaming in the spring sunlight. *I wonder how long it will be until those soldiers are lying here among these poor souls,* Freya thought now as she passed blood-soaked stretchers lined up by the washroom waiting to be cleaned. She glanced at the empty bottles of blood in a wire basket by the door of her ward and checked the handful of bloodstained bottle tags—each one marked with name, battalion, wound, date. *Thank God we managed to save the fresh supply in the ambulances.*

"Freya!" Tom called to her as she reached out to open the door.

"Hello, you." She checked to make sure no one was paying them any attention, and kissed him gently on the lips.

"I've been looking everywhere for you." He pulled her into the shadows of the storeroom.

"We were held up on the Madrid road."

"Christ, it's been busy. They have three tables working flat out down there."

He embraced her, sighed as he buried his face in her hair. The scent of ether still clung to him.

"Where have you been? I haven't seen you for days."

"There have been some problems." When he looked at her, Freya saw the dark circles under his eyes. "Darling, there's no easy way to tell you this. They are sending Beth back to Canada, and I must go with him."

Freya swayed, reached out for the rough wooden shelves. "You're leaving?"

"Come with me."

"Tom, I can't. My work is here." She shook her head. "When you see what they did in Guernica . . . It's only going to get worse."

"The bastards are trying to cover it up, you know. They're saying the planes were aiming at a military target, but then why the hell were forty-three aircraft from the Condor Legion bombing the town?" He grimaced. "They were mowing down civilians with machine guns as they tried to escape the fires." He gripped Freya by her arms. "You're right, it is going to get worse, much worse. The Nazis are using the Spanish cities as testing grounds for what's to come in the rest of Europe, you know that, don't you? It'll be Barcelona, Madrid, Valencia razed to the ground next. I can't bear to leave you here."

Freya leaned her forehead against his lips. "You know me, I'm bomb-proof, that's what everyone says."

"Freya, I'm serious." Tom took her face in his hands. "I love you," he said. "I want to spend the rest of my life with you. Come with me. We're not leaving until the end of the month. I've got to stick close to Beth, so I may not be around much over the next couple of weeks, but that will give you some time to think." He kissed her then. "Please think about it."

Freya's heart pulsed an irregular beat as she walked into the ward. She checked the charts, the words swimming before her eyes. All she could think was that Tom was leaving. Her brief moment of happiness was over, just as quickly as it had begun.

"Nurse . . ." a man groaned. She looked up, snapped into the moment as she walked toward him. His head was entirely covered with bandages. Where his hands should have been were two bloody, shapeless bundles.

"Hello . . . Simon," she said, checking his notes. "Let's see if we can't make you more comfortable." She knew he needed a transfusion, so she took the last bottle from the refrigerator. As it heated to body temperature, she double-checked his blood group, and sterilized the syringe. In a few minutes, she was all done. "Is that better?"

"Yes, feeling ticketyboo."

Freya smiled. She was always amazed how the men managed to keep their sense of humor. "Let's see how you are doing." She felt for the weak pulse.

"I feel so wretched," he said, his voice muffled by the bandages. "I've been in Spain only a couple of days. I've done nothing for the cause."

"Nothing?" she said. The courage of the man touched her. "You have done everything." She tucked the clean sheet in. "Rest now, if you can. Your pulse is stronger, you're doing well."

Freya wanted nothing more than to lie down on one of the beds and sleep for a week, but as she turned back to the ward and saw two rows of bed after bed stretching into the dim light, some with two men top to tail, each man as desperately wounded as Simon, her heart sank.

Early the next morning, Dr. Jolly's assistant found her sitting outside the hospital in the dawn light. Freya had her arms around her knees, and she was rocking gently.

"Freya? What's the matter?"

"I lost five men last night."

"Oh, God, I'm sorry." He sat down on the ground beside her, lit a cigarette, and handed it to her.

"There were six of them dying, and only me on duty. I had to choose." She raked her fingers through her hair. "One by one, they went. I was racing from bed to bed, trying to make them comfortable, trying to . . ." She fought the tears welling in her eyes.

"Frey, listen," he said gently. "You've been up at the front with the blood unit a long time now. I think it's time you had a break." He squeezed her arm. "I'll get Dr. Jolly to fill out the papers. Go to the Medical Aid reception center in Valencia. It will be better for you. Make lots of tea, keep the morale up. The cases are mostly convalescent over there—there will be less loss for you to deal with."

"This country . . ." she said. "This poor country. They are burning books in Cordoba, thousands of books. Little boys are marching in the streets with wooden rifles. Men are being shot like rabbits—and that man, that Queipo de Llano, with his broadcasts being shouted out across the country now the Germans have given him a transmitter: What was it he said? 'Tonight I shall take a sherry and tomorrow I shall take Málaga.' I hate it. I hate this ghastly war. I feel so helpless."

"That's why Spain needs us," he said, patting her shoulder as he walked away. "Take it day by day. There is no tomorrow, no yesterday for many of us now. There is only what we can do, what we can get through today. That is how you can help."

NINETEEN

Beneath the floorboards of Emma's bedroom lay a tiny photograph of a boy with dancing eyes. Sometimes, when the sunlight hit the crack in the shutters just so, a thin bright line broke through, penetrated the floor, and illuminated his face. The photograph lay among the dust of decades, alongside dressmaking pins and buttons that had slipped through the boards, and another photo that lay upside down, its edge just touching the boy. It was like he was waiting.

"I'm fine," Emma insisted, the phone resting against her shoulder as she fastened a diamond stud into her ear. "The house? It's not in such a bad state," she said doubtfully, glancing around as she reached for her other earring on the windowsill.

"Have you at least got a proper bed now?" Freya asked. "You must take care of your back, Emma."

"I'll order one," she said, distracted. She fumbled for the earring and heard it fall to the floor. She watched it spin on the polished wood, and disappear beneath the crack. "Damn."

"What is it?"

"Nothing, don't worry. I just dropped something. An earring that Joe gave me one Christmas." Emma sighed as she got down on her hands and knees. "Listen, I'll call you back later. I have a couple of appointments in town."

"Let me know how you get on at the doctor's, won't you?"

"Will do. Love you, Gammy."

Emma leaned against the board, testing it. It felt loose to her, creaking under the pressure of her hands. *There are some advantages to living in an old wreck,* she thought.

In the woodshed, Emma found a rusted crowbar, and she carried it back toward the house. Aziz looked up from the bonfire where he was burning all the brush he had cleared from the garden. "Can I help? You must not do heavy things, not with the baby."

"I need to lift a board in the bedroom. Do you think you can do it?"

It took only a few moments for Aziz to lever the board clear. "It is no good," he said, moving it aside. "These boards are all old. You need a builder."

"I know," Emma said, squatting down. She waved her hand, clearing the cloud of dust. "There it is!" She picked up the earring, and cleaned it off.

"Look at all this," Aziz said. He reached into the gap between the rafters and picked out the photograph.

"Oh! Isn't that wonderful?" Emma said as he handed it to her. "There's another one." She picked up the second photograph, and looked at them, side by side. "I wonder who they were?" She cleared the dust from their faces with her fingertip.

"Maybe you can ask the agent? Maybe he knows who lived here."

"Good idea. I'll call into the grocer's before I go to the city this afternoon and see if Fidel is around."

⁂

Emma loved the rhythm of her new life. After the weeks of turmoil, seeing the garden being cleared gave her real pleasure. At lunchtime as she walked to the gate, she glanced up at the "whoop-whoop-whoop" of the hoopoe that had taken up residence in the old bell tower, and smiled. She had always liked the autumn, and the scent of woodsmoke from the bonfire in the garden made the villa feel more like home.

She strolled out through the gate and down to the village, her arms filled with a bouquet of white Bianca roses. Outside the café a table of buoyant, boisterous old men with one grande dame holding court looked like they had been there for some time. A funeral was holding up the traffic, and cars snaked slowly past. Emma's stomach rumbled with hunger as she saw the woman dishing up paella from a large pan resting on a piece of corrugated cardboard. A man sitting alone eating eels with garlic and peppers dipped bread into a saucer of olive oil and tossed it to a tiny lithe black dog, who skipped off to join his gang of rude little street dogs, cocking his leg on the bottle of water someone had left on the street corner.

Valencian flags snapped in the air outside the town hall as Emma skirted around an old man in a checked shirt, who bent down, cigar in his mouth to squeeze the cheek of a baby in a pram. "*Qué bonita*!" she heard him say. Emma smiled at the mother. She was beginning to recognize faces in La Pobla, to learn its routines. She knew as she reached the end of the street that the old couple would be sitting on upturned orange crates peeling potatoes in the doorway of their crumbling baroque mansion. She knew as she passed Bar Musical that the sound of the Fallas festival band would be drifting out. Emma passed two band members strolling late to practice, autumn sun glinting on their French horn and trombone.

She stopped at the edge of the pavement, and waited to cross. An effigy of a saint in a tiled alcove above her looked down on a *policía local* officer directing the ballet of cars and scooters like a choreographer, his arms arcing, shaping the air. Girls in spandex pants and Puffa jackets clung to their boyfriends on scooters; the boys all had gelled quiffs, cigarettes dangling nonchalantly from the corners of their mouths as they sped among the snarled-up cars. The doorway nearby was strewn with palm leaves and petals for a wedding.

In the market, the smell of polished leather tack greeted her, then the smoky scent of charred meat. A chihuahua ran over the blankets of traders selling Peruvian ponchos and weavings, scurried past her feet. There among the bustle of vendors and villagers strolling to lunch, she saw Fidel's daughter's shop. She knew immediately what it was that his grocer's reminded her of.

When Emma was growing up, Liberty knew a woman whose young daughter had disappeared. The mother ran a tiny shop, a treasure house of hippie jewelry and patchouli oil in a quiet side street off the King's Road. All the local teenagers were drawn there through morbid curiosity. Stepping into the shop from the busy whirl of Chelsea was like stepping into a Victorian parlor laid out for mourning rather than trade. Grief permeated every item. It appealed to their maudlin sensibilities.

As she traveled, Emma came to realize that every town has a shop like that, a shop that time forgot, suspended in amber. They seem to exist in a customerless limbo, selling single pairs of underpants or dusty slippers. It reassured her, to find this constancy across the world. In America she loved the general stores, stocked with bric-a-brac, gasoline, and survival rations. In Europe she sought out the marvelous—the shop with a single doll's house in a glass arcade in Paris, an icon store in Florence. The contents varied, but all had the atmosphere of that small shop in her hometown, a quasi religious stillness, a sense of surviving loss.

Within days of settling in, she realized there were many shops like that in the backstreets of Valencia, selling fans, *mantilla* combs, but here only Fidel's had survived the modernization of the village, the encroaching of shiny *mil objets* stores and smart bakers. It stood tucked behind a flight of stone stairs leading up the side of the church. The displays of gleaming tomatoes, plump aubergines, and succulent melons lay beside a green doorway, half open, shyly inviting her in. Inside, a neat square of trestle tables covered in red-and-white-checked cloths supported baskets of fresh vegetables. There was, surprisingly, one other customer, an old woman with the look of a gypsy, who balanced a basket of red peppers on her hip as she chatted with Fidel's daughter. She glanced at Emma with dark-eyed curiosity.

"*Buenas*," Emma said once the customer had gone. "Is your father around?"

"*Sí*. He has just got home for lunch—he's out back." The girl pushed aside a heavy sage curtain, and directed Emma into a courtyard. As Emma glanced around, she remembered Fidel telling her that the family lived here still, above the shop.

"Ah, Emma," he said, appearing from the workshop. "How are you?"

"Good, thanks. These are for your family," she said, giving him the roses. "Thank you for helping my mother."

"You're very kind. Have you come about the display?" He flicked on the light in the old storeroom. "You can take whatever you like," he said, pointing to a rusty wrought iron flower stand. "It's seen better days, but if you'd like it . . ."

"I'd love it! It's beautiful."

"My wife, before she died, she used to sell flowers at the front of the shop."

Emma smiled sympathetically, reassured that her instinct had been correct.

"I'm glad that someone is selling flowers in the village again. So much better than the hypermarket's sorry bunches of carnations."

"You must let me give you something for it."

"Pah!" He waved his hands. "You'd be doing me a favor. This place is far too cluttered as it is." Emma looked around the immaculate whitewashed courtyard with its pots of geraniums and sparkling fountain.

"I don't know what to say."

"It's a pleasure." He cocked his head. "You don't strike me as a florist."

Emma laughed. "I'm not. I'm a perfumer by trade."

"Really? Well you have come to the right place. We love our perfumes in Spain. Every village has its own *perfumería*."

"Tell me, do you know anything about the history of the house, the Villa del Valle?" Emma fished out the photographs from her wallet and showed them to him. "I found these under the floorboards this morning."

"They look very old." Fidel shook his head, turned away from her. "No, I know nothing about the house. There were a few tenants over the years, but it has been empty for a long time."

"How long have you lived here?"

"My family, we came here in the 1940s. I am sorry, I can't help you." He thought for a moment. "You should talk to Immaculada. The de Santangel family have lived in La Pobla for centuries. When she comes into the shop, I'll ask her to drop by and see you."

"Thank you." Emma stepped out onto the pavement.

"So, how do you like Valencia?"

"I can't pin it down, yet. I mean, I love it, but it feels quite . . ."

"It's hard to get past the surface, perhaps. People are cautious. We are very different from the rest of Spain. We were in Muslim hands for many centuries, and have more of Catalonia than Castilla."

Emma nodded her head. "You can see that from the dialect—Valencian seems more like Catalan or French to me."

"I hope we grow on you. It is a friendly place, a good place, now."

"I'm hoping to stay," Emma said. "I want to make perfume here too, using Spanish ingredients."

"Ah, you should definitely talk to Immaculada then. The de Santangels are the largest landowners around." He shook her hand. "I will ask Macu to visit you."

Emma had an appointment with an English-speaking doctor in town, so outside the villa she tossed her handbag into the old yellow Land Rover she had bought, and headed for Valencia. As the traffic slowed passing over the dry Turia riverbed, she wound down the window, the breeze blowing in her hair. Her phone vibrated, and Emma hooked in the earpiece.

"Hello, Freya," she said.

"Just checking you remembered. Your appointment's in ten minutes."

Emma laughed. "I'm on my way. Stop worrying."

"He's good apparently. Your old GP on Sloane Street recommended him."

"I would have got around to finding a doctor . . ."

"You don't want to take any chances, darling. Anyway, I do worry. You're taking on too much, yet again. What on earth do you think you are doing opening a flower shop the minute you arrive . . ."

Emma indicated to turn into the car park near the bullring. "I'm just helping out a young Moroccan boy."

"Oh, Em. Not another good cause? You're as bad as your mother."

"He's doing very well, actually." Emma frowned. "And he's helping me out with the garden." Emma locked the car, and walked toward a shaded side street. She thought for a moment about asking Freya's advice about finding builders, but had visions of her project-managing the renovations from London. "I'm coping. I feel better than I have in ages."

"Good. That's good. Are you eating?"

"Yes," Emma said, laughing. "I'm putting some weight back on now. Still not much of a bump, but I'm sure the baby is fine."

"Libby was tiny when she was having you, right up to the last months."

"Talking of Mum, I wanted to ask you something." Emma paused to let a car pass by before crossing the road. "Gammy?"

"Yes."

Emma sensed her hesitation. "Do you know why Mum picked the house?"

"I don't . . . Well, you know how impulsive your mother was."

"I just wondered if you knew anything about it. I found some photos today, some old photos—a boy and a girl. In one of her letters Mum said—"

"Heaven knows, darling. An old place like that, they could be anyone."

Emma narrowed her eyes. She could tell from Freya's voice that she didn't want to talk. "I didn't ask if you knew the people, I asked about the house."

"I don't know anything," Freya said crossly. "What is this? The Spanish Inquisition?" They both fell silent, then burst out laughing. "Oh dear . . ." Freya said, catching her breath. "Your mother always loved Monty Python, didn't she?"

Emma smiled. This obviously wasn't the time to ask Freya about Liberty's letter. "Is everything OK with you?"

"We're pottering on. Ms. Stafford is back," she said, her voice taking on an edge. "But I can handle her."

Emma checked her watch. She didn't want to think about Delilah now. "Got to go," she said, walking quickly toward the door with a polished brass plaque on it. "I'll e-mail you the scan. Love you."

An hour later, Emma stepped out into the afternoon sunshine, a hazy image of her child in her hand. She paused in the doorway. "Look at you!" she said to her baby. She felt like dancing down the street, showing the scan to everyone she met. The blue domes of the city seemed more brilliant today, the sandstone warmer.

Emma strolled through the streets eating a vanilla ice cream, her dark coat swinging loose around her. She found herself in the cathedral square, and curiosity about the Holy Grail drew her toward the cathedral's vast doors.

"*Perdón*," a tall, smartly dressed man said as he squeezed by. She caught the scent of Acqua di Parma, leather, starched cotton as he passed. She noticed him immediately, drawn by the familiar citrus scent of Charles's cologne. Emma strolled along the colonnades and glimpsed him once or twice, walking quickly along the aisles. She paused beside a group of black-clad women praying before a reliquary containing the arm of St. Vincent Martyr. The incense-filled silence made her head spin. She walked on, her leather boots tapping on the tiled floor. As she crossed the nave, she felt someone watching her, and she turned quickly. A small boy stood alone beneath the altar, staring at her.

"*Hola*," she said, squatting down in front of him. "Are you lost?" The boy shook his head. "What's your name?"

"Paco!" the man called, and the boy flashed her a quick smile before he ran to his side. Emma stood, looked over at the man. The sun came out, and the golden light in the cathedral poured down from the stone windows like honey from the comb. She felt caught in time, for a moment, and the man raised his hand in thanks, the boy hugging his leg. As Emma walked, she couldn't help glancing over at him. The man was there again, keeping pace with her, occasionally looking in her direction as he talked to the boy.

Emma finally found the tiny chapel housing the Grail, and read from the guide she'd picked up by the entrance: *"The Santo Cáliz is a very ancient work and nothing can be said against the idea that it was utilized by the Lord during the first Eucharistic supper."* She sat in a pew and looked up at the bejeweled chalice in its glass case.

"Me puedo sentar aquí?" The man was at her side suddenly, holding the boy by the hand. "May I sit here?"

"Sí," she said, squeezing up to make room for them.

"You are English? American?"

"Both," she said, laughing. "Well, half and half."

"We wanted to say thank you."

Emma ruffled the boy's hair. "How old is your son?"

"My son? No, he is my nephew. My sister would kill me if she knew he had run off."

Emma glanced at him. He was well over six foot tall, and his dark hair fell to the collar of his linen suit. His temples were flecked with gray, she noticed, and she tried to guess his age. *Forty, perhaps,* she thought. It was hard to tell. There was an energy about him that made him seem ten years younger than the age the wrinkles at the corners of his eyes suggested.

"Tell me, is it really the Grail?" she said.

"Of course, they say it was from Palestine. Two thousand years old." He offered her his hand. "I am Luca."

Luca had folded himself into the cramped pew like an umbrella. There were no other seats in the small chapel, and Emma felt like a seabird sheltering in the shadows of a great cliff among the chattering gaggle of tourists and old women. Emma smiled politely as he went on, conspiratorially. "But a simple carpenter would not have had a cup decorated with gold and jewels . . ." His words washed over her. She watched his hands as his fingertips smoothed the polished wood in front of him. Emma had always found hands more expressive than faces—less easy to disguise. His were perfect, she thought—smooth oval nails, long, tanned fingers, strong, full palms. Gold cuff links gleamed at his wrists. "Maybe the little coralline cup is authentic."

A woman with a dark veil turned and pursed her lips "Shh." Emma's reverie broke, and she met his gaze for the first time. She felt like she had come to the end of a long journey.

"Some people will always believe what they want to be the truth," he whispered as they stood to leave. "I know you," he said suddenly, holding open the door for her.

"You just saw me in the cathedral!"

"No, from La Pobla. You are the flower woman?"

She paused and turned to him. "Yes."

"Wonderful." He smiled. "I wondered . . ."

"About?"

"The sign. The 'Perfume Garden.' You know the old book, by Richard Burton?"

Emma laughed. "I hadn't thought of that. I was thinking of my mother— she always loved the Song of Songs in the Bible." A smile played over her lips. "You mean *The Perfumed Garden?*"

"Exactly, the love text," he said, evidently pleased she had made the connection.

"Well, there won't be any concubines and aphrodisiacs on offer in La Pobla." Emma said, laughing.

He leaned toward her. "Too bad. It is just what we need in our lives, a little sensuality." Luca looked back at the Grail. "Do you believe in miracles?"

Emma glanced at him. *What if he is some sort of madman, or evangelist?* she thought. *No, he's too well dressed,* she imagined her mother saying. "Who wouldn't in a place like this?" she said.

"Good. The Virgin—you know the patron of Valencia?"

"Our Lady of the Forsaken?"

"*Sí,* the crazy, the dispossessed."

"Is she miraculous?"

"Yes. They say she was carved in the fourteenth century by a group of pilgrims who asked for four days' supply of food and a sealed room—the charitable society gave it to them. When the door was opened, the Virgin was there but the pilgrims had gone."

"How?"

"They were angels of course," he said. His face was solemn, but as he tilted his head he smiled. "Ask my mother."

"Shh!" The woman turned, hissed again. Emma watched him in profile as he apologized to her. His nose was like a Roman statue, maybe broken. It was only early afternoon, but already his skin was colored by the blue of stubble.

As the child walked ahead, Luca steered Emma out of the chapel, his hand in the small of her back. Some distant memory stirred in her. *This is how it feels,* she thought. *This is how it feels to be attracted to a stranger again.*

Pigeons rose from the square as they walked outside, toward the Basilica of the Virgin. Luca pulled a packet of cigarettes from his jacket the moment they were outside and past the beggars with their waxed Coca-Cola cups. He offered her one.

"I gave up," she said.

"Too bad." He shrugged. "We are a dying breed."

"That's why I gave up!"

"Then we shall just have to find another vice to share." His tanned face crinkled as he smiled, the cigarette gripped between even white teeth.

"Well, it was good to meet you," Emma said, digging her hands into the pockets of her loose coat.

"Welcome to Valencia," he said with mock formality. "I am Luca de Santangel."

"Emma Temple."

"Emma," he murmured. The clock began to chime. He fumbled in his jacket pocket and pulled out a card. "If you need anything, call me. We are neighbors now." She turned the card over between her fingers. "I am sorry, I must collect my mother." They walked as far as the Basilica of the Virgin, where hordes of small women dressed in black emerged like ants on a mission.

"A pleasure to meet you, Luca de Santangel." She glanced at his card. *Santangel?* she thought, remembering her conversation with Fidel.

"And you, Emma Temple." He held her gaze, and smiled. "It's a small place—I'm sure we'll bump into each other soon."

TWENTY

Freya stopped at the top of the street to catch her breath. The sunset radiating from the lavender mountains was jewel bright, like looking through cranberry glass. The windows glowed orange, golden against the rose sky. She picked up her suitcase, shouldered open the gate of the Villa del Valle, and strode along the neatly tended pathway. She knocked on the newly painted blue door and heard footsteps coming along the tiled corridor. The door swung open.

"*Sí?*" A young, pretty girl with her hair scraped back from her face popped her head around. A beauty spot between her brows, and dark almond eyes gave her an oriental air.

"Rosa del Valle?" Freya said. The smell of something fragrant cooking enticed her in.

"No, I am Macu. Come, Rosa is in the kitchen."

Freya followed her along the corridor to the kitchen. A young woman, harder-looking than Macu, was pounding herbs in a large stone mortar at the table. She was dressed in black. As she stood and wiped her hands on her white apron, Freya saw she was heavily pregnant.

"*Hola, buenas.*" Freya stepped forward and offered her hand. "I'm Freya Temple—Spanish Medical Aid. There's no room in the nurses' quarters, but they said you might have a room?"

"*Sí, sí.*" Rosa gestured for her to come forward. She went to take the case.

"Oh, no, I couldn't possibly. Not in your . . ."

"This? If my husband had his way, I would be out in the garden digging the cabbages." She took the suitcase. "Come, I will show you the room, you see if you like it."

Freya looked at the kitchen counter, saw the piles of fresh herbs. "Something smells good. What are you cooking?" she asked, pointing at the plants.

"Those? Medicine. It is a good time to pick the plants. Macu and I were busy last night." She mimed a headache. "I help people in the village who don't trust the doctor."

"We are both nurses then?" She followed Rosa to the hall.

Rosa's heels tapped as she led Freya up the stairs. "Maybe. I help them at the hospital when I can."

"So we'll be working together?" Freya turned to face her outside the door to her room. She liked Rosa immediately, sensed the humor dancing below the surface of her sad, dark eyes.

"There are only three rooms. Macu sleeps next door to you. This was . . . Well, this room is spare now. And I am with Vicente, there." She pointed down the corridor.

"Rosa!" a man's voice bellowed from downstairs. Freya saw her flinch.

"I'm sorry, I have to go. Vicente is home for his dinner, and he . . . Well, it's not ready." She backed away.

"Let me come and help."

"It's not necessary."

Freya opened the door, looked around the plainly furnished, clean room. Linen curtains billowed at the open window. "Perfect." She handed Rosa the first month's rent and sent her suitcase skidding across the floor to the end of the bed. "Right, let's cook."

"I am glad to be here," Freya said as they walked downstairs. "It's so awfully bloody on the front line."

"I know," Rosa said. "I was there, I fought in Madrid." She paused in the hall. Through the frosted glass window, she could see the bulk of Vicente's torso as he walked back and forth across the kitchen. "It is changing, now. There was such optimism." Her face fell. "Now it is gone."

"Rosa!" Vicente yelled.

"Come." Rosa beckoned her into the kitchen.

"Where have you been?" Vicente roared as the door opened. "I've been sweating in the shop all day—" He slammed down a joint of ham on the counter, then caught sight of Freya.

Rosa skirted around him, muttering under her breath. "This is Freya," she said. "She is going to stay here." Vicente narrowed his eyes. "She will pay." Rosa shoved the notes Freya had given her onto the counter. Vicente shrugged and pocketed them.

"*Encantado*," Freya said, offering her his hand.

Reluctantly, he took it. "*Buenas.*"

"My . . . husband," Rosa said, and Freya noticed her hesitation. "Vicente del Valle. He is *carnicero.*"

"Butcher?"

"Yes, butcher."

Vicente settled back in his chair at the head of the table, and Freya felt him watching her. His arrogance unnerved her. She rinsed a handful of tomatoes in the sink, and as she chopped she glanced up, catching his eye. He was handsome, certainly, she thought, but there was a weakness to his scarred mouth, a meanness there. Even at rest he looked like he was sucking sherbet.

"In here?" Freya pointed at a glazed earthenware bowl on the counter.

"*Sí, gracias,*" Rosa said. She placed the tomatoes, a loaf of bread fresh from the oven, and some cold ham on the table.

"Have you always been a butcher?"

"No, Vicente was a matador," Rosa said.

"Do you still . . . ?" Freya mimed waving a bullfighter's cloak.

"No." He leaned forward on the table. His gold teeth gleamed in the light of the oil lamp. "I am a butcher now. I get my revenge on the bull, eh?"

He scraped back his chair and went to fill his glass with wine in the scullery. Rosa whispered to Freya, "He was no good. To be a matador you have to face death squarely. But his brother, Jordi—"

"Why are you talking about him?" Vicente glared at her. Rosa quickly looked down at her plate. "My little brother, he was a *recortadore*—a bull leaper." Freya looked confused. "It is different. They jump the bulls, but we fight them." He mimed stabbing a sword into the arched back of a bull with the bread knife.

"Jordi was the best bull leaper," Rosa said quietly.

"You think?" Vicente gripped the knife. "Maybe he wasn't good enough to jump out of the way of the Nationalists' bullets, eh?"

"Don't." Rosa shrank into herself.

"If he was the best, why did he knock you up and leave you here, eh? Why did he get himself killed? If he is better than me, then why didn't he marry you?"

"He asked me," she said, her eyes filling with tears. She glanced at Freya. "If you are going to live here, maybe it is good you understand. Jordi, Vicente's brother, he was killed in Jarama." She pointed at a framed photograph of Jordi and Vicente on the sideboard. Freya wondered if two brothers had ever looked more different.

"I'm so sorry." *Jordi del Valle,* Freya thought. Why does that name ring a bell?

"My brother left his woman alone, with a baby, so I take care of her."

I bet you do. Freya forced an understanding smile.

"Rosa, she says she doesn't need a husband, but I made her see sense."

Freya weighed him up. She could sense Rosa's intense grief, felt her vulnerability beneath the tough front. *You knew when she was weak and just went for her like a predator.*

"Who is your husband now?" he said.

"You are," Rosa said, her voice barely a whisper.

"I can't hear you!"

"You are, you are my husband," Rosa said defiantly with tears in her eyes. Satisfied, he grunted and picked up his fork.

They ate in silence, Vicente staring resolutely at his plate as he wolfed down the ham and half the loaf of bread. Finally, he pushed away his plate and strode off outside without a word.

"Is he always so charming?" Freya waited for Rosa to look at her, and they smiled.

"Vicente is not comfortable with women. If you are not a wife, or a mother, or a whore, he doesn't know what to make of you."

Freya tidied the plates away. "No, no. You sit down," she said as Rosa tried to help. "You should put your feet up when you can."

"Thank you." Rosa sank back and rubbed her swollen stomach.

"When are you due?"

"Very soon."

"Is this your first? You must be excited."

Rosa hesitated. She wanted desperately to talk to someone and felt instinctively she could trust this Englishwoman. "Vicente . . ." Her face crumpled. "I have shocked you . . ."

"No, no." Freya sat down at the table, and took Rosa's hand. "Please don't cry. These are terrible times. You did the best thing for the baby."

"It is so bad."

"I'm sure we can sort it out. Now, where do you keep the tea?"

"Tea?"

"Chamomile, maybe?" Freya went to the cupboard Rosa indicated. "I'm going to make us a drink, and you can tell me the whole story. When will your husband be home?"

Rosa laughed bitterly. "He'll be hours. He's gone to the café to get drunk."

Freya took down two cups. "Jolly good. That gives us plenty of time to set the world to rights. Why don't you start at the beginning and tell me how you ended up in this mess?"

Rosa's story poured out as they talked late into the night. "The strange thing is, I never felt him go," she said.

"Who? Jordi?" Freya said.

"I feel him, here." She bunched her fist over her heart. "I see things sometimes. But I never saw him die."

"You mean visions?"

Rosa nodded. "My mother, and her mother before that were clever women, good with herbs—we call them *curanderas* but some, they call them *hechiceras*, white witches. They taught me to make medicine to cure people. They showed me how to gather herbs and plants at midnight."

"So you have the gift too?"

"*Sí.* I am one of two—I had a twin sister, she died when we were babies." Rosa paused. "And I have this." She pulled back the sleeves of her black cardigan, showed Freya her fingers, slender as a child's. By the side of the little fingers there were pale scars. "There were six, one extra on each side. The doctor removed them when I was born."

Freya raised her eyebrows. "Six fingers? Well," she said kindly, "people are always afraid of wise women."

"My family were gitano gypsies. They lived in the caves of Sacromonte, and that is where I grew up."

"I've heard of Sacromonte. Isn't that where people go to see dancing?"

"*Sí.* We dance all the time, for money, not for money. I can tell you stories of whirling dervishes, and Muslim prophets who came there long, long before the people came to watch us dance. That is where I learned."

"Flamenco?"

Rosa pulled a face, waved her hand side to side. "There is more to it than that. The music, the songs—the *cante jondo*—it is about . . ." She gestured to the floor, mimed something rising up. "It is about life, *duende* . . ."

"*Duende?*"

"Spirit. Some say it is evil, a ghost—but it's also magic." She thumped her heart. "Passion. You know Lorca? The poet?"

"I've read a little." Freya looked at her hands. "I heard about the awful, awful way he died."

"Federico was a friend of mine," Rosa said proudly. "People in my family, they worked for his family. His old housekeeper, she was my cousin. When I visited her, I met him. He came to Sacromonte to see me dance."

"Really? How wonderful. Did he ever read to you?"

"Yes. He was so kind, such a good man. He gave me one of his books." Rosa went to the dresser, pulled out a volume hidden behind some old cookery books. "I never read it, of course. I don't know how."

Freya flipped open the pages, saw where Lorca had inscribed the book to Rosa. "I could help you, if you liked, teach you the basics."

"Would you do that for me?" Rosa's eyes lit up. She took the book from Freya, ran her fingers across the cover before hiding it back among the cookbooks. "I put him here because Vicente never looks at the cookery books." She winked at Freya. "If you teach me to read Lorca, well . . ." Her gaze fell. "Jordi loved his poems." Rosa's face was haunted when she looked at her. "Every day I miss him, the man I love, the father of my child." Her eyes glistened. "When I met Jordi in Madrid, he made me feel so strong. For the first time in my life, he made me feel free. He told me all about the politics—he made me see for the first time. I wish you could have seen him talk, how he made people feel. Without him," she said, smiling sadly, "I don't feel so strong anymore. Not so sure. But I feel him, still. Vicente tells me he is dead, he says he saw the papers they took from the body."

"Why did you marry Vicente? Did he force you, Rosa? He hasn't hurt you, has he? I've met men like him before, you get a sense for them."

Rosa shook her head. "He . . . Vicente is clever. I was so bad, when he told me Jordi was dead. For days I couldn't eat, sleep. I wanted to die. When I said that to him, he told me to think about the baby." She looked at Freya.

"These are bad times. I want to give my child the only thing I can. Legitimacy."

"I understand."

"It is safe here, for now. I have Macu to help with the house. She is a good girl." Rosa smiled at Freya. "And now, we will be friends. You are meant to be here. I feel it."

TWENTY-ONE

The house drummed with the rhythm of falling water. Emma had run out of pots and pans to catch the drips, and she sat shivering at the kitchen table. When she'd gone to make coffee that morning, the stove had sputtered and died. The gas canister had run out, which meant no breakfast, and no hot water to wash in until the gas man's delivery to the square later that morning. She glanced down as the cat mewed plaintively at the back door.

"Hello, you again?" It blinked at her impassively. "Are you hungry?" Emma rummaged through the cupboard, and pulled out a tin. "At least you are all right." She opened the tuna, and set it down on the back doorstep for the cat. In the weak October light, she watched it eating. "Where have you hidden your kittens, eh?" She squatted down, tried to stroke its lean back. The cat hissed, ran off across the garden with a chunk of fish in her mouth. "Don't worry," Emma called after it. "No need for thanks." She leaned against the back door and surveyed the rainy garden. It looked worse, in some ways, now that the overgrown plants had been cleared. The lawn was stubbly and dead-looking, the perimeter walls in need of fresh paint.

Emma hugged her overcoat around her pajamas, slipped on a pair of Wellingtons, and decided to check the outbuilding for a spare gas canister. She grabbed the torch, and sploshed across the garden. The old storeroom was

dark and silent, dusty cobwebs hanging like old gray knicker elastic from
the beams. She swung the torch around. There was little of use in there, just
the lawn mower she had bought for Aziz to use, a jerry can of petrol. She
moved the beam of the torch back across the wall, and stepped toward a
door at the end she hadn't noticed, partially hidden behind old bamboo canes
and rusted rakes. She cleared them aside, tossing them onto the mottled
concrete floor. The wood had swollen, and she had to tug hard to open the
door. All she saw at first was row upon row of desiccated plants strung from
the slatted shelves of a deep cupboard, like a petrified forest. Then she
noticed something at the back of the top shelf, a dark shadow. She felt
up, her fingers tracing in the dust, and touched stone. Emma clambered up,
hoping the shelves would take her weight, and dragged down a heavy stone
mortar. *It's beautiful,* she thought. *It must be very old*. She clambered up
again, and peered over the shelf, looking for the pestle. It had rolled to the
back and was resting on a couple of old books. Emma dragged them down,
and staggered out into the garden, coughing with the dust.

At the door of the kitchen, Emma paused. A tiny old woman, dressed
in black and as frail as the skeleton of a bird, was wandering around inside, her hand stroking the old kitchen table as she walked. Her white
hair was swept back from her high forehead into a bun at the nape of her
neck, the widow's peak pointing to a beauty spot between her kohled
brows.

"*Buenos días,*" Emma said. "Can I help you?" She dumped the pestle and
mortar on the table. The books slipped to its side.

The old woman paled. "*Madre mía!*"

"Are you all right? I'm sorry if I surprised you."

She recovered herself. "I didn't hear you coming." She held her hard, pat-
ent leather handbag in front of her stomach like a shield. "I am Immaculada. Everyone calls me Macu. Fidel said you wanted to see me."

"Oh! I'm delighted to meet you. Thank you for coming." Emma dusted
off her hands. "I would make you a cup of coffee, but I've run out of gas."

"You are living alone here, like this?" Macu shook her head as she sat
on the chair Emma pulled forward for her.

"It's not so bad. I'm going to renovate . . ." She could see the concern on
the old woman's face. "It's nice to have a visitor. Most people seem afraid of
the house."

"The house?" She clicked her tongue. "Never fear houses, only people.
Ghosts perhaps." She shrugged, stared at Emma's stomach. "Are you . . . ?"

"Yes. The baby's due in January."

"You need help, especially in your condition. You have family here?"

"No. My mother bought this house, but she died."

"No family." She followed Emma's gaze to a framed photo on the windowsill. "This is your mother?" Emma sensed her surprise. "What was she called?"

"Liberty."

"And who was her mother?" Macu asked. Emma detected something in her voice, a tension.

"My grandmother? Her name is Freya Temple."

"Freya?" Macu looked up at her. "Is she still alive? Well I never . . ."

"You knew Freya?"

Macu settled back in the chair. "She was here, a long time ago."

"In the war?"

She hesitated. "Yes, in the war."

"Can I ask you something?" Emma pulled out her wallet and tipped the two photographs onto her hand. She passed them to Macu. "Do you know these people?"

Macu breathed in sharply, as if she had been struck. "These people are my friends. This is Rosa . . ."

Emma squatted down at her side to look at the photos. "And the boy?"

"He is Jordi. Jordi del Valle."

"So this was his house? I'd love to hear all about it. I'm so interested to know about the history of this place." Emma sensed Macu's reluctance. "I can't believe you knew Freya too. Did you work with her in the hospitals?"

Macu handed her the photos, closed her fingers over them. "I . . . I am so glad to meet you. To know about Freya, and your mother." She looked into Emma's eyes. "We will talk, one day. First, you must speak to your grandmother." She blinked, looked around her. "Oh, the things this house has seen. Now, look. It is falling apart."

"Like me," Emma said, laughing. She stood awkwardly and leaned back against the kitchen table. "Fidel said I should talk to you about local ingredients too. I make perfume."

"Do you?" Macu smiled. "My friend who lived here, Rosa, was good with herbs too. She made medicine, cures."

"Really? I'd love to hear more about her."

"My daughter is waiting in the car, so I have to go. You must come to our home, soon." Macu heaved herself to her feet. "We can talk properly then." She glanced around the dusty hallway. "In the meantime I will send you one of our housekeeper's daughters to help. Solé, she is good with babies, as well."

"Thank you. That's one less thing to worry about. Now I just need to find some builders," Emma said as she opened the door.

"Listen. You go and find my grandson, Luca. After this, go to the bar. He knows all about the farm, and he knows builders." She kissed Emma's cheeks. "He will help you put yourself back together again, you'll see."

"Luca de Santangel is your grandson?" Emma smiled. "We've already met."

Emma spotted Luca across the village square, sitting beneath the striped awning of the bar at a pavement table with a group of men. It looked like they had been there some time. Bottles of red wine and cognac littered the table. She waved, and he lifted his chin in greeting but continued his conversation. A chill wind lifted the awning, splashed rainwater onto the slick pavement in front of the bar. Emma turned up the collar of her coat, and began to walk toward the market. *If he's too rude to come and say hello, I'm damned if I'm going to go over,* she thought.

As she paused outside the *perfumería*, and gazed with a practiced eye at the window displays, she saw his reflection join hers.

"Good morning, Emma Temple." His face was close to her. She smelled alcohol, tobacco, vetiver soap. Her heart jolted.

"And I thought it was bad in London . . ." She turned to him and smiled. "It's not even midmorning!"

He looked at her quizzically. "What? The wine?"

"It's a bit early."

"Ah!" He waved a finger. "Just you wait. You will never see a drunk Spaniard. Not like in England. When I was in London I saw women—women!—staggering drunk and vomiting in the gutter."

"So now we can't drink?"

"It's not ladylike to get drunk," he corrected.

"That's so misogynistic!"

"It is the truth." He shrugged. "Women like that have no respect for themselves."

"But what about men?"

"It's different."

"No it's not!" She stepped aside to let an old woman with a shopping trolley pass her by. She eyed Emma curiously.

"*Señora,*" he said, and nodded at the woman as she passed.

"Your attitudes . . ." Emma sputtered.

"Old-fashioned, chivalrous . . ."

"Unreformed, traditional . . ."

"Stop it, you are flattering me!" He laughed. He leaned against the wall with one arm. "Tell me," he said quietly. "What is wrong with a man who provides for you, adores you, makes love to you like you are the only woman in the world . . ."

"I don't need to be made love to," Emma said, a smile playing on her lips. "I need a builder. Your grandmother seemed to think you could help."

Luca shrugged and nodded his head toward the café. "There are a couple of Polish guys in there looking for work. They are good. You can trust them. They did some work for my sister, Paloma."

"Thank you."

Luca folded his arms. "Maybe they can fix up the basics for you. Like a bathroom?"

Emma touched her hair. It was thick with dust. "Very amusing. I wanted to talk to you about some business too."

"Business? I'm disappointed. First builders, now business. I thought you were giving me the eye because you wanted to talk about pleasure."

"I was not giving you the eye!" She hoped she wasn't blushing.

"Yes you were," Luca said as he turned to walk away. He glanced back, smiling. "Look at you. Can't take your eyes off me, can you?"

Emma laughed, folded her arms. "Are all Spanish men this arrogant?"

"You'll see." He turned, walked backward for a few paces. "Macu called me. She wants you to come to the finca on Saturday. We can talk 'business' then."

In the bar, Emma beckoned to the waitress. "Are there any builders in here?" she asked the girl.

"Over here."

Emma turned. Leaning against the jukebox, a slim man in his early twenties was drinking Coca-Cola, a rucksack by his chair. To Emma he looked like a neon-lit angel, blond curls illuminated blue.

"You are a builder?" she asked.

"No, but my friend Borys is. I am a carpenter."

"Well, I need one of those too." she said. "What's your name?"

"Marek."

"OK, Marek." Emma jotted down her name and address in her notebook and tore out the sheet. "I live in the old white house at the top of the hill. If you and your friend can come over today that would be great. Say midday?"

"It's a date," he said, and pushed open the door of the café for her. Marek leaned against the frame, close enough for her to smell soap powder, chewing gum. "See you then, Emma."

At midday, Fidel arrived just as Marek and Borys were knocking on the door. Emma was relieved to see they knew each other. She had asked Fidel to help organize the build—she wanted someone on hand who could keep an eye on the job when she was in hospital with the baby.

"They are good workers," he said to her as they sat around the kitchen table. "For my brother they worked from dawn till dusk each day."

"Good," Borys said. "I am glad Señor Pons Garcia was pleased. Now, with this job, the garden will be last." He checked the list, making a couple of notes. "We will finish with the pool and the terrace. For now, we will set up camp out there with our tents, OK?"

Fidel looked at the rainwater dripping through the kitchen roof. "I think maybe you are better off in a tent out there too, Emma."

As they talked through her plans for the house, she discovered Borys was the builder, plumber, and electrician. Marek took care of the carpentry, plastering, and decorating, as well as the heavy lifting. "My back, he is not so good now," Borys said. Emma caught a glimpse of a thick leather belt beneath his waistcoat, and must have looked uncertain. "But don't worry I work like a superman."

"I'm sure you do," she said.

"Together, we make one big man!" Borys ruffled Marek's golden curls. "I know Marek since he was little boy—my best friend was his father. I promised to take care of him."

"Eh, I can take care of myself," Marek said. He glanced at Emma beneath blue-black lashes.

"Well, I am glad to have you both here." Emma started to clear up the mugs, but Borys stopped her.

"You go rest. We will be very quiet."

"Don't worry I could sleep through anything."

As he rinsed the mugs, he said, "You know you have a hidden room up there?"

"I wondered when I counted the windows outside," Fidel said. "Do you think so?"

"In between the main bedroom and the bell tower."

"Maybe there is a body in there?" Marek raised his arms like a zombie. "People say in the village this house is haunted."

"Well, I haven't seen anything," Emma said. "How exciting. Can you open it up?"

"For sure." Borys dried his hands. "It means breaking the plaster in the hall upstairs, but we do that anyway for electrics."

"Wonderful—why don't you start on that soon?"

"Yes soon, but first we make proper plumbing and electricity. You need heat and light for baby, yes?"

"But the secret room sounds far more interesting!"

"It can wait a few more weeks," Borys said. "It looks to me like it's been sealed up for years."

TWENTY-TWO

The taxi dropped her by a tall white wall, and Emma walked along the red earth track to the Santangel finca. An orangewood fire blazed at the side of the road where farmhands warmed themselves and drank cognac, crates of fruit stacked beside them.

A light breeze lifted the hem of her coat, and she pushed a loose tendril of her dark hair away from her face. In the distance, a small dark figure appeared on the path, a little white dog leaping at her heels. As Emma drew closer she could hear the woman chiding the dog. When the woman looked up, the words died on her lips. She skirted around, staring at Emma, her eyes narrowed.

"*Buenos dias, Señora,*" Emma said uncertainly. "Luca de Santangel, *por favor?*"

With a toss of her head, the woman indicated the sky. "*Qué pasa, chica?*" The woman smiled, but there was steel in her gaze. "What do you want with my son?"

"Señor de Santangel is your son?" She offered her hand. "My name is Emma Temple. Fidel suggested I should talk to your family . . ."

"Did he?"

"I've just moved into the Villa del Valle." She saw the woman flinch.

"Come." She signaled for Emma to follow her. As they walked, Luca's mother pointed upward. Emma stared at the sky. A small white plane banked above them, and she heard the engine note die down as it began its descent. The *señora* walked on, following the plane's path toward a clearing in the orange groves. By the time they arrived, the plane had landed on the strip and was taxiing toward a shelter. An old man dragged himself to his feet from the shadows and walked toward the plane, a high-tailed husky as large as a wolf racing ahead of him. The plane door opened, and Emma saw a tan, polished riding boot swing toward the ground. When she turned to talk to the woman, she found she had gone. Emma shielded her eyes from the bright winter sun, and saw the dog obediently lay down at his master's voice. Luca tossed the plane keys to the old man, and strode across the field, his dog at his heels. As he walked toward her, he tilted his head. "Emma Temple," he said, extending a hand. His skin was warm to her touch.

"*Buenas* . . . Hello, Señor de Santangel," she said uncertainly.

"Luca, please." He guided her toward the finca.

"Thank you for inviting me." Emma smiled, pulling her loose coat around her as they walked to the house.

"Are you cold?" Luca shrugged off his jacket, tucked it over her shoulders. The suede leather still held the warmth of his skin.

"Thank you." Emma inhaled the clean, familiar smell of Acqua di Parma, took in the flawless white cotton of his shirt, tucked into pale riding breeches. "I'm not used to such chivalry."

"Like I said, Spanish men still believe in *la caballerosidad*."

"Is that a good thing?"

"I don't know. Why don't you ask my sister?" He called out to a dark, slender woman unloading a gleaming black Volvo in front of the finca's main door, a little girl tucked into the crook of her hip. Emma admired the woman's understated elegance, her well-cut pair of light wool palazzo pants and cashmere wrap cardigan. Her bearing, and her black hair smoothed back into a bun at the nape of her neck, reminded Emma of her childhood ballet teacher. "Eh! Paloma! Do you think Spanish men are old-fashioned?"

"Why do you think I married a Frenchman?" she said.

"Paloma, this is Emma—Fidel sent her to see us." He kissed her on each cheek, and in turn she kissed Emma.

"Hello," Emma said, taking the toddler's outstretched, pudgy hand in her fingertips. The child had her mother's Chanel sunglasses in the other hand, and was chewing happily on the frame.

"You are English?" Paloma said.

"Yes. Well, I grew up in the UK, but I was born in America. Mum was a bit of a hippie at that point—Haight-Ashbury, Woodstock." Emma felt Luca watching her. "I lived in London . . . until recently. I don't really know where I'm from." She felt like she was talking too much. "Here, let me help," she said and took a couple of the Carrefour bags from the trunk.

"Thank you. Come inside, it's freezing." Paloma ushered her toward the kitchen as Luca walked away toward the stables. "Are you just visiting?" The warm scent of woodsmoke greeted them.

"No, I've just moved here. I'm renovating the old Villa del Valle." Emma hesitated as she saw Luca's mother at the kitchen table, carving serrano ham from a full leg with a glinting knife.

"Really? No one has lived there for years." Paloma put the groceries on the counter, and eased the little girl into her high chair. "Mamá, have you met Emma?"

"Yes, we met on the road," Emma said as the woman raised her chin.

"My mother, Dolores," Paloma said, a note of apology in her voice.

"I'm dying to find out the history of the place." Emma smiled hopefully. "Did you know the del Valles?"

"Me? No. I am too young. Talk to my mother." Dolores walked out, rubbing her hands clean on a red gingham cloth.

Luca glanced at his mother's retreating figure as he walked into the kitchen. "Sorry, I wanted to take care of Sasha—my dog."

"He's beautiful," Emma said. "I thought he was a wolf when I first saw him."

"Here." Luca directed her toward the fire. "Warm up. So cold! Can you believe it? Has anyone offered you a drink? Something to eat?" The scent of chicken roasting with lemon and thyme made Emma's stomach growl with hunger.

"I'm fine, really—thank you . . ."

"Nonsense! Paloma, who's coming for lunch?" From the room next door, Emma could hear adults chatting, the sound of children running and laughing.

"Just the usual. Olivier will be along once he's finished the lecture."

"My brother-in-law, the professor." He leaned toward Emma as he tossed a log onto the fire, spoke quietly. "I adore the man. He can talk the bark off a tree once he gets going." The fire hissed and cracked. "Let me take your coat," he said. "So you are here with your husband? Boyfriend?" Emma turned and shrugged off his jacket and unbuttoned her coat.

"Luca!" Paloma laughed. "Excuse my brother. Subtlety is not his strong point."

"No." Emma glanced over her shoulder at him. The fire reflected in his dark eyes. "I'm alone."

His lips opened to speak, but as she turned back to him his gaze fell to her rounded stomach. The thin silk of her dress clung to her curves.

"Ay dios mío . . ." Dolores exclaimed from the doorway, staring at Emma. Macu was on her arm. "This is my mother, Immaculada."

"Stop fussing," Macu said, shrugging her daughter off. "We've met already." She walked stiffly toward Emma. Her gaze softened as she reached for the gold locket that hung around Emma's neck. "Beautiful," she murmured. "So, how is the house?"

Dolores pursed her lips. "It is bad blood," she said. "That house is—"

"*Callate*! Enough!" Macu said. "You know nothing." She embraced Emma, kissed her on both cheeks. "Don't mind my daughter," she whispered. "She hasn't been with a man since 1971 and it shows." She shuffled past and poured herself a large sherry from a decanter on the kitchen table.

"Tell me, what business do you have with my son?" Dolores interrupted. Luca shrugged as if to say, It wasn't me.

Emma pulled herself up proudly. "Just that. Business. My family owns a company called Liberty Temple—"

"Of course!" Paloma exclaimed. "You're Emma Temple. I thought I recognized you. I'm a beauty buyer for the department store El Corte Inglés. We aren't lucky enough to sell your range, but I always stock up when I'm in New York or London."

"Thank you," Emma said. "I'm starting a new company. I want to try something different, based on aromatherapy. I need natural ingredients— the best."

"You're either a genius or crazy," Paloma said, laughing. "Some of our produce goes to the perfume manufacturers for sure, but why make your own? Maybe you want to buy essences from one of the big Spanish firms like Destilaciones Bordas Chinchurreta?"

Emma shook her head. "I want to do it myself, on a small scale at first. If it takes off, then I'll work with the big firms."

"Tsk." Dolores interrupted. "Why do young people make it so difficult, eh?"

Emma held her gaze. "I just have some new ideas." The baby danced in her stomach, a hand or foot striking out, sensing her tension. From the yard, a dog howled, a low keening.

"Are you staying for lunch?" Dolores asked.

"Thank you, I'd like that," Emma said.

"Well, sit down. A woman in your condition needs to rest." Dolores looked at the clock on the kitchen wall. "We'll eat when your Frenchman decides to turn up," she said to Paloma as she flung open the oven door.

"*Ay, Mamá*," Paloma murmured. "We have been married twenty years and still she can't say his name without crossing herself," she whispered to Emma.

As they walked through to the dining room one of Freya's favorite phrases came to Emma's mind: *You could eat off the floor*. The house was immaculately clean, the heavy, dark, wood-paneled doors waxed and polished, the brass candelabras gleaming from the beamed ceilings. The long table was laid for ten—the children sitting with the adults.

The hours passed unnoticed as the family chatted and leisurely ate their way through several courses. Olivier dominated the conversation, reducing them to helpless laughter as he told Emma stories about the scrapes he and Luca had got into as students.

"I was caught, on the drainpipe, climbing out of her room," he concluded his story. "Luca had to rescue me, cut my belt free. What was the name of that girl, Luca?" he called down the table.

"I don't remember," he said. "You had so many girlfriends."

"Luca!" Paloma put her arm protectively around her husband, pulled a face.

"Ah, there is only one girl for me, now," Olivier said, and kissed her forehead. "But then, well . . ."

Emma felt Dolores's silent disapproval snaking across the table like barbed wire.

"You are not hungry?" Dolores said to her.

"Thank you, it was delicious. I can't remember the last time I've eaten so much." The almond tart had finally defeated her, and Emma pushed her dessert plate away, smiling as the children raced outside. Immaculada had nodded off in her chair at the head of the table, and dozed content-edly, her lips working in her sleep. The sun sank low over the orange groves, warm light spilling through the doors to the terrace, gilding the silver candlesticks on the table as Dolores lit the wicks with a long taper. Emma still felt awkward around her, but as she leaned over to light the candle in front of Emma, she felt she should say something. "That was a wonderful meal," Emma ventured. "The chicken was perfect, and I've never had such delicious paella."

"It's not paella," she corrected her. "It is *arroz negro*—rice with squid ink."

"Ah . . . that's why it's black." Emma smiled. "I'd love the recipe." She took a sip of her water as one of the girls cleared away the dessert plates. "So, *Señora*, will your family be able to help me?"

Dolores shook her head as she sat down at her place. "Impossible."

"Nothing is impossible," Olivier said reasonably as he refilled their wineglasses. Emma liked him the moment she met him. He was affable, charming, bulbous-nosed. Clearly he still adored his beautiful wife.

"The thing is, I'm starting over again," Emma said quietly. "I want to get rid of all the . . . complications. I want only to work with the best suppli-ers." She held Dolores's gaze, glanced from her to Luca. "I heard you are the best. Can you tell me about the orange trees?" Emma said, cupping her chin on her palm as she leaned toward him.

"What do you want to know?" Luca said.

"Everything. I adore them. The oranges seem so improbable when you look out at the groves, like something a child would draw, and the smell . . ."

"Well, the finest of the flowers are from our groves in the south of Spain. The blossom is best after around ten years, and reaches its peak when the tree is nearly thirty years old."

Emma resisted the temptation to say "just like me."

"From each tree you get maybe five to twenty-five kilograms of flowers a year. Each worker can collect maybe eight to twenty kilos a day."

"What a wonderful job."

Luca shook his head. "No, it's hard work, it takes time and it is expen-sive."

"You probably know neroli relaxes you. People say walking in the groves is like"—Olivier waved his fingers near his temple—"Zen meditation. Maybe that's why we are so relaxed here."

"We have many different types," Luca said, "all across Spain. In the south,

we have land near Seville—those trees are best for fragrance. The flowers
are so sweet smelling, and the neroli is extracted from them. From the leaves
and twigs people take petitgrain, and bitter orange oil from the fruits."

"Perfect. Can I make a small order?" Emma said.

"It's been a good year." Luca took the wine bottle from Olivier and refilled his mother's glass, before topping up his own. "We have more than
enough for our regular customers. Where is your lab?"

"Lab?" Emma thought of the sterile laboratories they used in Paris.
She laughed. "I'm working in my kitchen, at home. I haven't got room
for all the equipment—distillers, enfleurage frames, presses, so I'll have to
outsource . . ."

"I know someone who can help you with that," Paloma said. "What about
Guillermo?" she said to Luca. "I heard his mother is retiring."

Luca smiled. "I'll talk to him." He looked at his mother. "What is there
to lose if Emma wants to play around?"

"Luca!" Paloma chided him. "It's hardly 'playing'—Emma is one of the
best young perfumers in the business."

"So, Emma," Olivier said, sensing the tension, "is your husband with you
here?"

"No, I . . . I lost my partner."

"How careless!"

"We were separated. And then . . ." She twisted the locket on its chain.
"He was in New York at the World Trade Center when the attacks happened."

The table fell silent. "I am so sorry," Paloma said. "Was he killed?"

"He's just disappeared off the face of the earth. It's . . ." Emma struggled
to explain. "I think for a while we hoped he'd just turn up. It's still hard to
believe."

Dolores's face softened. "The baby, did he know?"

Emma shrugged. "Joe was married to someone else by then."

"You poor thing, all alone . . ." Olivier started to say. At his kindness,
tears pricked Emma's eyes. She felt too hot suddenly.

"Olivier." Paloma kicked him under the table. "It is none of our business."

"I'm fine. I can take care of myself. And the baby." She sensed Luca watching her from his end of the table. He was leaning back in his chair, one elbow resting on the arm, his glass of wine raised. In the candlelight his face
had a softness she hadn't noticed before.

"Come," Olivier said, "we all need someone." He put his arm around Paloma's shoulders. "Maybe in time?"

Emma shook her head. "No. I was lucky. I had over ten good years with Joe. Now I have the baby, a new home, I am too busy . . ."

"Too busy for love?" Olivier laughed, breaking the tension. He covered his ears. "Stop it! You are killing me."

Paloma kissed his cheek. "My husband, the old romantic."

"Where are you staying?" he asked Emma.

"At the Villa del Valle."

"Really? Are you mad?"

"Everyone seems to think so." She laughed, relieved to change the subject.

"The place is falling apart. You're not living in the middle of all that?"

"It's not so bad, the builders Luca recommended are very kind. In fact, I enjoy the company."

Dolores muttered something under her breath. Emma glanced at her watch. "I should be going, I promised I'd be back to make some decisions on the joinery," she lied.

"Luca," Paloma called up the table, "you'll drive Emma home, won't you?"

"It's fine," Emma said. "I'll call for a taxi. My car is at the garage."

"You'll be lucky to get a taxi now," Luca said. "It's no trouble. I can drop you off on the way home."

They drove in silence for a while through the dark night, the headlights picking out orange trees, prickly pear cactuses on the side of the road, sometimes the flash of a wild animal's eyes. The warmth and comfort of the Range Rover relaxed Emma. "I assumed you lived at the farm," she said.

"Not all Spanish men live with their mothers." He glanced at her and smiled. "No, I have a room there, but my apartment is in El Carmen."

"I love that part of town. The museum is wonderful."

"The bars are good, it feels real still." He flicked on the stereo. Flamenco guitar played softly, round notes falling into the air like stones into still water, hypnotic and sensual. Emma let her head fall back. She felt pleasantly drowsy after the huge meal. The dark sides of the car seemed to shift toward her, to contract. She'd often noticed this feeling when she was tired, how her sense of space seemed to alter, become fluid. Emma glanced at his silhouette. Her eyes settled on his lips—full, and curved. He felt close. She thought of Liberty reciting the Song of Songs like an incantation in the garden: *"Let him kiss me with the kisses of his mouth . . . honey and milk are under thy tongue . . ."* Emma wondered idly how it would feel to kiss him. He turned and met her gaze.

"I like this music," she said quickly.

"He is good. He has *duende*."

"How do you know it is a man playing?"

"All great flamenco guitarists are men."

"That's outrageous!"

"It's the truth. You have great women dancers . . . but men make the music."

"Nonsense."

Luca turned slightly to her, gestured with his hand. *"Duende* is . . . the dark sounds, a certain magic."

"Passion?"

"Yes but more than that . . . like a ghost."

"Women can be passionate too."

"Of course, but it is different. Lorca said *duende* is like roots . . ." He sculpted the air with his splayed fingers. "Roots thrusting into the earth. He said we feel it, here." He touched his heart. "We feel *duende*. In the music we feel the touch of the earth and the spirits of those who have lived before." Just as she felt him opening up to her, he seemed to catch himself. Luca shifted in his seat, drove in silence for a while. "I am sorry about my mother," he said finally, and nodded at Emma's stomach. "I think she thought she was going to be a grandmother again."

"Why? Have you fathered many children around here?"

Luca glanced at her, smiled slowly. "Not that I know of. I meant Paloma's children. Mamá has her hands full helping her." He pulled up outside the Villa del Valle. "Here you are." He jumped out, came around and opened her door.

"Thank you," she said as he helped her swing down to the ground. She brushed the hair from her eyes.

"This will be beautiful one day," he said. "I've always liked this house."

"Yes, yes it will." Emma looked up at him. "Well, thank you. I look forward to doing business with you, Luca."

"It's a pleasure." His eyes wrinkled with amusement. "I'll talk to some friends. I think we can help with everything you need."

Emma leaned against her gateway and watched the taillights of his car disappear up the street. People strolled beneath the streetlamps, and lithe caramel-skinned teenagers on mopeds sped past, glossy hair streaming behind them like banners. As she lost track of Luca's car, suddenly she felt very alone. The baby stretched, and she winced, rubbing her stomach. *Lonely,* she thought. *Not alone.* She turned toward her house. "Come on, little one," she said aloud to her child. "Let's get to bed."

TWENTY-THREE

VALENCIA, MAY 1937

At nightfall, Rosa lit the lantern above the table. A spring storm rattled the windows of the kitchen, and a black cat seeped into the shadows of the hall. Rosa settled at the head of the table and shuffled the Tarot cards, her gold locket gleaming at her neck in the lamplight. "I don't know if I can do this. Since I've been pregnant, I don't see so clearly."

"You still haven't felt anything about Jordi?" Freya asked.

"No. I see nothing. It is all my fault. He went off to war to be a hero, to prove he is a better man than his brother. Which he is a hundred times over." She looked down at the deck. "If only I had kept him here with me."

"Jordi did the right thing." Macu tapped the table. "Talking of which, I want to know if I should accept Ignacio de Santangel's proposal."

"He is a good man, even if he is wealthy." Rosa split the deck a last time.

"Ignacio's mother says I am not good enough for him," Macu said to Freya. "He defies her."

"I thought the Republicans threw most of the landowners out of their homes at the start of the war?" Freya said.

"Or worse," Rosa said under her breath. "Ignacio's family survived because they are fair with their workers. You should marry him, Macu. I can tell you that without even looking at the cards."

"But what if there is no . . . boom!" Macu mimed fireworks exploding.

"You look at old couples in the village," Rosa said, tamping the cards down. "You think they still have 'boom'? How long do you think it lasts?"

Freya thought of Tom. *A lifetime.*

"Boom goes, trust me. Kindness lasts." Rosa began to deal.

Freya stared, fascinated, at the dog-eared cards decorated with strange images as Rosa dealt them out in a grid. *The Lovers,* she thought. "Would you read for me sometime?" she asked Rosa. "I have an important decision to make too." They heard the church bell begin to toll, and she checked her watch. "Damn, the bus. I'm going to be late for my shift." She put her arm around Rosa's thin shoulders, kissed the top of her head. "Don't wait up for me."

"Stay safe," Rosa said as she looked up at her. "The planes will come again tonight. Oh, by the way. Someone was looking for you earlier at the hospital—a young photographer. She said she was a friend of your brother's? Gerda someone?"

"I don't know her." Freya pulled on her mac.

"She was here taking photos of the People's Army." Rosa frowned as her gaze roamed over the cards laid out in the lamplight. "She showed me some of her pictures. It made me think of Madrid, the photos of the children on the barricades."

"It's surely better that the children have been evacuated now?"

Rosa shrugged. "I heard they are sending the Basque children away too." She rubbed her thumb across her lower lip, troubled by the cards. "Anyway, this Gerda says she will be here for a few days before she meets her partner, Robert someone."

"Capa?" Freya said. "He took that marvelous photograph of the falling soldier. If Charles has got to know him, he must be doing well."

Freya worked through the night as casualties from the bombings were brought in. She felt like she was drowning in the never ending stream of broken, damaged bodies, but she did what she could to alleviate the suffering of each of them. Early the next morning at the end of her shift, she went up to the wards to check on the soldiers convalescing after their operations. The words on the chart she was holding swam before her eyes, and she had to force herself to focus. "Jim Brown," she said aloud, and scanned through his notes. *"Chest wound, paralysis of left arm, possible nerve damage?"* one of the doctors had scribbled on his chart. Freya glanced up at his face. The boy had a little more color than the last time she had seen him. A blood transfusion had brought him back from the edge.

"Now then, Jim," she said. "Let's take a look at you. I'm just going to take your pulse." Jim's left arm shot up in the air, and Freya leaped back in surprise.

"The look on your face!" he said, laughing.

"How long have you been able to move your arm?"

"The pins and needles started a few days ago. I've been practicing. Wanted to give you a surprise."

"Well, you did that." She laughed, exhaustion and the reproachful stare of the Sister sending her into helpless giggles.

"Now that's a laugh I've missed," someone said.

Freya spun around to see Tom standing in the doorway, his cap in his hand. "Tom!" She ran to him, glanced back at the Sister, and pulled him into the nurses' station. "What a marvelous surprise."

He lifted her in his arms as he kissed her, her feet dancing above the floor. "God, I've missed you," he said, burying his face in her hair, breathing her in. "How are you?"

"You know how it is. I thought it would be quieter here, but they are bombing the hell out of the city each night."

"I went to look for you at the house where you're staying." He paused. "Frey, I hope I did the right thing. The girl who lives there—"

"Rosa?"

"She had a picture in the kitchen. Her husband and his brother. I was just making conversation while she made some coffee. She told me the brother had been killed. Jordi del Valle . . ." Tom frowned. "I told her that I treated someone by that name, and it sure wasn't the guy in the photograph. The man who died must have had Jordi's papers somehow."

"That's where I knew the name!" Freya slapped her forehead. "The transfusion. How did Rosa take it?"

"I don't know. First she laughed; then she cried. I hope I didn't do the wrong thing?"

"It's complicated." She stroked his face, concerned by how exhausted he looked. "Are you OK?" Freya took off her nurse's cap, shook out her hair.

"Things are getting kind of tense in Madrid. Beth's gone. He threw a glass ashtray at Culebras, one of the Spanish doctors, the other night. Even I'm in Beth's bad books."

She pulled on her mac, slipped her arm through his. They passed the young nurse taking over Freya's shift on their way down the stairs. "Have you crossed over to the 'misfits and shits' too?" Freya said quietly.

"'Fraid so."

They walked hand in hand out of the hospital. By the fountain, Tom paused, and turned to her. "The thing is, Freya, like I said, he's been sent back to Canada. Men like Beth are heroic, they give hope when they are in the right situation, but he was a liability here—all the great work we've done is being compromised. At least at home we can raise money for the Aid Committee."

"We?" Freya stopped walking. "You're definitely leaving too?"

"I wanted to tell you face-to-face. I have to go and help him get straightened out. There was a terrible scene the other day. He hid behind the curtains in the room where they were holding the disciplinary meeting. He heard exactly what everyone thought of him. When Ted Allan called him a "son of a bitch," he stepped out and gave his resignation. They don't even want him to stay on as a surgeon with the Brigades."

"But you could stay," Freya pleaded, the palm of her hand against his chest. "They'll need someone to run the transfusion service now."

Tom shook his head. "Culebras has won. It's in Spanish hands now. I'm leaving for Canada tomorrow."

"Tomorrow? Surely there must be a way for you to stay?"

"Beth needs help, Freya. He's brilliant, but all too human. Every time he falls down, he picks himself up and dusts himself down . . . but it's getting harder. He's exhausted, demoralized, and angry. He needs me."

"I need you, Tom." She laid her head against his chest. "How long do we have?"

"An hour, maybe, until my train." He raised her chin with his finger, forced her to look into his eyes. "I came here to persuade you to come with me."

"I can't. My work counts too." She thought of all the men and women she had treated, and of all those to come. She thought of Rosa, the baby, of Charles. "I'm needed here, Tom." She saw the flickering neon of a HOTEL sign, luminous in the morning light, took his hand. "Come on."

"Are you sure?"

"I love you, Tom. I don't know if we'll ever see each other again."

"Don't say that. Please don't say that."

"I'm tired, Tom. I just want to be with you, even for an hour. Just you and I."

In the faded luxury of the little hotel room, they undressed each other slowly, memorizing each line, each curve, the feel and scent of each other's bodies. They made love with an intensity Freya had never experienced before. Something bound them together forever, now. There would be no one but Tom for her. They lay curled like a shell, her pale back against his stomach, his arms holding her close. She fought sleep, the desperate swirling exhaustion that made her eyelids droop. She didn't want to miss a moment.

"I have to go," Tom said at last, his lips brushing the back of her neck.

"No," she said, burying deeper into the sheets, her arms holding his to her.

"I love you, Freya. After all this is over . . ."

She shook her head, tears coming to her eyes as she felt him slip out of the bed, heard him dress. "I can't bear it, Tom."

"I'm not going to lose you, Freya," he said, swinging his jacket on. "I wish I had something to give you, a ring . . ."

"There will be time for us, when this is done."

He checked his watch. "Damn, I'm going to be late." He leaned down to her, held her in his arms one last time.

"Be safe. Stay safe," she whispered, her face buried in his neck.

"I'll come for you," he said. "Just as soon as I can, I'll find you. I warn you, I'm not much of a letter writer."

"Just as well. I've seen your handwriting, I wouldn't be able to read a thing. Typical doctor," Freya said laughing, blinking back tears as she held him. She couldn't bear for him to see her cry.

"Wait for me. Don't let some other guy sweep you off your feet. Promise?"

Freya felt his arms release her, watched as he backed away from her toward the door. Her lips trembled as she smiled. "I promise."

"I'm not going to ask you to come with me again, though you know I want to desperately." He pulled on his cap, tilted the brim. "I'm not going to say good-bye . . ."

"Tom, wait!" Freya sat up in bed. "I . . ." Her throat was tight. This was her moment. She could go with him now, run to the station, sail for Canada. She could run, and never look back. *I'm needed here,* she thought. *I can't do it.* "I love you. I'll wait for you, however long."

He took one last look at her. "God, you're beautiful," he said, smiling, shaking his head.

The door swung closed, and Freya was alone. She looked at herself, reflected in the dressing table mirror, stretched out in the bed, a white sheet draped over the curve of her hip, her blond hair mussed up and tangled on the pillow. She touched her lips, swollen and red from their kisses. *Beautiful,* she thought. That was how he had made her feel. *Beautiful.*

TWENTY-FOUR

Emma sat on her new bed, propped up by plump goose down pillows. Empty boxes and carrier bags from El Corte Inglés littered the floor. She closed her eyes, took a speculative bounce, and sighed with pleasure, flinging her arms open. Even with the door closed, she could hear the sounds of the builders at work, the whine of the saw and the shuddering of the walls as Borys laid the new wiring. Above her, a cable dangled from the ceiling, waiting for the light fitting. A fire flickered in the grate in her newly painted white room.

She speed-dialed Freya's number, waited for her to pick up. Emma glanced over at the cat, sitting in a patch of warm sunlight on the window ledge. She inspected the fresh red scratches on her wrist. "Not mellowing much, are you?" she said to the cat. "You'll come round." The light outside was clear and wintry. Emma had been studding oranges with cloves that morning, tying them with red gingham ribbons to decorate the little pine tree Marek had dragged back from the market. She hadn't planned to decorate—the thought of her first Christmas without Liberty and Joe was breaking her heart, but when she saw how proudly Marek and Borys showed her the tree in the corner of the kitchen, she relented. Now, her fingers, holding the phone, were fragrant with spices.

Emma pursed her lips. Freya wasn't picking up. She wanted to talk to her about Liberty's suspicions, to ask her about Macu and Rosa as well. She had tried several times already, but Freya always managed to change the subject. She wanted to talk about Luca too, she realized. *Not that Freya is the best one to talk to about affairs of the heart,* she thought. *I wonder if she ever loved anyone?* Her thoughts trailed off as the answering machine cut in.

"Hello, Gammy, it's Em. Nothing special, just called for a chat. Anyway, love to you and to Charles. Speak soon."

Emma slumped back on the bed. She realized for the first time that she could no longer see her toes, wriggling in her thick wool socks, beyond the curve of her stomach. She was counting the time till the birth in weeks now, rather than months. She wished her mother was here. She would have the perfect advice for her. She always did. She imagined Liberty sitting at the end of the bed, chattering away, full of ideas and plans.

That's not how she was at the end though, Emma thought. She cast her mind back to the last time she had seen her mother alive, how Joe had carried Liberty to her room after the Easter dinner, like a broken bird in his arms. She was almost unrecognizable then, her face hollowed out, her hair gone. And yet she was Liberty to the last, insisting on joining the celebrations. *She always loved the holidays,* Emma thought. Freya had helped Liberty wind a cobalt blue Tuareg scarf into a turban, and slicked crimson lipstick on her pale lips. As everyone ate and drank with forced jollity, Emma had glanced down the table at her mother, propped up with cushions at the end between Charles and Freya, smiling benignly at them, unable to eat, or drink. She seemed to be ebbing away before their eyes. Emma saw Freya nod to Joe as Liberty's eyes closed, and he scooped her in his arms.

He had laid her in the bed, and kissed her forehead one last time, walked from the room unable to look at them, tears brimming in his eyes. Emma bathed her mother's face and hands as the nurse topped up her morphine under Freya's watchful eyes. They knew there would not be long now. Charles shuffled into the room and sat with her awhile, holding her hand, talking softly to her, telling her the stories he'd told her when she was a child, singing her the old songs.

Freya and Emma lay down beside her that night, keeping vigil, staying with her even as the last breath shook her body. Emma curled against her side, and Freya lay with Liberty's head resting in her arms, stroking her cheek, easing her into sleep as she had on a thousand other nights when storms and monsters had kept her awake.

Sometimes, even now, Emma caught herself thinking, *I must ask Mum where she found that fabric . . .* or wanting to share some small, inconsequential thing about the house or the village. She still found it hard to believe that her mother had gone. Emma blinked, and looked at the black lacquer box on her bedside cabinet. As she lifted the lid off, the orange interior reflected the fire. She flicked through the envelopes until she found the one she wanted: "On Love." She tore it open.

Em, what can I tell you about love? I am in no position to lecture you about romantic love, when you and Joe have made more of a success of your relationship than I ever did of mine.

Emma sighed, read on.

You have always done a wonderful job of loving, Em. You are the kindest person I know. What I'm going to ask you is to let yourself be loved. Let love in. Maybe Freya and I are to blame—we made you strong and independent. I think sometimes Joe struggles to keep up. Let him feel needed too. I hope you and Joe ride out whatever it is that's going on and you're not telling me about.

Emma raised her eyebrows.

Yes, of course I know. I'm your mother. I know everything. When you were little I managed to convince you I literally had eyes in the back of my head. I caught you once, when I was napping, gently parting my hair, looking for them.

Thing is, Em, what I've learned is that romantic love comes and goes. Sometimes the people you trust most with your heart are the least worthy. People are fallible, they screw up. It's up to you whether you can bear that, and forgive, or whether you should walk away. Sometimes life, and love, is as much about deciding who to let go as who to take with you on this journey. I hope Joe is worthy. Never let your capacity for love be diminished by the actions of others. Stay true to your heart. You've been so sad lately, closed yourself off. Maybe it was just you were hurting too much? Em, please don't give up. You can live a wonderful life, even if this love is coming to an end. If Joe's not the one, there is a man out there who will keep pace with you, even if you have to run alone for a time.

Maternal love, however . . . well, that's fierce and boundless, and it forgives everything. As you know, I never planned to have children. Freya and I never had the easiest of relationships; perhaps she put me off the whole idea. I'll never forget what she said to me about having a baby. She said that she would wake in the morning to my cries, and wonder how she would get through another day. Perhaps Freya wasn't a natural mother—some women aren't, I suppose, and it can't have been easy for her. When I found out I was expecting you, though—oh, I was so happy. I was terrified too, of course, because we ended up alone, just like Freya. I worried that I wouldn't be a good enough mother to you. But we muddled through, I think.

You were, and are, the most wonderful thing to have happened in my life. I am so sorry that I won't be there to hold your hand through that journey. I would give anything to be a grandmother, to hold a child, and love again. Oh, when I think of you as a baby—those gorgeous pudgy arms and legs, those ageless eyes. You'll see. I didn't know what love is, in all its terrifying vulnerability and fierce glory, until I had you. Look at me, assuming you'll have children! I can't imagine you not. You will be a wonderful mother, Em, far more consistent than me. But promise me you'll spoil them, once in a while? Let them eat a whole bar of chocolate in one go, for me.

Love, always.

Mum x

TWENTY-FIVE

"Where have you been?" Vicente slammed the door back on its hinges.

"I went into the city with Freya and Macu to hear La Pasionaria talk." Rosa let down her hair, brushed it through. When Freya was out, she still used Jordi's room to dress, refused to be naked in front of Vicente. He came and stood behind her now.

"You spend too much time with the Englishwoman."

"I like her. The work we are doing matters . . ." She could smell the cognac on his hot breath against her neck.

"I matter." Vicente spun her around, roughly pulled open her dress. He grazed her ear with his lips, cupped her swollen breast. She flinched as she felt the smooth metal of his teeth. "I am your husband. You did the right thing, Rosa. There is no shame now, for your child. I will take care of you . . ."

"I could care for myself."

"No." He turned her around, forced her backside to his hips, the edge of the dressing table pressing down hard on her stomach so that the baby squirmed. "You will see. You can see how the war is going. Franco will win, and then everything here will return to normal." His hand gripped her shoulder. "Valencia is a safe place. A decent place."

"Please, Vicente," she begged as he pushed her legs apart. "Not now . . ."

"If you are well enough to go and hear that woman talk, you are well enough to please your husband."

Rosa tried to distract herself, thought of La Pasionaria's beautiful voice, the warmth of her eyes as she talked of a free, democratic Spain. She had seemed more like a queen to her than a miner's daughter. "I want to go back to Madrid, to fight."

"No. This is your home now, and soon women will be at home with the children . . ."

"Just like the good old days?"

"Be careful, Rosa. Your Red child is protected now you have married me. I did the decent thing, I married my dead brother's woman. No del Valle will be a bastard."

"Decent?" Rosa cried. "You call this decent?"

Vicente tightened his grip on the back of her neck, forcing her head down. "I am a good man. I will be on the right side. The winning side." He yanked up her dress, grunted as he forced himself into her. "Jordi should have known better," he said, watching himself in the mirror. "He was so proud of you. He paraded you in front of me like a prize. He should have known the moment I saw you, I would want you . . ." His words trailed off as he tensed, gasped, his head rolling back.

Rosa forced him off her. "You pig." She went to slap him, and he caught her wrist, squeezed hard until she cried out. "At least it is over quickly with you."

Vicente put his face close to hers. "You think my dead brother was a better lover, eh? I take you like the bitch you are. Like an animal."

"He's not dead," Rosa said. She pulled her dress around her, covered her stomach with her arm.

"I saw the papers, soaked with blood."

"Whose blood?" Rosa stood up to him, raised her chin. "You tricked me. I believed you, but he's alive." She thumped her chest. "I know he is alive."

TWENTY-SIX

Luca watched the water in the fountain playing over the voluptuous backside of the reclining statue, lost in thought. His mind drifted, remembering Emma, walking away from him across the square the morning they met, the autumn sun filtered softly through the cotton hem of her dress. He saw the faint outline of her lower thighs, the sway of her hips . . .

"Luca, *qué pasa?*"

"*Joder*, Mamá . . ." He spun around.

"*Joder?* You say '*joder*' to your mother? I'll wash your mouth out with soap." Dolores covered one ear of the girl toddling at her side, pulled her into the silence of her skirts. "I'll give you *joder* . . ."

"You made me jump." He winced as she punched his arm with her free hand. Luca squatted down and tickled his niece's tummy, pulled a funny face. "I was just thinking . . ." he said as he stood.

"About that woman." Dolores pursed her lips as she did up the top button of her heavy black coat. "I know you."

"Emma is just a friend."

"And you are just a man." She clung to his arm as they walked away through the crowd spilling from the Basilica. "And that is exactly how these things start."

"Mamá, I am not looking for love." He dug his free hand into his pocket.

"Between my work at the finca, the responsibility of caring for our land, you, the families we support, I have no time for love." He thought of Olivier's laughter at the dinner, and his words sounded hollow even as he uttered them. Luca glanced down at his niece's bouncing brunette ringlets, the tender white parting of her hair. He loved his niece and nephews as his own—any aching hole in his heart was filled by them. There had been a time when he had wanted children, desperately, but that had gone. He had decided not to think about it anymore.

"I see how you look at her!" Dolores grumbled. "I have eyes. Just remember, Luca, she is pregnant with another man's child. And she is living in that house. It will bring nothing but trouble."

Luca slowed his pace to match his mother's shorter stride. Emma had unsettled him. His days had always seemed full, but now they felt restless and empty. In the evening, there had always been family dinners, or friends to meet at a bar in town. If he was lonely, there were a couple of women he trusted not to expect more than he could give. He enjoyed the peace of living alone—his apartment was comfortable, large enough for his books, a desk, a sofa, a huge TV, and a bed big enough to take his six-foot-three frame. He had shaped a life that suited him. He didn't realize he needed anything else, until now.

Dolores paused on the street to greet an old friend, and in the shop window of a bakery he considered his reflection objectively. His body was slightly heavier than when he was young, but he was at home in it, not running to fat like some of his contemporaries with their self-satisfied bellies pressed up against their desks and café tables. His hair was graying at the temples, but it was not thinning yet, and each morning he could still do two hundred sit-ups before walking Sasha in the orange groves. Each evening he swam at the finca, whatever the weather, his mother watching him from the kitchen window during thunderstorms as he cut through the water, backward and forward, oblivious to the lightning in the sky. He was not in bad shape, he thought. He wondered what Emma saw when she looked at him.

He had not meant to drop in to the Perfume Garden that morning, but he had bought the songbird for her on impulse in the market. He knew Emma would like it.

"*Buenos días, Señor*," Aziz said as Luca pushed open the door, the old bell tinkling.

"*Buenas*." Luca looked around the shop. "Do you have any gardenias?"

Aziz scratched his head. "I don't know. I'll ask Emma."

"No, don't disturb . . ." Luca's voice trailed off. He followed Aziz through the back of the shop into the garden, the bird trilling in its cage.

The house reverberated with the noise of the builders' drills, a cacophony of shuddering and whining.

"Emma," Aziz said, laughing. "Emma!" he shouted above the din.

She was dancing in front of the stove to the radio, her checkered men's pajamas tucked into warm socks and Wellingtons, a long blue dressing gown sweeping the floor.

She spun around, spatula in hand. "Luca? How long have you been standing there? I was just trying to warm up. Come in!" Emma laughed breathlessly. Aziz ushered Luca forward, and walked away toward the shop, smiling. As Emma kissed Luca's cheeks she felt that his were warm, freshly shaven. *I must look a wreck,* she thought, touching her freshly washed hair. She was flushed, hurriedly applied mascara smeared beneath one eye.

"You have a little . . ." He went to touch her cheek but hesitated, ran his index finger beneath his own eye instead.

"Oh damn," she said, wiping away the smudge. "I was just trying to make myself presentable. We have a new boiler at last, I can't tell you how exciting it was to have a proper shower."

"I don't want to disturb you." Luca offered her the cage. "I saw this little songbird, and thought maybe he would be a good Christmas present?"

"Thank you." Emma's eyes lit up. "What a lovely idea. I did this in Thailand . . ." She walked to the door, opened the cage, and the bird flew out into the garden, singing joyfully. The tabby cat tracked its path from the long grass, eyes gleaming.

"I thought it would be a good pet for you?" Luca followed her outside. Emma realized what she had done. "Oh dear, I am sorry."

Luca shrugged, smiling as the bird settled in an orange tree. "If it stays, then it is meant to be with you."

She set the cage down on the wall, leaving the door open. "Have you had breakfast?" she called over her shoulder as they turned back into the kitchen. In the corner of the room, the small tree shone with white lights.

"This is breakfast?" Luca's eyes widened as he looked at the flaming frying pan on the stove. He stepped forward, smothered the fire with a wet cloth.

Emma lifted the tea towel and poked at the peppers. "Tempted?"

"Of course," Luca lied.

"Would you mind putting a couple more logs on the fire? I'm hoping they'll get the heating up and running today, but it's still freezing at the moment." Emma clattered around in the kitchen, fetching plates and cutlery. The newly cleaned pestle and mortar sat in pride of place beside the chopping board.

Luca stoked the fire, golden sparks crackling and hissing up the chimney. As Emma cooked, she felt his presence warm her, the heat rise in her cheeks. She glanced over her shoulder, saw Luca pick up an old book lying on the table.

"I found that out in the store," Emma said as he flicked it open.

"Lorca?"

"I must ask Macu about it. He dedicated it to Rosa. I can't believe she met him. There was a cookbook too, of some sort. I can't make out much of the writing, but I think it belonged to her."

Somehow in the moments he sat at the table flicking through the poems, Emma conjured alchemy in the kitchen. The burned offering became char-grilled peppers, succulent, oozing virgin oil, to go with the ham and freshly baked bread.

"You are a magician," he said as she set the plate before him.

"I think we rescued it. My mother always said that love, dim lighting, and good ingredients are ninety percent of cooking." She looked away. "As for the other ten percent, well you can see how hopeless I am . . ."

"This box is beautiful." He pointed at the black lacquer chest on the table.

"It was for perfume." Emma eased the lid off. "When Mum died, she filled it with letters for me to read. I've only read a couple so far. I'm trying to make them last."

"Maybe you are trying to make her last?"

"Maybe."

"I know," he said. "I know how hard it is to let someone go."

Luca felt his mother tug on his arm, and they walked on along the street. Their slow pace irritated him. He caught the scent of the gardenias Emma had fashioned into a corsage for him, pinned to Dolores's coat. The heady fragrance made him think of Emma's hands, slender and graceful as they worked. Luca frowned. Everything seemed different now. He had always slept well, but his monastic bedroom suddenly felt like a cell. His wardrobe was full of the same clothes he had worn for years, yet he could no longer find anything to wear that felt right. He still sat at the same table in the bar in El Carmen each Tuesday to play chess and drink with Olivier, yet it seemed changed. He looked the same as he walked through the city, like any other man watching his niece running among the pigeons. Again and again, the toddler returned to them, arms and hands outstretched, laughter bubbling from her like freshwater from a brook. The world was new, and miraculous to her. No one could tell to look at him. No one could tell that in his mind he longed to run free across the square, laughing and running like a child with a light heart.

TWENTY-SEVEN

I never thought I would be afraid of the moon," Freya said. She leaned against the window of the storeroom, smoking. As she stubbed out her cigarette she carefully tucked the butt into a metal case in her pocket for later. A single searchlight flickered on, and off.

The clear night sky seemed to darken from the east, to clot with a pulse, a throb, a single note permeating everything. "Christ, they're coming again," a voice in the darkness called out.

Freya tensed. She waited calmly, certain of the carnage that was to come. The first bombing raid had terrified her, but now she knew they were powerless to do anything. She mentally tracked the path of the planes as they circled above Plaza la Reina. They were heading toward the hospital, coming closer. There it came, the whine, growing in intensity. The shrill scream of the bombs hurtling down. Would it be them this time? They huddled against the storeroom's strongest wall. Freya felt as if her body was three times its normal size, large and vulnerable. It seemed like the bombs were aiming directly for her.

"Put out that torch!" she heard someone yell on the street. "The militia will think we are signaling the planes."

Then it came, the crash, the shattering explosions—one, two, three. Close by this time. The wall against her back shook, but held. Above them, the ceiling cracked, plaster fell in slow motion. She glanced down at the man on the stretcher beside her, a white cloth over his face to protect him from glass and debris. Was that it? A fourth explosion, louder than the last tore through the building.

"*Madre mía!*" the Spanish nurse working with Freya cried out. A lightning flash illuminated the room, and as the rush of air knocked Freya to the ground, she saw the nurse's terrified face, caught like a photograph in the brilliance.

Night raids are normally easier, Freya thought as she stumbled to her feet. There was something unreal about watching a raid in the night, the silhouetted figures, the dance of light. It was the ghastly reality of the day raids she couldn't stand, the resigned faces of the adults, the sheer terror of the children. She covered her ears against the hysterical clatter of guns. Another blast. The windows flew open, glass cascading to the ground. Through the gaping holes she saw the star-bright flight of tracers, like silver lace against the sky. The even drone of the fascist fleet continued, unsatisfied.

Outside, she heard the clang of the ambulance bells starting up. Dim, blue-screened headlights washed the road. Silence fell on the city as they waited for the huge bombers to return. She heard the hurried footsteps of people rushing to the *refugios*.

Freya felt hopeless—she thought there was no point hiding in basements. She had seen huge buildings collapse like balsa wood when they took a direct hit. Then what? A slow, lingering death starved of light, starved of oxygen? Freya grimaced at the thought. The stone-walled storeroom was as good a place as any. It was all a gamble, a hideous lottery. She looked up as she heard someone calling her name.

"Over here!" she shouted. A slight figure scrambled over the debris in the hall, a camera swinging at her neck.

"Freya Temple? I'm Gerda, a friend of your brother's."

"Pleased to meet you."

"You'd better hurry. That little Spanish girl, Rosa—"

"Where is she?" Fear coursed like ice through her veins. Rosa hadn't shown up that evening for her shift.

"No, she's fine." Gerda smiled. "She's a couple of streets away. The baby is coming."

The planes dove low, and fast. The next bomb fell, the earth shuddering and jumping. Freya and Gerda cowered in a doorway, waiting for a break in the bombardment. Freya looked down the road and saw a villa appear to rise, intact, from its foundations, then crumple in a cloud of dust and debris, with a sound like the sea crashing against a cliff.

She coughed, the reek of smoke and burned dust in her lungs. "How much farther?"

"She's in the restaurant on the corner. According to the owner she stopped for a glass of water on the way to work." Gerda raised her voice as the planes circled overhead again. "They've bombed the station," Gerda yelled. "A train-load of Brigaders have just come in."

"Were they hit?"

Gerda shook her head. "But the casualties are bad. I saw women standing out in the open, holding their dead children. There was a doctor on the platform just blaspheming . . ."

Freya cursed in irritation. "What good will that do?"

Gerda raised her camera to her eye, took a photo of a plane banking overhead, silhouetted against the flaming sky. "Let's go." The girls ran down the street.

"I've been over at the morgue most of the day," Gerda said, "photographing people queuing to find out if their missing family members are among the dead. God, these people have guts. When you hear them talk about the bombers it's with dignity and contempt, not fear."

"They've endured so much. They'll survive this as well." Freya's shoes slipped on the broken bricks scattered around the tiled entrance to the restaurant as Gerda flung the doors open. They were greeted by the unmistakable keening cry of a woman in labor. "Rosa!" Freya cried.

"Where have you been?" Rosa yelled. She was on all fours under a solid stone arch beside the dining area, one hand reaching up to the marble column. "Everyone else has gone! The cowards are hiding in the basement. I said I'd take my chances here . . ."

"I'm here now," Freya said. She quickly washed her hands behind the bar. "Gerda, can you see if there is any hot water in the kitchen? Any towels?"

Rosa swore under her breath. "I tell you, I will never let a man near me again . . ." She gripped Freya's hand as a contraction tore through her. Freya stroked her sweat-streaked brow.

"Listen to me, Rosa. I'm going to check you now, see how far along you are." Freya positioned herself between Rosa's legs, lifted her skirt.

"Here's the water," Gerda said, squatting at her side. "Good grief," she said, wincing as she caught a glimpse of the baby's head crowning.

"Hold her hand," Freya said, "talk to her." Gerda scurried around to Rosa's side. "How long have the contractions been coming? You should have told me."

"A while. I don't want to have the baby in that house, not with him there. I thought I could get to the hospital." Rosa pursed her lips, panted short breaths.

"You're doing really well. Not long now. I want you to get ready to push. You're fully dilated and this baby is ready to come." Freya doubled up the towels, laid them on the floor. She rubbed her friend's thigh, soothing her as she would a frightened animal. "Breathe easily, if you can—"

"Breathe easily? I'd like to see you—"

"Right, push," Freya said as Rosa's words twisted into a cry. "Come on, Rosa!"

The three girls sheltered together in the flickering lamplight through the night, the electricity sputtering, finally plunging them into darkness. The crash of the bombs punctuated Rosa's cries as Gerda lit candles on the restaurant tables, and brought them to her. With each explosion, glasses behind the bar shook and tinkled. Toward dawn, as the last planes turned away from the city, Rosa's final, rending yell tore through the air, joined by the shrill cry of her child.

"It's a girl!" Freya said, placing the baby in Rosa's arms. "A beautiful, perfect girl."

"Of course she is perfect," Rosa said, tears streaking the dust on her cheeks as she slumped back against the column. She gazed into her daughter's dark eyes. "She looks just like her father."

"You were amazing," Gerda said, tucking a coat over them.

Rosa looked at the girls. "Thank you," she whispered. "Thank you."

"I'll never forget this." Gerda raised her camera to her eye, framing a shot of Rosa with the baby at her breast. "Damn," she said, checking her Rolleiflex. "Out of film."

"Can I ask you? Will you be godmother for my child?" Rosa asked Freya.

"It would be an honor."

Gerda kissed her fingers, placed them against the child's cheek. "May your life be a good one. Make it count," she said. She looked out through the restaurant window at the dawn sky. "That is all we can all hope for." She stood, tucked her camera into her jacket, and zipped it up. "I must get going."

"Thank you," Freya said. "When you see Charles, give him my love?"

"Of course," Gerda said, grinning. "I shall give him a kiss from you."

TWENTY-EIGHT

VALENCIA, JANUARY 2002

'm fine, it was a false alarm, just some Braxton Hicks," Emma said, tucking in the earpiece of the phone. She changed gear, and put her foot down, speeding through the orange groves. "I think the next litter of kittens are due any day now though."

"Kittens?" Freya said.

"The cat disappeared for a couple of weeks when she had the last lot, and I couldn't catch her quick enough to get her spayed. She's a funny little thing. She'll let me feed her, hangs around the house sometimes, but she still won't let me pick her up."

"Don't go giving her a name, Em. I know you."

"Well, the poor little thing's pregnant again, and no sign of the father."

"I couldn't give a fig about kittens, it's you I'm worried about. You're doing too much. Don't take any risks, Em." Freya's voice was full of concern. "When I think of the night your mother was born, she came awfully quickly, and you didn't hang around either."

Emma slowed at the junction, and indicated right toward the main road. "Gammy, I wanted to ask you about Mum, and the house. I met—"

"I'd rather hear about you, darling."

"Please stop worrying. Everything is under control. The house is fine, I have hot water, and electricity—"

"All the luxuries, then?"

"Don't be like that." Emma heard her sigh. "What's wrong?"

"Delilah has found out about the baby."

Emma leaned back in the seat. The indicator ticked on as her stomach knotted with anxiety. "How?"

"I feel so guilty. I've been dreading telling you."

Emma looked up into the rear-view mirror as the car behind honked. "I'm sure it wasn't your fault." She drove on.

"She says she was just looking for a file in my office. Well, we all know what she's like . . ." Emma heard Freya covering the phone momentarily and closing her office door. "She found a copy of your scan in my desk."

"I don't believe it. Now she's sneaking around looking at private papers?"

"Em, I don't want to worry you, but she's flipped out completely. She's put two and two together and figured out you must have slept with Joe after you had split up."

"Well, let her flip out. After everything she's done to me." She drove on toward the city. "Where is she now?"

"She's in Tokyo, trying to salvage the deal. You'd think she'd built Liberty Temple single-handedly the way she is walking around like some kind of martyr to the cause."

"I don't care anymore. Delilah can have it all." At the thought of her meeting with Luca, Emma smiled. "I have everything I need here."

She hadn't seen him since just after New Year, when she had dropped in to the finca with a poinsettia, a present for Dolores. *A peace offering,* she thought. Emma had found her in the kitchen, plucking a goose for the family's Epiphany dinner. The bird dangled upside down, its beak swinging just above the floor like the stamen of a strange flower among the black folds of Dolores's skirt as her grandchildren and their cousins ran from room to room, whooping with excitement. Paco had rushed past Emma, wearing the gold paper crown from the *roscón de reyes* cake.

Glimpsing the warmth of their large family, Emma keenly felt the loneliness of her own solitary Christmas and New Year. She had just wanted to get through the holidays as quickly as possible this year, distracted herself by painting furniture for the nursery and sewing curtains. Paloma had invited her to their party at New Year, but Emma had declined.

"Emma?" Luca had said with surprise as he walked into the kitchen and tossed his keys onto the dresser. "What a beautiful plant."

"Your friend brought it for me," Dolores said. She returned to the goose, tightened the grip of her thighs around its belly, and snatched at the feathers, tossing them to the ground.

The children rushed in, filling the awkward void in the kitchen, and Luca caught the smallest boy, flipping him over and dangling him by the ankles.

"Won't you stay for a drink?" he asked Emma, swinging the giggling toddler back and forth. "Paloma is around somewhere—I know she'd be glad to see you."

Emma glanced uncertainly at Dolores as she walked to the door. "Thanks, but I can see you have a houseful."

"It's traditional for all the family to come together," he said, scooping the boy up into his arms. "Now, you are lucky," he said to the child. "You have Father Christmas *and* the three wise men."

Emma smiled and turned up the collar of her coat against the cold wind as she stepped onto the path. "Enjoy your party. I've got to get going."

"I will call you, after the holiday," Luca called after her. "I think I have some good news for you."

I hope so, Emma thought, swinging the Land Rover through the narrow streets of El Carmen. She found a space on Calle Museo near the old convent, and walked around the block to Luca's building. Emma checked the address in her notebook and pressed the intercom button. Luca buzzed her in through the large, wooden doors that flanked the street. She walked through the shaded courtyard, and as she climbed flight after flight of pale stone steps to the top floor, she stayed close to the wall, trying not to look down through the open arches to the courtyard, vertigo sweeping over her.

Luca answered the door of his apartment wrapped in a white towel. "Emma, good morning." He kissed her on both cheeks, then ushered her in. He turned away, shaking the water from his hair. "I'm sorry, I was expecting Guillermo."

"Am I early?" She caught her breath. Her beating heart settled as she followed him through the shadows of the hallway to the living room, his bare feet padding across the parquet. His broad shoulders and narrow hips were silhouetted against the light from the terrace, his arms raised like the horns of a bull as he smoothed back his hair. He smelled wonderful to her; the creamy fragrance of almond soap, clean skin made the hair rise at the nape of her neck.

"No, no. I am running behind." He searched through a bag of freshly ironed clothes from the laundry for a shirt.

"Late night?" she asked. She glanced around his large, high-ceilinged apartment. It seemed monastic to her—dark, modern furniture, a monochrome palette of colors. It felt understated, but luxurious. On his desk, next to a silver paper knife, she glimpsed a photograph of a dark-haired woman.

"It was business," he said, laughing. "Would you like some coffee?" The sounds of the street drifted up from below. A half-smoked cigar smoldered in a Baccarat crystal ashtray beside a *cafetiere* on the balcony table.

Emma strolled outside through the open French windows and gazed out across the rooftops and blue domes of the city. She edged cautiously toward the table. "It's quite a view . . ."

"Why thank you." Luca leaned against the doorway, laughing.

"I meant the city."

"Of course you did."

Emma blushed, reached for the coffeepot. The buzzer sounded at the front door. "You're incorrigible."

"Help yourself. I'll just get the door."

Emma settled on the wicker sofa, glad to turn away from the dizzying panorama. She heard an exchange, male voices in the hall. It was cold out on the balcony, but exhilarating to be in the fresh morning air. She cupped the mug in her hands, and inhaled the smoky scent.

"Come in, have some coffee." Luca showed a small, athletic man to the balcony. "Emma, this is my friend Guillermo. I'll just put some clothes on."

Guillermo shook her hand, and settled back on a chair as Emma poured him a coffee. "Don't bother dressing on our account, Luca," he said, raising his eyebrows at Emma. "Not bad for an old man, eh?"

"Who are you calling an old man?" Luca laughed.

"What do you think, Emma?" Guillermo leaned toward her.

Luca glanced back at her as he walked away. "Are you two checking out my ass?" He smiled as he stepped into the cool shadows of the apartment.

"In your dreams!" She laughed.

"So, Emma," Guillermo said when they were alone. "You are a perfumer?"

"I am," she said. "I understand from Luca that your mother is too?"

"She is." Guillermo sipped his coffee. "Or should I say, she was. My mother, her mother, they have been perfumers for centuries, but now to

her great sorrow none of her children wish to carry on." He glanced at
Emma. "Which is why we may be able to help one another. Concepción,
my mother, she will not pass on her work to just anyone, but Luca tells me
you are one of the finest noses in the business. And soon to be a mamá?"
He leaned forward, rested his hand on her stomach. "When will the baby
come?"

"There're a few weeks yet."

"It's a wonderful thing," Guillermo said.

"Do you have children?"

"Yes, we are blessed with three."

Luca joined them, dressed in suede loafers, freshly pressed chinos, a heavy
pink shirt rolled at the sleeves. "Sorry to keep you," he said.

"You are too late," Guillermo said, winking at her. "Emma and I have
decided to have an affair. Why are you wasting time with Luca, eh?"

Emma laughed awkwardly. She glanced up to see Luca watching her. "We
are just doing some business. I came to see what was on offer."

"She was impressed, naturally," Luca said, smiling. He reached across
for his cigar, and sat beside her, his arm over the back of the sofa.

Emma turned to him. "So?"

He leaned toward her. "Ever since you came to dinner, Paloma has been
nagging me. She has always been obsessed with cosmetics, perfume, so I
didn't take her seriously at first."

"Women's things?" A smile played over Emma's lips.

"I never understand it," Guillermo said. "What is it with women and
perfume?"

"It's not just women," Emma said. "In some cultures, men buy just as
much fragrance as women."

Guillermo shrugged. "All you need is a little cologne to feel fresh."

Emma shook her head. "No, perfume is more than that. Perfume is . . ."
She thought of her mother's letter. "It's love, it's the key to our past . . ." She
frowned as Guillermo laughed. "Perfume makes people feel alive." She struggled to find the right words, motioned in the air with her hands. "You know,
when you're learning to memorize fragrances, they make you keep a notebook of associations. Every perfume is linked to a memory." She thought
of Liberty's last notes in her book: *Jasmine? Orange blossom, yes!*" "When
you are weaving the top, heart, and base notes of a fragrance together, that
is how it feels: like you are conjuring a moment in time, like you're tran-
scribing memories in perfume."

"Ahh . . ." Guillermo said. "You will like my mother. Where did you train?"

Emma sensed that behind his relaxed charm, he was testing her. "My mother taught me everything she knew, and I studied in Grasse too."

"You learned from your mother? That is always best, generation to generation."

"I looked into your work," Luca said. "You didn't tell me you are a genius, Emma."

Emma felt the heat rising in her cheeks. "Is that what Paloma said? I don't know about that . . ."

"I think the people in your industry would disagree." He glanced at Guillermo. "I stayed up half the night reading about Emma's business on the Internet."

Emma glanced at him in surprise. "It wasn't just me. I worked with my mother. I don't . . . I still don't know how I'm supposed to carry on without her."

"Well, Paloma says you have a great future ahead of you," he said. "She said your career is just beginning, whatever happens to your mother's company, and we would be foolish not to help you. She said one day you will be a major customer." He glanced at Guillermo. "Between us, we have contacts across Europe, and in time we can introduce you to suppliers, laboratories, whatever you need." Luca looked at Emma. "You will make a success of it, I know. Your mother would be proud."

"Thank you." At his kindness, she felt her throat tighten. "It's strange, starting from scratch again. I keep thinking how much fun she would be having with all this."

Luca sensed her discomfort. "Tell me something, Emma," he said to distract her. "With your expert 'nose,' how do I smell to you?"

She looked up, surprised, and smiled. "You?"

"Ha!" Guillermo laughed. "You smell of late nights and broken hearts." He grinned as Luca scowled playfully at him.

"You smell of Acqua di Parma. It was one of the first things I noticed about you," Emma said. "My great-uncle Charles wears the same cologne."

"Ay." Luca ran his hand through his hair, wincing. "So I smell like an old man to you?"

"I didn't mean that . . ."

"No, it is too late now," Luca said, his hand falling to his heart. "I am crushed." He glanced at Emma, and smiled.

Emma nudged him. "I'll make you a deal. You help me get this all off the ground, and I will create your very own fragrance." She looked him square in the eye. "Something unique, like you."

Guillermo raised his eyebrows. "Lucky man."

"Well I need someone to be a guinea pig for my new experiments," Emma said, tilting her head as she waited for his answer. "I'm afraid it may take awhile."

"All great art does. I always wanted to be a Muse." Luca smiled, holding her gaze. "So, we will help you, and Concepción . . . ?" He looked at Guillermo, who nodded.

"It will all be arranged," he said. "My mother will adore you, Emma. She will expect you in Cuenca as soon as you can get out there. We have sold the house, and my mother needs to sell on her whole stock. She will pass on all her knowledge, her suppliers, and her recipes or formulas or whatever you call them . . ." He shook his head. "I am sorry, I am a businessman. I know very little about her work."

Emma's mind danced with possibilities. She thought of old apothecaries' chests filled with herbs, spices, pictured stands of gleaming glass flasks with handwritten labels. She thought of the recipe book she had found at the house. "Wonderful," she said, excitement brimming over. "In fact, I have an old book I'd be interested to show Concepción. I think the woman who owned my house made perfumes, or cures, from the herbs she grew in the garden. I'd be interested to try to re-create some of them, but I can't work out the ingredients."

"I am sure she can help you."

"Please thank your mother. I'll come as soon as I can."

"Thank you, Guillermo." Luca shook his hand. "You will like Concepción," he said to Emma. "She is the best perfumer in the whole of Spain." He paused. "Maybe now, the second best."

TWENTY-NINE

At dawn, Charles woke, sunlight flaring through the open window. Outside on the street he could hear *madrileños* going to work. He was—as usual—instantly alert. It had always amazed Freya when they were children how his eyes would flick open like a switch, and he would be up and about. She used to tease him that he was half machine.

He picked his way through the sleeping men lying on the floor, the bed, the sofa—a soft landscape of gently rising rib cages, a warm blanket of vapors from last night's cigarettes and whiskeys drifting over them. In the bathroom, he performed his ablutions quickly, then stood before the mirror. Deliberately, he did not shave—it had taken days to get a semblance of five o'clock shadow, and he hoped it made him seem older, tougher—more like the men asleep next door. He riffled through his sponge bag and found some pomade, slicked it through his fair hair. He tried to make it seem even half as luxuriant and untamed as Capa's. Around his throat, he loosely tied a silk cravat. *Too much?* he wondered. Gerda was so beautifully turned out, even on the front line, he hoped she might appreciate a touch of dandyism, a shot of color. The men had teased her about wearing lipstick and high heels to the battlefront, and he had been rather disappointed to see that recently she had stuck to rope-soled shoes. She seemed tired since returning from seeing Capa in Paris. At the thought of his friend, Charles felt guilty. He knew Capa loved Gerda. *But I can't stop thinking about her,* he thought. *I'll regret it for the rest of my life if I don't tell her how marvelous I think she is.*

As he studied his reflection, Charles thought back to that wonderful night at the beginning of June. They had all spent the day on the Navacerrada Pass, finishing up the last shots there, and had dined with General Walter in front of his bunker. Gerda had shown no fear that day. To Charles she had seemed like the spirit of liberty, her fist raised to the sky, yelling "Forward!," her slight figure, topped with a dark beret, running across the open ground, heat shimmering on the horizon. She captivated every man she met. Walter had joked he had never seen so many men in his unit clean-shaven.

As they sat drinking in a bar on the Gran Via in Madrid later that night, Charles watched Capa and Gerda forlornly. "What's he got that I haven't?" he said quietly to Hugo.

Hugo looked up from his notebook. "Capa? Apart from irresistible charm and more talent in his little finger than you'll—"

"All right, all right. I get the picture." Charles wearily rubbed the heel of his hand between his brows, and took a hit of whiskey.

Hugo chewed the end of his pencil thoughtfully. "Capa is one of life's adventurers. Men want to be him, women can't help loving him."

"I just wish . . ."

"The little red fox has got under your skin, eh?" Hugo laughed softly. "Every man I've met here has a crush on Gerda."

"Hey, Charles?" Capa called across. "Do me a favor. I'm playing cards tonight. Can you make sure Gerda gets back to the Alianza safely?"

Charles's heart leaped. "Of course."

Gerda slung her camera over her shoulder as she walked toward Charles. "Honestly. The way he worries about me. If I can handle myself on a battlefield, I can certainly find my way back to my rooms."

"Where are you heading tomorrow?" Charles said.

"We're going to hang around in Madrid for a while, then maybe head down to the south again. You should come along."

"Thanks. I'll think about it," Charles said, wondering if he could stand the exquisite torture of being around her and Capa all the time.

"I'm going to report from the International Writers' Congress in Valencia next month. They're touring Valencia, Barcelona, Madrid. Everyone will be there—Neruda, Hemingway. Malraux is guiding a group of writers who couldn't get visas down through the Pyrenees."

"That should be interesting." Charles felt flustered even talking to her. "Who are you working for now?"

"*Ce Soir,* and *Life* magazine. I'm hoping the pictures I've taken in Valencia will get me out of Capa's shadow."

"My sister, Freya, is in Valencia, with Spanish Medical Aid."

"Didn't I say? I remembered you mentioned I should look her up at the hospital. I met her the other night. She was amazing—this little Spanish girl went into labor. Freya delivered the baby."

"Did she?" Charles smiled at the thought. "Good old Frey."

"I ran out of film. I could have kicked myself. It's exactly the kind of shot I want more of, the women and children away from the front line."

"I got some lovely pictures the other day. There was a memorial in a village a few miles from the front—all the women were dressed in white, carrying flowers up to the cemetery. It was terribly somber, but when they opened the gates, the entire place was filled with blue flag lilies. It was like the sky had come down to earth. But in the middle was a square, pricked with black crosses for their fallen soldiers. The women scattered white flowers on each grave, on all the pathways. It was quite beautiful."

"I wish I'd been there."

I wish you were with me, always, he thought. Charles picked up the heavy Eyemo movie camera from beside the bar door. "May I help you with this?"

"Thank you." Gerda smiled up at him. "Useless thing. Well, not entirely useless. Ted says it's good as a shield from the bullets."

They walked along the deserted street, the cobbles slick with warm rain. "Where did you learn to take such good photographs?"

Gerda glanced up at the clouds as the heavens opened. "André taught me everything I know."

"André?"

"Bob, as you all call him." She laughed. "Capa. Gosh you really are a cherry boy, aren't you?" Charles blushed. She looked at him, brushed her wet hair from her face. "Hey," she said. "I'm sorry." Charles stopped walking, and turned to her. They stood alone, only the sound of the summer rain drumming on the roofs. "You're very handsome," she said softly. "That's why he asked you to look after me, you know."

"I don't understand."

"He thinks you're too decent to do anything, now you're my protector. He saw the way I looked at you the other night . . ."

"But why? You're obviously together, I wouldn't . . ."

"André and I are together, that's all—*copains*. Oh sure, he's asked to marry me a hundred times, but I don't know if I want to settle down yet ..." They leaped onto the pavement as a truck thundered past, showering rainwater up in an arc. Gerda skipped into a shop doorway, laughing. Charles thought there was a lightness to her he had never seen in anyone before. He felt, somehow, if he reached out and touched her, his hand would pass right through her, like the shimmering image of a projector. "Shall we wait a moment? The rain must stop soon." She shivered as Charles ducked in beside her.

"Are you saying you believe in free love?"

Gerda laughed. "You English are so formal." She looked up at him, so close he could feel her breath on his cheek. "I believe in love, life"—with her index finger, she touched his right cheek, then his left—"and the pursuit of happiness." She tapped her finger playfully against his lips. Desire coursed through him—it was as though her touch had branded him. She tilted her head, waiting.

"Gerda, I . . . I can't. You're with Capa."

"Don't you get it?" she said, laughing. "I am Capa—at least half of him. Without me, André wouldn't be Capa."

"I'm confused."

"He is more than André, more than me. Robert Capa will be a legend."

"You mean, he's an invention?"

"Precisely. We invented the greatest war photographer in the world, and raised our prices. It worked." She shrugged. "As for André, I have no illusions about the times we are apart. He doesn't like to be alone."

Charles saw a darkness pass across her face, as fleeting as a cloud moving across the sun. "But you love him?"

"Love?" She laughed. "Of course I love him. But after the writers' congress, André is going to Paris, and I shall be coming back here to stay at the Alianza." She hesitated. "I don't imagine for a moment that he will be lonely in Paris. Why should I be lonely here?"

"Gerda . . ."

"Do I shock you, Charles?"

"No, I . . ."

"You are sweet." She kissed him then, the lightest, briefest touch of her lips against his cheek, and Charles was lost.

Gerda, Gerda, Gerda . . . his thoughts were a sigh of longing, he felt himself become aroused even thinking of that kiss, that single, brief, glorious kiss.

"Come on, old chap, there's a queue forming out here," someone called, thumping on the door. Charles quickly rubbed some toothpaste along his teeth and unlocked the door. "Good grief, it smells like a tart's boudoir in here, Temple. What are you hoping to do? Knock the rebel lines out with your aftershave?"

"Shut up," Charles said as he barged past the older man.

He grabbed his Contax on the way out the door and jogged down to the lobby. He scooped up a copy of the day's paper, and scanned the headlines—heavy fighting near Brunete. He knew the village had been won and lost twice—the fascists were advancing again. "Gerda!" he called. He saw her and Ted loading up a car just outside. Gerda was wearing khaki overalls. She seemed more beautiful than ever. *The face of an angel,* he thought. He realized he was staring, and sauntered over, trying to seem casual. "Where are you two off to? Morning, Ted."

"Charles." Ted frowned, put a protective arm around Gerda as he helped her into the car. "We're heading out to Brunete."

"Who's up there now?"

"Líster and Walter's divisions, and several others."

"They need all the men they can get. The Nationalists are pushing in again," Gerda said. "I can't bear it. We mustn't let them pass."

"Is there room for another in the car?" Charles said hopefully.

"Of course—" Gerda started to say.

"Sorry, old boy," Ted interrupted. "We'll be full up in here once we get the Eyemo loaded up. Why don't you take the car behind?"

Charles eyeballed him. "Yes, I understand." *I understand completely,* he thought. He stalked away to the next car and jumped in alongside some reporters he knew vaguely from the bar.

As they bumped along the country roads to Brunete, a glorious July day unfolded. The rising sun bathed the landscape in gold, like silk unfurling from a roll. The entire journey, Charles kept his eyes fixed on the back of Gerda's head. Snatches of their singing drifted back in the shimmering, hot air—"Los Cuatro Generales." She always seemed to be laughing, always full of joy. Charles had never envied anyone more than Capa. He imagined taking her delicate, fair hand in his, looking into her sea green eyes. "I adore you, Gerda," he would say. He wanted her so badly, it was an exquisite pain just looking at her. Let alone imagining holding her, making love to her . . .

"Christ!" The reporter next to Charles swore as a massive explosion broke Charles's reverie. A billowing cloud of smoke and dust rose on the horizon. "They've started early." The car ahead stopped. There was obviously an argument going on. The driver got out of the car and came over to his colleague.

"No farther," their driver said, indicating they should get out.

"What? That's ridiculous! We've paid you to take us to Brunete," Charles said.

"No." The driver shook his head obstinately and opened their door.

"Forget it, we'll walk," Ted called across.

Charles shot out of the car and was at Gerda's side, striding through the golden wheat field. "May I help with anything?"

"Thanks, Charles," Ted said quickly and handed him the heavy Eyemo camera. He walked on ahead at Gerda's side. She looked over her shoulder and gave Charles an apologetic look.

"It will be a good chance for some action shots today," she called.

"Are you afraid?" Charles shouted.

"Always!"

By the time they reached General Walter's offices, sweat was trickling into Charles's eyes, running along his spine. Walter looked up. "What on earth are you lot doing here? I've just sent a bunch of your fellows packing. It's not safe. Franco's troops could be here any minute."

"Then we're just in time," Gerda said, and smiled.

Charles huddled down in the dugout as the biplane swooped low again and the "rat-tat-tat" of machine guns chopped the air, bullets whizzing overhead. The noise was deafening, the Condor Legion's Stukas and Heinkels thundering through a sky black with smoke and fire, pounding the retreating Republican troops with bombs and gunfire.

"Gerda, it's the camera lens!" Charles shouted. "The light catches the lens—they are coming straight for us!"

Charles cowered next to Gerda and Ted, horribly aware that his backside was sticking up out of the foxhole. He couldn't bear the thought of being shot there, willed his buttocks to contract, to disappear into the earth.

"We can't lose Brunete . . ." Gerda's fists were clenched in fury. They had been shooting film all morning, and she was packing away the last of the rolls. "Damn it, this is some of the best work I've ever done, but we can't lose this battle." She leaped to her feet to photograph twelve bombers in formation.

"For God's sake, Gerda, get down!" Ted cried, trying to pull her down beside him. Another explosion blew her back, the earth heaving like the sea before them, fountains of soil pluming into the air.

"*Scheisse,*" she said, spitting earth from her mouth. She ducked down. "That was close." She calmly rolled over and photographed a biplane as it swooped low toward them, spewing bursts of fire between the propeller blades as the bullets rained down on them.

"Don't give up!" she yelled at the retreating Republicans.

Charles checked his watch. It was half past five. Men were streaming around them now, running from the front. He saw a man blown from his feet by the force of the blast. "We should go . . ."

"Fight on, comrades! *No pasarán*! They will not pass!" Gerda's voice was drowned out by the thunderous assault from the sky. "Oh God," she said as she slumped down. "When you think of all the fine people killed in this battle alone, it seems unfair to be alive."

"Gerda, he's right. We've done all we can. Let's get the hell out of here." Ted dragged her up, shielding her with his body and slung the camera over his shoulder. He turned to Charles. "Well? Are you coming?"

Charles sprinted after them, panting for breath. He ran blindly from the front through fields of the dead and dying, stumbling over twisted bodies. It seemed to him they were running through a furnace, a vision of hell far worse than anything Goya had painted. The shouts, the noise of screams and the crashing engines of tanks behind them thundered in his ears. At any moment, he knew it could be his fragile body on the ground, broken and bleeding, feeling life ebb away. He ran faster, and faster, caught up with Ted and Gerda as they reached the Villanueva road. Tanks and jeeps bounced across the rutted ground at high speed, in retreat. One of the tanks slowed to allow the three of them to scramble aboard, and they clung on.

Charles gasped for breath, the vile metallic taste of battle, of smoke and oil, of sweat and fear and death was in his mouth. The tank thundered down the road, and he began to come back to himself. It seemed strangely quiet after the battlefield. His eyes smarted still from the smoke, but here the wheat swayed peacefully in a breeze coming down cool and welcome from the mountains.

"Once we get through here, we'll be clear to Madrid," Ted yelled.

Charles closed his eyes. He was shaking with adrenaline and fear. He wondered what on earth had compelled him to come to Spain in the first place. This was not the world he remembered. He longed to be in the hills above Yegen again, in the sunlit grass, stalking Mazarine Blues with his net, the clean light and clean linen, the silent air— The tank lurched as it rejoined the main road, dragged him from his daydream.

"Over there!" Gerda cried. "It's Walter's car."

They leaped down, and raced past a whitewashed farmhouse toward the retreating car. Charles heard Ted asking if it could take them as far as El Escorial. Clouds drifted lazily in a cobalt sky. Charles could see the car was already loaded down with wounded soldiers. Gerda and Ted were ahead of him, and he saw Gerda bend her head in concentration as she sped toward the car, and make a leap for the running board. Ted leaped onto the other side. They turned to Charles, their faces illuminated with triumph. *My God,* he thought, *they're in their element here.* He realized at that moment he would never be a part of their world.

"Bad luck, Charles!" Ted hollered.

"See you at the hotel, Charles. I must get these pictures wired to Paris," Gerda called. "Tonight we'll have a farewell party in Madrid—I've brought champagne!" She waved to him, smiling broadly.

"Gerda!" Charles yelled, waving madly.

She laughed, waved back.

"Gerda!" he screamed. There was nothing he could do. A tank, out of control, careered toward the car, slammed into Gerda. He watched helplessly as she was crushed, thrown aside like a rag doll. Ted flew through the air, limbs dangling, the car mangled and broken like a dinky toy, shoved along the road.

A thundering phalanx of aircraft bore down on them. Someone grabbed Charles by the arm, dragged him to the ditch. He hunkered down as ammunition pounded the earth around them, thumping into the soil, the shuddering waves passing through him. Above the noise, he could hear Gerda crying out. And he could not reach her. He could hear Ted calling to her, saying he couldn't move. Charles blinked, his head filled with dancing lights. He curled up in a ball, trying desperately not to pass out, forcing air into his lungs. He wanted to be sick.

People around him began to clamber out of the ditches as the aircraft dispersed. He staggered, shaking, to his feet. He could see a group of men around Ted, pulling him onto a stretcher. His legs dangled helplessly.

"My legs!" Ted cried out. "I can't move my damn legs. Gerda!" Charles ran over to him. "Where is she? Charles, find her." His face was contorted with pain. Charles nodded. Ahead, he saw an ambulance, and on a stretcher a familiar pair of tiny feet beneath a sheet. He ran over, nauseated, afraid of what he might see.

It was Gerda. Her face was pale and her hands were clamped across her stomach, dark blood drenching the sheet. Charles felt the bile rise in his throat as they placed a blanket over her. "Charles," she whispered, smiled at him. "Where are my cameras? Do you know? Are they smashed . . ."

"I don't know." He fought back tears as he bent and kissed her forehead. "Don't worry about them. I'll look for them, I promise."

"It was my best work, you know," she said, drifting into unconsciousness.

He looked after her helplessly as they loaded her into the ambulance, which then raced off up the road. Charles stood entirely alone as men and vehicles streamed around him, retreating to Madrid.

THIRTY

Emma browsed through the shelves of CDs in Fnac. The store was busy, full of weekend crowds and teenagers flirting, listening to music on the headphones at the end of each aisle. She strolled through the store and stopped in the English books section, leaning down to search the bottom shelf. Someone slapped her backside gently. She wheeled around, her angry expression dissolving.

"Sorry, couldn't resist," Luca said.

"Well, try!" She smiled in spite of herself as she kissed his cheek. "This is unexpected."

Luca shrugged. "I told you, it is a small place. You bump into people." He took the book from her hand. "*The Diving Bell and the Butterfly*? This is very good."

"You've read it?"

"Olivier is determined my brain won't waste away down here," he said, smiling. "He keeps me up-to-date on what I should be reading. He's forgotten more about literature than I'll ever know."

"I think you're being modest. Paloma said you met Olivier when you were at the Sorbonne."

"Did she? It was a long time ago." He slipped his hand in his pocket. "My father was French. It seemed a good idea to study in Paris."

"He was French? I was wondering why you use de Santangel."

"My name?" Luca shrugged. "In Spain you take the mother and father's names, but here de Santangel means a lot. After my father left, my mother quietly dropped his name from ours."

"He left? I'm sorry." Emma paused. "I know what it's like to grow up without a father."

"It was OK. There has always been a lot of family around—I loved my grandfather, Ignacio. He was a good man, more of a father to me than my own."

"You're lucky, then." Emma walked on, gazed at a poster advertising *Jazz in Paris,* a black-and-white image of lovers embracing beneath the Eiffel Tower. "Wow ... Paris. I'd have loved to have studied there. Mum wanted me to join the family business though. After I trained in Grasse she shipped me off to America. I think she wanted to toughen me up a bit."

"Did it work?"

"You tell me." Emma's laugh faded. She had loved Grasse, the steep hills filled with the scent of mimosa. Sometimes she wondered what would have happened if she had stayed in France. "Still, I met Joe, and now ..." Her hand caressed her stomach. "I can't really regret any of it."

"Olivier and I had a great time." Luca stepped aside to let a group of teenagers pass. "We had a tiny apartment overlooking Sacré Coeur. We shared everything ..."

"Wine, bread, women?"

Luca smiled. "But then Paloma managed to escape Mamá's hawklike protection of her virginity long enough to board a train to Paris. As luck would have it for Olivier, I was out that night with a girl, and by the time I got back, Olivier had asked her to marry him. With them, it was love at first sight."

"Paloma said she thinks Olivier wanted to have you as a brother just as much as he wanted her as a wife."

"She mentioned you had lunch together the other day." He gestured for her to go ahead through the crowd.

Emma glanced at the CDs in his hand. "What are you buying?"

"I don't know. Do you think a teenage boy will like these?"

She flipped through them. "What did you listen to when you were ... ?"

"Seventeen. It's for Benito, Paloma's eldest."

"It's his birthday?" Emma asked.

"Yes—on Saturday. You should come."

"I don't want to intrude if it's a family thing."

"I know Paloma would be delighted. The food may not be up to much. Olivier and I are making paella."

"I'd love to," Emma said. "OK, so what did you like at that age?"

"Punk, if I could get away with it." Luca laughed.

"There we go." Emma led the way to the Sex Pistols, handed him *Never Mind the Bollocks*. "Any seventeen-year-old boy would love this. Then get him a gift voucher so he can choose stuff he really likes."

As they paid, Emma turned to Luca. "Now you have to help me buy my present for Benito. What do you think he would like from me?"

"I don't know," Luca said. "Why don't we have a coffee and think about it."

"How is the flower shop doing?" Luca asked her as they walked among the stalls of the Mercado Central. It was bustling, the cool, vaulted halls filled with echoing voices, footsteps, the mingled salty tang of shellfish and sweet fruits. "There have been so many weddings and funerals lately in the village it must be booming, or blooming."

Emma laughed. "The Perfume Garden," she said, pausing by a fruit stall, "is doing very well, thank you." She picked out a melon, inhaled its summery, mouthwatering scent, pressed her fingers into its firm flesh, testing it. "God, I feel like I've swallowed one of these." She rubbed her hard, round belly.

"Not long now," he said, handing some money to the stall holder. "You look beautiful, anyway."

"Thank you." She didn't want him to see how pleased she was, and busied herself tucking the melon in her bag. They walked on to the next stall. "Did I tell you I've been experimenting with making some scented candles for the shop? I've found a wonderful old firm to work with, and once I have the scents perfected we'll go into production."

"I can't keep up with you." As Luca stepped aside to let a porter pulling crates of fish on ice go past, he caught something in Emma's expression, a fleeting concern. "I mean, I think it's wonderful, how creative you are. That you see so many opportunities around you."

"Do you?" Emma's face relaxed. "Thank you. Mum . . . well, she said in one of the letters she left for me that maybe I'm too . . . I don't know. I do too much."

"No good ever came from someone trying to be less than they are." He gazed down at her. "Be everything you should be."

"You make it sound simple."

"It is. My grandfather always said do what you love, and do it as well as you can. There's no other way, for me."

"It's funny, I always thought it would be great to have a flower shop and now I have one on my doorstep." She thought for a moment. "After all these years of running a big company, it's been satisfying making a small idea come true."

"But you will go back to your real work, as a perfumer?"

"Yes, of course," she said. "Once everything is tied up in London." She paused. "It's fun though, seeing how flowers give people immediate pleasure. With perfume, I was always stuck in the studio, or the lab. Then, once Mum decided I should take over, I was on the road seeing our big buyers. I lost touch with the customers, I think." She shrugged. "I love it now, watching people coming and going with flowers Aziz has sold them, thinking how happy their friends will be with a spray of gerberas, or how their lovers will feel to get a huge bouquet of roses."

"You like making people happy, I think." He nudged her gently. "But the name—you have a very wicked sense of humor. If only the good little women of the village knew they were buying their carnations for the Virgin from a sensualist."

"Sensualist?" Emma glanced at him. Luca stepped closer, reached over for a basket of strawberries. He lowered his head to them, inhaled. He offered them to her, and she smelled them, covering his hand with her own.

"Like you said in the cathedral—Song of Songs, Burton's ancient erotic texts . . ."

"Well, from what I remember from the book, they knew what they were talking about with their aphrodisiacs. You wouldn't believe what you can do with a little ginger and cardamom." She flashed him a quick smile.

"I'll bear that in mind."

THIRTY-ONE

"Capa?" Charles crooked the telephone against his shoulder, and squeezed the bridge of his nose between his fingertips. His eyes were red rimmed. On the bar, several French newspapers lay in front of him, each open at the pages covering Gerda's funeral. "Can you talk? I don't want to disturb you."

"No, no . . . it's good to hear your voice, Charlie."

Sunlight struggled through the blinds, picking out the stooped figures of exhausted men, empty glasses littering the tables. Charles was wearing an old black roll-neck, in spite of the stifling heat. "I'm so sorry about Gerda, Bob. I'm sorry I couldn't get to Paris for the funeral . . ."

"What the hell happened?" Capa's voice was thick, choked with grief. "She never should have been out there."

Charles hung his head. "It all happened so quickly. I tried—"

"I'm not blaming you, Charles," Capa cried. "No one but me could have made her see sense. I could have saved her."

Charles picked up a packet of cigarettes. "Damn," he said, and threw the empty pack down. He drained his glass, and signaled to the bartender.

"I just feel so . . . I've been a little crazy since . . ."

Charles thought of the reports of Gerda's funeral in Paris, how Capa had to be carried from the grave.

"Teddie told me about what happened in the hospital. You know they gave her a blood transfusion, and she said, 'Whee, that feels better now.' She survived the operation . . ." Capa's voice was muffled. "I should have been with her. This never would have happened if I had been with her . . ."

Capa rambled on and guilt tightened in Charles's heart like an over-wound clock. "She loved you," Charles said quietly.

"Of course she loved me! I don't need anyone to tell me that," Capa cried. "She was mine, and I was hers. We belonged together." Charles waited in silence. "I'm sorry, Charlie. I shouldn't take it out on you."

"No. You go ahead."

"Everyone loved Gerda," Capa said. "But she chose me. We were going to be married."

"I know, old man. I'm sorry."

"The funeral was so beautiful. There were so many flowers." Capa talked on, telling him everything that had gone on in Paris, but Charles felt like he knew it by heart.

He looked at the photographs in the newspapers laid out before him. Since her death he had tortured himself by reading every detail, every word of the coverage of her life and funeral. He had had no idea how much her work was valued. The papers declared her an antifascist martyr, a latter-day Joan of Arc. Tens of thousands of people lined the streets of Paris when her body was taken to Père Lachaise cemetery on August 1 to the strains of Chopin's funeral march. It would have been her twenty-seventh birthday. In one paper, among the images of the funeral, the crowds, the banners, the flowers, photographs that Gerda had taken were reprinted, including one he knew perfectly well was by Capa. *Does it matter?* he thought. *They were always going to end up together, André and Gerda, Gerda and Capa, two halves of the same coin.* "We invented the greatest war photographer in the world" he remembered her saying as they sheltered from the rain. "Capa will be a legend." Now, he knew, they would be bound by that legend forever.

Charles stared down at the newspaper as Capa talked on. In Gerda's photos of the war he saw the bright, hopeful faces of young militiawomen training on the beaches in Barcelona in '36, peasants in Aragon harvesting straw, war orphans in Madrid. *These were the people Gerda cared about,* he thought. Charles's head slumped to his hand. Gerda's photographs pierced your heart, took your breath away.

"She was so beautiful," Charles said quietly as Capa fell silent. He perched on the edge of the stool. "So beautiful. Her photos . . . maybe she gave too much of herself, took too many risks . . ."

"Why did no one call me, for Christ's sake? I would have come straight down if I'd have known she was planning to head out to Brunete again. I had to read about it, can you believe it? I was in the dentist's waiting room, Charlie. I read it in the damn paper." Capa sighed. "You know, I shoot a line—happiness is a game of poker, a bottle of Scotch, and a pretty girl. But she was my world. I've never known peace and happiness like it. Never will again."

"I hope, in time, you do, Bob." Charles stood, and scooped up the papers. "Listen, when are you coming down?"

"Not for a while. I just want some time alone. I'm going to head to the States and see my family."

"I understand." Charles hung his head. "See you around, Capa. Look after yourself."

"Right back at you, kid. Stay lucky."

Charles heard Capa hang up the phone. *You're lucky, Bob,* he thought. *She loved you.* He took a last look at the photo of Gerda in the pages of *Ce Soir. Some of us can only dream of love like that.*

THIRTY-TWO

There's no hurry. We can go to Cuenca once the baby has come," Luca said. To Emma's secret delight, Luca had taken to calling in at the Perfume Garden every few days, sometimes for flowers, sometimes just to chat. "Concepción is quite happy to wait to talk about selling her business. In spite of Guillermo's encouragement, I get the feeling she is in no hurry to stop work just yet."

"Good, I'm glad the meeting can wait." Emma stood from the stool behind the till and stretched, her hand at the small of her back. "I don't find long car journeys terribly comfortable at the moment."

"That's new, isn't it?" Luca pointed to the flower stand.

"Fidel gave it to me. I've just finished renovating it." She ran her fingertips over the newly painted wrought iron.

"His wife used to sell flowers."

"He told me."

"Did he? You're certainly getting to know the locals."

"We have a business to run." Emma scooped up the trimmed stalks of the flowers she was arranging in iron buckets, and tossed them into the bin.

"Talking of which, where is the boy? You shouldn't be working . . ."

"It's fine. Aziz needed to take his sister to the doctor. I'm just helping out."

"Don't let him take advantage of you."

"I can take care of myself."

"I know you can." Luca passed her an iron bucket filled with fragrant freesias.

"Thank you." She slotted it into one of the hoops on the stand, stepping back to see how the display looked. "When did Fidel's wife die?"

"Years ago. It was tragic really."

"What happened?"

"It was Fallas time. You know, the festival in March when everything goes crazy in the city and villages."

"I've seen pictures. Do they really set fire to those huge figures?"

"Every year," Luca said.

"It seems rather dangerous."

Luca shrugged. "Normally people are careful. They douse all the buildings in water. That year there was an accident in the village . . ."

"With a firework?"

"No, with one of the bonfires."

"She burned? How awful." Emma imagined the bacchanalian scenes she had read about, the towering fires and crashing explosions, and then, among the revelers, a single figure at a flaming window.

"She was visiting her mother in the old part of the village. I heard they had built one of the fires too close to the house, and the whole lot went up."

"Her mother died as well?" Emma shivered. "He seems like such a lovely man too."

"He is. They were a devoted couple."

"He must be lost without her."

"I guess."

"You sound uncertain."

"It always seems to me that the people who have had the best relationships manage to move on from their grief, somehow."

Emma fell silent for a moment. "I'd never thought of it like that."

Marek jogged toward them. "Emma," he said. "Come see. We've knocked through the wall upstairs."

Emma waddled through the garden to the house and climbed the stairs, followed by the men. Borys stood panting against the broken-down wall, covered from head to foot in dust. Marek took up the sledgehammer. "Look."

Behind the plaster, the doorway had been roughly boarded up. He anchored the hammer, and pulled hard.

Luca coughed. "Emma, come. Wait until they are finished. This dust is no good for you."

"No, it's fine." She stepped forward. The handle was clear now. Squinting, she reached in, felt the cool brass knob beneath her hand. It turned, and Marek helped her push the door open. In the half light, Emma could make out blue-and-white *azulejos,* tiles with swirling floral patterns running in a frieze around the room. "It's beautiful!" She supported her stomach with her hand as she ran down the hallway and returned with a torch. As the light swept the room, she could see a bed still made up, a dressing table, a wardrobe. Then as she swung the beam of light, she made out a face, and cried out.

"What is it?" Luca was at her side instantly, pushing Marek aside. The boy scowled.

Emma's heart was pounding with excitement. "I don't know . . ." She peered into the darkness, then began to laugh. "Oh! It's a poster, an old print." She stood up, and turned to Borys. "Well done, both of you. Can you get all of this down? I can't wait to see inside."

An hour or two later, Marek came to find her. Emma was sitting alone in the flower shop, thinking about her conversation with Luca. She was staring into space, twirling a peony stem in her hand. *I wonder if that's it?* she thought. *Luca's stuck, somehow. Maybe he hasn't been able to move on from whomever he lost?*

"It's done," Marek said.

Emma jumped. "The room? Sorry, I was miles away."

He followed her upstairs. Emma stepped through the ragged doorway and over the pile of rubble just as Borys threw back the shutters and sunlight flooded the room. Emma looked around, a slow smile forming on her lips. The blue-and-white room had been untouched for years, it seemed. The poster on the wall was life-size—a bullfighter, she thought, judging by the arena in the background, the roses at his feet. She cleared the dust from the paper. " 'Jordi del Valle,' " she read. "It's the boy in the photograph under the floorboards! This must have been his house, his room."

Marek pointed at the dressing table. "But if it was a man, why are there perfume bottles in here?"

"His wife, perhaps?" Emma picked up one of the glass bottles, uncorked the stopper. When she inhaled, she smelled something dark. *Iris?* "Would you mind?" she asked Borys. "I could do with a moment alone in here."

Once the builders had gone, Emma turned slowly in a circle, taking in the room. "Why would anyone have sealed this room up?" she said aloud. She stopped in front of the wardrobe, half afraid of what might be inside. Her hand rested on the tasseled key in the lock. The door creaked open, her reflection in the cracked mirror swung away. The clothes inside were simple—dark, understated, all but a red silk dress with a sweeping train. "Who were you?" Emma whispered.

In the dressing table, she found coral beads, a black paper fan, an embroidered silk shawl. In the central drawer there was an empty tube of red lipstick. As she tried to push the drawer back in, it stuck. Something was jamming it. Emma reached her hand in, felt up into the roof of the drawer. Her fingers ran across the leather cover of a notebook, tucked against the struts.

She turned the book over in her hand, and sat on the bed, a cloud of dust rising in the morning sunlight. "Rosa Montez" it said, in a childish, slanting hand on the flyleaf. As Emma turned the pages, she realized it was a diary for 1938. Some dates were marked—a cross every four weeks, occasional birthdays and anniversaries. In May she saw "Loulou, first birthday" on the seventeenth.

Loulou? She gasped. Her mother's birthday. Emma looked around the room, felt like a door had opened in her mind.

THIRTY-THREE

Rosa hummed a lullaby, rocking in the lamplight, tracing the sleeping face of her child with her fingertip. "Little Loulou," she said. "He can christen you Lourdes if he wants like his mother, but you are my Loulou."

Freya leaned over them, and smiled. "How are you feeling?"

"Me?" Rosa said, glancing up at her. "I am fine. A little tired. She seems to like to be awake all night, and sleep all day. How about you? Is your stomach better?"

"Much better, thank you. The herb tea you made me has really done the trick."

"Are you sure you're not . . ." Rosa mimed a rounded stomach.

"Me? Pregnant?" Freya laughed aloud. "Don't be silly." As she looked at the baby's face, she was filled with longing. She counted the days. *September first is tomorrow,* she thought. She hadn't had a period for months, but then several of the girls were the same. *Is it crazy to hope I might be, that I might be carrying Tom's child? Then, at least I will have a part of him forever.*

Rosa stood and gave the baby to Freya. "Will you take her for a while?"

"I'd love to."

Macu sat at the kitchen table embroidering sheets for the baby while Rosa pounded herbs with the pestle and mortar. Freya stretched back in the chair, her reading glasses pushed up into her hair. She was exhausted. Every time she closed her eyes, her mind filled with the horrors she had seen at the hospital that day. She was glad to be at home, at peace with the girls, and with the thought of her cool, narrow white bed awaiting her.

"It is nice when Vicente's away," she murmured as she closed her eyes. She stroked the baby's back as she lay on her chest, loved the warmth of her, the weight of her.

Macu laughed. "You think it's nice for you? Imagine for poor Rosa, how nice. No beating, no bothering her in the bedroom."

"Macu," Rosa chided.

"It's true!" she said. "So soon after the baby. It's not right . . ."

"Enough!" Rosa's cheeks colored. "He is my husband, it's his right. I knew what to expect when I married him."

Freya looked at her. "Rosa?"

"Mm?" She stopped working away at the mixture.

"I know why you married Vicente—it made sense, for you to have security for your child. Why did he want to marry you?"

Rosa looked down at the bowl, stirred the mixture slowly. "Jordi had something he couldn't have. Jordi has something, he can never have," she corrected herself. "One day—"

A pounding on the front door interrupted her. The girls looked up in surprise. "Are you expecting anyone?" Freya said.

"No, no one."

Freya tucked the baby into the woven Moses basket and strode into the hall, carrying the heavy brass candlestick. "Stay there."

"Wait." Macu grabbed the poker from beside the fireplace. "I'll come with you." As Freya unlocked the bolts, she stood ready, the poker raised above her head. "Leave the chain on."

Freya inched open the door, and peered out. It was a man, huddled over. Silhouetted against the moonlit sky bright with stars, she couldn't make out his features. She could tell from the uniform that he was Republican. The cicadas hummed, frenzied in the warm night. "*Qué pasa?*" she said.

"Freya?" The figure stumbled forward. "Thank God, they said you were here." As the man slumped on the doorstep, Freya frantically unhooked the chain.

"Help me," she said.

Macu dropped the poker with a clatter, and pulled back the door. The man fell backward onto the floor, his handsome, filthy face illuminated by the moonlight. As she gazed down at him, her lips parted.

"Who is it?" Rosa appeared in the doorway.

"It's my brother," Freya said as she knelt beside him, and brushed his hair from his brow. "It's my brother, Charles."

Between them, they carried him to a bed, stripped him of his filthy, louse-ridden uniform and boots full of holes. In spite of having seen hundreds of men naked and wounded in the last months, Freya felt it would be wrong to see Charles in a state of complete undress, so she left Macu to clean him while she and Rosa burned his uniform in the courtyard. Freya wrinkled her nose with distaste as she poked at the smoldering cloth with a stick of orangewood.

"Ugh, that awful smell. Sometimes I think I shall never get rid of it."

"Blood, sweat, and worse. Thank God for perfume, eh?" Rosa nodded in understanding. "You bathe tonight. I will give you some of my rose bath oil."

"Oh, no," Freya turned to her. "I didn't mean . . ."

"Please." Rosa patted her hand. "You have had a big shock. It will help you sleep too. You need to be strong for your brother. He needs you now."

Charles lay on the bed in the candlelight, his limbs as loose and guileless as a child's in sleep. Macu stepped forward tentatively with the enamel bowl of steaming water.

"*Señor*?" she said gravely. Charles did not move. She put the bowl down, shook his arm gently. "*Señor*?" She thought for a moment he might be dead, and panicked. She laid her head on his chest, listened to the steady thump of his heart. No, not dead then, but as good as. She added the essences that Rosa had given her to the hot water, and gently she set to work, bathing him. Several times, she returned to the kitchen for fresh water as she washed the filth from his skin. She had helped Rosa and Freya at the hospital caring for the wounded soldiers, but this was the first time she had been alone with a man. When she started on his face, she soaked a fresh towel and wiped away the dirt from his cheeks, his soft pink lips. Macu paused. He was so young, almost a boy. She rinsed his hair, like spun gold beneath the mud and grease, supported the weight of his head in her hand. At last she stepped back, pulled a clean white sheet up to his shoulders, covering him. He looked like an angel, she thought. Macu crossed herself, ashamed of the thoughts that filled her mind.

"*Cómo está?* How is he?" Rosa appeared at the door.

"He is good." Macu scooped up the last bowl self-consciously. Rosa blew out the candle.

"Well done. He is to be your special responsibility. If Vicente comes home"—she paused, thinking quickly—"we'll tell him Freya's brother is visiting from England. Tell him he was with the conference of writers, that is better. He is sick, and he is staying with us." Rosa pulled an amber bottle of oil from her apron pocket. "Every morning, and every night, you are to rub this into his body. Mix a few drops into almond oil, and massage, like this . . ." She mimed a circular motion. "I would do it myself but I have the baby, and Vicente would not like it."

Macu blushed at the thought. "*Sí,* Rosa. I will do it. I will make him better again."

"Good girl," Rosa said, closing the door with a smile on her lips.

THIRTY-FOUR

Sitting in Plaza la Reina in the heart of Valencia, Emma thought how every single person in that square was there because for one night or one stolen moment their parents loved one another. Sex, pure and simple, made the world go around, east and west alike. Every stranger passing by her table had been born as their mother endured the worst pain of her life, had been held up: "It's a boy!" "It's a girl!" Their backsides had been wiped and wailing hunger sated, their clothes washed and beds made for years to get them where they were today, busy on the way to work, talking into a mobile, or searching a trash can for a crust of bread.

As her due date drew closer, she had spent the past week in a near frenzy of activity. Paloma had dropped by the evening before to invite her for lunch.

"What on earth do you think you are doing?" Paloma had cried.

Emma teetered on the chair, muslin billowing over her arm. "You made me jump!"

"Get down from there at once." Paloma held her hand as she clambered down. "Don't you have a proper ladder?"

"I was just trying to hang some curtains. I'm hopeless with heights," Emma said, laughing. "I thought I could reach . . ."

"Even more reason why you shouldn't be climbing up there, then. Marek!"

she called. "Borys!" Paloma launched into the builders, told them in no uncertain terms that Emma was not allowed to lift a finger until after the baby comes.

Instead Emma focused her nesting urge on gathering supplies for the weeks after the birth. In the echoing halls of the Mercado Central she stockpiled food for the freezer. The market closed at lunchtime, and the traders cooked paella with the day's leftovers in vast pans outside the door, orangewood fires sending plumes of smoke up to the sky. Emma stopped to watch them cook. She carried bags of tortoiseshell *mantilla* combs from Nela, and fans to send home to Freya as a "thank-you" for holding the fort in London. In Prénatal she couldn't resist buying a tiny footed pajamas with ribbon fastenings, the first part of her baby's wardrobe. As she held it up for inspection now she couldn't believe that soon she would be dressing her child in it.

"Oh!" Paloma cried as she spotted Emma. "It's so cute! Adorable! You can't believe they are that tiny at first! I have a stack of baby things you can have, I must dig them out for you."

"That would be wonderful. After everything that's happened in the last few months I haven't wanted to tempt fate by buying too much." Emma felt embarrassed. "It's silly. It's not like me to be so superstitious."

Paloma patted her hand. "No, I understand. I will make up a bag of clothes for you."

"What if you have more?"

"Nooo." She shook her head. "Three is plenty. Olivier would have a football team, but I have my career to think of now. Benito we had very quickly, but we had to wait for Paco, and the baby. Olivier has his daughter now." Paloma ordered a glass of wine. "I'm sorry I'm late. Have you been waiting long?" She rooted around in her handbag for her mobile. "Mamá . . . Well. You've met her now. She was meant to be taking care of the children tonight so that Olivier and I could go to the theater, but we had a falling-out." She mimed a bomb exploding. "So I asked Luca, but he won't be back from Madrid in time. I have to call Olivier and cancel."

"I'll have them," Emma said.

"No, I couldn't ask you."

"Really, I'd love to. Why don't you drop them off at teatime? I can get them ready for bed. Then Luca can pick them up later."

"Are you sure?" Paloma's face brightened. "It's been so long since we had a night out. I've forgotten what it feels like to be out on a date with my husband."

"It will be good practice for me." Emma eased herself back in the chair. "So, have you managed to find out anything from Macu, about the house? I'd love to know why that room was sealed up."

Paloma shook her head. "She wants to talk about it, I can tell, but something's stopping her. Mamá knows too, I'm sure, but she won't tell me." She leaned forward. "I think there is something shameful, for our family."

"I don't want to make trouble for you. I've asked Freya, but she won't talk about it either." Emma swirled the water in her glass, the bubbles sparkling in the sunlight. "I wish she'd open up. I get the feeling she's carried a burden for a long time."

"I think a lot of people who lived through the war . . ." Paloma hesitated. "They think memories should stay buried."

"Which side were your family on?"

Paloma's eyes flickered at the directness of the question. "It is not as easy as that. Many families just wanted to get by, to live a peaceful life. Ignacio, my grandfather, was a good man, but it was hard for them because . . ." She sat back and sighed. "I think it was known Macu was Red, so was Rosa. I think they were in some kind of trouble. It is a small place, people talk. Mamá . . . she likes to do the right thing. She cares a lot about the honor of the Santangel name. Past is past."

"Is that why your mother dislikes me? Is me living at the house stirring up old memories?" Emma held her gaze. "So that's why she doesn't like me working with Luca."

"She tries to protect him, but my brother is a big boy," Paloma said, smiling. "It is thanks to him that the Santangels are successful. He has doubled our land, our wealth."

"Really?"

"My brother the dark horse." She sipped her wine. "Maybe in the last few years he has been working too hard."

I know the feeling, Emma thought. "Tell me about Luca."

"What do you want to know?"

Emma blushed, fiddled with the stem of her glass. "Is he seeing anyone? I mean, I know he's not interested in me . . . but why isn't he married with an adoring wife and a troop of kids?"

"You know, he has a lot on his plate. He has a lot of responsibilities." She looked Emma in the eye. "Some guys are like that—caught up with work . . ."

"But, I mean, he's so . . . There must have been women?"

"Sex? Of course he's had—has girlfriends. He's just not a family man."

"No," Emma shook her head. "I've seen something in his eyes when he is playing with your kids—it's love, but it's edged with something . . . grief, maybe. He's been hurt. I know that feeling—I recognize it."

"Many, many women have hoped to steal his heart and failed. I like you, Emma. Don't set yourself up for more pain. You've been through too much. If you want a relationship, a father for your child, I know heaps of men who would adore you. Just don't pin your hopes on Luca."

"Of course not. No, I don't need anyone. It's taken me nearly a year to feel strong again. I'm not going to take the risk of . . ."

Paloma leaned back in her chair, her head slumped onto her hand. "You've fallen for him, haven't you?"

"No!" Emma felt the color rising to her cheeks. "I mean, maybe if everything had been different . . ."

"People grow old waiting for everything to be perfect," Paloma said. "My brother is a wonderful man, but he has suffered a lot." She hesitated. "He has a lot of ghosts."

"Don't we all?" Emma stared at the doves rising from the square, wheeling against the blue domes and cerulean sky. "Would it have made a difference if I wasn't pregnant?"

"No, it's not that. If he trusts you, maybe he will tell you everything when he is ready. It's not my place to talk behind his back. I adore you, Emma, I hope we will become great friends . . ."

Emma reached forward and took Paloma's hand. "Same here. I understand."

"If he hasn't explained why he's alone then I can't, I just can't."

That night Emma enjoyed the sound of laughter in the house, cartoons on the television, the pounding of small feet up and down the upstairs corridor. *A house like this needs the laughter of children,* she thought. After tea, she bathed the two children, dressed them in their cotton pajamas and brushed their hair as she had watched Paloma do. The warmest room in the house was the kitchen, so she tucked them up with blankets on the sofa in front of the fire, and told them a story about magical creatures who lived in the orange groves before humans arrived, about unicorns and lions, talking tigers and snow-white flying horses.

At the end of the story, she sat enjoying the silence, the dozing children, the warmth. A low, mournful cry stirred her, and she struggled to her feet. "Cat?" she called. She tracked the cries to the kitchen sink and pulled back the curtains beneath it. There, tucked in the corner on a nest of rags, she saw the cat, licking the first kitten. "Well done!" she said, settling down on her hands and knees. The cat looked at her impassively. "Good girl," Emma said. "You tell me if you need help, OK?" Emma tucked the curtain across and left her in peace. She settled back on the sofa, the wind rattling the French doors to the terrace, and stared at the flickering fire.

She must have nodded off herself, because she woke to find Luca leaning in the doorway watching them, smiling.

"No," he whispered as she stirred, "don't move. You all look so peaceful." He lifted Paco into his arms, squeezed onto the sofa beside them all. As his arm stretched over the sofa, Emma felt his hand brush her shoulder. She smiled sleepily at him. "Have you had a good day?"

"Yes. But not as much fun as you've had." He glanced at the piles of paintings on the table and the toys all over the floor.

"It's a mess. I was going to tidy up before you came." The baby sighed in her sleep, curled up against Emma's side, her arm stretched over her bump. Luca affectionately stroked the back of her little hand. "Guess what—we have kittens!" she whispered. "Do you think Paloma would like a couple for the children once they're weaned?"

"I'm sure. In fact, we could do with a couple of cats on the finca. Our old tomcat disappeared."

"They do that sometimes when they get old."

"Perhaps, or maybe wild dogs."

"Let's hope he went peacefully in a sunny spot under an orange tree, eh?" Emma stifled a yawn.

"You're tired. I should get these monkeys home." He scooped his niece and nephew into his arms and stood. "It's a shame to disturb you all. This is what men dream of coming home to."

"What? Woman with a bun in the oven, a troop of kids, dinner on the table?" Emma laughed as she staggered to her feet.

"No." He looked hurt. "You are a businesswoman, I know. Maybe we want different things."

"Luca." She caught at his sleeve.

"Thank you, Emma." The barriers had gone back up again. *"Hasta luego."*

THIRTY-FIVE

At sunset, Freya dragged herself up the hill to the Villa del Valle. She pulled her coat around her as the chill wind whistled down, bringing the earthy scent of onions from the fields. Every bone in her body ached. All she wanted to do now was sleep.

"*Buenas*!" she called, pushing open the kitchen door. She leaned down and kissed the top of the baby's head where she sat in her high wooden chair at the table.

"Busy day?" Rosa asked. She was labeling bottles of essences, rows of amber glass bottles gleaming in the lamplight.

"The hospital is crazy. I wish the Spanish doctors wouldn't give us such a hard time."

"They have their way of doing things, you have yours. I'll come back soon. Macu can help more with Loulou now she is bigger."

"Where is Macu?"

Rosa raised her eyes. As they stopped talking, Freya heard the unmistakable squeak of bedsprings overhead. "They are saying good-bye, I think."

Freya blushed. Over the last weeks she had seen Charles transform from a broken shell of a man to his old self. "Of course. He's leaving for Barcelona tonight."

"Everyone is leaving for Barcelona," Rosa said bitterly. "First the government runs here, now they flee to Barcelona." She glanced at her child, thought of the children being sent overseas. "Freya, I want to ask you . . ."

"Yes?"

"If anything happens here, anything bad, will you look after Loulou?"

"Of course. But nothing is going to."

"Who knows? The war is not going well. Every day, I hope that Jordi will walk in that door. Every day, but there is nothing."

"No word from Vicente either?"

Rosa shook her head. "Who knows what he is up to. I don't trust him. It is good, I think, that your brother is leaving."

"I'm glad that Charles and Macu are . . ."

"Lovers?" Rosa put down her pen, and gestured at the bottles in front of her. "Love is the best medicine there is. Macu has experienced her 'boom,' and your brother is well again. When he goes, I think she will be happy to marry Ignacio now. He is a good man, and she will grow to love him."

Freya folded her arms and laughed. "You planned all this, didn't you?"

"I don't know what you mean . . ." A smile played on her lips.

"Being with Macu has made him happy, and I think writing his book is helping." She glanced down at Rosa's work. "Your handwriting is really coming on, you know." Freya peered down at the neat, childish script.

"It's all thanks to you, and your brother." Rosa pulled over a new notebook. "Look, I am writing out my recipes. Maybe one day Loulou will make medicine too."

The steady pulse of the bedstead against the wall upstairs quickened. Freya cleared her throat. "Shall I make some tea?"

Charles flung himself back against the pillows, and Macu curled in his arms. "I'm going to miss you," he murmured into her hair.

"Take me with you, Carlos."

"I can't. You know that. You're safer here."

"I would be no trouble, I promise. I will fight with you as Rosa did with Jordi . . ." She touched his face. "I love you." She waited. A tremor passed across her lips. "I don't expect you to feel the same. I know you have to leave, I—"

"Oh, Macu." Charles closed his eyes as he kissed her. He couldn't say it. *It's not fair,* he thought, *to leave her with hope.* A line furrowed between his brows as he thought of Capa's grief for Gerda. *I have to let Macu go, in case*

I don't return. She can't wait for me. "You dear, dear girl. Without you . . . I don't know what would have become of me." He thought of the weeks he had spent recovering with the girls, the warm last days of autumn working in Valencia, away from the front line for a time. "You've put me back together again."

"Only for you to go and fight, maybe be killed?" She held him closer. "That is what we women do, what Freya and Rosa do in the hospital. They mend the men, only to send them to the front again."

"That's the way of war," Charles said.

"Do you love me, Carlos?"

"Macu, I will never forget you." He smiled down at her. "You were the first."

She looked up at him, surprised. "I thought—"

"No." *My first love,* he thought, his heart heavy at leaving her.

"There has been no one else?"

"No one." He thought of Gerda.

"I can't believe that." Macu pushed him away playfully.

Charles hesitated. "There was someone I admired, a great deal—"

"See?"

"But she was with a friend of mine, and . . . and she was killed, a short while ago."

"Carlos, I am sorry." Macu touched his face.

Charles pushed down the emotion welling inside him, forced a smile. "So you see, you are my first love."

"Let me come—"

"No. I shall never forget you, but your life is here, and I must go back to finish my work." She started to protest, but he touched her lips. "I don't want you to wait for me. Promise you will be happy? Marry that chap in the village who proposed—"

"Ignacio?" Macu blinked, looked away. "I didn't think you knew?"

"Rosa told me." Charles smiled sadly. "And every time he sees you, he can't take his eyes off you." He traced her collarbone, the curve of her shoulder with his fingertip. "I can't blame him."

"I promise you, there has been nothing between us. Ignacio has asked me to marry him many times, but he is like a brother to me—"

"You don't need to explain."

"What about you, and me?"

"Macu, no one knows about us." He gazed up at the ceiling, unable to meet her urgent gaze. "These weeks with you have been the happiest of my life, but I can't promise you the future Ignacio can."

"I don't want—"

"Well I do." Charles turned to her. "I want you to be happy for both of us. Love for both of us." He stemmed a tear at the corner of her eye. "I wish you love, Macu. Love, a family, a long life—all the things I can't guarantee." He glanced at the clock. "I must get ready. The car will be here soon." He slipped out of bed and packed his few belongings. His hand hesitated over the camera. "Macu, may I take your photo, to remember you by?"

"No one has ever taken my picture before." She lay back in the bed, her dark hair gleaming against the blue-and-white *azulejos* tiles. A white sheet draped across her body, emphasising every curve.

"I want to remember you like this."

"Wait," she said. She reached over to the bedside table and snapped open a black fan. She held it to her face, gazed steadily at the camera with glistening eyes full of loss, and love, at Charles standing naked before her.

They walked downstairs arm in arm. "I will miss you," she said.

"And I, you." Charles kissed her. "Thank you."

"Don't be silly."

"No." He looked into her eyes. "I'll never forget you, Macu. You may just have saved my life." A car's horn sounded outside. "I'd better say goodbye to . . ." His words trailed off as they heard the terrace door burst open, and Vicente's shout.

"Look at you with your potions!" Vicente yelled. "Witches the lot of you!"

Charles put his kit bag down. "Excuse me, Macu."

Vicente staggered drunkenly across the kitchen toward Rosa, knocked the carefully labeled bottles on the table flying. The baby began to wail with fright.

"Where have you been?" Rosa yelled.

"None of your business." He pushed her roughly aside.

"Don't you touch her!" Freya cried.

Vicente wheeled on her. "You? You stuck-up English bitch, you whore . . ."

Charles tapped him on the shoulder, and as Vicente turned, thumped him squarely on the nose. Vicente staggered back, fell onto the floor.

"That, sir, is my sister, and that's no way for a gentleman to talk to her."
He flexed his hand. "Damn, that hurt."

Rosa calmly stepped over Vicente's prone form and hugged Charles.
"That's no gentleman. That's my husband." She kissed Charles's cheek. "You
go now. It's better you are not here when he wakes up."

THIRTY-SIX

The night was perfectly still. No dogs barked. Moonlight spilled through the muslin drapes, bathing Emma's bed in silvery blue light. She lay awake as the baby turned cartwheels in her stomach. She stroked her tummy, soothing the child with her soft words. "It's OK." Her voice faltered as she thought how hurt Luca had looked that evening. She rubbed her stomach along the curve of the baby's back, and the child stilled at her touch. It was no use, she was wide awake now and needed to pee— again. She swung her legs out of bed with difficulty and slipped on her Moroccan tan leather slippers, pulling a heavy wool gown around her. The house was cold and silent. She didn't even bother flicking on the bathroom light—she made this nighttime journey so often now she could do it in the pitch-dark. Tonight, in the moonlight, the house was filled with a strange and beautiful glow. *Tea and toast,* she thought as she washed her hands, her reflection luminous in the mirror.

In the kitchen, she raked the embers of the fire in the stove, and tossed on a few more orange tree branches. The kettle hissed on the range as she stared out across the moonlit mountains. Snowflakes fell hypnotically beyond the window. "Well look at that," she said to the baby. "Snow in Spain, who'd have thought it?" She shivered, and took a mug of tea to sit by the fire. She leaned her head against her hand, watching the flames dance, her eyelids heavy, drooping closed. "Moon River . . ." she sang softly to the baby.

"Wider than a mile . . ." A male voice joined hers.

She glanced up. Someone was sitting in the shadows by the fire. "Joe? How did you . . . ?"

"Who were you talking to?"

"Our baby," she murmured. "Joe, how did you find me? I thought you were . . . You've been missing for months."

"I've been busy, baby." He knelt down before her, placed his hands on her stomach. "Man, you are huge!" He laid his head against her. "I can feel him kick."

"How do you know it's a boy?"

"Of course it is!"

"Could be a girl."

"Nah! This is little Joe in here, isn't it?" The baby kicked twice in response.

"I missed you so much. I miss our life . . ."

"Hey," he said gently. "Where's my pal? Where's my buddy? Nothing fazes you, Em. You're tougher than anyone I know."

"No I'm not." She bit her lip. "I don't know how to do this without you."

Joe sat back on his heels. In the firelight his face seemed softer than she remembered—golden, radiant. "That doesn't sound like the girl I know. I remember the first time I saw you. You were so confident, striding across the quad in one of those long black coats we all used to wear."

Emma shifted away. "That wasn't me, Joe, that was Lila. She had a long coat, not me."

"Oh?" He gave her his best little-boy-lost smile. "You know me and my memory—it's funny, it isn't what it was . . . Hey, don't cry." He took her hand.

"Why did you do it, Joe? Why her?"

Joe shrugged. "I guess I got tired of saying no to her. She needed me . . . and you, you didn't seem to need me anymore." He kissed her fingers, laid his cheek against her hand. "You've got to move on, baby. We had a good time . . ."

"We had a great time. I loved you, Joe." She felt all the anger well up inside her, everything she had wanted to say. "You lost faith in me, in us. You took something people search a lifetime for, and threw it away. Even if we had got together again for the sake of the baby, it would never have been what it was."

"It could have been better."

"No. Nothing could be better than what we had. I loved you, Joe. I trusted you. You didn't love me enough."

"Em, people screw up. They can be selfish, impulsive."

"I'm not just talking about your affair. You lied to me, even when I had all the evidence and gave you chance after chance to confess. You lied and said it was one night. You treated me like an idiot. You didn't have the decency to be honest with me."

"I hoped you wouldn't find out."

"You humiliated me."

"Not everyone is perfect."

"Meaning what? That I am?"

"No, baby . . ."

"That's what Lila said, when I confronted her. That I was Miss Head Girl, too perfect, too closed. Business first. Now look at me, no business, no relationship, just the baby."

"I'm sorry, Em." He took her hand. "But you know, if I knew then, when I met you, what was ahead I wouldn't change a thing." Tears pooled in his eyes. "We had some great times. The best. I loved you, Em, but we've had our time. You need to find a new life, for you and little Joe."

"Josephine."

"Nah!" Joe laughed softly. "You'll see. It's up to you now. You can do this. I'll be watching, you know. Make sure he grows up to be a better man than his father." Joe wiped away a tear from her cheek. "I'm sorry I wasn't the man you deserve, Emma."

"It was both of us. We took our love for granted."

"Don't make that mistake next time."

"Next time?"

"Oh yeah." Joe smiled. "Just you wait." He picked up the blankets from the sofa arm and tucked in beside her. "It's all still to come, and he'll be the luckiest guy in the world."

"Thanks, Joe." Emma sighed sleepily.

"For what?"

"For coming all this way."

Joe kissed the top of her sleeping head. "You have no idea, baby, you have no idea."

The sound of a siren on the road swung through the night, and Emma woke with a start. She blinked, confused to find herself alone. "Joe?" she said. The cat yowled in response from her nest under the sink. "Wow," she said, stirring from the sofa. "That was . . ." She stared out at the snow drifting by the window. "That was strange." Emma wrapped her arms around herself as she gazed out of the window. "I miss you, Joe," she said quietly. For the first time, she felt he had really gone. There was no doubt in her heart.

Emma padded across the room and picked up her mother's box of letters. She settled back on the sofa, and smoothed the lid. It was covered with dust from the builders, and her breath bloomed on the surface as she blew it away, cleared the black lacquer with the sleeve of her pajamas. As she opened it, the firelight illuminated the orange interior, gilded her face. Emma flicked through the remaining envelopes. "On Loneliness," she said, and glanced at the cat. "That seems right for tonight."

Em, let me share something with you which has taken me sixty-four years to learn. I hope it saves you wasting time, as I did.

It's an illusion that we are all alone. We are more connected than we think. It was spending so long in hospitals recently that made me see clearly how much we all need one another. We are all connected at some basic level, but people forget. They forget to connect. They get caught up in the race, in the illusion of "me" and "you" when what matters in this life is "we." I felt so lucky to go through this last journey with you, with all of you at my side. I saw so many lonely people, Em. I saw the isolation, the fear in their eyes. If doctors prescribed friendship they would save millions on drugs. I looked at some of the old people who had no visitors day after day, and thought, "When was the last time someone hugged you, or held your hand?" So that's what I did when I was in hospital, I went and talked to them, gave them a hug. And you know what? It helped me feel less afraid and alone too. Loneliness is a blight—we're not meant to go through this life alone.

This is what I learned. People spend a lifetime looking for this, or that—a place, a house, a person that completes them. But your home is within you, you carry your place in the world. I was always a free spirit, alone in the traditional sense for years—no security, no home, no husband, and I was always searching for something I couldn't name. Then you came, a glorious, wonderful surprise. You taught me something that all the ashrams in India and retreats in California couldn't—you taught me that to give, to love selflessly, fearlessly is the key. You taught me that the only way is to open yourself completely to life. Loneliness closes people off—people get hurt, or scared, and shut down. It comes to us all at some point in our lives—when your father left us, I thought I was broken. I thought I'd never survive. But I did, for you. Times like that are sent to test us, I think. It's your moment of truth. Will you close down, or will you grow stronger than ever?

As a parent, you wish you could spare your children this. I hate to think of you alone, Em. I remember you walking away from me on the first day of school. You looked so vulnerable, and uncertain. I just wanted to scoop you up in my arms and protect you, but I had to let you go. Every stage of life I've seen you go through I've felt like that—when your first boyfriend broke your heart, when you moved to France. You taught me that love is letting go. I had to step back. I feel like I am stepping back a last time, now.

Let go, Em. I know you—you will be missing me just as much as I miss you already, even thinking about not being there for you. But take it, take all the pain, and loss, and loneliness and send it back to the world as love. Give it wings: let love shine through you in your work, in your family, in the home that you make. Transform your pain, Em, send loneliness flying. Connect with your life, with the people you meet, the beauty around you. As you walk through life embrace the whole magical experience. God knows why we are here, and what it all means, but at the end of my life I see we don't have to understand, we just have to have faith, to feel it, to embrace the everyday miracle of being alive. I wish I had known this sooner.

I feel so lucky to have lived, and loved, and to have been loved by you.

And I do love you, Em, so very, very much.

Mum x

THIRTY-SEVEN

Charles cowered in the abandoned tank, writing by candlelight. He glanced up as another explosion shook the earth.

It looks like the pause in the bombardment has ceased.

As you know, nothing happens during the two to four o'clock siesta. That is one thing I have learned—if it is hot, you will find the Nationalists in the shade, if it is raining, look under cover. They are predictable in that way at least.

The fighting is bloody here in Teruel, Freya. All the old gang has been here—Capa, Hemingway, and Hugo. Each evening we retire to a hotel sixty miles away in Valencia to file our reports. I'm sorry I haven't had a chance to come and see you girls. Do give my love to Rosa and Macu.

Hemingway left for America on Christmas Eve. He plans to raise funds for the Republicans with the film he has made. I fear it may be too late. We are losing this war because of extremists blinded by dogma to the bigger picture. If only the factions supporting the Republican Left—the anarchists, the Communists, and the unions—could put their differences aside. It will destroy me if we lose against fascism because of the petty infighting of the political parties.

Thank you for my Christmas parcel of Cadburys and Players. I was so grateful I almost wept. I thought of you on New Year's Day. I woke early and went out to the courtyard for a cigarette. Snow was falling, and there were pigeons fluttering above. It was like a fairy tale, the perfect silence. It reminded me of the snow globe you loved so much when you were little. Do you remember, the one I broke? When we go home, I shall buy you another one.

This whole city is like a snow globe. Teruel is a glittering ice city, spiked with turrets, the cathedral spire. When the bombs come, the snow rises up like the ghosts of the dead. We had to use cranes to lift the vehicles up the steep mountain road. The dead are stacked like log piles on the side of the road, frozen stiff, abandoned among broken furniture and burned-out trucks. God, war is a hideous mess.

At least the line has held, and the city is in our hands. The battle rages on. I have just seen militiamen lead fifty people who have hidden in a basement for two weeks to safety. You never saw a more pitiful sight.

They say the first ten days at the front are the worst. After that, if you have survived, you are an automaton. You have seen too many good men die. Hemingway says there is nothing fitting about modern war—men are dying like dogs for no reason. But when I look at the men around me—the determined, hard faces of the Commies and the weedy intellectuals like me—as each wave of battalions goes forward to face death squarely, it always seems to me there is almost an ecstasy about them. Men who fight together, who hope together, have a nobility and strength they could never achieve alone. War is bloody, but it brings out the truth in man. It seemed like a fairy tale, a simple case of good versus evil, but honor is dying.

Some time later, Charles returned to his letter, continued in a different pen.

The shelling is getting worse now. It is near the end. We have gone in hand to hand. Freya, I killed a man.

I will never forget his shocked, angry eyes. He was older than me, in his forties maybe, but God he fought back. I was never more alone. It was him or me. The horrid pushing, and shouting, the ghastly gleaming blade of the bayonet. Oh, I have shot at men before, from the safety of dugouts and trenches, but I think many in this war aimed to miss. But this, oh God, this will be on my conscience for all eternity.

I am trying to keep the truth in me, the qualities you know. I have changed, but I will not let it change "me," if that makes sense. I want to still see the beauty in the world, Freya. I need to. I am not Capa—he writes the poetry of war with his pictures, a tragic poetry. I feel a dilettante in comparison. He is haunted, passionate, impulsive—everything I am not. I wish I were more like him, Frey. I wish I did not know what it is like to kill a man. Let's never talk of this again.

Happy New Year.
Your loving brother,
Charles

Charles folded up the letter, and sat for a time with his head in his hands. He scrambled from the tank, the metal cold beneath his blood-caked fingers. He jumped down into the snow, and clicked his lighter. From the flame, he lit his last cigarette, then the corner of the letter. He lifted it to the wind, watched the gold flame lick around the paper, curling, charred as it leaped into the air, the frozen city behind.

THIRTY-EIGHT

Snow fell steadily beyond the window as Emma sat at her desk, Liberty's notebook in front of her. She had spent hours unpacking the vials of fragrance Liberty had collected, arranging them in family groups of citrus, spicy, herbal, floral, woody, leather. The other packing boxes from London littered the house now, unopened. All she had wanted to do was assemble the "organ," to somehow conjure her mother here with her.

Emma carefully unwrapped the last bottle, a boronia absolute. It joined the hundreds of other bottles of essences and absolutes. On one shelf, Emma placed her empty bottles and labels, on another her ingredients. Finally, she centered the scale at the middle of the tiered shelves, and placed an empty glass jar on it, ready to work, but she didn't know where to begin. She knew the fragrance she wanted, like a half-remembered melody she couldn't sing but would know instinctively the moment she heard it. She felt restless, and she snatched up the notebook, paced in front of the window, her warm socks padding on the newly polished floorboards. She read the list she had just written:

SPAIN—SOMETHING WONDERFUL:
The seduction of white flowers
Woodsmoke and saffron

Lavender mountains, cranberry sunsets
Blue domes
Lemon trees
Floating bridges
Immense night skies pricked with stars . . .

Luca's wrists, she thought. *The indentation at the base of his throat. His hair in the wind.* Emma frowned as she selected a few vials from the tiered shelves of her desk. She wanted to transform what she was feeling into fragrance. She closed her eyes, thought of blossom, cedar . . . When she thought of him, the fragrance deepened, became mixed with earth. With glass pipettes, she measured out a few drops from each vial, replacing them on the shelves as she noted down the amounts she used. Memories, associations danced in her mind—colors, odors, textures—as she inhaled the mix. Since training in Grasse, Emma could imagine in three dimensions the way the molecules of fragrance worked together at a microscopic level, connecting, transforming. She always pictured the fragrance in motion, like a mobile in a chemistry lab.

She needed something else. She selected three more bottles: neroli, bitter orange, petitgrain, sniffing each in turn, clearing her "nose" by smelling coffee beans in between each. Emma jotted down some notes. The scent relaxed her—she remembered Olivier saying that the smell of orange blossoms was associated with meditation, a Zen state. *There's still something missing.*

Emma thought back to walking in the orange groves with Luca that afternoon, how he had run his hands through the earth. She pulled on her boots and walked out into the snow. The night air seemed alive, made anew, sparkling. She kicked at the ground. *This is my earth,* she remembered Luca saying, *it made me.* Emma squatted down, scraped the soil with her fingertips, inhaled. What was missing? Emma touched the locket at her neck. What did she need?

The mountains had seemed close that afternoon, sparkling with fresh snow beneath a cobalt sky. She had felt like she could reach out and touch them. Luca had offered her his hand. A fresh gust of cold wind had ravished her as she stepped down off the road into the grove.

"What a day." She had felt the Morse code of her heart pulsing strong in her. Luca whistled for Sasha, and Olivier and Paloma walked arm in arm ahead, the children throwing snowballs.

"That dog has a mind of his own," Luca said. "He is a real Spaniard. Hates getting up in the morning, won't eat much before lunch, but once he's been out for his evening *paseo,* he's like a different animal."

"I've never seen a dog who can look so exhausted." Emma buried her cold nose down into her soft pink scarf.

"It's like he has a hangover every morning." Luca laughed. "When he wakes up, he has bags under his eyes."

"You can imagine him rubbing his chin in front of the mirror, getting ready to have a shave." Emma laughed.

"Or ordering strong black coffee at the same little café each day to ease himself into the morning." Oblivious, the dog crisscrossed among the trees ahead of them, nose to the ground, tail high, tracking the course of something. "Are you all right? You're not too tired?"

"No, I'm fine." Her hips were aching painfully but she wasn't going to let anything spoil this glorious afternoon. "I'm bored of sitting at home, waiting for this baby to come. It's wonderful to be out, exploring." She glanced at Luca. "You've never thought of leaving here, of traveling?"

"I've traveled all over the world. At least enough to know that I always want to return here." He smiled, squatted down on his heels, raked through the snow to the ocher soil. "This is my earth. It made me. When I die, I want to be here." Sasha ran over, sniffed his face, and Luca laughed. He tossed a snowball off into the groves and the dog chased away. "We belong here."

"You're lucky." Emma pushed a branch out of her path as they walked on. "I wish I felt like that. Sometimes I don't know who I am, especially now Mum has gone."

"Is your father alive?"

"Dad? Yes, but he has a whole other family now. I spent some time with him recently, but we're not close. He just . . . Well, the birthday cards stopped when I was about nine, put it that way."

"Perhaps now is the time to choose your own life?"

Emma glanced at him. "A clean slate? Maybe you are right."

"Have you managed to find out anything more about the house?" he asked as they walked on.

Emma shook her head. "Freya won't talk to me, and I don't want to push Macu too much." She dug her hands into her pockets. "I'd just love to know the truth about what went on."

"The truth?" Luca smiled and shook his head. "Sometimes there are many truths. It depends on how you look at something." He scuffed the snow with his boot. "You are happy here?" he asked her after a while.

"In Valencia? Yes, yes I am."

"I am glad. I thought, perhaps, you would not stay long."

"Looks like I'm here for the duration." Emma spoke quietly, sensing that he was trying to say something important.

"Emma . . ." Luca began. Sasha barked suddenly, a low, mournful cry more like the howl of a wolf, and another dog's bark snapped in the cold air. "Sasha!" Luca ran ahead into the orange grove. Emma followed at a distance, struggling through the snow, the green branches of the trees catching at her. The cries of the dogs grew fiercer.

In a clearing, Emma came upon them. A muscular black Alsatian stalked around Sasha, its teeth bared and ears hard against its head. Sasha reared up, his silver hackles raised, and brought his front legs down on the dog. They locked, snarling, striking at one another. Luca leaped toward them, pulling Sasha clear. The Alsatian snapped at him, catching the flesh of his hand in its teeth. Luca roared, and kicked out at the dog, which ran off into the trees.

"Let me see," Emma said, taking his hand. He shook a white handkerchief from his pocket as she inspected the bite.

"It's nothing," he said, stemming the blood with the handkerchief.

"You should have it checked," she said. Luca snorted and shook his head. "The dog might have rabies." Emma tied the handkerchief tightly around his hand and Luca winced.

"No, it was tagged," he said. "They are always fighting, these two." He looked over to where Sasha lay, head on the ground, waiting to see what would happen next. "You . . ." he growled, and the dog rolled over on his back.

"Men." Emma sighed. "Just don't know when to let it go, do you?" She winced as her stomach hardened with a contraction.

"Emma?" He touched her arm.

She breathed out as the pain ebbed. "Don't worry. It's just Braxton Hicks—the baby isn't due for a couple of weeks yet. Just a false alarm."

Emma frowned now as another contraction set in. She exhaled slowly, her breath a cloud of white, and looked out across the sleeping garden. She imagined the summer to come, and all the summers after as the garden came back to life. In her mind, she conjured the perfume of flowers, the dappled shade of the trees on fresh grass, the sound of running water in the fountain. *Perhaps now is the time to choose your own life,* she remembered Luca saying. She looked up at the moon, said a silent "thank-you" to her mother. *I choose this,* she thought. *I choose this place, this life.*

THIRTY-NINE

VALENCIA, JULY 1938

Rosa swung in a hammock in the garden, the July sun beating down through the leaves where she lay, her child asleep in her arms. The village was quiet at siesta time, and all she could hear was the water dancing in the fountain. It seemed impossible that the war was drawing ever closer, at the Ebro river now. She closed her eyes, felt the steady rise and fall of the child's rib cage beneath her hand, brushed the damp curls from her hot brow. She felt afraid now, not for herself, but for her daughter. Rosa jumped as the latch on the gate clicked. She raised her hand to her eyes, shielding them from the sun.

"*Quién está ahí?* Who's there?" she said. She heard the crunch of gravel beneath boots, and struggled to her feet, laying the child down to sleep. As she turned, the man took her in his arms, pulled her to him.

Rosa fought back, pushing him away. As she struggled, she saw his filthy beard, smelled the stink of his ragged clothes.

"Rosa," he said. "Don't you recognize me?"

At the sound of his voice, she stilled, her heart thundering beneath her ribs. "Jordi?" she cried. "Jordi?" She started to shake, to weep. She took his face in her hands, and looked into his eyes. "Oh God, you're alive. I knew you were alive!" They clung to each other in the dappled light as their child slept on beside them.

Macu came around the side of the house, carrying a tray of peaches. When she saw them, her hand slipped, the fruit tumbled to the ground.

"It's like you saw a ghost, Macu." Jordi turned to the sleeping baby.

Rosa watched his face. "She is your daughter," she said, a tear trickling down her cheek.

He stepped forward, reached out his hand, dark against Loulou's pale cheek, her white dress. He hesitated, his hand trembling. "I can't . . ." he whispered, his voice tight with tears. "She is too perfect."

Rosa lifted the child into his arms. "She is yours, ours." Jordi buried his face in her hair. "She is beautiful," he said, and kissed the top of Rosa's head. "You haven't changed."

"You have." Rosa tugged his beard. She thumped his chest. "Where have you been? They told me you were dead. They showed me your papers."

Jordi thought back through the months of combat, hazy memories rolling into one another. "I lost my papers. I gave my jacket to a comrade who was badly injured."

"You're alive. That's all that matters." She thought of Vicente. "Jordi, there's something you need to know . . ."

The shutters upstairs rattled open, and Vicente appeared on the balcony in his pink dressing gown, stretching and yawning after his siesta. "Rosa!" he bellowed. "Rosa!"

Jordi looked from her anxious face to his brother and knew.

"They told me you were dead," she said, clutching at his shirt.

Jordi thrust the baby into her arms and pushed her away. "You, and him? How could you?"

"Please, he told me it would be best for our daughter, for Loulou."

Vicente leaned on the balcony, looked down into the garden. "Who's there?" Jordi gazed up at him, his eyes full of anger and pain. Vicente began to laugh. "Well look, it's the prodigal son."

"Do you love him?" Jordi said to her. His eyes scared her. He looked like the man she loved, sounded like him, but his eyes were dead. He had the look of an animal that has been beaten, its spirit broken.

"Are you mad?" she said. "I love you, Jordi, I have always loved you. He told me I had to marry him, to protect our child."

"You married him?" Jordi took a step back.

"*Sí,*" Vicente said, folding his arms.

Jordi stuck his cap on his head. "Then there is nothing to be done."

"I will divorce him!" Rosa whispered, clutched at his hand. "Jordi,

I have heard nothing from you, nothing, for over a year. If you had written . . ."

"I can't write. You know that."

"You could have got a message to me."

"I have been fighting, Rosa, all over Spain," he said, his voice cracking with anger. "And now, not far from here, the bodies of my friends are on the banks of the Ebro." He flinched as he thought of the swollen bodies washed up along the river, buzzing with flies.

She saw the madness in his eyes flare then, the damage the war had done.

"We have been trapped in the bottom of a valley for days." He wiped his mouth with the back of his hand. His throat thickened again at the thought of the heat, the dust. "Marco's brother was killed trying to cross the river. We brought him home."

"You're going back?" she said incredulously.

"Of course, the battle is just beginning there. To resist is to win." He clenched his fist. "We may lose five thousand, but they will lose four times that many."

They sat in silence around the kitchen table at nightfall. Jordi had bathed for the first time in months, changed into fresh clothes. His hair hung wild and dark to the collar of his white shirt, and where he had shaved his beard, his skin was a lighter caramel against the dark angles of his sunken cheeks. The child slept in his arms at the head of the table. At the opposite end, Vicente cleaned his nails with the tip of a knife.

"Would you like some wine, Jordi?" Freya asked, offering him the jug.

"I don't drink," he said. He looked at her, as if seeing her for the first time. "Your nurses are wonderful," he said to Freya. "So brave. They work in a train in a tunnel near the front, they work in caves near the river where you cannot stand up. It was dark where they tried to save Marco's brother. That is where my friend died, in a cave. An Englishwoman held his hand, right to the end."

"We never let a boy die alone," Freya said quietly.

"Then your nurses will hold a lot of dead men's hands in the next months." Vicente folded his arms and stared at his brother.

Jordi scraped back his chair, walked around to Rosa, and handed her the child. "It is time for me to go."

"So soon?" She looked up at him, her gaze pleading with him to stay.

"Be safe, little brother," Vicente said, without getting up from the table.

Jordi snatched up his jacket and marched toward the door. Rosa bundled the child into Macu's arms and ran after him.

"Wait," she cried out, running along the path after him. "You can't just leave."

"There is nothing here for me now."

She caught his arm, forced him to stop. "Jordi, I am here. Your child is here."

In the moonlight he looked younger to her again, the scars of the war softened on his face. "I thought you would wait."

"Surely you know, if it had just been me . . ." She took his face in her hands. "I love you. I love you," she said, over and over again, her lips brushing his. She held him close.

"If you loved me, you would never—" His voice caught, he tried to push her away, but Rosa clung to him.

"Vicente forced me to marry him."

"If he has hurt you, I'll kill him—" Jordi started back toward the house.

"No!" Rosa blocked his path, felt the lean muscles of his stomach flex beneath her palms. "No. He said the only way our child would be safe is if I married him. So I did." She waited for him to look at her. "I married him only for our child. Please, believe me."

"The thought of you, with him . . ."

"He does not have me." She took him in her arms again, held him tight. "Only you, Jordi. Only you." She felt him breathing hard, the beat of his heart against her face.

"Come, tomorrow, to Sagunto. We have a camp in the ruins. I will wait for you before I return to the front."

"Tomorrow?"

"Are you scared?"

"With you, never." She kissed him then, felt life rising up in her again.

The front door banged open, and they broke apart.

"Rosa," Vicente yelled from the house. "Come back inside."

She hesitated. Every fiber of her body told her to run with Jordi now, run and keep going. Then she saw Vicente had the child in his arms. On the street she could hear Marco's mother crying, begging him to stay. She lowered her voice. "I will come, tomorrow."

Jordi leaned down, whispered in her ear. "Better the lover of a hero than a coward's wife."

"Come with me," he said. Jordi held Rosa close to him beneath the rough blanket, her cheek against his smooth chest. She felt his heart steadying as they lay, limbs entwined, sated. Beneath them, in the moonlight, the ruins of Sagunto slept.

"I can't, you know I can't." She buried her face in his neck. "If I go with you, he will never rest. He will come after me, and I can't leave our child."

"I won't let you do this." He cupped her face in his hand.

"It's the only way, for now." As her gaze searched his face, her eyes filled with tears. "I love you, Jordi. I will always love you."

"I'd rather die than be without you." Jordi screwed his eyes shut. "Promise me, if I don't come back, you will never love him." His voice broke, and when she looked at him, she suddenly saw him for the boy he still was. He was not a soldier, she was not the great dancer he had fallen for. They were just a boy and girl in love.

"Never."

"I can't bear it. My own brother, how could he . . ."

"He said he was doing the decent thing."

"Decent?" Jordi's voice was low, angry. "I should kill him. I trusted him. It was always the same, when I was a child. If I made something, he would break it."

"He can't touch us," she said. She lifted his hand to her heart. "When it is safe, send word to me, and I will come to you."

"What about the child?"

"If I can, I will bring her. If not . . ." Rosa's voice trailed away. "Children are being sent to safety all the time. Freya tells me she is being sent home soon. She will go to a hospital at the border. If I have to, I will take Loulou there." Her chest tightened as she thought of being separated from her child. She forced down her tears. "There is no good here, for her now. If we lose the war, no child of ours will be safe."

"Can you trust the Englishwoman?"

Rosa looked at him. "Yes. Yes, I can. Freya will take care of her until we are free. We can escape, together. There's still time."

He reached between her breasts. In the firelight, the gold locket swung from a fine gold chain.

"See?" she said. "I wore it tonight. Me and you. I will always be with you." He kissed her eyes as she began to cry, her lashes darkening into points. "Always."

"We will leave in a few days, go north. We will fight to the end."

"If we only have days, we must make them last a lifetime."

He leaned down and kissed her breastbone near the locket as she lay back on the earth. "I love you, Rosa," he murmured as he fell into an exhausted sleep.

Rosa lay awake all night, into the cold gray dawn. She did not want to miss a moment with him. She thought of the Lorca poem that Freya had read to her, and she understood as she looked at Jordi, his skin dark against the earth. *We are the same,* she thought, *we are all of this earth.* She stroked his sleeping face, remembered Jordi's words: *"We have hours, not years together, perhaps—but they are full hours, full of you, and me, and our love."* He rolled over in his sleep, his muscles twitching from exertion. She breathed in the scent of crushed pine branches beneath them, and her face stilled as she remembered what else he had said. *"I face death head on. I am not afraid anymore, now I have you in my arms again."*

FORTY

Freya swirled her brush in white spirit, wiped the bristles clean. *Woman's Hour* was on the radio, and she listened to the discussion about Afghanistan as she sorted through the tubes of oil paint at her side. She squeezed a bright, ultramarine blue onto her glass palette, and turned to the large canvas on her easel.

Charles tapped on the door. "Do you want anything from Waitrose? I'm just popping out for a paper." He shuffled over to her, peered down his nose through his half-moon glasses. "Oh, I like that. It's coming on really well." He laid his hand on her shoulder.

"Thank you." Freya tilted her head, looked at the mountainous landscape taking shape on the canvas. "I haven't felt like painting Spain for years."

"I remember that view," he said. "It was from your room, in the villa, wasn't it?"

"I'm surprised you remember the view." Freya raised an eyebrow. "As I recall, the view was the last thing on your mind when you were recovering in that room." She patted Charles's hand. "Can you get a couple of yellow peppers? I thought I'd make gazpacho tonight."

Charles buttoned up his winter coat, tucked the empty sleeve in. "Any word from Em?"

"She's fine. A few contractions," Freya said. "It won't be long now."

"Good." Charles hesitated by the door, looked at the dog-eared photograph of Rosa with Liberty as a baby that Freya had recently framed and hung on the wall. "I remember taking that."

"It feels like yesterday."

"You know she's going to want to know the whole story, don't you?"

Freya's brush hovered over the canvas. "I know. It's time she knew." She thought of the mountains, the luminous light. She flexed her hand and winced.

"Rheumatism playing up?"

Freya nodded. "I think it was washing all those sheets in freezing streams. I've never been the same since Spain."

"You want to go back, don't you?"

"Could we?" She turned to him.

"I don't know."

"Think of the baby, Charles. We could help Emma."

"Get under her feet more like." He coughed, caught his breath.

"She has no idea what to expect, how exhausted you are at first. Do you remember Libby, with Em?" Her eyes took on a softness. "She didn't think she needed us either, but she didn't have a clue, bless her."

"Liberty never thought she needed anyone, always charging through life trying to control everything. Look at that box of letters she left for Em. She couldn't let go even from beyond the grave."

"I think they are bringing Emma some comfort."

Charles laughed through his nose. "Lord knows what words of wisdom she's doling out. She was always a willful girl."

"She was that." Freya sat back and looked at her painting. "Maybe I tried too hard to protect her."

"Libby loved you. She soon came running once she was knocked up and Mr. Free Love didn't want to know. You put her back together again, just like you always did." Charles raised his chin. "We did our best for her. I'd do the same again in a heartbeat."

"Same here." Freya picked up her walking stick. She shuffled over to Charles, smoothed down his collar. "No regrets?"

"Regret is a useless emotion."

Freya thought of the nights she had found him, head slumped on his desk, surrounded by photographs of Hugo and their friends. "It's time, Charles. Think about Spain, at least."

"Spain? I think of little else."

She kissed his dry, wrinkled cheek. "You and me both."

FORTY-ONE

BARCELONA ROAD, JANUARY 1939

Well, we made it. The last of the last-ditchers, eh?" Charles rolled his head toward Hugo as the planes dove down toward them again. "Who would have thought it, a couple of cherry boys like us, staying at the Hotel Florida with Hemingway and Capa . . ."

His voice was drowned out by the "rat-tat-tat" of machine guns, the frenzy of feet and screams from the road. Four hundred thousand people snaking along the road toward the French border, diving for cover like a column of dominoes, falling.

Through tear-filled eyes he watched as children with bloody rags tied around their arms and feet struggled by, crying from pain and hunger. Some clung to their parents. Many were alone. Across from him huddled a woman with a newborn child at her exposed breast. Next to her, an old woman who had given up hope lay down by the side of the road to wait for death. The people on the road stepped aside, pulled their donkeys and mules to the verge as trucks thundered past, taking the Prado's Goyas, El Grecos, and Velázquezs to safety.

"Look at that, Hugo. They're saving the bloody paintings, but what about these poor people, eh?" Charles's voice trembled with shock. "Do you remember what we said in Barcelona, Hugo? When La Pasionaria told the Brigaders that we could go proudly?" His throat tightened at the memory of the Brigades marching one last time through the streets as flowers rained down. "We said we couldn't leave these people. We'd stay, join up with the Republican troops. 'Together to the end,' that's what you said. Well it is the end. It's over, Hugo." Charles cowered in the ditch beside the Barcelona road as the planes swooped low again. He screwed up his eyes as he heard the planes come closer, closer again. The last wave had caught them. He had been running at Hugo's side, saw the plane bank down, head directly at them. The line of people ahead of them parted like a dark tide, bodies and carts lurching to the side of the road, screams mingling with the metallic "rat-tat-tat" of the machine guns, bullets weaving a deathly path through them.

"Over here!" Hugo had cried, dragging Charles toward a shallow ditch.

"Wait!" Charles spotted a small boy of two or three over his shoulder. The child was standing in the middle of the road, wailing, openmouthed with distress, separated from his mother. A woman was running up the road toward him, screaming. Charles ran back, Hugo at his heels. The plane was so close now, he could feel the thud, the vibration of the bullets hitting the earth. Charles grabbed the child, and Hugo dragged the woman to safety, diving for the ditch too late as the planes swept over and the bullets found them.

The mother and child sheltered next to him now, rocking in silence, pale with shock. The woman could not look at Charles. He remembered landing in the ditch, the thud of the earth against his chest, a seeping wetness through his coat from the slush and mud. He remembered Hugo, falling on top of him. "It's over," he mumbled. His words slurred as he slipped in and out of consciousness. A numb, throbbing pain began to register in his left arm. He tried to move it, and found he could not. "This was our war, wasn't it? Hugo? Such a picturesque war—a savage, bloody mess, but god the country . . . so glorious. And the women . . . I miss women, Hugo. God muddled with men, but the women he got right. Is there anything so perfect?" He drifted for a moment, the image of Macu's face floated to the surface as darkness descended on him. He felt like he was underwater, the sound of the assault raging around him muffled and far away.

"Home," Charles mumbled as he returned to consciousness, the throbbing in his arm making him wince as he tried to move. "I want to go home . . . to my butterflies. They are wonderful. God was having a good day when he invented butterflies . . ." His eyes rolled. "I think perhaps it's possible to know the truth of the world to be ghastly, and yet still see the wonder in being alive. What do you think, Hugo?"

"This one's alive!" he heard someone call. Then the scramble of feet.

"How will they report this one, eh, Hugo?" he said. "What to do when you and I have seen so much, and seen the truth, and they tell something different? I hope to God this is the end of it. Imagine a world built on lies, and nonsense . . . is that what we have fought for?"

"Wait! I know him," a man shouted from the road. "Get a stretcher over here!"

Charles felt someone reaching down to him, dragging something away at his side. Pain, sudden and sickening flooded in from Charles's arm.

"It's time, Charlie," Capa said.

"Wait . . ." Charles mumbled, delirious with pain. "Hugo . . ."

"He's gone, Charlie." Capa leaned over him. "I've been looking all over for you."

Charles glanced at Hugo, gulped back a sob. "I got the shot, Capa."

Capa looked into Charles's eyes, compassion on his face. "I think this time, Charlie, you got too close." He helped the ambulance driver heave him onto the stretcher. "Let's get you out of here. I'll see you in France."

"Yes . . . France." Lights danced before Charles's eyes. "Wait . . ."

Capa turned. Charles tried to unhook his camera, and he helped him. "Would you like me to send the film on to your newspaper?"

"Yes. Then take it. I have no use for it now."

"I can't . . ."

"No, really. I'd like you to have it. It's a Contax. Should have bought a car, like Hugo said."

"Thank you." Capa squeezed his right hand.

"Take extraordinary pictures with it. Show the world."

The medic tucked Charles in on the stretcher, gently covering his bullet-shattered left arm. "Come on, laddie, let's get you out of here."

Charles's head rolled to the side as he was lifted away, and he gazed for the last time into Hugo's unseeing eyes.

FORTY-TWO

After walking the length of the village, Emma was out of breath. She dipped her hand in the fountain near the church, cooled her wrists. Doves swooped down into the square, white against the ocher paintwork and the dazzling blue sky, already streaked with the gold of sunset. She sat down on the low white wall, and rummaged through her basket for a bottle of water. She sipped at it, and wiped her lips. From the basket, she took the picture she had just picked up from the framer's. The gilding gleamed in the evening sun as she tore back the bubble wrap. The photographs of Rosa and Jordi were mounted together now, safe behind glass.

"Who were you?" Emma said quietly. She gazed at Jordi's face, so proud and strong, and Rosa. Emma looked up as an elegantly dressed woman emerged through the church door. The woman turned to talk to a waiter at the café next door, and Emma waved as she recognized Macu. She wore a white silk shirt beneath her winter coat, loose dark wool trousers, and loafers. As Emma swung her bag over her shoulder and began to walk toward her, Macu's eyes opened wide in surprise.

"What are you doing out here in the cold? You should be resting before the baby comes."

"I'm so bored, sitting around the house." Emma kissed her. "I just walked to the framer to pick this up."

"These are the photographs that you found?"

Emma realized Macu wasn't looking at her, she was looking at the locket. "Yes. They were under the floorboards, in the house."

She looked Emma in the eye finally. "I was hoping I would bump into you. Let's get a drink," she said, and they walked arm in arm to the café, her cane tapping against the pavement.

They sat at a table near the counter, and Macu sipped at her cognac before reaching for her handbag. She slid an envelope across the table to Emma. "I wanted you to have this. You'll have to get another frame."

The sounds of the café, the hiss of the coffee machine, the chatter of the customers seemed to fall away as Emma lifted open the flap. Inside, there was a photograph. She recognized Rosa immediately. "When was this taken?"

"The autumn of 1937. Not long after Loulou was born."

"The baby?" Emma gazed at the battered photo. Rosa sat in the garden of the Villa del Valle, a child in her arms.

"Oh, Emma," Macu said, taking her hand. "Look at Rosa closely, do you not see?"

Emma squinted, searched the grainy image of Rosa's face. Then she saw it. "The locket," she said. Her hand flew to her neck. "She's wearing my locket."

Macu touched Emma's hand, her face full of compassion. "Jordi gave it to your grandmother."

"To Freya?"

"No, *cariño,* he gave it to Rosa."

FORTY-THREE

Oleander, jacaranda, oleander, jacaranda . . . Freya thought as she strolled up the hill to the Villa del Valle, running her hand along the railings. Glossy dark leaves waited for the brilliant pink and white flowers to come. The light was falling, and as she reached the wall of the villa, Freya sighed wearily. It was to be her last night in the house, and her bags were already packed, ready to leave for the Spanish hospital on the border. The thought of all that lay ahead, the desperate plight of the refugees, of gray, rainy London, depressed her. She was going to miss Spain, in spite of all she had lived through. She noticed a chink of light coming from Vicente's shop, and heard the sound of male voices talking low and fast. She glanced around the street to check she was alone, and sidled over to the door.

"It's over," a man said. She could hear the arrogance, the boastfulness in his voice. "The Reds are fleeing like rats. Soon Madrid and Valencia will fall."

"And we will be ready to welcome the great generalissimo." Freya recognized Vicente's voice. "Our time is coming, my friend."

"I'll be fine," Rosa had said when Freya had told her that afternoon it was time for her to leave. Behind her defiance, Freya sensed her uncertainty. Rosa stroked the child's head as she slept in her arms, a tiny hand grasping the lace at the collar of her blouse. "Would you mind giving me some water?" Freya took the beaded net from the pitcher and poured a glass for her. "Thank you," she said. She felt Freya watching her. "Really, I'll be fine."

Freya looked her in the eye. "This . . ." She indicated the scar on Rosa's cheekbone. "It will get worse, you know."

Rosa turned her head to the fire, stared into the flames. "He hasn't hit me since. He was angry that I disappeared. I told him I was with Macu, helping with her wedding trousseau, but he didn't believe me. He would kill me if he knew I had been with Jordi. Vicente has promised . . ." She frowned as Freya snorted with disbelief.

"Vicente is a thug, a bully."

And now, Freya thought, *it turns out he's Fifth Column. I must warn Rosa.*

"What have we here?" A strong hand shot from the shadows of the alleyway, gripped Freya's arm, dragged her into the shop. "Look, Vicente, these Red nurses are making house calls now." The man threw her forward toward the counter, blocked the door.

Vicente had his back to her, arranging his knives on the wooden board. Freya recognized the man at his side from the village. There was a plate of almonds and Manchego cheese on the counter, and the man was chewing, dark eyes watching her. The muscles beneath Vicente's tight white shirt rippled as he turned to Freya, the knives gleaming in the light of the oil lamp. "Well. I hear you are leaving us?"

"Yes, that's right." Freya pulled herself up to her full height. Her heart was thundering.

"She was listening outside," the man said from the doorway.

Vicente clicked his tongue. "Silly girl. What did you hear?"

"Nothing. I heard nothing. I just came to say good-bye."

He stepped toward her, slowly. His nostrils flared, sniffing the air. "You know, when you fight the bulls you learn to smell fear."

"Fear?" She glared at him. "Why would I be afraid of you?"

"You should be." The light caught the blade of a short knife Vicente still had in his hand.

"As I said, I came to say good-bye."

"You know, only liars tell the same story each time."

"I didn't hear—"

Vicente pushed her back against the counter, forced his thighs between her legs. She felt his breath, hot against her neck, and then the blade. "I think maybe before I kill you, we will have some fun."

The man by the door laughed. She heard the sound of the street door closing, the bolt sliding in.

"Please don't," Freya begged, struggling. He forced his tongue, thick and bitter with almonds, into her mouth. They held her down then, and Freya screwed her eyes closed and tried not to cry.

"Vicente!" Rosa rattled the back door of the shop. "Vicente!"

He grunted, turned his head to look at the door. Freya felt his weight shift, and she reared up, bit down hard on his ear. Vicente roared, stepped back, clutching the side of his head.

"Let me go," Freya said, her voice shaking, but firm. She pushed her skirt down. "Let me go now and I will tell no one. I'll leave, immediately." She raised her sleeve, wiped the blood from her split lip.

Vicente buttoned his trousers and nodded to the man by the counter to undo the door. Rosa marched into the shop with the child on her hip and looked in disgust at the men. She took Freya's arm and led her to the house. "I am so sorry. I saw," she whispered. "I saw in my head what he did to you."

"Rosa!" they heard Vicente bellow, not far behind.

"Come with me." Freya was shaking violently. "I can't leave you with that . . . that monster. The Medical Aid convoy is leaving tonight."

"No," Rosa said as they ran upstairs.

"But why?"

"Freya . . ." Rosa shook her head. She locked the bedroom door behind them. "I have nothing." She cradled Loulou's head. "This was Jordi's home, and it is hers."

"So you would stay here, for the sake of a house?" Freya said incredulously.

"It is more than that. You wouldn't understand. Her life will be different from mine. My child *tiene ángel*—she has grace." Rosa put her fingertips to the side of her head. "It is not just a house. I have seen it, seen that the future of our family is here. A woman of our blood will be here, long after that bastard Vicente is gone."

"How can you possibly trust him?" Her face contorted with disgust. "He could turn on you at any time, tell them you fought for the Republicans . . ."

"I know!" Rosa cried. "I know," she said, lowering her voice. "But I must wait for Jordi to come . . ." She hesitated. "I am pregnant again."

"Oh God, Rosa," Freya said. She rolled her eyes, and her shoulders sank. "I wondered why you were dressing like that. Hasn't he noticed?"

"Vicente? No, I am careful—it is like with Loulou, I didn't show much til the end with her either. He said I am getting fat and I agreed with him."

"Surely you could have taken precautions?"

"Precautions?" Rosa laughed bitterly. "It is Jordi's child, not Vicente's." She shifted the child on her hip. "It's not his, I know this. I tell him I have my period when I am most fertile. For a butcher he is very squeamish about blood if you see what I am saying. Other times he is too drunk to notice—I am careful, tell him he is such a big man he make me bleed a little . . ." She turned her pale, tired face to Freya.

"Rosa!" Vicente bellowed up the stairs.

"I'm coming!" she called. Freya followed her as she raced downstairs. In the doorway to the kitchen, she stopped dead. Vicente was on a chair, hanging a photograph of Franco above the fireplace. As he stepped down and turned, he looked at her, his eyes narrowed in defiance. Blood caked his wounded ear.

"There, everything will soon be as it should." He put his arm around Rosa, pulled her roughly to him. "Barcelona has already fallen, and we are ready, for when they come. I'd like to say I will miss you . . ." he said to Freya.

"But you can't?"

"It's only because you are a friend of Rosa's that I do not kill you now."

"You can't scare me," Freya said quietly, walking over to him. Rosa's eyes warned her off. "I'm a nurse, not a soldier."

"How do we know that, eh?" He sneered. "You could be a spy. We have ways of finding out, you know."

"You'd like that, wouldn't you?" she goaded him. "Do you get a kick out of hurting women, Vicente? Is it more fun than taunting bulls?"

"Why you . . . !" He raised his hand.

"*Señor!*" Macu interrupted. She strode through the door, carrying a huge pan of steaming paella from the oven outside. Beyond her, in the garden, the flames leaped, the orangewood gleaming, cracking, smoke rising.

"Vicente," Rosa said. "We must eat."

"To hell with that." He kicked out, knocked the paella pan to the floor. Saffron-tinted rice scattered, and Macu fell to her knees, cowering.

Vicente turned on Freya. "Look at you," he hissed, his face close to hers. "What man would want you? Skinny whore . . ."

"Vicente!" Rosa pulled at his arm. He swung around with his free arm, knocked her against the counter.

"Get off me, woman. You are no better."

Rosa doubled over, panting.

"You animal!" Freya cried. "How can you hit her when she is carrying a child—" The words died on her lips as Rosa looked at her frantically.

A sly look crept over Vicente's face. "Is this true?" He pulled Rosa to him, crushed his lips against hers. "Ha!" His chest puffed out, his head slanting back with the arrogance of the matador. "Now you really are mine," he murmured. Loulou began to cry.

"I must see to her," Rosa said.

"Leave her," Vicente said. "Leave the little bastard." He grabbed her wrist as she started to walk away. Rosa flinched.

"You're hurting her!" Freya cried.

"This?" He leered. "This is just the beginning." His knuckles were white as he squeezed her arm. "Every day, you will pay . . . and when she is old enough"—his mouth twisted cruelly—"then she will pay too."

The bile rose in Freya's mouth. "No," she said. "I won't let you."

"You?" He pushed Rosa aside. "What can you do? You are nothing. Get out of here." He picked up Freya's suitcase, threw it out onto the path. "I do what I want." He leered. "This is my house."

"It is the del Valles' house—Jordi's as much as yours by right," Rosa said quietly. She stepped forward, hugged Freya. "I am sorry. So sorry, for what he did to you. Forget it. Forget all of us."

"No." Freya screwed her eyes closed, hugged Rosa tightly. "I will never forget you, and Loulou. I'll wait for you. There is a hospital at Cerbère, that's where I'll be," she whispered. "I'll wait for you."

FORTY-FOUR

Macu settled back in her chair, cupped her empty glass with her hands. Beyond the café windows, the lights of the village square sparkled like jewels in the night. "That is the last time I saw Freya."

Emma sat with her head in her hands. "I had no idea."

Macu looked tired to Emma. She seemed to be far away in her thoughts. "She was a good woman, a brave woman. I understand why she spared you all this."

"Poor, poor Freya. I still don't understand how she and Mum escaped. What happened to Rosa?"

"She ended up in Mexico."

Emma's eyes widened in surprise. "Mexico?"

"I have no idea about Freya and your mother's story, you will have to ask her, but in prison I asked Rosa—" Macu glanced at her watch as they heard Dolores's voice on the street. "I will tell you another time. My daughter has come to pick me up now."

"But wait, why was Rosa in Mexico?" Emma's mind whirled with questions as Macu heaved herself to her feet.

"She cared for the refugee children there, taught them to read and write." Macu paused. "She died in a nunnery. She was not old."

Emma looked down at the photograph of Rosa and Liberty. "A nunnery? I thought Republicans didn't believe in the Church?"

"The Church supported Franco, and many Republicans were atheists, but it was a big mistake taking on God. Simple, working people like Rosa and me grew up with God's love in our hearts. We could not let go." Macu looked at Emma. "When Rosa lost her faith in man, maybe . . ." She paused. "Maybe God was all she had to turn to."

"Mamá!" Dolores bustled through the café. "Why are you here?" She glanced at Emma and grudgingly nodded.

"I was talking to Emma. I was telling her about her family."

"I'm sorry," Emma said as Dolores scowled. "It's getting late for you."

"We will talk another time." Macu patted her hand.

"Please, there's still so much I don't understand. Tell me what happened when Valencia fell."

"It was a bad time, a very bad time. When Catalonia fell, and Madrid, and our own Valencia . . ." Macu took a deep breath. "I remember it like yesterday. It was cold, but sunny. As the tanks rolled into town, I remember the sun glinting on the Nationalists' bayonets. There were thousands running ahead of them, trying to get away." She paused. "Those who stayed welcomed Franco. There was no choice."

"Macu, did you stay?"

"Me? Yes, I stayed. I married Ignacio shortly before the Nationalists arrived."

"And Jordi, what about him?"

"I don't know. Jordi came back from the front, just as he had promised." Macu hesitated. "But Rosa had gone north with the child, your mother, to take her to Freya. I heard Jordi and his brother arguing one night in the kitchen. Vicente said he would make sure he and his comrades got away safely if he left Vicente and Rosa in peace. If not, he would betray them to the Nationalists."

"I don't understand. I thought Vicente was just a butcher . . ."

"A butcher? Ha! He was that all right. He was Fifth Column, the enemy within. All along he had been for the fascists. All along."

"What happened?"

"Stop it." Dolores took her mother's arm, whispered in her ear. "For the love of God, stop. What good can come of this, of digging up the past?" She glared at Emma, said clearly, "We have to go. Now."

Macu stepped awkwardly from the table, the chair scraping on the terrazzo floor. "I can't talk about this now. My daughter, she is bossing me around."

"Wait! You said you spoke to Rosa in prison?"

Macu spoke quickly, angrily to her daughter. "Yes," she said to Emma. "Yes, I saw Rosa." She paused. "I was with her in prison. I will come and see you soon. I will tell you everything I know." She took Emma's hand. "I understand why Freya didn't want to talk about this. After what that *hijo de puta* did to her before she left for the border . . ."

"Mamá!" Dolores cried.

Macu embraced Emma. "Before we talk more, call Freya. She is a good woman. Do not blame her for hiding all this from you."

FORTY-FIVE

Still they came. For weeks the refugees had poured down from the Pyrenees to the French border, an endless stream of gray, broken figures materializing like spirits from the mist and the sleet, huddled in blankets, stooped by the cold wind blowing in from the sea. Freya did what she could for them as they passed through. She exchanged bread for the guns that the soldiers dropped at the border. She wrapped blankets around the shoulders of shivering mothers clutching silent, dark-eyed children in their arms. She bathed their cold and bleeding feet with freezing water from the stream. And she waited, day after day, for that one precious face among the masses; she waited for Rosa.

As she walked along the corridor of the old château they were using as a field hospital, the sole of her shoe flapped. She had gone forty-eight hours without sleep, and the babble of voices seemed muffled to her. She pressed her hand against the cold stone wall, swayed slightly. She hesitated by the hall, searched the crowd in case she had missed her. People clustered around the great stone fireplace, spooning thin soup from tin cups into their mouths. A father held his young child closer to the crackling brushfire, trying to warm her feet, his hand dark and rough against the pale skin of her calf. Everywhere that smell, that awful smell that she thought would never leave her skin, her memory. The smell of blood, and filth, and smoke—the smell of defeat. As she blinked, she felt the world falling away, the corridor shifting around her.

"I hope you're on your way to bed, Nurse?"

Freya turned to the woman who had spoken. "Yes, Sister . . . I . . ."

"You're exhausted," she said. "You're no good to me in the theater if you don't get some rest."

"But . . ."

"I know you're worried about your friend, but you can't spend every waking moment looking for her."

Freya nodded, stumbled to the dormitory. Another nurse was dressing, the paraffin lamp illuminating the cathedral arch of her rib cage as she pulled a white vest over her head. Freya's old gramophone played quietly, a Casals cello suite bubbling from the shadows.

"I hope you don't mind?" the girl said. "I just couldn't bear the silence."

Freya collapsed on her bed fully clothed. "It's funny, isn't it," she murmured, "how used you become to the noise." Her eyes drooped. "Mimi?"

"Mm?" The girl turned, hairpins in her mouth as she fastened dark tendrils of hair.

"You'll wake me, if you see her? She has a child, a baby with her."

"Show me the picture of them again." She took the dog-eared black-and-white photograph of Rosa in the garden with the baby. "Who is she? A friend?"

"They are more like family, to me," Freya said, and as her eyes closed she knew that was true.

At dawn, fists pounding on the door woke Freya. Her dreams were of dazzling color—running through the orange groves with Tom, her hand trailing against blossoms, the scent of neroli on the blue, blue air. Her peaceful expression faltered as she came to. "Yes? Come in." She forced herself up.

"Mimi sent me," the boy said. "Your friend—"

Freya raced past him, the worn leather of her shoes slipping on the steps. She ran outside, snow falling in the pale light beyond the cover of the stone arcades, muffling her pounding feet. She ran past a young mother, her baby at her breast, an old woman sheltering them from the wind with a patched blanket. Across the mountainsides, a chain of campfires flickered bravely. There, at the border, she saw a huddled figure. "Rosa!" she cried out. The woman looked up.

"I have found you . . ." Rosa shook her head as they embraced, careful not to crush the child strapped to her chest.

"You're alive. Thank God, you're alive. How is she?" Freya stroked the sleeping child's head, her thatch of dark hair like spun silk beneath her fingertips.

"Cold, but well," Rosa said. "We managed to get a lift in a truck most of the way here."

"Come." Freya took Rosa's papers from the guard. "We'll get you blankets, something to eat." Rosa began to untie the sling from around her neck. "Rosa?" As she saw the sudden grief on her friend's face, Freya felt nauseated. "No . . ."

"I am going now." Rosa blinked back tears as she looked at her daughter's face. "I only brought her to you. I must find Jordi. If he is alive . . ."

"No," Freya pleaded. "If he's alive, he can take care of himself. Think of your baby . . ."

"I am thinking of her. How can I let her think her mother just left her father behind? Negrín demanded that Franco make no reprisals, but we cannot trust that man."

"I know. But what if they catch you?"

"What more can they do to me?" She breathed in the scent of her baby, pressed her lips to her head. "Be safe, *cariño*," she whispered, and handed the child to Freya.

"Please don't. I can't . . ."

Rosa shook her head. "You told me, you would do anything for me. Well, I have nothing." She pounded her fist in her palm. "They took everything from me, my home, my life, my love. All I have is my child."

"Please stay. I've been posted to the maternity hospital at Elne, you'll be safe there, you can help me until the baby comes . . ."

"No. Promise me you will take her away from here. Go, soon. Never let them catch her. Take her to England with you."

"I can't! I'm not married, I . . ." Freya could see tears welling in Rosa's defiant eyes.

"You must! This is why I came. You told me, you would help us . . ."

"I meant both of you—there are boats leaving for Mexico. You could have a new life. You can't just abandon her."

"Abandon?" she snapped. "I love this child more than life, so I brought her to you." Rosa wiped at her cheek. "You were there as she was born. I trust no one but you with her."

"Don't go." Freya shook as she thought of Vicente. "You mustn't go back to that house, to him."

"I have no choice." Rosa's voice broke. "For Jordi, I have no choice."

Freya held her gaze, then screwed her eyes shut tight, and nodded.

"Thank you." Rosa unclipped the locket from around her neck, flicked open the catch. She slipped the photographs of her and Jordi into her pocket, then pressed the necklace into Freya's hand. "This is all I have for her." Tenderly, Rosa held her child's head in her hands. She whispered to her, a blessing, a last good-bye. She pressed her lips to her forehead, tears trickling into the child's downy hair. "Be safe," she said. She glanced up at Freya. "Keep her safe. Give her a new name, a new life." Rosa tore herself away, stumbled as she began to push through the stream of refugees.

"A new name?" Freya called. "But what? What shall I call her?"

Rosa paused. "*Libertad*. Call her Liberty." She raised her fist, and turned back to Spain.

Freya watched her solitary figure disappearing into the snow and the mist as thousands upon thousands walked toward her. The child stirred. Freya looked down, pulled away the covers as the child stared at her, reached up, encircled her finger with a strong, fragile hand. "Hello, Liberty," she said.

FORTY-SIX

Luca leaned against the kitchen table, his arms folded across his chest. "How are you?"

"I'm . . . I'm fine." Emma's eyes were red and puffy. "I just didn't sleep very well last night, after I spoke with Freya."

"Macu told me she spoke to you. She's worried about you." Luca waited for her to look at him. "I'm worried about you."

Emma blinked away fresh tears. "She told me. Freya told me how Rosa left Mum at the French border with her." She put her arm around her stomach protectively. "How could anyone do that? How could you leave your child?"

"They were terrible times. Macu can maybe help you understand. She is coming here after the market. She wants to explain everything." Luca settled back. "Were you working?" He nodded toward the notebooks scattered across the counter, the chemical formulas and diagrams.

"Just experimenting, trying to distract myself." Emma pointed at the old recipe book on the table. "I think it was Rosa's. I thought at first it was a cookbook, but when I started looking through they seem to be instructions."

"They look like spells," Luca said, laughing uneasily. "Maybe she was a healer? These must be recipes for simples. You should ask my grandmother."

He paused at a page with a drawing of a flowering plant. "I hope you are not making this?"

Emma peered over his shoulder. "Poison? What plant is that?"

"Oleander. You have to be careful with it."

She stirred the pestle and mortar. "No poisons today," she said. "Just a mint massage oil for tired feet. Mine are killing me."

His face softened. "It gets better, after the baby comes. I remember . . ." Luca paused. "Paloma was tired too." He rolled up his sleeves. "Here, let me try for you."

Emma blushed. "No, I couldn't . . ."

"It's fine. Macu will be a while."

Luca guided her to the old armchair by the fire, and pulled over a stool. He draped a towel over his knee and lifted her foot onto his lap. Emma wiggled her foot out of its sheepskin Ugg boot. "No Wellies today?" he said as he eased her foot free.

"No, too cold. Oh, that feels good." Emma's head fell back against the chair as warm oil dribbled between her toes.

"Soon you will feel like you are walking on air." He cupped her foot in his hands. "It will all be OK, you know."

"Do you think so?"

"It is a big shock, I imagine?"

"I don't know who I am anymore." Emma frowned as she thought of her conversation with Freya, how upset she had been. "I feel terrible, I think I took it out on my grandmother . . . on Freya." She paused. "I can't believe she lied to us all these years."

"Perhaps she was protecting you the best way she knew how?"

FORTY-SEVEN

VALENCIA, MARCH 1939

Rosa ran, her breath catching fast in her throat, a sharp pain in her side. The truck had dropped her on the back road, and she ran through the orange groves as fast as she could, an electrical storm chasing down from the mountains, lightning forking up into the charged air. The rusted back gate of the Villa del Valle banged in the wind, and she wrenched it open, gasping.

"Thank God, you are here! They are going to kill each other!" Macu ran to her.

"Who?"

"Jordi and Vicente, come quickly." The girls ran toward the house. "Jordi just showed up. Vicente went crazy." Macu caught her breath. "The Nationalists are having a victory party in town. He expects you to dance."

"To dance? He's mad!" Rosa flung open the terrace door. The kitchen was in chaos, chairs upturned, plates and glasses smashed across the floor. "Stop it!" she screamed as Vicente lunged at Jordi again, wrestling him to the floor. She tore at his shirt, dragging him away. Vicente swung at her.

"No!" Macu yelled. "Think of the baby." The brothers held fast to each other, breathless.

"Get out of here," Vicente said, turning to Macu. "Ignacio is waiting for you." As he looked away, Rosa touched her stomach briefly, and nodded, holding Jordi's gaze. *Yours,* she mouthed.

"Rosa," Jordi said, starting toward her, but Vicente tightened his grip on his shoulder, pinning him down.

"Where have you been?" Vicente said to her.

"Where do you think? I took my child," she said, looking at Jordi, "our child to safety."

"Good riddance," Vicente said.

Jordi cried out, used all his strength to push Vicente away. He struggled to his feet, wiped at his bloodied lip with the back of his hand.

"I came back for you," Jordi said, glancing at Rosa. "Come with me now."

"I don't think so." Vicente grabbed her by the wrist, pulled her to his side. "You see, Rosa is having a child, little brother. My child. If she stays with me, I will let you go free."

"I will not leave Rosa."

"What choice do you have?" Vicente sneered. "I'll arrange for a boat to come to the beach we used to go to as children near the Albufera in a few hours' time. They will take you and Marco to safety. If you stay, now that Valencia has fallen to our great general, you will be rounded up and shot like all the rest."

"Why are you helping me?" Jordi squared up to him.

"I want you gone, for good."

"No. I won't go," Jordi said to Rosa.

"You can, and you will." She wrenched her arm from Vicente's grip, and took Jordi by the hand, leading him toward the terrace.

"Farewell, little brother," Vicente called.

"I'll see you in hell!" Jordi glared at him.

"Leave him," Rosa said under her breath, dragging Jordi into the garden. "Where is Marco?"

"Saying farewell to his mother."

"They will take her too, there is no one to protect her—"

"Not like you? You have the great Vicente, Fifth Column bastard—"

"Stop it. There is no time for this." She held Jordi's face in her hands. "There is no time for us. The reprisals are beginning already. You have to leave, now. Our daughter is safe with Freya, and I will do all I can to keep our baby safe too. Forget about Vicente, I will take care of him once you are safely away. I'll find you, Jordi." Their kiss was urgent, filled with all there was no time to say.

"I love you, Rosa." He glanced up at the sound of a low whistle from the dark orange groves. "That is Marco."

"Go," she urged him, her voice breaking. "Go safe, my love."

As the candle guttered, her reflection in the mirror darkened. Rosa watched herself disappear. She twisted the gold tube of lipstick, scraped the last crimson traces out with her thumbnail and rubbed them slowly across her mouth, a split in her nail catching at her lip. She traced the scratch with her tongue as the light died. Her hand shook as she placed the lipstick on the dressing table, the metal clicking on the glass. She thought of the day she had bought it in Madrid—her first and last luxury, how it had made her feel like a woman. *The great Rosa Montez, muse of Lorca, the greatest dancer in all of Andalusia,* she thought. *Who am I now? Nobody. A shadow.* In silhouette against the light from the hall, as she pinned up her hair, she saw the familiar shape of her profile, arms, breasts, the dark sheen of her red dress, but her heart, her soul had gone. She screwed up her eyes, wished herself gone, wished she was with Jordi. She picked up the tall tortoiseshell *mantilla* comb, and eased it into her hair. The teeth dug into her skin, pulled taught against her scalp. In silhouette she looked like a queen.

"Rosa!" Vicente yelled from downstairs.

There was still time to run. Her fingers instinctively searched for the gold filigree locket around her neck. It had gone. Rosa opened the windows wide, looked out across the garden she had grown to love. She reached into the pocket of the old black dress she had been wearing earlier, pulled out the photographs of Jordi and her. She had looked at the camera with a passion and defiance she felt no trace of now. This was the only picture she had of him. Jordi smiling, his eyes dancing, full of love. She smoothed it with her thumb, remembered how it had felt to run her fingers through the warm dark curls that hung down to his shoulders, remembered how his eyelashes had brushed her jaw as he kissed her neck. *I love you,* she thought. *I will always love you.* She did not know what to do with the photographs now they were not safely in the locket. Vicente would destroy them. She crouched down, searching for a crack in the floorboards. She remembered the loose board by the bed in her room, and ran through the house silently. She stooped by the side of the bed and slipped them through, letting them fall softly into the darkness. She could rescue them later.

At the sound of her heels, clicking lightly on the staircase, Vicente turned. His irritation thawed as he walked toward her, desire pumping through his veins, molten and unstoppable. "Rosa, Rosa . . ." he whispered, caressing the gentle swell of her stomach through the full red skirt of the dress. "Just in time. The general has sent a car," he said proudly. "Well? What do you think?" His hand swept over his new uniform.

"You look like a fascist pig."

He wavered, no longer the hero. But like all predators he smelled fear, and as he saw her eyes flicker uncertainly, his snapped back hungrily to hers. He was in charge now.

As they drove through the darkness toward the city, Rosa wondered, *Is this how it feels when you are on your last journey?* She thought of all the men who had "taken a walk" this way. They passed houses dark in the night where she was used to seeing warm light spilling out, the sound of music, voices. All gone. The people fled, or disappeared. The closer they came to the city, the stronger the smell of burning, of carnage.

"Close the window, Rosa, it's not—"

"No. I want to remember this."

At the first checkpoint, the car slowed. Soldiers checked their papers, scanned the passengers. Vicente leaned over. "Hurry up," he barked. "Move these people out of the way. The general is expecting us." Rosa saw the young soldier's eyes open in surprise.

"Yes, sir."

Rosa touched the cool glass as they passed streams of people pale with exhaustion and fear. Her heart beat harder—what if she saw him among them? What if Jordi hadn't made it to the coast in time?

The beautiful blue domes of the city gleamed in the half-light as they always had, the Turia river flowed on. But all around them, everything had changed. As they joined a convoy of military vehicles, Rosa saw a man being dragged from an apartment building, his wife clinging, screaming, to his leg. Soldiers bundled her back inside the courtyard, pushed back terrified children who hovered in the shadows of the doorway. As they drove by, Rosa craned her head, caught the woman's cries of "No, no, no!," saw a dark-uniformed soldier raise the butt of his rifle and bring it crashing down on the side of the man's head. He crumpled to the gutter. Rosa swore under her breath.

"This is just the beginning," Vicente said. "They are going to rout out the rot."

"Are you threatening me?"

"You, my dear?" He cupped her face. "No. You are mine. And Macu? Well, if your little friend keeps her head down then she will be safe with de Santangel too." He patted his pocket, pulled out a leather case. "Can't you drive any faster?" he said irritably to the driver as he lit a cigar.

"I'm sorry." The driver indicated the trucks and tanks ahead.

He checked his watch. "We will walk from here. Pull over."

"Are you sure it is safe, sir?"

"Are you questioning me?"

"No, sir." The driver looked straight ahead as he drove slowly to the side of the road.

Vicente walked around to Rosa's door. As he checked the street, she gazed at the holster at his waist. *I could shoot him,* part of her thought. She imagined them walking the backstreets to the palace, turning, kissing him, falling into the shadows of one of the patios—and then, a single shot. She saw herself running barefoot through the streets, taking a simple cotton shift from a washing line. She imagined walking through the night, hiding from patrols, then reaching the coast at dawn just as the boats arrived, racing down the beach to Jordi, embracing, laughing in the surf. Vicente opened the door, and she blinked, stepped mechanically from the car. She glanced around: four soldiers stepped out from a car behind them. Of course, they had an escort.

Glancing down the street, Vicente pulled his pistol ostentatiously from its holster, and took her arm. He guided her along the familiar backstreets and alleyways to the Palacio del Marqués de Dos Aguas. At this time of night, she thought, the cafés should be open, the children playing in the street with the little dogs racing and yapping as the parents sit talking under the stars, eating tapas and drinking. But the streets were eerily silent. The smell of burning hung heavily in the air. Shops and cafés were shuttered. All Rosa heard was the sound of the soldiers marching behind her, and her own breath catching in her throat.

"Is he safe?" she said quietly.

"Not now . . ."

She yanked her arm from his. "Is Jordi safe?"

His eyes hardened. "I made a deal, didn't I?"

"If I ever find out you betrayed him . . ."

"You'll what?"

Rosa stumbled deliberately, bent down to check her shoe. Slowly he squatted down beside her, the snout of his pistol grazing the cobbles. Without looking at him, she said quietly, "I will make you pay." She raised her eyes to his. "You have me now. You have my word. I am buying his freedom with my body. But you will never, ever have my soul."

Vicente clasped her wrist, hard. "Stupid woman." He leaned close to her. She felt his hot breath on her ear, smelled the scent of stale tobacco. "It's not your soul, or your heart, or your love—whatever it is that you prize so highly—that I've ever been interested in." She struggled, but he held her firm. "Tonight, and every night, you will be in my bed. I will make you forget my brother ever existed." Her stomach lurched with nausea as his gold teeth caught at her earlobe, his tongue traced the dip against her neck. "I have you. And you have our child." He released her, and she shivered as she stepped away.

"Are you cold?" he said, loud enough for the soldiers to hear.

She glanced back at them, shook her head. As they walked on, they passed a courtyard lit with flares. The heavy double doors were open and Rosa glimpsed Nationalist soldiers laughing and smoking around a fire, and beyond them, a body lay, bare and grimy feet emerging from the shadows of a wall scarred with bullet holes. She swallowed hard as Vicente slipped his arm around her waist, guided her to the street.

"You're a sensible woman, Rosa. You may think you are doing this for love, but my brother was a fool, a young fool. You're smarter than him. You're a survivor."

"No." She shook her head.

"Yes, you are." His fingers dug into her hip bone as he pulled her closer. "It's a new era, Rosa, and it pays to be on the winning side." His arm swept out across the city. "All of this will be ours. Our great city will rise again, and this time we will be in charge. We will have status, riches."

Rosa gazed up at the elaborate carvings of the palace door, the twisting bodies and writhing plasterwork like the icing on a demented wedding cake. Her stomach tightened with fear.

"What's this, del Valle?" An officer laughed. "No car?"

"It's a beautiful evening for a stroll with my wife."

"Your wife?" He eyed her with a mixture of curiosity and lust. "Congratulations. Where have you kept this beauty hidden?" He bowed low, kissed her hand

"A wise man keeps his treasure at home," Vicente said.

Rosa blinked as the doors swung open and they left the dark street behind. The light was dazzling, glittering from chandeliers, sparkling in the fountain as they crossed the tiled courtyard. She lifted the hem of her gown and they swept up the staircase to the state rooms, passing soldier after soldier.

"The general is in the *fumoir,*" the soldier said, leading them through to a side room. "Come, pay your respects." Rosa heard the sound of male voices, harsh laughter drifting out on the cigar smoke. She raised the back of her hands to her lips, inhaled the fresh scent of orange blossom.

"Say nothing unless you are spoken to," Vicente hissed as the noise swelled. The room made Rosa think of a chess set; everything was black and white— the tiled floor, the ebony furniture inlaid with ivory, the muted uniforms of the soldiers. There at the heart of the room sat the conquering general holding court. He glanced over as Vicente guided Rosa toward him.

"General." The officer clicked his heels. "May I introduce Vicente del Valle, and his wife. They were most helpful with the war effort from behind the lines."

Rosa flinched. It was unbearable to be included in Vicente's double-dealing.

The general eyed her as he flicked ash from his cigar into a marble ashtray at his side. "I was just wondering what had happened to our dancer."

Rosa glared at the man. She could see him coolly assessing her. He could tell, she knew it. He could tell she was descended from gypsies, that she was a Republican. She imagined them dragging Jordi from a side room, throwing him down on the floor before her, bloodied and broken. She saw herself clinging to him, kissing his dear face, unafraid of dying as long as they were together. Rosa raised her chin defiantly.

"My wife is a famous dancer, General." Vicente bowed low. "Of course Rosa would be delighted to dance for you."

"I must congratulate you, del Valle. It looks like you have tamed a wild one here. Very beautiful, but perhaps you should clip her wings? Pull her claws?" The men around him laughed indulgently. Rosa felt their ambition and desire ebb around her like black oil on water.

"Thank you, General." Vicente flushed with pleasure.

The general slowly exhaled a plume of gray smoke. "You will dance for us tonight."

"I will dance," Rosa said, "but for Spain."

The general's eyes narrowed at the slight. Vicente's palms grew clammy with sweat. It was over before it had begun. He could have risen through the ranks, earned untold riches—but this, he could tell from the expression on the men's faces, this would never be forgotten. They would be lucky if they were not soon "taken for a ride." Rosa swept out to the ballroom, where the women already sat at chairs arranged around the dance floor.

As she strode through the room, silence fell. Her heels clicked on the wooden floor. She scanned the faces, recognized many of them. Landowners' wives, bankers' wives, women she knew from the church and the market. Ordinary local women, showing their true colors now, she thought. Or were they just afraid, like everyone else? Their gazes followed her, some sad and fearful, others jealous and vicious, snapping at her as she walked. They were the ones who would betray their neighbors, even incriminate the innocent for old debts or slights. Then there, at the edge of the circle, she saw Macu. Don Ignacio de Santangel was helping her settle into a chair. He had not collaborated with the general, she knew, not joined the Nationalists, like Vicente, but he had kept his head down and enough of his wealth would survive. The men and soldiers filed in behind Rosa like a black stream, flowing in to join the women until the room was full. As the general took his seat, Rosa noticed Vicente had been taken aside, guided to a chair farther away. *Good,* she thought, *it has begun.* She glanced at Vicente's wounded, furious face, and knew she would be punished that night. *Do what you will. I am stronger than you. You will never break me. I will buy time for Jordi, and then I will be free.*

Rosa paced, center stage, eyes closed, barely listening as someone introduced her, told the crowd that there would be an addition to the program tonight. Beneath her, she could hear a guitarist tuning up. The notes drifted to her through vents in the ballroom floor, from a hidden room below. In decades past an orchestra would have been secreted down there, playing for the dancers above. *Who is playing?* she wondered. *One of ours, no doubt. Perhaps he had bought his life, or his family's, by agreeing to perform like a circus animal for the great general too?* Each note rose up in her like a fragile bubble, surging through her legs, her torso, her arms, her neck, as she rolled her head, loosening up, freeing her spirit. She paced like a caged animal, her blood quickening to the vibrations of the notes, sensed the eyes in the darkness watching her. As the guitarist stopped tuning up, she stood still, waiting. Breathing. Her eyes rolled back, lips parted, and with a stamp of her foot it began.

She recognized the singer immediately. The woman's husband had been taken the moment the troops rolled into town. The keening pain of the woman's voice gave Rosa's movements edge and precision. *Duende* rose from the bowels of the earth, forked like electricity through the notes, the voice, her limbs. As the music flowed, she lost herself. It was always like this. This was a dance that was in her blood, her bones. She had performed so many times, in the caves with her family. She had danced in the shadow of the Alhambra for Lorca. Her hand snaked above her like vines. She remembered him reciting, an incantation, how even the wind seemed green, how the branches came alive. Her feet pounded like thunder, her dress whipping through the air. She danced as she had for Picasso in the Albaicin, as she had for Jordi, in the firelight, on their last night together in the ruins at Sagunto. There she had felt the warmth of the ancient stones answer the life in her limbs. That had been her greatest dance, she knew, her passion, her love, drawing the spirits of the earth, the ghosts from the ruins. She would never dance like that again for anyone, and this, tonight, was only an echo of that, an aftershock. This would be her last dance.

The music gathered pace now. Rosa sensed the pain, the passion in the melody. She wondered if they could hear her feet dancing above them, the answering staccato stamps and beats. As she turned, she fixed first the general, then Vicente with her eyes. They would never take her spirit. She danced for the man and the country she loved.

On and on, faster and faster the music and dance welled up. Her limbs melted into the air. She was not there. She saw Jordi, running for the coast. They were behind him now. Vicente had betrayed his brother, she was sure of it. The dogs and soldiers were close by. She saw Jordi and Marco racing through the rice fields to an old Barraca farmhouse, hiding out in the steeply pitched roof as the farmer's wife said, "No, I haven't seen anyone here." She saw them, lying on the dusty floorboards, gazing down at the soldiers as they dragged the woman outside.

"We can't let them take her," she heard Jordi whisper to his friend.

"They'll kill her anyway." She saw Marco shake his head. "Everyone knows the family are anarchists."

She saw Jordi check his pistol. "Would you rather die like a hero or live like a coward?"

"If they just shot me, I wouldn't mind so much," she heard Marco reply. "I just don't want to be taken alive."

"Come on then." Jordi embraced his friend. "What are we waiting for?"

The music was in her now, racing and swirling in her blood. Somewhere in the room, she was aware of cries—"Olé! Olé!"—the clapping of hands. But she was not there. She was flying above the earth now, running like the wind behind Jordi, willing him on to the sea. The bullets were flying with her, past her, as she tried to shield him. Marco fell. Jordi ran back.

"Go," Marco cried, clamping his hand to his side, blood seeping through his fingers to the sand.

"No! I'll not leave you." Rosa watched Jordi glance up, catch sight of a small fishing boat on the horizon. "I'll carry you."

Marco cried out as Jordi tried to lift him. "Leave me!" There were shouts nearby. "But leave your pistol too. Go, now," he whispered as Rosa saw Jordi press the gun into his hand.

Rosa's feet beat an impossible rhythm, staccato, quick-fire, raining down like sparks as the music reached its crescendo. In the heat and the fire, she saw Marco lift the pistol to his temple. Crack, went the heel of her shoe. She was running again then, running at Jordi's side to the boat.

"We are Spaniards," he had said to her when they were last together. *"Life is a tragedy to us."* They had shared one last, desperate kiss. *"Salud, Rosa!"* he'd cried. *"We despise death, our love defies it!"* Faster and faster, she danced on, the dance of her life, her thundering feet, one, two beats more and it stopped, suddenly. His arms flung into the air. She raised hers as he raised his, twisting above her. She felt herself losing him. As he fell, she fell, and the spirit drained from her. She lay panting on the floor as the applause thundered around her. She closed her eyes tight and searched for him. Was he diving? Swimming to the boat she had seen on the horizon? Had he outrun them? She breathed hard, lights flashing behind her eyes as she came back to herself. Or had they shot him down? Were his arms flung upward to heaven as he died, or in victory as he escaped to freedom? As she lay still

in the pool of light from the chandelier above her, her red dress spilled out around her. The applause raged on, and her body sank against the floor, willing it to swallow her up. "Jordi," she murmured, her ribs pressed down, her knee pushed hard against her stomach. And in response, a tiny foot pressed back, flexed, kicked out to freedom.

FORTY-EIGHT

VALENCIA, JANUARY 2002

Emma struggled into a loose gray sweater and sprayed Chérie Farouche on her brush. Just as she ran it through her hair, her mobile rang.

"Freya?" Her face set hard.

"Em, darling." Emma could hear the panic in her voice. "Are you all right? Is the baby all right?"

"No, I'm not all right," she said. "How could I be after our conversation?" she cried out. "Of all the people I thought I could trust . . ."

"Emma, please."

"I can't believe it's all a lie. You lied to me! Who am I, Freya? Who am I?"

"Darling, please calm down. Let me explain . . ."

"No. No more lies." Emma heard voices downstairs. "I'm going to talk to Macu. I'm going to find out what happened to Rosa. Did you know that she was in prison?"

"Prison? Oh God, no." Freya's voice shook. "I was always afraid of that."

"I have so many questions just running around and around in my mind." Emma's chest was tight, and she was breathing heavily as she staggered downstairs. "How did you and Mum get home, to England?"

"I'd told Rosa where I would be, at Cerbère, and I'd managed to get a post at a maternity unit they had set up in an old mansion in Elne. I hoped she'd come with me there." She paused. "But when she went back for Jordi, I stayed at the border, and managed to track down Charles. It was chaos. They were machine-gunning the refugees, the bastards. That's how Hugo was killed, and Charles lost his arm. By the time they reached the medical center with him, gangrene had set in. Poor Charles. Eventually, once he was strong enough to travel, we left together."

"With Mum?"

"Yes."

"And nobody stopped you? You just took a child from Spain to England, and raised her as your daughter?"

Freya hesitated. "It wasn't quite as simple as that."

"How could Rosa just abandon Mum?"

Freya sighed. "I've never understood it myself, how anyone could give up their child. She said she had no choice, but she did. She chose Jordi."

"She knew Mum would be safe with you."

"Perhaps. Those militiawomen were incredibly strong. I remember one girl saying to me she would kill her own child rather than be unable to fight at her husband's side."

Emma glanced up as she heard Luca calling. "I've got to go."

"Emma, please understand, I had my reasons . . ." She paused. "Very good reasons for hiding the truth. I was only trying to protect Liberty, and you."

"Did Mum know?"

"Not until very near the end." Freya's voice was thick with emotion. "She forced it out of me finally."

"Is that why she came to Spain? Is that why she bought this house?"

"Yes. She made me promise that I would tell you, eventually. It never seemed like the right time, and now . . ." She sighed. "It's funny. Rosa said to me once that her female descendents would live in the Villa del Valle, and she was right. I think Liberty wanted to give you something she felt she never had."

Roots and wings; Emma thought of her mother's words. She grimaced as her stomach hardened with a contraction. "I have to go. I'll speak to you later."

"Love you, Em. You will take care—" Freya's words cut off as Emma hung up.

"Emma!" Luca yelled from the kitchen.

"I'm coming." She winced, her hand against her side. "What on earth's the matter?"

"You need to come and see this."

Luca led her through the kitchen, and pointed at the pit Marek was digging for the pool in the garden.

"*O mój Boże . . .*" Marek said. "My God!" He yanked the lever back on the digger and stopped the engine. "Borys!" he yelled.

"What is it?" Borys ambled around the side of the house, carrying boxes of deep blue tesserae ready for tiling the pool.

Marek scrambled up onto the digger scoop, and dug his hand into the ocher earth. Borys put down the boxes with a grunt, dust flaring at their base. He turned to Marek, muttering under his breath in Polish. His mouth fell open, and he crossed himself. Silhouetted against the sunlight, Marek was holding up a skull—a human skull. He turned toward the house and saw Emma standing with Luca at the door, staring at him. Marek lifted the skull to show them, the morning sun glinting on its gold teeth.

FORTY-NINE

"Where have you been?" Macu wrung her hands. The oil lamp in the kitchen swung in the breeze as the back door banged open, light swinging around the shadows. Rosa calmly placed a woven basket full of glossy green leaves on the kitchen table, and the wind rolling down from the mountains lifted her hair.

"Vicente has sealed up Jordi's room. He's crazy!" Macu cried.

Rosa thought of the photographs hidden beneath the floorboards in her bedroom. At least they were safe. *Together forever,* she thought. She dragged the heavy black cauldron from the fire, and checked the boiling water.

"Let him," she said quietly, shoveling in the leaves.

"It's like he's trying to wipe out his brother entirely. It's like Jordi never existed."

"He is guilty," Rosa said as she wiped down the pestle and mortar.

"Guilty? Who is guilty?" Vicente said, barging into the kitchen. He was stripped to the waist, his muscular, scarred body gleaming with sweat. He marched over to Rosa. "Where have you been?"

"Gathering food and snails for dinner, Vicente." When she looked at him, her eyes were black pools. "I am cooking your favorite." She pointed at the skinned rabbit in her basket.

"Good." He grunted and strode outside. They could hear him shoveling plaster into a bucket. When he walked through, rain slicked his face, and he left muddy footprints through the house.

"Aren't you going to say anything?" Macu whispered to her.

Rosa shook her head as she pounded the leaves. "All in good time."

Macu checked the paella, testing the crispy layer of *socarrat* at the bottom of the pan. She stepped back from the fire. "It is ready," she said. "Shall I call him?"

"Yes." Rosa tipped most of a bottle of cognac down the drain, then placed it on the table. She was breathing slowly, though her heart leaped in her chest. She listened to the dull thump of his feet across the landing above her head, followed his path as he walked down the wooden stairs. Rosa poured herself a small glass of cognac, and sat down to wait for him.

"About time." Vicente strode through the kitchen. He washed his hands in the basin of water at the sink, ran them over his sweating face.

"Macu, would you serve my husband?" Rosa said calmly. Macu scraped the paella pan with a large metal spoon, filled a bowl with the steaming rice. He started to eat without acknowledging her.

Rosa sipped her drink. "Vicente?"

"Nngh?" he grunted, without looking up from his food.

"Why have you sealed Jordi's room?"

"Jordi?" Vicente sucked a snail, tossed the empty shell aside. "He has no use of a bed where he is now."

Rosa's face was pale as she looked at him. "What do you mean?"

"Jordi is gone." Rice clung to his glistening lips as a cruel smile formed. "Haven't you heard? The Republicans surrendered formally at eleven o'clock this morning. Franco is victorious. This is all mine now."

"You said you would help him. You said you would make sure he reached the boats."

Vicente laughed. "The coast is crowded with fifty thousand people trying to escape. Maybe he was lucky, maybe he wasn't."

"Vicente." Her voice was low, her fists clenched under the table. "What have you heard?"

He shrugged, his face full of conceit. "A little bird told me they were running for the boats off the beaches near the Albufera." He lunged at the bottle, poured out what was left. "There are thousands and thousands," he repeated, draining his glass, "jamming the coast like rats. Marco was shot."

"Oh God, no," Macu said, her hand on her face.

"And Jordi?" He pulled a face. "Who knows . . . What do you think? The two of them against the great generalissimo's troops." He turned on his wife, his face coloring with anger again. "Who cares, anyway? That is the past. This is the future, you and me." He pushed back his chair, strode around to her. Vicente placed his hand on her stomach. "Our child."

Rosa glanced at Macu. She saw her fighting to compose herself. "Of course, Vicente," she said.

"Jordi got what he deserved. Never forget I could have the troops here like that, if I wanted." He clicked his fingers in Macu's face.

"Why don't you then?" she said.

"Maybe a few of your friends got away, but most are being rounded up for the prisons and the bullrings." He mimed cocking a gun, pointed his index finger at Macu. "You? You're not worth the effort it would take me to go into town." He waved his hand, dismissing her. "Good-bye and good riddance to you. This is a great day. The flag of Old Spain flies again from our balcony." He pointed his glass at Rosa. "And you, my love, my little dove, are my wife again. No more of this *'mi compañera'* nonsense."

"Let me get you some more cognac." Rosa dragged Macu into the pantry and closed the door.

"How can you stay here? The man is an animal! The things he has done . . ." Macu was shaking with emotion, trying hard to control herself. Rosa calmly unlocked the corner cabinet and sorted through the glass bottles, selecting a blue one. "Rosa, what is that?"

"Just a little sedative. I don't want him to touch me tonight."

"I wish I'd had some when he came for me."

Rosa turned to the counter, and steadied herself. When she looked up, her eyes were dark and determined. "Macu," she said, taking her old friend's hand. "I am sorry. If I had known . . ."

Macu's face fell. "It is nothing. Compared with what he does to you, it is nothing. But you can't let him get away with this."

"I have no intention of doing that," Rosa said steadily. "He threatened my daughter, he betrayed the man I love, his own brother . . ." She uncorked a bottle of cognac, a stream of expletives falling like a curse from her lips as she poured some away. "Enough," she said. Macu watched in silence as Rosa picked up the dark blue bottle and turned it to the light. She came and stood at her side. "For what he has done to me, to Freya, to you, to Jordi, he will pay. Will the world be a better or worse place for one less fascist?" She tipped the entire contents of the bottle into the cognac. She took the cloth from the white bowl she had left steeping on the side, ladled in the mixture through a funnel.

"Rosa, what is that?"

"No, don't let it touch you. It is the leaves I cooked earlier. Oleander," she said simply. "A few drops would kill most men. For Vicente, I use more."

"I can't let you do this," Macu said quietly.

"It's nothing to do with you," Rosa said. "This is my decision. Vicente will never stop, he will never let me go." She clenched her fist. "You go now. It won't be long until the troops come to search the village. It is safer if you are at home, with Ignacio. You must never come back, never see me again."

"No." Macu hugged her tightly. "I will stay. I will help you."

Vicente's head lurched up as Rosa carried the bottle over to him, the fire-light gleaming through the dark amber liquid. "*Joder!* You took your time." He thumped the table, threw down the newspaper.

Rosa looked down at the headline: *LA CONQUISTA DE VALENCIA Y ALI-CANTE HA PUESTO DEFINITIVO TÉRMINO A LA PESTE ROJA. Peste roja,* she thought. *Red plague—exterminated.*

"Well, what are you waiting for, eh?" He shoved his empty glass toward her. In the bloodshot eyes, the flaccid face, Rosa glimpsed what he would become, how his looks would desert him as his true character etched itself on his face. She filled his glass and placed the bottle on the counter.

Rosa dished out more of the paella into the earthenware bowl and carried it to him. He drunkenly scooped mouthful after mouthful. Rosa knitted quietly in the lamplight as he ate. He struggled to his feet, staggered across the kitchen like a bull at the end of a long fight, ribboned banderillas streaming from its bleeding flanks. He refilled his glass, sat down, and knocked back the drink. As his eyes drooped, Rosa put down her knitting, and waited.

The minutes ticked by, only the crack and hiss of the fire, and the thunder rolling overhead breaking the silence. Macu finally crept across to the table. "Rosa?" she whispered. "Is he . . . ?"

"He should be," Rosa said. Her face was set hard with bitterness. They heard rain begin to fall harder, drumming down on the roof of the house.

"Is he breathing?" Macu tiptoed toward him. "I'll check." She stepped forward, her hand reaching to touch his neck. Just as she reached him,

Vicente snorted, reeled forward. The women cried out as he stumbled to his feet.

"What have you done to me?" He clutched his stomach, grimacing. His words were thick and heavy. "You witches! I curse you!" Rosa backed away, but he grabbed Macu by the neck. The storm raged outside, the wind screaming through the garden, through the open door. Macu began to choke, her feet dangling above the floor. She clawed frantically at his huge hand.

"Help!" she rasped. "I can't—"

Rosa tried to drag him off her, but Vicente's hands were clamped tight, his muscles contorted, bulging in his back. She wheeled around, seized the heavy stone mortar in her hands, raised it high, and brought it crashing down on the side of his head. He released Macu with a gasp, and by the time he hit the floor, dark blood was flowing from his temple into the shadows. "*Hijo de puta.*" She spat on him. "You son of a bitch."

The women stood in silence above him, shaking, catching their breath. They both jumped as lightning cracked across the sky. "You must go," Rosa said, turning to Macu.

The girl shook her head. "No. You are my friend, for good or bad." She took Rosa's hand, and looked down at Vicente. "What do we do with him?"

Rosa looked out at the dark garden. The lightning illuminated the pile of plaster where Vicente had been working, the shovel stuck into the earth. "First we dig a hole," she said. "I will go and find another shovel in the shed." She gathered up the cookbook, Lorca's book of poetry and the heavy mortar, and staggered out into the garden with them, the rain streaming down her face. She shouldered open the storeroom and heaved them onto the top shelf. As she crossed the garden, she pulled the gold ring from her finger and tossed it into the well. She gazed down into the dark water, and the shimmering image of a woman she no longer recognized looked back. The ring fell, in slow motion, turning and gleaming, down to the smooth rocks and the silence below. *It is like I was never here,* she thought.

Macu ran out to join her, and the two women dug the ocher earth, the storm raging around them. "It's taking too long!" Macu cried. After half an hour, the pit was only a few feet deep. "He is too big!"

Rosa looked back into the kitchen, saw Vicente's twisted body lying on the floor. She glanced at the pile of lime plaster beneath the awning of the shed, waiting to finish the wall. "No. It will be fine. I can do this." She put down the shovel. "Macu, help me drag him to the shop. I can take care of it from there."

"The shop?" Macu grimaced. "Rosa, what are you going to do?"

Rosa marched up the path to the kitchen. "I am going to tidy up. By the time I have finished, you would never know we have been here." She thought again of the photographs, beneath the floor upstairs. "The house will go to sleep for a long, long, time, like in a fairy tale." The girls grabbed a leg each, and heaved Vicente out of the kitchen, his head bumping down the stone step. His arms dragged behind him as they pulled him through the orange trees, across the grass slick with cold rain.

Rosa caught her breath as she opened up the back door to the shop. She turned to Macu. "I can manage now." Lightning cracked the sky again, and Macu glanced into the dark room, saw the rows of silver knives illuminated, gleaming darkly. Rosa took her shoulders. "Macu, forget all about me. Forget all of this."

"I can't. You are my friend."

Rosa hugged her, felt her shaking in her arms. "Go, and make a good life with Ignacio. You can have everything, Macu—a home, a life, a family." She kissed her on both cheeks. "Be safe."

Rosa heard Macu's feet running away through the garden, waited until she heard the back gate swing closed. She looked up at the house, the wind blowing through the orange trees. Bile rose up in her throat as she thought of what she had to do, and her fingers trembled, reaching across the cold tiles of the counter. "It's time, Vicente," she said quietly. "It's time."

FIFTY

Not those ones, these," Macu said, pointing toward the white lilies at the back of Aziz's display.

"*Sí, Señora.*" Aziz eased the stems from the steel bucket, heads nodding in the breeze. The heady scent of incense licked the air from their white tonguelike petals.

"*Buenos días*, Macu," Emma said, stopping to kiss her cheeks. "Those are beautiful, Aziz. Are they for something special?"

"I'm taking them to the cemetery for my Ignacio," Macu said.

"Morning," Fidel said. He carried a wooden crate of fresh vegetables into the shop. "I have your order here. My daughter asked me to drop it by for you."

"Thank you. What do I owe you?" Emma reached for her wallet.

Fidel patted her hand. "Nothing. It's a pleasure. You need all the fresh fruit and vegetables you can eat. It is good for the baby."

"Are you all right?" Macu said. "You are very pale."

"I'm fine." Emma leaned against the counter. "I've just . . . I've had a bit of a shock. They've unearthed a skeleton in the back garden."

"A skeleton?" Macu paled.

"It's the strangest thing—it has gold teeth."

"I tell you, this house has *mala sombra*—bad energy," Aziz said as he handed Macu the bouquet of flowers.

"Rubbish," Emma said. The sun was shining, but she felt suddenly cold. "Luca's called the police. I think they are going to bring an undertaker to deal with the remains."

"Come," Macu said. "It will be a while until they are here. We need to talk." She took Emma's arm. "Let's walk to the cemetery together. You too, Fidel."

They ambled along the dusty pavement, in silence except for the tap of Macu's walking stick. Fidel pushed open the squeaking iron gates of the cemetery and ushered the women inside. Emma pulled down her sunglasses against the glare of the white walls, the fierce light glinting off the polished headstones and gilt vases. On each neatly tended grave there were fresh flowers. *I can see why Aziz is doing well,* she thought, grimacing as her stomach contracted.

Macu walked along the gravel path, and stopped at a large marble tomb. "Can you help me?" she asked Emma, pointing to the wilting carnations in the vase at its base. Emma leaned down awkwardly, emptied the vase. She looked at the list of names inscribed in the marble. Beneath Ignacio's, she saw: *ALEJANDRA RAMIREZ VILLANUEVA 1971–1999. She was the same age as me, whoever she was,* Emma realized. Beneath that, there was a simple *XAVIER DE SANTANGEL RAMIREZ 1999.*

"Here," Fidel said, and passed her a penknife to trim the base of the lilies.

"It's so peaceful," Emma said.

"I like to come here each week and talk to Ignacio." Macu stepped back and sat on the stone bench against the wall with Fidel. She let her head rest back and raised her face to the sun. "So, ask me whatever you want."

Emma slid the last of the lilies into the vase, and settled down on the bench beside them. "Why will no one tell me the truth? Please tell me what happened here, after the war, I mean."

"They were very bad times," Macu said quietly. "I was lucky. The Santangels, they were a big family, they protected me. I tried to help Rosa, but when she came back after leaving your mother with Freya . . ."

"She was trying to reach Jordi? What happened to him?"

"Nobody knows. So many people disappeared."

"And Rosa?"

"She was rounded up with the people at the docks. She was sent to prison." Macu paused. "There were rescue vessels in the harbor, some of them even took women and children on board. But those bastards broke their agreement. The Nationalists said they would give safe passage to the refugees, but Franco's men made every last one of the refugees disembark. It was a trap, a hideous trap. They caught them like butterflies in a net." Macu's breath shuddered. "There were men, brave men like Jordi and Marco, embracing on the docks and shooting each other's brains out so they wouldn't fall into fascist hands. Rosa told me she saw men do it, saying, 'On three: *uno, dos, tres . . .*' Boom. Can you imagine? What a way to die."

"Macu," Fidel said, "maybe we should wait. It is not good for Emma, for the baby."

"No. Emma wants to know. If she is to make a new life here, she must know the truth about our families." She closed her eyes. "The people who had no bullets to kill themselves with were herded into the bullrings and prisons. There was no food, nothing for the children, only the clothes on their backs."

"They took the women and children too?" Emma said.

Fidel nodded. "Just being the wife or girlfriend of a Red after the war was enough. After Barcelona and Valencia fell, they rounded up thousands, hundreds of thousands in the prisons."

"No one talks about what went on there," Macu said, "or the concentration camps."

"You mean like in Nazi Germany?" Emma said.

Macu nodded. "It was horrific. People were treated like animals, in Spain, in their own homeland, and in France." She looked out across the graveyard. "You know, they swept aside the abuses of Franco's regime when he died in 1975—everyone wanted an easy transition to democracy. There have been no trials. No one wants to break this unwritten pact of silence. They think if they don't remember it is better." Macu sighed. "But even the dead have rights. We must talk, we must make sure this never happens again."

Fidel wrung his hands in his lap. "There is no peace here. So many families destroyed, so many children without their parents. People look at Spain and see the land of sun, the holiday homes, but underneath . . . It is not so bad here you think, but there are still people who will not buy from me because my family were Reds." He paused. "Sometimes I wonder if the fire that killed my wife, her mother . . . I wonder if it wasn't an accident."

"Surely not?" Emma said.

Fidel shrugged. "My mother was in prison too. She was one of the people rounded up at the docks, just like Rosa." He hung his head. "You know, so many children died."

"They kept the children with the women?" Emma's stomach twisted.

"Yes. They gave the women maybe one herring a day, a few noodles in seawater. Mothers, their milk dried up, their babies died. It was terrible, terrible," Macu said. "A warder told Rosa: we don't want to convince you we are right, we want to punish you." She looked at Emma. "They treated the women like animals."

"You know, they said we were mentally deficient," Fidel said. "The scientists, they experimented on our men—the International Brigades, they were among the first."

Emma thought of Charles, felt nausea welling up in her. "I understand," she said, her voice a whisper. "I understand why people want to close this away. I feel like I've opened Pandora's box."

"No. It is right that you know the truth." Macu hesitated. "I want you to know that your grandmother, she was very brave." She took Emma's hand. "You know, I managed to see Rosa. By then they had sent her to Ventas prison, in Madrid. They were moving prisoners back to their point of origin. It was built for five hundred women, but they held over five thousand, mothers with small children. Oh, they were cruel."

"Where I was, they believed children should be removed from the parents," Fidel said. "They took me from my mother." He screwed his eyes shut. "I remember walking in the yard, that freezing yard, with the other children, looking up at the bars—all the mothers would gather there, pushed against the windows, trying desperately to see their child. I was maybe four, five years old. I missed my mother so much."

"You have to remember, most of these women had done nothing," Macu said. "They were the daughters, the wives of Republicans. That was their only 'crime.' That is why they were dragged naked through the streets with their heads shaved, humiliated, tortured, imprisoned."

Emma felt her head swimming. "Tell me what happened to Rosa."

"I only managed to see her because they thought she might die, after losing the baby."

Emma turned to her. "The baby?"

"*Sí.*" Macu nodded. "She had fallen pregnant again, with Jordi's child. They had been together, before he went to fight in the last battles of the war." She looked at Emma. "I remember the sound of the doors locking behind me. I was terrified I might not be allowed out. The toilets were overflowing with excrement—God, the stench. All you could hear was the sound of children weeping. Rosa told me five, six children a day were dying. Dysentery, meningitis—measles was a death sentence."

"What about the baby?"

Macu slowly shook her head. "She gave birth in prison. Can you imagine, bringing a life into the world in that place? Rosa said they took the baby away to clean him up—they told her it was a boy. So my friend, my dear, brave Rosa waited, and waited, lying there cold and alone and bleeding. Finally they came back and told her the child was dead." Macu's voice caught, a tear trickled down her cheek. "He had been stillborn." She pulled a lace handkerchief from her pocket and wiped at her face. "She asked to see the body but they said they had already buried him, with the other children."

"Oh God," Emma said, her hand across her stomach. "Poor Rosa."

"Maybe they lied. They took children all the time," Fidel said. "They gave them to 'good' Nationalist couples who raised them to salute the generalissimo."

Macu clenched her fist around the handkerchief. "It happened too much. Rosa thought she would be executed now that her baby had gone—that happened to a woman she knew. Rosa said it was the worst thing she had seen in all the war. They tore the child from her arms, and the woman was dragged away, screaming for her baby. Rosa was broken by the time I saw her."

There was a tight knot in Emma's throat. "Oh God, this is too much to take in. How did she get out? How did Rosa get to Mexico?"

"I helped her. When I saw what they did to her . . ." Macu twisted the handkerchief in her hands. "I knew she would die if she stayed there. So, we switched clothes, papers. Rosa walked out of Ventas in a fox fur coat, to the waiting car. My driver took her to the coast. I lay low long enough for her to get away, then pretended she knocked me out. I banged my head against the wall to make a bruise, and cuts." Macu's frail fingers traced her hairline. "Ignacio came and saved me. He knew, I think, what I did. But we never talked about it."

"He was a good man," Fidel said.

"Rosa was right about him," Macu said to Emma. "He defied his parents, and he married me. He loved me, and I grew to love him. For sixty years, we had a long and happy marriage. Neither of us were 'Red' or 'fascist,' we just loved each other, and loved our country. He had powerful friends and he got a pardon for Rosa."

Emma hugged Macu. "Thank you." She held the old woman in her arms. "Because of you, my grandmother escaped."

Macu patted her back. "She was my friend. There is not a family in Spain, I think, without a grief to nurse. Fidel's generation are the lost children," she said. "We will bear this anguish until the day we die."

"What is worse," Fidel said, "is that even those who escaped, the children who were adopted in Russia, Mexico, England—Franco would not let them rest. He killed their parents; then he went after them. The Falange foreign service hunted the children down. Even with new names, new families, they were not safe."

Emma thought of Liberty, of Freya's uncharacteristic panic every time Emma wandered off as a child, and understood at last.

"Tell me about when my mother came here," she said to Fidel.

"It was a long time ago, now," he said. "February last year?"

Emma thought for a moment. "I had to go to New York." She frowned. "Mum said she was going to Cornwall, one last time. It wasn't long before she died."

Fidel's face softened. "She wanted the house to be a surprise for you. I am sorry that I could not tell you when we first met. I took her up into the mountains, so she could see the land of her fathers. I showed her the village, and the Villa del Valle." He smiled at the memory. "She said 'This is it, this is it! My whole life, I've felt I was homesick for somewhere I'd never known.' She told me that in Britain, where she grew up, the Celts called it '*hiraeth*'—a longing for home."

Emma smiled. "I'm so glad that she was happy here."

"That is what she wanted for you. She said that she hoped this would be a new beginning."

"It is what Rosa would have wanted too," Macu said softly. "You know, she escaped to Mexico on a boat, the SS *Sinaia,* from Sète in the end. Nancy Mitford and her husband had set up an office in Perpignan to help refugee mothers escape. Rosa worked with her." Macu smiled. "Can you imagine your grandmother in the middle of that chaos? All these people with cardboard suitcases, donkeys, goats, and dogs all over the place. It must have been bedlam." She shook her head. "I had one letter from her, once she got to Mexico. Rosa went on the boat as a nurse to help the children. She never came back." Macu gazed out across the cemetery. "After she died, a nun sent me the photograph of her that I gave you the other day. Our friend Carlos took it in the autumn of 1937, and Rosa treasured it." Macu glanced at Emma's necklace. "We did not have many photographs in those days." She smiled at the thought of her old friend. "Rosa loved that garden. I know she would be so happy that you are making it good again."

Emma squeezed her hand. "Thank you. I know how hard talking about all this must be."

"Not being able to talk is hard." Fidel's voice shook. "People think the old wounds have healed. Well, not for our families. My father, he was taken." He wiped away a tear. "So many Republican families have nowhere to go still, nowhere to grieve. On November first, where do they take their flowers to honor their dead?" He offered Macu his hand, and they walked across the cemetery. The temperature dropped as they stepped into the shade. He ran his hand over the pockmarked plaster of the far wall. "See here? These are bullet holes. They rounded up the men of the village who had supported the Republicans, and made them dig a big hole. They shot them, and threw their bodies in. My father is here, somewhere." He opened his palms, swept them over the green, green grass. "All I want is to find him. He should be buried properly, over there, like Franco's men," he said, pointing at the neat rows of well-tended graves beneath a war memorial. "It is all I want."

"There are graves like this all over the country," Macu said. "People were thrown down wells, cliffs, ditches. Maybe one day Spain will open its eyes. We are a democracy now. Some people say the past should stay buried, but until people like Fidel's father are laid to rest, the old wounds will not heal."

"I wonder who was buried at the house," Emma said, frowning.

"Him?" Macu said. "That was your grandmother's husband."

"Jordi?"

"No, not Jordi," she said with anger in her voice. "That son of a bitch, Vicente."

"But how did he die?"

Macu hesitated. "He had many enemies. Who knows?"

Emma's face contorted. She placed her hand against the wall, gasped.

"Emma," Fidel said. "Are you all right?"

Macu looked at her, full of concern. "We have upset you. I did not want to tell you all this, not at the moment."

Emma pursed her lips, exhaled slowly. "No. I'm glad I know. But I think . . ." She gritted her teeth as another contraction began. "I think I need to get to the hospital."

FIFTY-ONE

A red Triumph Dolomite careered down Pond Place, past the workers' cottages, showering Freya and the pram with filthy water. "Damn you," she said under her breath as she slicked back her rain-drenched hair, fumbling for the key with her cold fingers. "Shh . . ." She rocked the pram with her foot as she opened the door to the cottage. She hoped Charles was in a better mood. Since his return from the convalescent home, he had been unable to see or speak to anyone. Freya readied herself. She remembered the words of the matron in Spain: *"Just when you think you can't take it anymore, smile. Always smile, girls."* The door was grimy with soot, and from each chimney, a thick plume of gray smoke rose into the darkening sky. Freya coughed, her chest aching. She hadn't been able to shake her cold. The door bumped open, sticking on the damp carpet where it had swollen. She was greeted by the sound of Billie Holiday on the gramophone, and a haze of cigarette smoke.

"There you are. Where have you been? It started tipping down hours ago," Charles said. He heaved himself up from the sofa. The house was freezing, and he wore a couple of sweaters and a scarf. Freya dragged the heavy pram into the room.

"You look—"

"I look dreadful." She glanced at the coffee table littered with empty bottles, glimmering weakly in the light of the coal fire.

"Can I get you a drink, old girl?" Charles inspected a glass dubiously and set it back down on the table. His hand shook as he reached for the bottle of brandy, and the glass tumbled off the table, smashing on the hearth. "Oh ruddy hell," he mumbled and tried to kneel to pick up the shards of glass.

"Just leave it," Freya snapped. The baby's shrill wail increased in pitch.

"No, no. I can do it," Charles slurred. "I'm still getting used to doing things with one hand."

"Leave it!" she yelled. "For God's sake, Charles . . ." She burst into tears.

He stubbed out his cigarette and stepped cautiously toward her. From his jacket pocket he pulled a clean handkerchief, waving it like a flag of surrender.

"Thank you," she said, wiping her eyes. "I am sorry. I don't normally . . . I don't know what's wrong with me."

He put his arm around her shoulders. Freya looked up at him forlornly, tears pouring down her cheeks. "Can I get you anything? A cup of tea?"

Freya shook her head, fighting to compose herself. "No, thank you. I'm just so terribly tired. I've walked miles, trying to get her to sleep. She won't stop crying, I just don't know what I'm doing wrong."

"May I?" He untucked the blankets from the pram. Liberty's lips were pale, her legs drawn up to her stomach as she cried. "She has colic, I think."

"I know. I've tried everything. I don't know if it's the food, or . . ." Freya began to sob again. "I didn't know it was going to be so hard. It just never stops. Day and night."

"There, there." Charles patted her on the shoulder. "It will get easier, I'm sure."

"Oh God, I hope so. I don't think I can handle much more."

"Listen, I have an idea," he said. "Why don't you have an early night? I'm quite sure I can cope."

"No, it wouldn't be right." Freya eyed the table of glasses.

"Nonsense. I'm not paralytic, Frey. Now," he said, crooking the child on his hip as he gazed into her eyes. "Young lady, you have one of England's finest young lepidopterists taking care of you. I know nothing about rusks, but I can bore you silly about butterflies." Charles winked at Freya as she laughed through her tears. "Go to bed."

That night, as Freya had her first unbroken night's sleep in weeks, Charles paced the living room. He had a muslin draped over his waistcoat, and jiggled Liberty up and down on his shoulder as he walked.

"Gosh, you have amazing stamina," he said. He paused, his eyes turning toward the child. "Oh dear, I think you've . . ." He pulled a face. "I do hope you're in a nappy?" Charles walked wearily to the kitchen. "Let's see. I think Freya has a bunch drying over the range."

He laid the child down on a clean towel on the kitchen table, and she gazed at him, sucking her thumb. "I think you're feeling better after that?" he said quietly. "Now. How does one . . . ?" Charles scratched his head. "I've seen Freya do it. It can't be that hard." He looked around. "Some warm water? Cotton wool or something?"

Charles rummaged around under the sink and filled a bowl with water from the kettle, mixing it with cold. He scratched his head. "I know! I have some cotton wool in the study." He returned clutching a glass jar. "Messier work than chloroforming butterflies, but there you go." He gingerly unbuttoned Liberty's vest. "Oh Lord, it's . . ." He grimaced. Charles felt hysterical laughter bubbling inside him. He pulled down some clean nightclothes from the airer. "Shall we try these?" He pursed his lips. "Eugh. Lord, how can such a small person make all this?" He turned his face away as he cleaned her. "I say, can you give me a hand here? You just put your foot in it."

He finally managed to get a clean nappy and pajamas on the child. "There, not too bad, and we didn't impale you with the nappy pin." He stepped back to admire his work. The clean nappy bulged down to her knees. "It doesn't look terribly smart but hopefully it will hold until morning." He carried her through to the living room, and stretched out on the sofa with her resting on his stomach.

Freya woke to the sound of milk bottles being placed on the doorstep below her bedroom window. As always, her first thoughts were of Tom. She had heard nothing from him as the months dragged on, and finally, yesterday, she had told herself it was hopeless. He had forgotten about her. *"Smile, girls."* Her matron's voice came to her. *"No tears, be strong."* She sighed and stretched. *What a blissful night's sleep.* Her eyes flew open. "Liberty!" she cried aloud, and sat bolt upright. The cot at the foot of her bed was empty. "Charles!" she yelled, dragging her old blue flannelette dressing gown on. She shot out of bed, ran downstairs. "Charles, where's—" She stopped dead, and began to smile. There, on the sofa, Charles lay snoring, the child tucked safely beside him, reaching up to play with a mobile of multicolored paper butterflies that he had made for her.

FIFTY-TWO

LONDON, JANUARY 2002

"Freya!" Charles stumbled through the conservatory. "Freya!"

"I'm in the kitchen," she called. The theme tune from *The Archers* drifted through the cottage. Freya looked up from the heart-shaped tarts she was making.

"She's in labor, Frey. A chap called Luca something just rang."

"Luca de Santangel. He's Macu's grandson." Freya dusted off her hands.

"Good Lord, Macu has grandchildren?" Charles slumped down at the kitchen table.

"Charles, she has great-grandchildren. How old do you think we still are? Twenty?" She carried on spooning strawberry jam into the cases.

"Yes, I suppose I do, sometimes," he said. "Is Macu still alive?" He shrugged as Freya rolled her eyes. "You don't like to take anything for granted at our age."

"Did it never cross your mind to find out?"

"I . . ." Charles ran his hand through his hair. "Never mind. I can't believe our Em is going to be a mother."

"Have you decided?"

"About what?"

"Spain, Charles. If you won't come, I'm going to go by myself."

"I'll see. It would do you good, I think. A little break in the sun after all the problems you've been having with Delilah."

"I can handle her." Freya looked down at the neat rows of hearts. "I'm just worried about Emma. I couldn't bear it if all this came between us, not after all this time."

"Secrets have a nasty habit of revealing themselves." Charles traced his finger in the flour on the table. "I said we should have told them the truth years ago."

"You did not!" Freya said. "You were the one who started it. Because of you, our whole life was built on a lie."

"Frey, I remember clearly telling you when Libby turned eighteen we should—"

"Poppycock." She staggered to her feet, leaning heavily on her cane. "If we'd have told her, the first thing she would have done was race off to Spain to try to find Jordi and Rosa, and it still wasn't safe. The reprisals went on for years." Freya tugged on the old oven door. "Damn," she said, the handle coming off in her hand.

Charles muttered under his breath. "Leave it to me." He stood, took the handle from her, and wiggled it into place.

"You said you'd get this fixed."

"Another lie?"

"Don't start, Charles, just don't." Freya swung around with the tray of tarts, and stumbled. The tray clattered to the floor. "Look what you made me do!" she cried, looking at the broken cases and jam oozing onto the old wooden floor.

"Sorry, Frey," he said. Ming stalked over and took a speculative sniff of a tart, before turning tail. "Even the cat thinks your pastry looked a bit dry." Freya laughed, in spite of herself as she reached for the broom. "What are you doing baking hearts anyway? It's not Valentine's Day for a couple of weeks."

"I was going to post a box to Em," she said as she swept up the mess. "Don't you remember? We used to make them every year." Freya blinked quickly.

Charles caught the tremble in her voice, and shuffled forward, put his arm around her. "Come on, old girl . . ."

"Don't you dare say 'stiff upper lip.'"

He turned off the oven. "I was going to ask you if you fancied a Bloody Mary at the club, wet the baby's head."

Freya tossed the broom aside, and took his arm. "Now that is a good idea. Do you think Em will ever forgive us?" she said as they hobbled through the house. "She sounded so angry when I spoke to her earlier."

"She's had a big shock." Charles lifted down her gray wool cape from the pegs by the front door, and handed it to her. "We'll soon know."

"I can't bear it. I always knew this day would come." She smoothed down Charles's scarf. "I've been afraid of losing them my whole life."

"Will you tell her?" Charles couldn't look at her. "Will you tell her what I did?"

"What *we* did," Freya reassured him. "No, not unless I have to. Emma's been through enough."

FIFTY-THREE

The trolley wheeled through to the operating theater, wheels squeaking on the linoleum. Emma watched the lights flickering above her. The room was dark when they pushed her in. As the fluorescent tubes buzzed, illuminated, the sound of a radio drifted in, playing 1980s pop.

"Now, Emma," the anesthetist said kindly, "relax." He took her arms, strapped them cruciform to a plank of wood across the operating table. Emma closed her eyes.

The hours had rolled into one another as Emma lay in the hospital room. "Please, can't I walk around?"

"No." The nurse looked up from between her legs. "It is no good. Your waters have broken, but you are still only two fingers . . ."

Emma groaned. The contractions were coming hard and fast now, and the pain tore through her.

"Be quiet," the nurse said.

Emma thought, *What? Be quiet? You bitch, you have no*—and another tidal wave of pain ripped through her. "*Necesito control . . . dolor*," she gasped, the correct vocabulary abandoning her.

"No, impossible." The nurse shook her head.

"Epidural." Emma gritted her teeth and forced her head up. She glared at the nurse. "Now!"

The nurse pursed her lips. "I will ask your husband."

Husband? Emma thought as she followed the nurse's green figure retreating down the corridor. Her vision blurred as the pain returned. She breathed through it, but it felt like every atom of her body was contracting then expanding at lightning speed. She heard voices. Luca. *Thank God.* He had driven her to the hospital and must have stayed. She craned her head to look up at him.

"If you are not her husband, you cannot sign the papers," the nurse said.

"I am as good as her husband." Luca took Emma's hand. She gripped hard as the next contraction came. He watched, helplessly, as her face contorted with pain. "Try to breathe," he said gently, wiping her hair from where it had stuck to her brow. "What can I do to help you?"

"Epidural, now," she gasped.

"Get her an epidural," Luca said to the nurse. "Get the doctor! I will sign whatever you want. I am with Emma, we are lovers, the baby is mine." He glanced at her for confirmation.

"Yes." She cried out again.

"Do I have to get the doctor myself?" Luca turned to the nurse.

He held her hand as they administered the injection. Ice cold, numb relief flooded through her. She came back to herself, breathed easily. "Thank you," she whispered. Luca stroked her hair. "Thank you for staying. I don't know what I would have done . . ." She was suddenly aware that she was wearing a blue surgical gown, and her backside was hanging out.

"When I saw them take you away, you looked so lost . . . and so brave. I couldn't leave you here alone." His eyes were red rimmed, dark circles beneath them. "It reminded me—" He shook his head. "It doesn't matter. I hope you don't mind, what I said? That I am with you, and the baby . . ." He took Emma's hand. "I spoke to the doctor." He lowered his eyes. "The reason you have such bad pain. The baby, he is stuck."

"Oh." Tears welled in Emma's eyes as she looked at the monitor tracking her baby's heartbeat. "Is . . . Everything is going to be OK isn't it?" The room filled with doctors and nurses.

"Yes of course it is. Emma, I—"

"Emma," a man in scrubs interrupted, leaning down so she could see him. "Your baby is in distress. We have to get him out as quickly as possible."

"Oh God. Please, save my baby." Tears rolled down her cheeks. She turned to Luca. "If anything happens to me . . ."

"Don't." Luca kissed her forehead as they prepared to lift her onto the trolley. "Everything will be fine. I'll wait for you."

She could hear the sound of metal on metal now. Behind the screen hiding her stomach, she felt nothing but a tugging push and pull. Then he was there. A cry. Startled, she opened her eyes as the anesthetist dropped the screen slightly. "Look, Emma," he said. "Your son." She glimpsed a curved back, narrow vernix-covered hips lifting clear of her body. Her head shook with the effort of holding it up to look at him. The screen went back, and she slumped down, grinning. She wanted desperately to hold him. As they worked on her, she listened to her baby, a stranger suddenly, crying in an adjacent room. She tried to turn her head toward him, drifting in and out of consciousness.

"*Eh, Mamá!*" she heard a nurse say. "*Rubio! Qué bonito!*" The woman lowered the baby to her side. He looked just like Joe in miniature. Fathomless dark eyes returned her stare. She tried to lift an arm to touch his hand, the soft blond hair on his head, but she was still strapped down. She longed to hold him, but all she could do was move her head a little.

"Hello, baby," she whispered. He blinked at her. She felt as if he knew everything, the secrets of the universe and the meaning of life. The baby was lifted away, and Emma closed her eyes, exhausted.

When she awoke she was in a room on the maternity ward. The sound of other babies crooning and crying disturbed her. It was dark. *Where am I? How long have I been asleep?* she thought. Her body ached, icy pins and needles coursing through her. She was tucked up to her chin in blankets. She licked her lips. She had never been so thirsty in her life. *Oh God, the baby! Where's the baby?* She rolled her head to the side, and found Luca dozing in a chair, the baby curled up in a blanket, sleeping peacefully on his chest.

"Luca," she whispered.

"Hey, you're awake." He cradled the baby as he leaned forward and kissed her forehead. "Look what you have done." He held the baby so she could see him. "He's perfect, beautiful."

Emma lifted her arms clear, trailing drips. Gently, Luca placed the sleeping child in her arms. She kissed his tiny fingers, inhaled his soft, clean scent.

"So, there you are." She smiled wearily at her child. The baby stirred at her voice, dark eyes blinking reflectively. A knitted hat covered the blond fuzz of his hair.

Luca stroked her hair. "You were incredible."

"I thought . . ." Her eyes filled with tears.

"You are both fine, you'll recover. And he has ten fingers, ten toes—and a great set of lungs."

"Ah! You're awake." A nurse bustled in. "Let's check a few things."

"Water . . ." Emma murmured. "Please, can I have some water?"

"No, no liquids for a few hours."

"You're kidding?"

"No liquids, then *dieta blanda*." She checked the morphine drip, and tidied the sheets. "When he wakes, you can feed him, OK? Your husband is staying with you?"

"I don't . . . Do you have to go?"

"Not if you don't want me to. Paloma is coming to see you in the morning."

"Stay, I'd like that."

The nurse glanced curiously from Emma to Luca. "Good. Get some rest."

Luca stooped and took the baby from her arms, settled back into the arm-chair at her side, murmuring softly in Spanish to him. "What will you call him?"

Emma looked at them together. The baby seemed tiny in Luca's large, tanned hands. "Joseph Luca Temple," she said quietly.

"Really?" A smile broke across Luca's face, his teeth white and even against the dark stubble of his chin. "Hello, Joseph Luca." He kissed the baby's head. "You won't give him your partner's family name?"

"We were never married. Now he's gone, I want the baby to feel connected to my family at least."

"Do you still miss him?"

"No." In that moment, Emma realized it was true. "Not anymore. I did . . .

I mean, you can't be with someone for years and just stop loving them, can you?"

"No." Luca looked very tired suddenly. "No, you can't. Even when someone leaves you, once the pain dies down, the love is still there."

"Is that what happened to you? Did you lose someone too?"

"Yes." Luca glanced at her. "I loved someone very much, and they were taken from me. My wife, Alejandra. A couple of years ago, she lost a baby, lost her life giving birth."

"Oh, Luca, I'm so sorry." Emma reached for his hand.

"There was nothing I could do. Nothing I could do to help her."

Emma looked at him, compassion filling her heart. "Would you be Joseph's godfather?"

"Thank you," he said, smiling. "It would be an honor." Luca reached over, stroked a strand of hair away from her cheek. "Get some sleep."

At dawn she woke to Joseph's cries. Overnight she seemed to have grown a new body. She laughed with disbelief as she looked down at her breasts. At least at first it seemed funny. The baby wailed with hunger, and yet he couldn't feed. Luca left to shower and have breakfast and a steady stream of visitors for the girl in the next-door bed stared impassively at her. Sore and bloodied, too proud to ask for help, she finally broke down and sobbed.

"Emma!" Paloma arrived bearing a huge arrangement of birds-of-paradise. "Oh you poor girl, what you've been through! Luca told me all about it!" She kissed her on both cheeks, glanced at the family next door *"Buenas,"* she acknowledged them. "Why have they got no bloody curtains in this place?" She rearranged the chairs to try to give them some privacy. "Now, who's this making all the noise? Joseph Luca? Eh, *cariño* . . ." She soothed him, laid the baby along the flat of her arm, rubbing his back. "Colic, eh?"

"Is it? I don't know. I'm not very good at all this." She gestured at her breasts. "I can't get him to feed."

Paloma perched on the side of the bed. "Don't worry. I hadn't a clue either," she said gently. "Can I help you?"

"Oh please, I'd . . . we'd be so grateful."

Paloma glanced over at an elderly uncle who was staring at the spectacle. "Eh!" she chided him. He looked away, picked up a magazine. "Sometimes

I think they should paint a sign above the door of every maternity ward: 'Leave your dignity here.'" She laughed. "Now then, show me what you have been doing." Gently, she helped Emma get the baby into position.

"Oh!" Emma's eyes widened in surprise as the baby latched on. The relief was instantaneous. "It's working! You did it!"

"Hola." Luca stood shyly at the door, with an armful of dusky pink roses. "I can come back . . ."

"No, it's fine, I'm getting used to an audience," Emma said, laughing. "Your sister has worked miracles."

Luca slumped into the armchair. He had shaved, and she caught the reassuring scent of Acqua di Parma. "Olivier's just parking the car. You look better."

"Nurse Ratched finally let me have a glass of water," she said.

"Oh God, I remember that," Paloma said. "And it's like a greenhouse in here. *Dieta blanda?*" Emma nodded. "They'll have you on gruel for days, then noodle soup if you are lucky. I tell you, by the end of the week you'll think *natillas* pudding has never tasted so good."

"How long will you be in for?" Luca asked.

"A week at least." Emma winced as she moved.

"I'll come as often as I can." He caught Paloma watching him.

"I don't know what I would have done without you," Emma said.

"It was very brave of you," Paloma said to him. Emma looked from brother to sister, aware now of the secrets that Luca held.

"It's helped, I think." He reached out for the baby's hand, stroked it with his index finger. "For years I was afraid . . . Then to see this little man, my godson . . ."

"Oh!" Paloma cried. "That's wonderful! We must have the christening party at the finca."

"I couldn't impose—" Emma began to say.

"It would be our pleasure," Luca said. "Joseph Luca is family now." He smiled at Emma. "Can I get you anything?"

"A cold bottle of water would be wonderful."

After Luca had gone, Emma gingerly edged out of the bed with Paloma's help. Her breath was tight and short. "It will get easier," Paloma said. "The anesthetic makes it hard to breathe. Can you manage?"

"I'll be fine," Emma said, taking tiny steps. "I just need the bathroom." She stepped noiselessly to the en suite, and heard the sound of Luca and Olivier talking in the corridor.

"Look at you, like a proud father," she overheard Olivier say.

"Godfather," Luca corrected him.

"Paloma tells me you stayed with her in the hospital?"

"I couldn't leave Emma alone."

"Be careful, Luca. You're playing with fire."

"I don't know what you mean."

"Luca, it has taken ages for you to put yourself back together again after Alejandra. You've only just recovered."

"Emma is a friend."

Emma frowned, looked down at her hand resting on the door handle. *What was I expecting?* she thought. *I've been kidding myself.*

"Do you really know what you are doing? It's too complicated—she doesn't belong here, she has another man's child."

"I told you," Luca said. "Emma is just a friend. That is all. I felt sorry for her, here alone." Emma heard the defensiveness in his voice.

He felt sorry for me.

"Good, good," Olivier said. "I was just worried."

"Well don't. There's nothing to worry about."

Just a friend, she thought, hope fleeing. *I'm just a friend.*

FIFTY-FOUR

Freya unlocked the door of the cottage and threw her medical bag down. She kicked off her shoes at the door and sighed. It was quiet, but she could hear Charles in the kitchen, laying out the dinner plates on the old table.

"Hiho," she said, stopping to check Liberty, who was lying curled up asleep on the sofa by the fire with her friend.

"You're late," Charles said as she walked into the kitchen.

"It was a long delivery." Freya yawned. "Poor girl was a child herself." She looked at Charles. "Has everything been OK here? Did Libby and Matie play nicely?"

"They've been fine. I picked Matie up this afternoon. They said they will collect her tomorrow morning."

"Did you do their tea?"

"Yes, they're ready for bed." He tossed the cloth onto the wooden draining board, and frowned. "Listen, we had a visit this morning. I think you'd better sit down, Freya."

"What is it, Charles?" She perched on the edge of the old pine table.

"You know I've been keeping an eye on what the Falange are up to in England?"

"Yes?"

"I was talking to one of the girls on the Basque Children's committee. The damned fascists are coming after the refugee children."

"What will we do? What if they come for Liberty?"

"The thing is, nowhere is safe. The Falange have been getting a lot of help from the English fascists. There are cells all over the country now—London, Bristol, Glasgow . . . Freya, they are stepping up their efforts to repatriate children. You've heard of the Special Delegation for the Repatriation of Minors?" Freya nodded. She was dreading what was coming. "Well, responsibility for rounding up the children has been transferred to the Falange's Foreign Service. Pius XII has even issued a papal edict saying that the children must go back to Spain or face being accused of apostasy."

"What? They'll throw them out of the Church? Oh, good grief."

"A papal envoy has approached the children's committee." Charles raked his fingers through his hair. "The fascists are being clever—much of the repatriation is being done through diplomatic channels. The British press aren't helping—all the cockamamie stories they are printing about the children stealing."

"It was the same in France, with the refugees. They thought they were criminals. There is such small-minded, bigoted . . ." Freya wrung her hands in frustration. "When you look at those beautiful, innocent children in the refugee colonies at Hammersmith and Barnes. Do you remember how beautifully Matie and the Basque children sang at that fund-raiser? How can anyone look at them and call them criminals? We can't let the fascists kidnap them."

"I don't think the Falange are going door to door snatching children."

Freya snorted. "You want to bet? After what we saw in the war, I wouldn't be surprised by anything they did. What does this mean for us?"

"I spoke to one of the chaps in Hammersmith this afternoon. The relief organizations are sending many of the children home."

"To Spain?" Freya looked through the kitchen doorway to where Liberty lay sleeping quietly on the sofa, firelight dancing over her face. Her blood chilled. "No. No, they can't take her."

"The thing is, a chap *did* arrive on the doorstep today. He gave me this." Charles slid an envelope across the table to her.

"And you say they aren't hunting down children? How did they find us? I don't understand."

"They are saying the Republicans committed an atrocity sending children overseas."

"An atrocity? Taking children out of a war zone is an atrocity?"

"Their country isn't at war anymore, ours is. Frey, they're evacuating children from London at the moment." Charles tapped the headline of the *Times*. "Children are being killed every night in the bombings." He lit a cigarette. "The chap who came today, well, he said the children deserve to be brought up as Spaniards."

"As good fascists, he means. I—" Freya stared at the envelope. Her words faded as she recognized Rosa's childish handwriting.

"Not all Nationalists are fascists." Charles waited. "Frey?"

She closed her eyes, rubbed the bridge of her nose. "Like not all Republicans are Commies? Tell that to the bitch of a matron who got me fired from my night job when she found out I'd been in Spain—'We can't have Red nurses on our ward, Miss Temple.' It's unbelievable. I went as a humanitarian! I went because I wanted to help ordinary, working people like us. Not only are the veterans from the Brigades not getting a pension, we are *still* being persecuted."

"Maybe it's no bad thing, losing that job. You're doing too much, Frey. Volunteering at the colonies with the refugee children, working as a midwife, taking care of Libby."

"What choice is there? The children need help, and we need to eat."

"I told you. We'll get by."

"What about the men who can't? The dockers and builders who lost arms and legs?" Freya put her head in her hands. "We're broke, Charles." She was close to tears. "It's never going to stop, is it? Not while Franco is in charge. They are going to keep coming after the Republicans and their families."

"We have to face it. Children are being sent back from the USSR, from France . . ."

"From England?"

"Yes, from England. I spoke to a lovely woman who was working with the Quakers. They took a group of children down to the Spanish border, and handed them over. She said it was one of the worst things she has ever had to do. But the parents of the children had written asking for them to be returned to Spain."

"Like Rosa?" Freya tapped the envelope on her thumb. "I don't believe it. It terrifies me, the thought of whatever they did to her to make her write this." Freya ripped it open and scanned the letter. "Look at this, it was written just after the end of the war. Why has it taken so long to get here, eh?" She read on and began to laugh. "Good old Rosa. Listen to this: 'Send

Lourdes home to the bosom of her family to be raised as a good Spaniard. Remember how Vicente doted on her? There will be plenty more of that.'" Freya ran her finger over Rosa's signature. "What did they do to her to even get our address?" she said quietly. "The letter is a warning, Charles. We mustn't let them get Liberty, whatever happens."

"The thing is, Frey, they've found her now. They know she's here." He took her hand. "They're coming for Matie in the morning, and they want to take Libby too."

A wave of nausea swept over her, and Freya shook her head. "No, no, no. I promised Rosa she would be safe. To hell with them if they think we are morally unfit to raise a Spanish child." She got to her feet, pacing the kitchen as she thought. "Nothing, no scheme thought up by fat, rich, frightened men is going to beat us. We can't let them win, Charles."

"It will never stop."

"Then neither will we. They can be as devious and cruel as they want, but they will never destroy truth and courage."

"But what about the agents? They are coming back."

"Then I'll have to run, with Libby." Freya looked at her brother, his pale unshaven face. "I'll adopt her, change her name." She walked through to the living room, and Charles followed. "Do you think . . ." she whispered. "Libby and Matie get on so well. Couldn't we take her too?"

"No, Frey! They're not like kittens. You can't save every Spanish child, you know."

"I was thinking—the cottage in Cornwall . . ."

"It's hardly habitable, Frey. Don't you remember how run-down it is? It was the only place we could afford with that last bit of our inheritance. I bought it thinking of our future, but we haven't had any money to do it up yet."

"Charles, after the conditions we lived in in Spain, it will seem like a palace." Freya took his hand. "It wouldn't be forever. You could come too."

"No, one of us has to work, and I'd not be much use as a fisherman with this." He nodded at his missing arm. He thought for a moment. "I shall go back to my butterflies. At least you only need one arm for the net, and I'm sure my old college would take me back to teach. I'll write to Imms." He looked at her. "You've been so terribly brave, Frey. Matie will be fine, the committee will make sure of that. I promise you, I will take care of you and Liberty." He looked at the girls sleeping on the sofa. "Whatever it takes."

FIFTY-FIVE

Just before the Fallas party, Emma tossed the last of the empty boxes into the Dumpster. Padding barefoot through the rooms, she enjoyed the peace. Over the last few weeks, the house had come together. In Emma's room, Joseph slept quietly, a fire crackling in the stove, split logs piled ready at its side. Down the corridor, she could hear guitar music drifting from Solé's room, the sound of her shower. It was taking some time to get used to having her around the house, but Macu had been right, Emma had underestimated how exhausting the first few weeks with a new baby would be, and she needed all the help she could get. Solé was a kind girl, if a little too trusting. Borys and Marek enjoyed teasing her—so far she believed that Polos were Poland's main national export, and Borys's "Chopin" vodka was bottled directly from an underground stream at his house. Emma smiled as she flopped back on her bed, stretched out her arms, luxuriated in her new white covers. It felt, finally, like everything had come right.

Emma rolled her head to the side as her mobile beeped. It was a text from Freya: *"Em, don't want to disturb you, but: Warning—Delilah on her way."* Emma's stomach lurched as she read on. *"Japanese ready to sign. She's coming to persuade you face-to-face. You hold all the cards. I'm sorry. Love you. F x"*

She dressed slowly, taking time with her hair and makeup. It was the first time in a month she had managed anything more than sweatpants and her old sweater. *If Delilah's on her way, it's just as well I'm reentering the land of the living,* Emma thought. She had been dreading the time when she would have to face her old friend, had pictured it a thousand times. Delilah would be dressed in her favorite gray silk shirt, pencil skirt, Louboutin heels, smoking in the shadows like a Veronica Lake heroine. Emma would no doubt be in a milk-stained T-shirt, with unwashed hair and saggy leggings.

The thought of Delilah had thrown her. Emma hadn't spoken to Freya since their argument, but now, she realized, she wished she was there to help her deal with Delilah. *I'll call her in the morning,* she thought. *We can't carry on the way things are.* Emma pulled a couple of dresses from her wardrobe. Nothing seemed quite right. She padded through to the blue bedroom and flicked on the light. From the wardrobe, she lifted the red dress. She was the same height and build as Rosa, and it was as if the dress had been tailored for her. With a pair of delicate heels, and a spritz of her new jasmine perfume, she was ready for the night. Emma raised her wrist to her nose, and inhaled. The balance of neroli in the top notes was not quite right yet, but the heart of it, the creamy, carnal indole scent of the jasmine, made the hair rise at the nape of her neck. She was getting close. *There's no hurry . . .* She thought of her mother's letter on perfume. *It takes time to create a great fragrance.*

Marek let out a low whistle as she walked downstairs.

"Emma, you look so beautiful," Borys said, clutching his old cap in his hands. "We came now, to say good-bye. We will stay in the inn near the bus station tonight."

"Are you leaving already? Won't you come to the dance?"

"I am too old to dance," Borys said, easing his back.

"I may come along later." Marek stepped forward, pointed at the chimney breast. "We hung the picture for you. Who are they? The girl is very beautiful."

"It's Rosa, my grandmother," Emma said. "Thank you," she said. "What a lovely surprise. I'd been meaning to get around to it." She tilted her head and smiled at Rosa's beautiful, defiant face. The house felt complete now, somehow. "I can't believe it's your last night," she said, turning to Borys and Marek. "I'm going to miss you."

"We have a last surprise for you." Marek led her out to the courtyard. "OK!" he called. Borys flicked a switch, and the pool illuminated, the new blue mosaic gleaming.

"Oh! It's beautiful!" Emma cried. "I didn't think you'd have time to do this. I'll think of you every time I swim here with Joseph."

"We should celebrate," Borys said.

"Do you like cava?"

"Cava? Yes, of course."

"Well, let's open a bottle. Joseph is staying with Solé at Macu's tonight, so for once I can relax," Emma called over her shoulder as she went to the kitchen. She came back with three glasses and handed the bottle to Borys. The cork exploded, shot across the pool.

"To our last night," she toasted. "To coming home."

Salsa pulsed along the streets of La Pobla, the rhythm like a heartbeat in the night. Emma felt young, and alive. Walking with Paloma toward the market square they drew cries of "*Guapa*!" and "*Mi amor*!" The night sky was like blue velvet, stars sparkling above the white lights hung in the trees.

"Is it always like this?" Emma asked, laughing as Paloma pushed through a group of men. The dark streets thronged with people, the cool night air laced with the smell of woodsmoke, roasting meat, the sharp explosions of *traca* firecrackers. Children dressed in traditional black smocks and blue-and-white-checked Fallas neck scarves wove among the legs of the adults as they embraced and danced. Music pulsed from the open doorways of bars. The night felt full of possibility.

"Tonight, anything goes." They weaved through the crowd. "By the way, everything is ready for the christening party tomorrow."

"Thank you. It's so kind of you all."

"It seemed like an appropriate time to celebrate little Joseph's arrival, and we are family now. Joseph is Luca's godson." Paloma nodded her head. "Talk of the devil."

Luca pushed through the crowd. "Emma, would you like to dance?"

"Go, shoo . . ." Paloma gestured toward the dance floor as she took Luca's glass of wine. "I am going to find my husband."

Luca took her in his arms, and the music lifted her. Emma gave in to the rhythm, her hips loosening, moving easily with his. She lost herself, swept away by the melody, the closeness of him, the crush of the crowd. *Just friends,* she told herself. She closed her eyes, remembered seeing him for the first time, the way time seemed to stop. He held her closer. She smelled his familiar, clean scent of leather, cologne, warm skin. She remembered how she felt the first time, sitting with him in the cathedral. She wished she could stay like this forever.

"You dance well," he said.

"Sorry?" Emma strained to hear over the music.

Luca pulled her closer, his lips against her ear. "I said, you dance well."

Emma smiled. "It's in the blood." The beat picked up, and as she spun away, their fingertips parted. A girl in a tight black dress cut in, dancing hard and close to Luca. He looked for Emma in the darkness, but when the girl kissed him, forced her lips to his, Emma backed away. She glanced back over her shoulder as she walked, crestfallen, to the bar.

"Where's Luca?" Olivier asked. Emma nodded toward the dance floor. She tried to hide her disappointment.

"Not her again," Paloma said.

"Again? Who is she?" Emma tried to sound casual.

"Just one of his girlfriends," Olivier said.

"One of the many, eh?" Emma picked up her bag.

"One of the regulars," Olivier said, turning away. "Luca has many admirers, some more serious than others." Emma caught the confusion on Paloma's face.

"Listen," Emma said. "I've had a wonderful time, but I'm tired."

"No, wait. So soon?" Paloma reached for her hand.

"Really." She glanced quickly at the dance floor. The girl was grinding against Luca, laughing as she swung her leg to his hip.

The music ended, and Luca walked to the bar, followed by the girl. "Maybe I'll join you for one, Luca, for old time's sake?"

"Suit yourself." He shrugged as he lit a cigarette, and scanned the crowd. As he glanced down the girl took the cigarette from his lips. Annoyed, he reached for another one.

The girl inhaled deeply, blew a long plume of smoke from pursed lips.

She leaned on the bar, pushing her breasts into a deep cleavage. "I don't have to work tonight," she murmured. "We could . . ."

"No." Luca said. He knocked back his glass of cognac, poured another.

"Hey, we always have fun, don't we?" She traced the back of his hand with a scarlet nail.

"I said no."

"No strings . . . just like always."

Luca stuck the cigarette into the corner of his mouth, and reached into his pocket. He tossed a wad of notes onto the counter, and picked up the bottle of cognac.

"You're leaving? What's changed?" Her brow furrowed. "Ah," she sneered. "The perfume woman?"

"I don't know what you're talking about."

"I saw you dancing with her." The girl leaned toward him. "I love perfume. You know what you smell of, Luca?" she whispered in his ear. "Sex. Always, since we were children. It's such a waste. You saved yourself for Alejandra, your childhood sweetheart, now you keep yourself for her . . ."

"Go to hell."

"You need to remember who your friends are, Luca," she whispered, dipping her finger in the cognac, running it over his lips. "You were glad of a friend when Alejandra—"

"Don't talk about my wife."

"Does the perfume woman know?" she called after him. "Does she know her rival is a ghost?"

FIFTY-SIX

"One, two, three..." Charles began to count to one hundred as Matie and Liberty ran giggling through the cottage to the garden, looking for somewhere to hide. Once they were out of earshot, he slumped down in the armchair by the window, and rubbed the bridge of his nose. He had just taken a phone call from a friend at the Barnes colony. It was time for the children to return to Spain, and they would be coming to get the girls soon.

Charles gazed out of the grimy window at the empty street. They had been lucky, so far. The bombs were falling nightly on London. Unlike many who cowered in shelters and the underground during the attacks, he and Freya carried on as normal during the bombing raids. Freya had joked that morning that they were "bombproof," but he wondered if life would ever seem simple and safe again. He thought of the girls' conversation at breakfast.

"I am going home," Matie had lisped, spooning up her porridge.

"Home? Where is home?" Liberty swung her legs on the chair.

"My home is Spain. I am going to Spain."

"Uncle Charles, where is my home? Is my home Spain?"

Charles had looked up from his newspaper. "No. Your home is here, Libby, with your Mummy—Freya, and me."

Spain, he thought now, his stomach tight with emotion. He bit at a piece of loose skin beside his thumbnail as images kaleidoscoped in his mind. He was no good alone with himself these days, unable to rest, to shake the memories, the ghosts in the back of his head. Charles covered his face with the palm of his hand, raked his hair as if he were trying to push them away. "Ninety-nine, one hundred," he called. He strode through the house, making straight for the conservatory. But for a pair of dusty old Lloyd Loom chairs, it was empty now—he hoped that one day it would be full of plants and butterflies. His footsteps echoed across the cracked tiles. "Coming, ready or not!" He knew that Liberty always hid in the little alcove in the corner, and he scraped back the door.

"Not fair!" Liberty pouted.

"Right, Libby," Charles said, his heart racing. "Let's play another game. I won't tell Matie where you are hiding. I want you to stay here, do you understand?" The child nodded. "I want you to be very, very quiet."

"Like a mouse!"

"Yes, like a mouse." Charles glanced at his watch. They would be here any minute. "Stay here until I come and get you."

He pushed the cupboard door closed, and locked it.

"Matie!" he called as he went out into the garden. "Matie!" He heard giggling from behind the potting shed. "Found you!" He picked her up and hugged her, a lump forming in his throat. Charles carried her into the house, and she clung to his neck. "Now, Matie, some nice people from the committee will be here soon, with some other people, from Spain."

"From home?"

"Yes, Matie, from home. Libby is hiding," he said. "She's hiding very, very well. So these people mustn't find her, Matie. If they ask you where Libby is, you say she has gone away. You say you were playing last night and Libby went away."

"Yes, Uncle Charles."

"It's a game," he said quietly. "Just a game." There was a knock at the door as he walked through the house. "It's time to go home," he said as he opened the door. His face set grimly as he looked at the men on the doorstep. A woman from the rescue committee stepped forward and took Matie's hand.

"Good-bye, Matie," he said, screwing his eyes closed as he kissed the top of her head. "God bless."

"You have the children's papers?"

"Yes. One moment." Charles reached into his pocket, and handed them to the man.

"Where is the other child?"

"Didn't they tell you?" Charles held his gaze. "There was an accident. Lourdes del Valle was killed in a bombing raid."

"I'm sorry. We will of course investigate." The man shook his hand. His eyes narrowed, glancing at Charles's missing arm. "This must be very difficult for you. I can assure you the child's future is in Spain."

Charles looked at Matie's bright, hopeful face in the back of the car. She waved at him. "Take care of her," he said quietly, and closed the door.

Charles leaned against the wall, listening to the car pull away. His heart was thumping, and he stumbled as he walked toward the kitchen. He poured a large whiskey from the bottle on the dresser, and picked up the phone.

"Hello," he said, his hand shaking as he held the receiver. "Is that the children's committee? This is Charles Temple. I'm afraid I have some bad news. The little girl staying with us, Lourdes del Valle. Yes . . ." He listened as the woman sorted through her paperwork. "We were caught out last night during the bombing raid." He listened as the woman at the other end of the phone talked. "I'm afraid she was killed. Yes, the rest of us are unharmed, a few bruises. No, they haven't been able to recover a body yet. Yes, of course. I'll come in and sign any paperwork you need. Thank you. Yes, we are all devastated."

"Charles?" Freya said. He wheeled around, saw her standing in the kitchen behind him, her face ashen. She was carrying a basket of groceries ready for the journey to Cornwall.

"Good-bye," he said and hung up the phone.

"Charles, what have you done?"

"Freya, I had no choice. They came for Liberty."

"What did you do?" she yelled.

"Matie has gone home, but Libby is safe."

"What are you talking about? Have you gone mad? How could you pretend she's dead? I wanted to adopt her, legally." Freya walked to the telephone. "I'm going to call the committee, tell them you'd been drinking, tell them you'd lost your senses."

Charles pressed down on the phone, disconnected the line. "They will take her. They will take Liberty from you, just like they took Matie. Do you understand?" He gripped Freya by the shoulder. "I promised you I would protect you and Liberty."

"So what are we supposed to do? Run, and hide all our lives?" Freya shook her head in disbelief. "You're insane!" She rubbed the back of her hand over her lips.

"From now on, Spain never existed," Charles said. "Rosa, Jordi, they are gone. Lourdes del Valle is dead." He hugged her, whispered into her hair, "Liberty Temple is your daughter, Freya. No one must ever know the truth."

"I can't do it, Charles. I can't build our whole life on a lie."

"Well you have no choice. They will take her, if they find out, Frey. They have the letter from Rosa and that's all the authority they need. We can do it, Frey, we have to, for Libby. I don't know if they are going to fall for it. Children are being killed every single day in the raids, but they'll be suspicious. They'll be watching us." He turned to Freya. "I think it is best if you and Liberty leave for Cornwall immediately. It's not safe here, the Falange have spies everywhere."

"The suitcases are almost packed."

"Good. I'll bring the car around and take you straight to the station." He thought for a moment. "In case they are watching the house, we can hide Libby in one of the cases, tell her it's part of the game."

"Part of the game?" Freya cried, cupped her hands over her face, rubbed wearily at her eyes. "I can't—"

"You can, Frey. We can do this, for her." His voice shook. "If we save one child, just one child from . . . from, *that*," he said, screwing his eyes shut as images of the war powered into his mind. He shook his head, and looked at Freya. "One child, one precious child makes a difference."

"We'll never get away with it."

"We will. We're at war—people disappear all the time. The authorities are overworked, people slip through the cracks." Charles thought for a moment. "Once you get to Cornwall, just tell them we lost everything during the Blitz, all our paperwork, her birth certificate. Tell them she's your illegitimate daughter, that you had her in Spain." He took her hand. "Liberty is your daughter now, Freya."

"Where is she?"

"She's hiding in the conservatory. I locked her in the cupboard."

"You did what?" As Freya ran through, Charles drained his drink, listened to her talking calmly to the child. Freya pushed past him, holding her, Liberty's legs wrapped around her waist.

"Where is Matie, Uncle Charles?" Liberty said over Freya's shoulder.

"She had to go home." Charles held Freya's gaze, his eyes hard and determined. "Now, darling," he said, "we are going to play a game. Let's pretend . . ."

FIFTY-SEVEN

Emma had not missed hangovers. She searched through the new cupboards in her bathroom but couldn't find any Tylenol. She chewed two children's aspirin and grimaced, letting her head rest against the cool mirror. As she closed her eyes, she saw again the woman seductively dancing with Luca. "God, I'm such a fool," she said under her breath. She straightened up, and ran her hands through her hair. Reflected in the mirror, she could see Rosa's red dress still on the floor where she had thrown it the night before. Emma picked it up, and put it on a hanger on the bathroom door, smoothing the heavy silk. She remembered how wonderful she had felt, dancing with Luca, his hand warm against the small of her back, the music moving through them, around them. She closed her eyes again, hot with humiliation. *Such a fool,* she thought. *As if he'd even look twice at me.* Luca's words, overheard in the hospital came back to her: *she's just a friend.* The sound of distant church bells tolling roused her, and she glanced at her watch.

"Solé," she called down the stairs, hopping as she zipped up her boot. "It's time to go." She could hear voices in the kitchen, and furrowed her brow. She grabbed her favorite Nicole Farhi jacket and ran downstairs.

"The service starts in quarter of an hour," she said, looking down as she fastened Rosa's locket around her neck.

"Well, look at you, stranger," Delilah drawled.

Emma's head shot up. Delilah was standing in the middle of the kitchen, with Joseph in her arms.

"Your nanny tells me you're on the way to Joe's christening." She looked down at the baby. "I feel like the bad fairy, turning up without an invite."

"What are you doing here?"

Delilah stepped toward her. "He's beautiful, Em. He looks just like his daddy." She waved her hand around the room. "And all this. It's perfect. But then you always do everything to perfection."

"I'm not perfect. I've never tried to be perfect."

"You don't have to try to be anything—you just *are* perfect. Face of a successful company, homemaker, beauty, loyal friend . . . you had it all, and now you're the mother of his child." She leaned in to Emma. "Congratulations."

"This wasn't to get back at you, if that's what you think."

"You fucked him, after he was with me," she said under her breath. "You have his baby. It's not fair, you still have part of Joe."

"We're both grieving," Emma whispered, glancing at Solé.

"Yeah, except I'm not allowed to. I was the bitch who broke you up."

"Play the victim if you want to, Lila, you were always very good at that."

"He loved me. He married me."

"He loved us both, and nothing is ever going to change that." She looked at the clock. "Solé, would you mind taking Joseph on to the church? I'll see you there in a few minutes. Luca is waiting for you."

"Luca? Who's Luca?" Delilah asked as she handed the baby to Solé. Emma tried not to show her relief.

"Joseph's godfather. A friend."

"How nice. Just like me."

Emma waited until she heard the front door close. She rounded on Delilah. "You gave up any rights to my friendship the first time you slept with Joe."

Delilah held up her hands. "Forgive me."

"Give me one good reason why I should."

"Because I'm sorry from the bottom of my heart." She tilted her head. "Because I bet you haven't stayed up all night talking and listening to James Taylor with anyone else. Do you remember?" She began to sing " 'You've got a friend . . .' "

Emma picked up her handbag and slung it over her shoulder. "For the love of God, don't start singing at me," she said walking away.

"Yeah, I could never hold a tune." Delilah followed her outside, slipped on a pair of sunglasses, the gilt tips catching the sunlight.

"Listen, this is a bad time."

"I'm not going to stay long. I just want you to sign the papers."

"I'm going to need to think about that." Emma said as she locked the front door behind them. "Where are you staying?"

"Here."

"You've got to be joking?"

"What are you going to do, throw me out? We need to go over the Japanese deal. No need to thank me by the way . . ."

"Thank you?" Emma cried.

"Without me, the entire sale would have fallen through. You want a clean break? Fine. That's what I'm giving you." The women strode out through the gate and headed toward the village. Delilah glanced at Emma. "You look too good for a woman who has just had a baby."

"Flattery will get you nowhere." Her headache was still thumping, and she winced in the bright sun. "Do you know, Lila, when I first knew for sure you and Joe were having an affair? I was driving to the office, and saw you walking along the King's Road. I waved at you, slowed down to give you a lift—I know you saw me, and you walked away."

"I don't remember."

"You were so guilty, you couldn't look at me."

"That was after the first time," she said quietly.

"So where did this happen?"

"What?"

"When did your affair begin?"

"Don't, Em . . ."

"No!" she yelled, stopping dead. "I want to know. How many nights do you think I cried myself to sleep, Lila? Wondering how and where it started."

"Brighton," she said quietly.

"Brighton?"

"We'd been working late. It was a beautiful evening. I said to Joe, 'Why don't we drive down to the coast just for fun, like we all used to in the old days.' "

Emma remembered the three of them in Joe's convertible, Lila normally hungover and asleep in the backseat, the wind lashing her face as they raced toward the coast.

"It should have been me," Delilah said quietly.

"What?"

"I waited all that time for him. He'd been dating that girl at home . . ."

"Clare?"

"Yeah, that's right. Square Clare. All through the first year at Columbia, he stayed faithful to her. I tried my best . . ."

"I'm sure you did."

"Then I heard he'd split up with her. That first night of our last semester, I was going to tell him I was in love with him." Delilah laughed bitterly. "But there you were, pitching up for your stupid little course like a breath of fresh air, vibrant, beautiful." She sighed. "Joe confided in me that night—can you believe it? I could see you had both fallen in love at first sight." She looked Emma in the eye. "I'd missed my one chance. You stole my moment. I hated you."

Emma held her gaze. "You hid it well." She turned and walked on to the church.

"I didn't want to lose him. If I showed you how I felt, I'd have lost Joe too. They always say love is just a different way of looking at a friend. I had to learn to make my love for Joe look like friendship."

"So none of it . . . *Our* friendship, it was all a sham?"

"At first. But you—you're just so damn lovable. I think it was when I had flu that winter I first started to warm to you."

"Me, or my ginger chicken soup?" Emma remembered the endless hot water bottles she made for Delilah, the hours spent poring through old copies of *Vanity Fair* and *Vogue* on her bed, surrounded by tissues. "I don't know how I never caught it."

"You? You're never sick. You have the immune system of a hippopotamus."

"Are they healthy?"

"God knows." Delilah riffled through her handbag and lit a cigarette. "Oh, what a mess, Em. I'm sorry."

Emma stopped on the steps of the church, and looked at Delilah. This was the woman who had destroyed her life. *But she's hurting too,* she thought. Reluctantly, Emma hugged her. "I forgive you."

"Really?"

"What else can I do? We both . . ." She hesitated. "We both lost him."

Delilah held her close. "Thank you. Life's too short, Em, that's what your mum said to me once." Emma stiffened at the mention of Liberty, but Delilah held on. "She was right, as always. Let's put the past behind us."

Uprooted tree stumps ready for the bonfires towered in a pile on the outskirts of the village like a funeral pyre, roots crusted with balls of red earth. Beyond them, figures walked across the open land, like the souls of the dispossessed in the gray light of the late afternoon, eyes to the ground.

"What are they doing, the people out there?" Delilah said as she swung the car past, tires squealing.

"They're gathering snails," Emma said from the backseat. She tucked Joseph into his car seat with a blanket. "It's Fallas. Everyone is cooking paella."

"What do they do with them?"

"Put them in a bag with herbs, clean them, and eat them. You should try them."

"Eugh, sounds disgusting." Delilah's rental car bumped along the road. "Damn," she muttered as they hit a pothole. "Maybe we should have brought yours. This is going to bugger up my tracking. I don't know how you can live here. I mean look at this shithole—the whole country is like a building site. Mangy dogs everywhere. Look at that . . ." She gesticulated toward a flock of brown sheep grazing the dusty earth in the shade of an olive tree. "It's like the fricking biblical times."

"I like it here."

"Oh don't get defensive, darling. I'm just worried about you, Em, that's all. This is hardly what you're used to." She ran her hand through her glossy blond waves. Emma was always surprised by how small Lila's fingers were, like a child's, tapering to tiny red nails from a soft, round palm. "You do seem awfully on edge."

I wonder why, Emma thought. She couldn't believe Delilah had charmed an invitation to the party out of Dolores.

"Have you spoken to anyone? I mean a lot of women get depressed after having a baby." Delilah glanced in the rearview mirror.

"I'm not depressed!"

"Come on, darling, look at you. You've let yourself go a bit, haven't you? When was the last time you had your hair done?"

Emma took a deep breath. Up ahead at a farm a furnace glimmered darkly. A group of six or seven men were bent intently over a stone plinth. Four dark legs thrashed above them.

"What the hell is going on there?" Delilah cried.

"Don't look," Emma said, remembering the effect blood had on her. She winced at the piercing shrieks of the animal. "They're killing a pig."

"What is this? Lord of the fucking Flies?" Delilah raised her fist as the car roared past. "Bastards!"

"You eat bacon. Where do you think it comes from?"

"I don't want to know!" Delilah checked her reflection in the rearview mirror, ran her tongue over her teeth.

"Turn here." Emma indicated the long drive to the de Santangel finca.

"Well . . ." Delilah said as they swept up to the front of the house. "This is more like it. Your friend has looks and money. Quite a package."

"*Hola,*" Luca said, opening the door for Emma. He kissed Joseph's head, then Emma on both cheeks. "It was a lovely service. Come on inside."

"Thank you." Emma forced a bright smile. If he could behave like last night was nothing, then so could she.

Delilah climbed out. "Hello, everyone, what a beautiful place. I . . ." She strolled around, her voice trailing off as she saw the caterers carrying a freshly slaughtered lamb to the fire pit for roasting "Oh God!" she gasped and fainted. Luca lunged forward and caught her in his arms.

"Not again," Emma said. "She always does this at the sight of blood."

Luca carried her to a bench, reached into the fountain, and splashed water on her brow. Delilah fluttered her eyes.

"Slap her," Emma muttered. "That helps sometimes."

"I apologize, Delilah," he said.

"I could forgive you anything." She gazed up at him. "Do call me Lila, all my friends do."

Emma stalked toward the house as Paloma came out to meet her, arms open wide in greeting. "Here's the guest of honor!" She took Joseph in her arms. "Where's your friend?"

Emma nodded toward the fountain. "Draped over your brother."

Paloma's eyes narrowed. "Ah. I know her kind." She leaned in to Emma. "My guess is she doesn't have many girlfriends?"

Emma realized suddenly Lila hadn't. Emma still had people she'd known since schooldays in her life. *Loyal friends,* she thought. *Delilah had only me.*

"Luca's no fool."

Unlike me. Emma frowned. She wasn't going to let Delilah spoil the day. She looped her arm through Paloma's. "Thank you, this is so beautiful," she said as they walked through to the party.

"It's our pleasure. How about a drink? Let me get you some juice."

"Juice? No, thanks—I'd love a glass of wine."

"Wine? Welcome back to the land of the living!"

As the guests mingled, Joseph was passed from person to person, old ladies cooing over him, giving Emma advice she hadn't sought but accepted with good grace. On the terrace, Paloma had set a table with white linen, strung lanterns from the shady tree overhead. The meal was simple, but delicious. Luca sat at the head of the table. Emma noticed Delilah made sure she was sitting at his side. She had always tolerated Delilah's flirtatiousness toward every attractive man she came across, but now her every move, her voice, her laughter grated on her nerves. Emma selected a fig from the bowl on the table, inhaled its clear green notes, and woody, earthy scent. She picked up a small, sharp silver knife, sliced it open. *I think what I am feeling is close to hate.* Emma's senses were acute. She felt like she was seeing clearly for the first time in months. Her teeth sank into the sweet fruit, soft on her tongue. She looked up, felt Luca watching her.

Night fell, and the adults sat talking while children ran, laughing, across the lawns. Benito dragged the stereo outside, and in the courtyard people began to dance.

"He's been very good." Luca paused beside Emma's chair. He stroked the baby's face as he slept in her arms. "I said I would show your friend Valencia tomorrow. Why don't you come along?"

"I'll think about it." Emma glared at his back as he walked over to talk to Delilah.

"Ah, Joseph's sleeping at last," Paloma said, leaning over.

"It's been quite a day," Emma said, watching Delilah.

"Don't make it so obvious," Paloma whispered to Emma, evidently reading her thoughts. "No one here knows the history. As far as they know she is your best friend, come over from England for the christening. You will come off badly. Someone like her is very good at charming everyone— like Machiavelli, a semblance of goodness, no? When underneath, I'm guessing . . ."

"Thank God you're here." Emma squeezed her hand. "No one would believe it anyway, would they? Look at how easy and charming she is. No one would believe she stole the love of my life."

"Was he?"

"Joe?" Emma hesitated. "I . . . I don't know. He was the first man I ever loved. I was practically a child when I met him."

"Then don't speak too soon." Paloma caught Luca watching them. "Perhaps the love of your life is still to come."

FIFTY-EIGHT

Charles sat at a picnic table, sipping a Styrofoam cup of tea in the courtyard beside the Chelsea Gardener. He was reading the newsletter from the International Brigade Memorial Trust, waiting for Freya. An obituary for one of the doctors who had worked with Bethune's blood transfusion service caught his eye. *What was the name of that chap?* he thought, casting his mind all the way back to a day in 1942.

He had been lolling around in the cottage one afternoon, trying to get up the nerve to call Freya down in Cornwall. It took several thuds of the door knocker to rouse him.

"Who the hell is that now?" Charles had staggered to his feet, knocking over an empty bottle. The kitchen table was littered with glasses and dirty plates, and the cat stood in the middle of it, licking a bowl. He stumbled through the living room, tripping on a pile of books and newspapers. There was another knock on the door. "I'm coming!" he yelled, wrenched open the door, and peered out. The light was fading as evening fell, and he squinted at the man standing on the doorstep. "Can I help you?"

Tom took off his trilby, and tucked it under his arm. "Hello," he said, and offered Charles his hand. He folded up the piece of paper with the address written on it.

Charles glimpsed Freya's handwriting. He looked suspiciously at the bouquet of white roses in his hand. "Do I know you?"

Tom laughed. "No, we've never met. I'm Tom Henderson. I'm a friend of Freya's. You must be her brother, Charles."

"I'm afraid she doesn't live here anymore." Charles leaned against the doorway. His head was spinning, and Tom's face swayed before him.

"It's been a while. I've been in China, with Bethune's blood unit."

"Bethune? I remember him."

"He died in '39, sadly, but we've been carrying on his work."

Charles had the horrible sensation that he was about to be sick. "She's gone," he said brusquely.

"Do you have a forwarding address? I wrote to Freya a couple of times, but never heard back. I'm going home to Canada, but I hoped . . ."

"She married some time ago," Charles lied, thinking guiltily of the letters he'd destroyed. "She has a daughter." He saw Tom's face fall with disappointment.

"I'd still like to write to her, to explain—"

"No, that's quite impossible." It was too dangerous. He wasn't going to risk anyone connected with Spain being a part of their life. He lived in fear of the knock at the door, of the danger that Liberty could still be taken from them.

"Could you just tell Freya I came?" Tom reached into his pocket for his wallet and handed Charles his card. "I understand it's too late, that I lost . . ." He paused, and shrugged. "I lost my chance. I should have guessed she'd have married."

Charles wavered. It was clear this man loved her. *No,* he thought. *Freya must never know.* The only way they could be safe was to cut off from their past entirely. Out of sight, he crumpled Tom's card in his fist. "I'm sorry. You had a wasted journey. She's not coming back."

Charles heaved himself to his feet now, and tossed his cup into the bin. He shuffled through to the garden center and spotted Freya up ahead, choosing bedding plants.

"Frey!" he called. She looked up, and smiled. *Still beautiful,* he thought, walking toward her. It was like a painting: the dazzling flowers in the fading light setting off the angular lines of her gray bob and her stooped, slender body in its trademark black polo neck.

"I'm not done," she snapped. "You know I don't like to be rushed. I told you to have some tea and wait for me."

"Stop bossing me around, woman." He tapped the newsletter sticking out of his jacket pocket. "Another one gone—some chap who ran the blood transfusion units."

Freya's face fell. "Not Tom Henderson?"

"No, but that's the name I was searching for. Who was he?"

"Tom?" Freya touched the petals of the deep blue pansy she was holding. Charles noticed how her face softened, the sadness in her eyes. "Tom was . . ." She shrugged and put the plant down. "We were in love. I hoped . . ." She sighed. "Well, it didn't work out. The last I heard, he went off to China with Bethune. He forgot all about me." She hugged herself. "I never forgot him though. Maybe that's why I never married. None of the other men could hold a candle to Tom."

"For heaven's sake, woman, all this time? Why didn't you tell me about him?"

"I don't know why I'm telling you now." She walked on through the Chelsea Gardener, gazing at the rows of multicolored plants laid out for the spring. "I think it's Emma, having the baby. It feels like a new beginning for us all. After Liberty, and poor Matie . . ." Her voice trailed off. "My own problems didn't seem to matter anymore. I buried myself down in Cornwall, made a new life." Freya followed him with her gaze as he walked on. "You know, it's the christening this weekend, and Fallas."

"Oh, Frey, I still haven't made up my mind."

"I'd like to be there, for Emma. Delilah is on her way, and I don't trust her one bit. Not one bit."

They shuffled home along the teeming streets, headlights starting to illuminate as night fell. Cars beeped in frustration as they took too long to cross the road, and Charles flicked a white van the V-sign once they were safely on the pavement. He was puffing for breath as he pulled out the front-door keys.

"Why didn't you tell me all this years ago?" he said as the door closed behind them. "The Canadian chap turned up in London, you know."

"Tom?" Her jaw dropped. "Tom came back for me?" Freya felt behind her, lowered herself onto a chair by the front window.

"Yes, very pleasant fellow. I told him you were married, had a child."

"Oh, Charles." She shook her head as she flicked on the lamp. "Why?"

"Well, you still weren't talking to me, and it was so soon after they tried to take Libby. I thought it was safer if we cut off all links with Spain. I was trying to protect you both." He squeezed her shoulder. "There were letters too . . ." Charles winced as Freya cried out.

"Why didn't you tell me?"

"Christ, I'm sorry, Frey, if I'd known . . ." Charles pulled his glasses from his top pocket. "You never talked about him. If he mattered so much, why did you never try to contact him?"

"I was scared." Freya looked at her hands. "When I heard nothing, I was scared Tom had found someone else, or that what we had would have changed. I was scared I loved more than I was loved." She glanced at Charles.

"Ridiculous. I've never known you to be scared of anything." He shuffled over to his laptop. "I always thought you could have done more with your life. Perhaps because of this Tom chap you never took the risk."

"More than what, Charles? I worked, I raised a family. Has it ever occurred to you that I have done everything I always wanted. I lived, Charles—"

"And loved?"

"Yes, I loved. I loved Tom, very much, very passionately even though we were together a short time." She rubbed her eyes. "Anyway, you're a fine one to talk, Casanova," Freya said. "You were so caught up in the war, you missed what was right in front of you. Whatever you say, you wasted your life on regret too, Charles."

Charles slumped down into the desk chair. "You're talking about Immaculada, aren't you?"

"You missed your chance, Charles. She adored you. If you had asked, she would have gone with you."

"Do you think I haven't been over this a thousand times in my mind? What if I had taken her with me? What if Hugo and I had just left after the Brigades disbanded?" He raked his hand through his hair and glanced at the sideboard. "Is there any Scotch left?"

"No. And you know you're not supposed to—the doctor warned you about your liver."

"Frey, I am eighty-six. Let me live a little." He polished his glasses. "She was a beautiful girl," he said, his face growing wistful. "I expect she married that sensible boy who followed her around like a puppy. What was his name?"

"Ignacio."

"Yes, Ignacio." Charles pressed his lips together, and shrugged. "Maybe we both missed our chances. But it's not too late." He flexed his fingers over Freya's laptop. "There's no time like the present."

"What are you doing?" Freya struggled to her feet, looked over his shoulder. Charles typed "Dr. Thomas Henderson, Canada" into Google. Seconds later, an address appeared. "Oh, I don't know. I can't . . ."

"Too late now." Charles dialed through the number on screen, and handed her the headset.

"Good morning, Dr. Henderson's office."

"I can't do this, Charles . . ." Freya began to say. "Ah, good morning. Is that Dr. Tom Henderson?"

"Yes, good morning, ma'am. How can we help?"

"Is it possible to have a word with him?"

"I'll put you through. May I ask who is calling?"

"Freya Temple."

"One moment please."

Freya was shaking, and Charles stood to let her sit down. She heard the sound of a phone being picked up. "Good morning. Tom Henderson." Her heart was beating hard.

"Tom? Is that you?" He sounded the same to her, exactly the same. It couldn't be possible. She felt the years fall away, remembered how it felt to hold him, how his eyes crinkled when he smiled, how she loved him.

The man laughed. "Yes, it's me. Who is this?"

"It's Freya." Perhaps he had forgotten her, after all this time? "You may not remember . . . we worked together with Beth."

"Beth?" She heard him pause. "Dr. Bethune? Oh, I get it. You must want my dad? Tom Henderson Senior?"

Freya clapped her hand to her head. "Of course."

"Say, are you *the* Freya? The one he always talked about after Mom died?"

The Freya, she thought. "I hope so."

He laughed. "Oh man, he would have loved this."

Her heart sank. "Do you mean Tom's . . . ?"

"I'm afraid Dad died last spring."

"I'm so sorry." Freya felt tears coming to her eyes. "I'm so terribly sorry for your loss."

"Hell . . ." He sighed. "I miss Dad every day. But, you know, my son is the spitting image of him."

"Did he . . . did you all have a good life?" Freya wiped at her cheek, her hand trembling.

"The best," he said. "After Dad came back from China in '42, he married my mom. They had six kids—"

"Six?" Freya laughed through her tears.

"You know what Dad was like, he always loved kids."

Freya thought of him playing with the children on the street in Madrid, clowning around, handing out sweets. The thought of this other life, the one they had no chance to share together, clutched at her heart. "I expect he was a wonderful father."

"Mom and Dad had fifty good years together. Lived to see his grandkids, that's what he always wanted."

Freya pictured him, the patriarch of a brood of dark-haired children. "I'm so glad to hear he was happy," she said, trying to keep her voice steady.

"He never forgot you, Freya," he said. He fell silent for a moment. "Man, you guys saw some times."

"We did," she said, and stemmed a tear. "We certainly did."

"He wondered . . . I don't know if I should even ask you this. Dad talked a lot about you, after Mom died. He wondered sometimes whether you regretted not waiting for him."

"But I did. I did wait for him." Freya thought of his handsome, open face, how she loved him. She took Charles's hand, squeezed it in reassurance. "There was a misunderstanding. I never married."

"I'm so sorry—"

"No, don't be. I have had a wonderful life too—" She closed her eyes, held on to the memory of the last time she saw Tom, when he walked away from the hotel room in Valencia, his smile as he waved good-bye. "But every day I've thought of Tom. Every single day."

FIFTY-NINE

"Open your mouth," Luca said, looking at his watch.

"Why?" Delilah said.

"Trust me! The Mascletà fireworks . . ." There was a huge explosion. The air shook, and cheers erupted from the packed city square.

Emma's eyes widened with shock. It felt to her like the air was shimmering, disintegrating—the noise was like a physical blow, the acrid smoke overwhelmed her. "Why do they do this?" she shouted.

"It makes you feel alive!" Luca laughed, guiding them through the festival crowds to where they had parked near Plaza la Reina. An effigy of the Virgin as tall as the cathedral towered over them beneath blue-and-white awnings. Fallas queens bearing carnations passed the flowers up to men who clambered around the scaffolding, threading the stems in, weaving the Virgin's robes. As the crush thinned out, he turned to them. "What would you like to do now? See the coast, or eat? The bullfight perhaps?"

"Oh, the bullfight!" Delilah took his arm.

"Are you sure? We don't want you fainting again," Emma said.

"I'm sure Luca will take care of me, and you should try everything once." Delilah lowered her sunglasses and stared at him from beneath sooty lashes. "Or twice, if you enjoy it."

Emma fought the temptation to punch Luca in the arm as he laughed. Her eyes bored into Delilah's slender back as they walked on, striding ahead of her. Her shoulders were thrust back, outlining the blades, her spine a sinuous indentation above her backside, undulating like an inverted heart. She was wearing pink. Emma knew this meant she wanted to appear feminine, vulnerable. Emma glanced nervously at Luca. *Oh God, he can't take his eyes off her. I feel like I'm wearing a tent.* The breeze lifted the loose white cotton dress that Emma wore.

Emma hadn't wanted to risk leaving Delilah alone with Luca, so she had joined them, leaving Joseph at home with Solé.

"Shotgun!" Delilah cried, jumping into the front seat of Luca's car. He opened the door for Emma, and she slipped into the back.

Luca edged through the backstreets and pulled out into the swirling traffic on Guillem de Castro. "So this is your first time in Valencia, Lila?"

"It is. I think it's marvelous." She leaned forward, gazed up at the twin towers of the Torres de Quart. "Look at that gorgeous castle! It's like something from a fairy tale. Like Rapunzel."

"It's not a castle. They are part of the old wall. I think it was a women's prison for a while."

"When was that?" Emma looked at the huge Gothic towers and thought of Rosa. *Was she imprisoned there, before Ventas?* She imagined all the women crammed in the cold stone rooms with their children.

"I don't know. A long time ago. You know the story of El Cid?" Luca drove on. "Charlton Heston rode from that tower, strapped to his horse."

"How romantic!" Delilah said, gazing up at the huge stone towers, pocked with the marks of cannonballs. Through the archway she glimpsed several huge papier-mâché figures. "God, they're a bit macabre, aren't they? Were you serious when you said they are going to burn all those things tomorrow night?"

"Of course," he said. "It's the last night of the Fallas festival, la Cremà. The whole city will be ablaze."

Delilah craned around to look at the towers. "Look, there are people up there—we should go up later." She glanced back at Emma, and pulled a face. "Oh, of course we can't. I'd forgotten about your vertigo, Em."

Emma folded her arms. "Don't let me stop you."

"You like architecture, Lila?" Luca said. "We have a little time before the bullfight. I'll show you the new City of Arts and Sciences."

Luca drove out over the Calatrava Bridge. Emma gazed up at the white ribs arched against the cobalt sky. They seemed like bleached bones to her. The dazzling white buildings, set in shimmering tesserae pools, reminded her of vertebrae, ribs, eyes. She thought of Vicente's fractured bones, scattered beneath the lime. "It is too late to know what happened here, but it must have been during the war," the policeman had said. "There were so many atrocities . . . this man had been cut limb from limb." Emma leaned her head against the window. At least his remains were now safely interred in the del Valle family grave. She was not superstitious, but she had definitely felt the atmosphere in the house change. Emma was so lost in her thoughts that when the car stopped near the bullring after circling the city, she looked up in surprise. Luca came around and opened the door for her.

"Thank you," Emma said.

"You're very quiet. Are you enjoying yourself?"

"It's very entertaining." Emma folded her arms. "The way you've been flirting with Delilah."

"Flirting? I was being kind to your friend, that's all."

"Very kind."

"Now you're being unreasonable."

"Unreasonable?" She couldn't stop herself now. "I'm always reasonable, Luca. Good old reasonable Emma."

"What is wrong with you today?"

"Nothing. I told you, I'm just tired."

"Would you like to go home?"

"Yes."

"We're not leaving are we?" Delilah joined them. "Come on, don't be so boring, Em!"

Emma bit the inside of her cheek. The thought of spending any more time with Delilah didn't appeal. She checked her watch. "You two go ahead. I should get back for Joseph."

"Are you sure?" Luca said.

She backed away from them. "Have fun. I'll get a cab and see you back at the house." She caught the triumphant look on Delilah's face as she turned away.

In the Plaza de Toros, a searing blue disk of sky looked down on the churned ocher earth.

"I hope these seats are all right?" Luca ushered Delilah in ahead of him.

"I'm sure they are perfect."

"I like the sun. When you buy tickets for the *corrida* you choose, *sol* or *sombra*. Sun or shade."

"Fascinating." Delilah gazed around the arena. "Does Em enjoy this?"

"I don't know. We've never been."

"I doubt she would. Bless her, she can be very moody." Delilah pulled a red lipstick from her bag, pouted her lips. "So, tell me what happens."

"The matadors go to the *capilla*—"

"The what?"

"The chapel. Before they fight, they ask the Virgin for protection." The crowd roared. "Now, this is the *paseíllo*—the parade."

Delilah yawned. "Who sits up there?"

"That is the box for the president, or the most important person here. Today it is the mayor, and with him a vet and an artistic consultant."

"Art?" She laughed through her nose. "They call butchering bulls art?"

"It is."

"Oh come on, it's a funny little man in a shiny suit—"

"It is the suit of lights, the silk is strong, like armor."

". . . goading a great big bull."

"If you saw the matador's bodies, there is nothing funny about it. Each one is a mass of scars." He folded his arms. "You don't understand. We identify with the bull and the matador. It is the intensity of the relationship—"

Delilah cried out, burying her head on Luca's shoulder as the bull staggered under a blow, deadly bright banderillas sticks fluttering, hooked in its back. When she raised her head, lipstick had smeared across his shirt. "I am sorry . . ." As she went in to kiss him, Luca stood abruptly.

"No, I am sorry. You have made a mistake."

He pushed his way out of the bullring, and reached for his mobile phone as it buzzed. He looked at the message: *"Cuenca, tomorrow? Em x."*

Emma sat on the terrace, watching the flaming sunset, the phone at her side. She mulled over her conversation with Freya. She had told her about Delilah's arrival in Spain, and Freya in turn told her the story of her affair with Tom. Emma had never heard Freya talk so openly before, and she longed to see her, to comfort her.

"Don't miss this moment," Freya said finally, her voice catching. "If you think you have a chance of happiness with this Luca chap, don't let Delilah ruin everything before it's even started. Fight for him, Em."

Emma was surrounded by the last of Liberty's letters, the empty box gleaming. She sipped her wine and gazed out across the mountains, bats looping lazily above the orange trees. In her hand lay the final envelope: "In Case of Emergency." She picked up the silver paperknife, gilded by the last rays of the sun. She hesitated for a moment, then slit the envelope open.

Darling Emma,

First off, whatever it is is nowhere near as bad as you think. If you have reached one of those moments in life where you are at a crossroads, stop and think. Change is the one sure thing in life. As much as we cling to the familiar, everything is transient. Life can be beautiful or dreadful—often simultaneously. When it is dreadful, it is good to remember that everything changes. It will pass. Think of the possibilities ahead—seek out the beautiful.

Stop, and listen to yourself. The answer is within you. Make your decision, then act. It really doesn't matter much whether you have made the perfect choice. You have made a choice. You are determining your own fate, not buffeted around by chance. This is why so many dreams remain just that—people fail to follow their gut instinct, Em. Trust yourself. Take that step. If life knocks you down, get back up. If it knocks you down again, get back on your feet and look it in the eye—every time.

There will always be something or someone to battle against. Most often, that battle is with yourself. Choose your fights carefully, and your friends. Life is short, and trust me it goes by too fast. Don't waste time on people who sap your energy, Em—surround yourself with people who give you strength. Don't let idiots push you around. Be strong. Fight back. Don't let them pass the line you have drawn. If your heart and soul are strong, you win—every time.

You are stronger than you can ever realize, and I am always, always covering your back.

I love you, Emma. You can do it.

Mum xxx

Emma smiled. This was the advice she had been looking for. *Thanks, Mum.* She looked at the letters scattered across the table. All the other advice, about business, family, friendships, each letter would have its day. She picked up her mobile and fired off a text to Luca. Next, she unscrewed the lid of her Montblanc and flipped through the Japanese contracts for Liberty Temple. She initialed each page, and paused when she reached the final one. For a moment, she imagined going back to London, staging a buyout, forcing Delilah out of the company. Emma looked out across her garden at the sunset, the lavender mountains. *Seek out the beautiful.* This was where she belonged. This was worth fighting for.

With a flourish, she signed her name next to Delilah's signatures, and tossed the contracts aside. She kicked off her flip-flops and padded barefoot into the garden, breathing in the green scent of the cold grass beneath her feet, the spice of the herbs. It felt like an enormous weight had lifted from her. She walked around the perimeter walls, her head held high. Her fingertips brushed the leaves of the plants, and she imagined the flowers to come. Rosa's garden was coming back to life, and aromatic basil, mint, rosemary scented the air. In her mind she conjured the perfumes, imagined a whirlwind of petals raining down. "Awake, O north wind," she said quietly, reciting from the Song of Songs, as Liberty had so many times to her as a child. "And come, thou south; blow upon my garden, that the spices thereof may flow out. Let my beloved come into his garden."

After checking Joseph in his cot, and lighting the fire in the kitchen, Emma came back outside. She wrapped a thick wool cardigan over her dress, and settled down to wait for Delilah, watching the sun sink low.

The garden door flung open. "The next time I go to a bloody bullfight remind me to buy *sombra* not *sol*, OK?" Delilah stalked out to the terrace. Her face was sunburned, her eyes halos of white. "You could have told me how strong the sun is here. Why are my suitcases in the hallway?"

Emma turned to her. "Because you are leaving." She calmly packed up her mother's letters into the lacquer box, and tucked it under her arm.

"What?"

"I said," Emma repeated, striding toward her, scooping up the contracts on the way, "you are leaving." She shoved them into Delilah's hand. "I've signed the papers. Sell the company, take the money, and get out of my life."

"Is that it?" Delilah cried after her. "After all these years?"

"Good-bye, Delilah. Close the door on your way out."

"You can't just walk away from me. How can you?"

Emma paused, shot a glance over her shoulder. "It's easy. Watch."

SIXTY

The seat belt sign went on. Freya looked down at the sparkling carpet of lights below them, the roundabouts and roads that hadn't been there sixty years ago. The roads glowed orange, pulsed like synapses in the early morning light. "We're here, Charles. We're back."

Charles opened his eyes, gazed out of the airplane window at the rose light refracting in the glass as the plane banked into Valencia airport.

"I was just thinking, Frey. Do you remember? When they tried to take Liberty from us?"

"I'll never forget it. Never."

"I thought you'd never forgive me for saying she'd been killed."

Freya took his hand. She remembered how, after several months, Charles had appeared one day in Cornwall. She had ignored his letters, his calls. He walked toward her along Bamaluz Beach, broken and disheveled, buffeted by the wind. They had stood and looked at each other as Liberty played, splashing in the surf, oblivious to everything that had gone on. Freya had taken the first step, and they had clung to each other, their strange little family reunited beneath a soaring, dazzling sky. "It was a long time ago." She looked down at the Spanish coast, the sea glittering in the distance. "I hope Emma will be pleased to see us. She's still so angry with us."

"Can you blame her? The poor girl's just discovered her whole life is a lie."

"Thank you, Charles. A great help you are."

He patted her hand. "She'll come round. Emma loves you, Frey."

"She loves us both. And we're all the family she has now." Freya looked at him. "Why did you change your mind, about coming back?"

"Maybe it was learning about you and that Tom chap. I sat there, yesterday, thinking about how we'd missed the christening, and Delilah showed up, and we weren't there for Em."

"She understands now, about Spain."

"It's too easy for lives to fall apart. I was just thinking about Rosa, how the worst thing that can happen is losing a child. We've already lost Liberty, Frey, and she was our child too." He blinked quickly. "We lost her. Let's not lose Em."

"Where did all the years go, Charles?" Freya said, a wistfulness in her voice. "If only we'd—"

"If only? You can waste a lifetime thinking of all the 'if onlys.' There is no happily ever after. There's contentment if you are lucky. But happiness—true happiness—it's like one of my butterflies. It's dazzling, and unlikely, and you find it when you least expect it." He looked at Freya. "It goes too soon."

Freya squeezed his hand. "Not if you catch it on the wing."

SIXTY-ONE

The road to Cuenca cut through rolling hills, climbing into the mountains. The earth was red and ocher against the early morning sky, like the blood and sand of the bullring. The drive unfurled the tension in her. She was happy just to be with Luca, to travel in silence knowing that a whole day lay ahead of them. They parked outside the town and walked across the stone bridge to the cliffs. Above them, the houses clung to the rock, their wooden balconies jutting out into the abyss.

"In the summer the fields round here are full of sunflowers," Luca said. "Each face is raised to the sun in perfect formation, the heads turning through the day."

"I'd love to see it. And I'd love to stay in this *parador*." She glanced in at the beautiful old hotel.

"There is one in the grounds of the Alhambra too, in Granada." Luca guided her toward the bridge. "I've never stayed there, but every time I go to the gardens, I see people . . ." He hesitated. "Couples. It always seems so . . ."

"Romantic?"

"Yes."

Luca guided her to a narrow alleyway behind Cuenca's cathedral. "It is quite different from Valencia, no?"

"Completely." Emma gazed up at the dark, ancient walls, sensed the shadows, the relics inside. She shivered. "I still haven't got to grips with this feeling here, the dark and the light."

"*Sol y sombra*. It is Spain."

"I have to be honest, I find the dark rather frightening still."

"Perhaps you are meant to." They paused outside a studded wooden door, and he knocked. Emma heard footsteps coming toward them along a stone floor, and the door creaked open. "Concepción," Luca said as he leaned down to embrace a tiny woman dressed in black.

"Luca, Luca," Concepción said, cupping his face in her hands. "Look at you. You are working too hard still? When are you going to settle down and have some sons who can work for you, eh?" Emma sensed him tense, but he smiled.

"Concepción, this is my friend Emma. Emma, Concepción Santos."

"Come in." She stepped aside to let them enter. The door closed behind them, and the shadows, the scent of sandalwood, spices embraced them. A black cat wound its way around Emma's ankles like a skein of silk around fingertips.

"So, you are a perfumer too?" she said to Emma. It sounded like a challenge.

"Emma's family is from Valencia," Luca jumped in. "Her grandmother was from Granada, Sacromonte. She was a friend of my grandmother's."

The old woman folded her arms. "And what are you going to make? My son showed me your company on his computer." She waved her hand dismissively. "It seems very modern, all about packaging."

"That's all gone," Emma said. "I've shipped over my mum's organ of fragrances, but I want to build one of my own for the first time. I want natural essences that are rooted here." Emma thought of *duende,* something rising from the ground, a spirit, a passion. That was the magic she wanted in her work.

"It will not be easy." She pursed her lips. "People will tell you using natural ingredients is too hard."

"I'll start with simple formulas, perhaps colognes using the blossoms."

Concepción clicked her tongue. "Valencia is not the place for blossom. The best are from Sicily, and Andalusia."

"Emma knows that. We can help her with some of ours from the south," Luca interrupted.

"Of course, I will have to use ingredients from all over the world—that is how perfumery has always been—and eventually, if it all works, production will need to be on a big scale. But I want the company to have its roots here. For now, I'm going to concentrate on making bespoke fragrances."

"That is how it was in the old days," Concepción said, "before all the synthetics came along. I am glad that perfume is returning to nature. Perhaps it will become more holistic again."

"And when it takes off, will you travel again so much?" Luca asked Emma.

"No," Emma said. "The balance was all wrong before. I'll employ someone young, who wants to be on the road all the time. I'm going to stay home, and do what I'm good at."

"Making perfume, love, and babies." Concepción laughed. "Like me. I am nearly ninety and I have spent my life doing what I love." She beckoned Emma closer and whispered, "You know, in the Alhambra the concubines in the harems would eat musk so that when they made love their sweat was perfumed. I can show you some old recipes." She patted her hand, and gestured for them to follow. Emma sensed she had passed some kind of test. As they walked along the dimly lit hallway, Emma felt the temperature dropping. It was like walking into the hillside, into a cave. Concepción unlocked a side door, and flicked on dim candle lights.

"I appreciate you letting me see your studio . . ." Emma began to say, her words trailing off as she stepped into the room. It was windowless, hung with deep-red velvet drapes. Before her stood a massive mahogany table, the tiers of shelves filled with tiny glass bottles, each with a handwritten label, some with worn gilding around the stoppers. "Oh, this is incredible." She felt like a child again, remembered going to the corner shop each Saturday with Charles to select a quarter of sweets from the glass jars of gobstoppers and rainbow crystals. Hundreds of vials of pure perfume, extracts, absolutes, essences and attars glittered around her.

"I've never seen . . . do you call it an 'organ' in Spanish too? It makes my desk look amateurish." As she turned, and her eyes adjusted to the light, she saw that the back wall was stacked with shelves of jars, each filled with herbs and gleaming liquids.

"My family have worked with fragrance for centuries," Concepción said. "My ancestors came from Arabia—they created scents for Boabdil, the sultan, at the Alhambra."

"I think some of these bottles have been around since Boabdil's time," Luca said, laughing.

Concepción ran her hand affectionately over the worn wood of the work-table. "I think 'organ' is a good word. When you make a great perfume, it is like hearing a melody become a symphony. You compose a scent, it is like music."

"I've still so much to learn," Emma said, turning slowly on the spot.

"There is no hurry. All the best perfumes take years."

"That's what my mum used to say."

Concepción's face fell. "Now there is no one left in my family who is interested. I am the last." She waved her hand toward the far wall. "Some of these ingredients have been macerating for years. Like wine, some crops and some years are better than others. See what you think," she said and left them alone.

"This is amazing," Emma said as she leaned down to examine the labels. *Ambergris,* she thought. *Of course.* "Some of these bottles look like they are hundreds of years old. This glass looks Venetian."

"Concepción is like my grandmother, they never throw anything away," Luca said. "Since the war, I think they like to feel they have enough put away."

"You know, when I trained in Grasse, I learned to memorize three thousand smells," she said. "I think there are some here I've never even thought of." She opened a vial, and inhaled. "There are only a few hundred naturals. That's what I'm interested in now."

"Won't that limit you?"

Emma shook her head. "Perfume's rooted in nature, and the combinations are almost infinite. I love that. Mum always said the oil is the soul of the plant, the flower. To her, perfume was sacred."

"And you agree?" Luca smiled as he saw the excitement in her eyes. He settled back on the high wood stool by the table. "What is that one?"

"Close your eyes." As she approached him, his knee brushed against her thigh, and he peeked through one eye. She put the bottle down and unwound the red pashmina scarf from her neck. She covered his nose, his lips. "Breathe," she said. "This will clear your nose, your palette." Luca's fingertips jumped on his thigh as she blindfolded him. "No cheating," she whispered, her breath against his ear. "Trust me." Emma lifted the bottle toward him. "Now, what do you smell?"

"Sandalwood," he said. "That's easy."

"Very good." Emma took a clean flask from the table, and measured out a small amount, dropping it into perfume alcohol. She turned, and Luca sensed her hips shifting close to him. Every noise, every smell intensified. "Now, what's this?"

He inhaled. "Spice." A warm, woody scent intoxicated him. "Cinnamon, or clove?" He reached out blindly for her, found her waist.

"Excellent," she murmured. Emma worked quickly now. He heard the delicate "chink" of the glass bottles as she sorted through the vials, felt the shift and curve of her back as she conjured the fragrance.

"What are you doing?" He reached blindly for her hand. He was aware of his breath, the beat of his own heart. Snatches of fragrance came to him like the notes of a melody—lavender, orangewood, neroli, leather . . . something he couldn't name, like earth after rain.

"Patience!" she said, laughing.

He heard the glass dropper "chink" a final time, and his lips parted as the fragrance came to him: warm skin, summer air, sex. "All I can smell is . . ."

"You," Emma said. She took his hand, dropped a little of the mix against the inside of his wrist, and massaged it in with her thumb. "What do you think?"

Luca lifted his hand, still in hers, breathed in. His senses swam, he felt like he was waking up after a long sleep. Emma loosened the scarf, he felt it fall away against his cheek. "I think you are a magician." He took her face in his hands, closed his eyes as he kissed her then. The air around them seemed to dilate as their lips touched. The scarf fell to the floor, to the shadows as they held each other. He murmured her name as he kissed her neck, his hands in her hair, hers tracing the curve of his shoulders, his back.

"What did you put in that?" He smiled as he caught his breath.

"A secret." She touched his lips with her fingertips. "I didn't think . . ."

"That I wanted you?"

"That you felt the same." Emma lowered her gaze, but Luca cupped her jaw in his palm, made her look at him.

"I wanted you the moment I saw you," he said.

"But, you said to Olivier we were just friends—"

"What else could I say? That I had fallen for a woman with a broken heart?" Emma's lips parted. "Olivier is my closest friend. He was worried that I would be hurt again, after Alejandra. That is all."

"He was trying to protect you?" Emma thought of the night of the dance.

"I had to give you time, Emma, time for you to grow strong enough to love again." Luca glanced toward the door. They could hear Concepción's footsteps tapping along the corridor.

"I don't want to wait any longer." Emma turned to the desk and wrote out a label, attaching it to the vial. Her stomach was tight with desire, senses quickened. She eased in the stopper as Luca pulled her to him. He kissed her then, a kiss like she had never known. She felt herself falling, fearlessly. The door creaked open, and she stepped away, breathless.

"*Oh, me gusta.*" Concepción tottered toward them carrying a tea tray with a decanter of sherry, cut glass twinkling in the dim light. "Very masculine. Very . . ." She looked at them both, her gaze dancing. "It reminds me a little of Peau d'Espagne."

"I'm glad. That's exactly what I was aiming for," Emma said.

"But there is something extra . . . it is not musk?"

"Ambergris."

"Ah, interesting." Concepción put the sherry down and glanced at them, knowingly. "I like the balance. Very aphrodisiac. You have the start of something here, I think. What will you call it?"

Emma smiled. There could only be one name. *"Duende."* She turned to the old woman. "You must let me pay for the ingredients," she said, reaching for her bag.

"I won't hear of it." Concepción clapped her hands. "So, what do you think?" She poured them all a glass of sherry, offered around a plate of salted almonds.

Emma looked at Luca, and she saw her desire echoed in his gaze. She licked the salt from her lips, felt the sherry coursing warm down her throat. "It would be an honor to continue your work. I'd love you to teach me everything you know," she said to Concepción.

"What will you do now, Concepción?" Luca asked her.

"I shall retire. My sister lives in Málaga. She has been asking me to come and live with them. This house has already sold. They are going to turn it into some kind of tourist attraction." She waved her hand at the perfumes. "All I care is that this goes on."

"I think," Emma said, looking at Luca, "it is only just beginning."

SIXTY-TWO

On the drive home from Cuenca, Emma leaned against the open window, the wind rushing through her hair. She pressed her lips against her hand, suppressing a smile. Joy bubbled in her like freshwater. She held the memory of that afternoon like a jewel, remembered the diffuse light playing on the high white walls of their room in the *parador,* the warm breeze lifting the muslin curtains, the golden hours they spent discovering each other. These were moments waiting to be found. She glanced at Luca as he drove, and he reached for her hand, lacing their fingers together. It felt to Emma that the wall between them had fallen as effortlessly as a tower of children's building blocks, and the easy intimacy she had longed for was there all along. After that stolen afternoon, their lives fell into step together.

Luca pulled up outside the Villa del Valle, and turned off the engine. In the village, the bonfires had been lit, and the breeze through the open window was scented with orangewood smoke. They sat in silence for a time, listening to the distant music in the market square, the engine ticking as it cooled, unwilling to break the spell, to return to the world. Emma sat with her bare feet tucked up, her arms wrapped around her legs. Luca turned to her as he took the keys out, and laid his arm over the back of her seat.

"So." He tilted his head, smiling.

"Coming in?" Emma said.

"I thought you'd never ask."

He came around to her door, and opened it for her. Emma stepped out onto the pavement, her tan leather sandals swinging from one hand. The pavement was warm beneath her feet, and her body ached pleasurably as she walked. She felt alive, renewed.

Luca buried his face in Emma's hair as they reached the front door of the Villa del Valle. "You smell wonderful."

"I smell of sex," she whispered as she turned to him. The sunset flamed amber and rose above them. When he kissed her she felt the pillow fullness of her bruised lips.

"If you could create a fragrance that makes people feel how I feel at this moment . . ."

"We could do that, something aphrodisiac." She breathed in the scent of her jasmine perfume, a new deep pulse where it had melded with the fragrance she had created for Luca in Cuenca. This was the perfume she had been searching for. *If I have to work a lifetime,* she thought, *one day I'll capture this moment.*

"More than aphrodisiac." He traced her jawline with his fingertips. *"Duende* . . . magic . . . love."

"You love me?" She laughed softly. "You. Love. Me . . ."

"I've loved you from the moment I first saw you." Luca kissed her, her back arching to him.

"Excuse me," Solé said, opening the front door. She slung her bag over her shoulder, and sidled past.

"Solé!" Emma brushed back her hair. "Is everything OK?"

"Sure." She glanced at them, a smile playing on her lips. "I heard your car—"

"Of course, you want to get to the Fallas."

"We'll see you later at the party?" Solé said.

Luca glanced at Emma. "Perhaps."

"Have fun," Emma said as Solé walked away.

"Do you want to go?" he asked Emma.

"I'd rather have a quiet night in." She dropped her bag inside the door. "We have the house to ourselves, Joseph is asleep, it's early still . . ." She reached up to Luca, her fingers sliding inside the stiff collar of his shirt.

"Ah," Luca said, pointing at the arc of lights flickering on the baby monitor on the hall table. "You spoke too soon."

Emma padded back into the kitchen with Joseph in her arms. "Here we are," she said. Luca had lit the stove and the lamps, and a bottle of wine stood open on the counter beside the old pestle and mortar. He looked up from stoking the fire as she walked in, and Emma felt a jolt of happiness.

"Hey, little man." Luca dusted off his hands, and took the baby from her.

"Are you hungry? I could—" Emma started to say. A knock at the door interrupted her. "Who can that be?" She strode toward the hall.

Luca lifted Joseph up until they were eye to eye, and pulled a face, waiting for the reward of a smile. "Ah, tonight, Joseph Luca," he said, grinning back, "we are the happiest men alive."

Dread filled Emma's heart. *What if it's Delilah? I can't believe she left that easily.* She could see the silhouette of a slim woman in the frosted glass, and as she reached for the door handle, Emma steeled herself.

"Freya?" Emma cried out. "What are you doing here?"

"Surprise!" Freya said. She opened her arms, hopefully.

"More like a shock," Charles said, stepping out of the shadows. "Hello, Em."

"I don't— No, it is. It's a wonderful surprise." Emma embraced them in turn.

"We thought you might need a hand with Delilah," Charles said. "But it seems we are too late."

"The office left a message on my phone that I only picked up after we landed," Freya said. "'Miss Stafford has closed the deal.'"

"I know, I signed the papers and kicked her out," Emma said. "I can't believe she went so easily."

"Really? She never gave a damn about any of us. She's a wealthy woman now," Charles said. "She has everything she wished for—"

"Except Joe," Freya interrupted. "You have to be careful what you wish for. Sometimes the price is too high."

"I'm just glad it's over," Emma said. "Good luck to her."

"Good riddance, more like," Charles said. "Now what, Em?"

"Now this." Emma gestured at the house. "A fresh start. I should have called you, I'm sorry. It's just been—" Emma glanced back into the house toward the kitchen and smiled. "Come in, come in," she said, ushering them through the door. "Where are your bags?"

"We didn't want to assume," Freya said. "We've booked into the little pension in town tonight."

"There was no need to do that. We'll get your things in the morning. There's lots of room." Emma gestured up the stairs. "I think you know where everything is." She glanced at Freya and smiled. The kitchen was empty when they walked in, the doors to the terrace open.

"Where have you been?" Freya said. "We've been sitting in the café down the road all day. Your phone was off."

"As usual," Charles muttered. He looked around the kitchen. "Remarkable. It hasn't changed at all." The sky had darkened outside, and he jumped at the sound of the first firework. "Isn't it the Cremà, St. Joseph's Day, today? By tonight the whole of Valencia will be blazing."

"Talking of Joseph, where is the baby?" Freya said.

"With Luca, they must be in the garden." Emma started to walk to the terrace. She heard him talking to someone, voices drifting around from the front of the house.

"Darling, wait." Freya took her hand. "I'm so sorry." She held her gaze. "We both are."

"Sorry?" Emma said. "For what? For saving Mum's life?"

"For all the lies." Freya blinked, her eyes gleaming.

Emma embraced her, held her tight. "I love you, Gammy. It changes nothing," she said. "I know now, I know what you both went through here." She stepped back and took Charles's hand, looking in turn at them both. "You did what you did to protect Mum."

"Thank you, Em," Charles said, blinking quickly. He looked over at the terrace door as Luca walked in. "How do you do?" He stepped forward. "You must be Luca? This is Freya, and I'm—"

"Carlos?" Immaculada stepped out from behind Luca.

"Macu?" Charles said.

Freya laughed, clapped her hands together. "I don't believe it." She hobbled forward, embraced her old friend. She glanced at Charles, saw the color had risen in his cheeks.

"Of course, you all know one another?" Luca said.

"What a marvelous surprise," Macu said, linking her arm through Freya's. "We were all on the way to the Fallas, and Olivier saw Luca's car." She tilted her head as she looked at Charles. "You haven't changed at all," she said, her gaze softening.

Emma took the baby from Luca, and handed him to Freya. She cradled him in her arms, and smiled down. "There, there," she said as he grizzled. "You don't know me, do you?"

"This is your great-grandmother," Emma said, putting her arm around Freya. She heard Freya gasp. "And this is your great-uncle Charles . . . Carlos." She smiled as Charles shuffled over.

"What a handsome fellow," he said. "Hello, young man."

Freya gently shifted the baby in her arms. "Doesn't he look like Em?" she said. As Emma went to greet Paloma and Olivier, Freya looked up at Charles. "I can't believe it," she said quietly, her voice catching.

"See? I told you she'd forgive us."

"Poppycock. You were as worried as me."

"This is what it was all for, Frey." Charles's eyes glistened. "Everything we fought for, everything we did to protect Liberty." He smiled as the baby gripped his finger tightly.

The air in the garden was rich with the smell of woodsmoke and cordite. From the village came the flash and crackle of *traca* firecrackers, echoing the booming explosions from Valencia. The night sky pulsed and glowed as one by one flames engulfed the papier-mâché figures of dragons, princesses and knights in the village square.

Luca opened a bottle of champagne, and handed glasses around. "To us," he said to Emma, chinking his glass against hers.

"We should make a toast," Olivier called to them. He caught Luca's eye. "This is a celebration."

Emma raised her glass. "To family," she said. "To all of you. To Mum, who made all of this possible."

"To Liberty," Charles said. Emma followed his gaze to where Freya and Macu sat, with Joseph in his Moses basket between them.

"*Viva la libertad*!" Macu said, smiling at Charles.

"Oh, we shall tell you some tales," Emma heard Freya saying to the baby. "The most incredible story in the world . . ."

"Come." Luca stepped close behind Emma, slipped his hand into hers. "There's not much time," he said. He led her away, across the cool lawn to

the steps of the bell tower, and they climbed up into the darkness. "Are you
OK?" he said as they reached the top. "You don't like heights?"

"I'm not afraid." Emma caught her breath, and placed her glass on the
white wall. Luca put his arm around her shoulders, and they turned toward
Valencia just as the first fireworks soared above the city, showering the deep
blue velvet sky with silver and gold. *I'm not afraid anymore,* she thought,
leaning into the warmth of his embrace.

Emma looked out across the orange groves. Above the golden halo of
light from the fires in the city the sky shone with thousands of stars. She
thought of her mother as she looked at them. She felt again the ache, the
longing for her soft embrace, the warm scent of roses. She thought of Rosa,
dancing for Jordi in her red dress in the firelight, of Freya and Tom, walking through the Spanish hills arm in arm, full of such precious joy and happiness. She thought of all the lives, the loves, cut short by war, all the years
that might have been. She thought of Joe, reading her message in the Twin
Towers as the shadow of a plane passed over the streets of New York. She
looked at Luca as he watched the sky, and honored the woman he had loved,
who had loved him. She saw all their lives written out across the night.

"Who knew it could end like this?" Luca said, gazing down at the garden. "Look at what you have done. Isn't it beautiful?" Strings of white lights
shimmered among the orange trees, and the pool reflected the fireworks soaring overhead.

Emma saw the people she loved most in the world gathered there in the
garden, and the past, the present, the future fell together as one. She touched
Rosa's locket at her throat, claiming this moment, forever, for all of them.
"The end is never the end," she said, turning to Luca, ready, at last. "It's always the beginning of something."

AUTHOR'S NOTE

In July 1936, forces led by Francisco Franco and a group of rebel generals staged a military coup against the democratically elected government of the Second Spanish Republic. It is estimated the Spanish Civil War of 1936 to 1939 that ensued cost the lives of half a million people. Another half a million Spaniards fled as refugees. This battle was the prelude to World War II. Franco's rebel Nationalists gained support from Hitler's Nazi troops and Mussolini's Italian fascists.

Nearly 60,000 volunteers from over fifty countries joined the International Brigades as combatants and noncombatants to fight with the Republican Army against the Nationalists and their supporters. These included 2,800 American volunteers who fought with the Abraham Lincoln Brigade and other battalions.

Among the International Brigades' volunteers were many women, who mostly worked with medical units. Spanish women like Rosa both helped behind the lines and fought side by side at the front with the men on equal terms. Some 200,000 people died in combat—4,900 of them from the Brigades. The other 300,000 who lost their lives during the war and the reprisals that followed the Nationalist victory were murdered, executed, or killed in bombing raids. Many of these victims were women and children. Valencia held out against the Nationalists until the end. It was the last major city to fall in Spain. Veterans from the International Brigades and Republican exiles went on to fight fascism in Europe in World War II.

The Spanish Civil War divided the country and individual families. Until 2007 there was a national *pacto de olvido,* a pact of forgetting. The Spanish writer George Santayana said, "Those who cannot remember the past are condemned to repeat it." Now, thanks to the Law of Historical Memory, the history of the war is being rewritten. This account of women at war, and their families, blends fiction with the real events of that time. The true memories of those involved bear witness to the extraordinary sacrifices ordinary people make for freedom.

ACKNOWLEDGMENTS

Many people have generously shared their knowledge and experience during the research for this book. Particular thanks goes to Professor Paul Preston, Jim Jump of the International Brigades Memorial Trust, Emilio Silva of the Association for the Recovery of Historical Memory and Cynthia Jackson of the Robert Capa Archive at the International Center of Photography for their extensive help and research suggestions. I would also like to thank Stuart Christie, Angela Jackson, Natalia Benjamin of the Basque Children of '37 Association, James Cronan of the National Archives, Mónica Moreira, Harriet Batchelor Patrizi, Piers Garnham, Reverend Alison Craven of St. Luke's and Christ Church, Tim Birch, Susana Gil, Pilar Ballesteros, Ivan Llanza Ortiz, David Barros, Jorge Garzón, John Muddeman, Julian Donohue of the Lepidopterists' Society, Mark Ritchie of the Royal Borough of Kensington and Chelsea, and Lisa Wood of John Rylands University Archive. Thanks also to Drs. Rookmaaker, Foster, Friday and Asher of Cambridge University, Elaine Oliver, Jonathan Smith of Trinity College Library and Tracy Wilkinson of King's College Archive. Isabelle Gellé and Luca Turin were generous with their inspiring advice about perfumes.

I would like to thank Peter Stanford, and David Whiting of the Cecil Day-Lewis Estate for permission to quote the beautiful extract from "Walking Away."

My thanks go to Leila Aboulela, to Sherry Ashworth, Nicholas Royle, my MA group at MMU and the maniacs of Moniack Mhor for their help with the story.

Thank you to my wonderful agent, Sheila Crowley, and all at Curtis Brown. Thanks both to the team at Atlantic in London, and to all at Thomas Dunne Books, particularly my editor, Anne Brewer.

To paraphrase Marcel Proust, the "charming gardeners" who make my soul blossom have supported me with great patience in the writing of this book—to my children, and to my family, with love and thanks always. Don't forget to smell the flowers.

1. Which story line did you relate to most, and why—the contemporary or historical?

2. Do the "real" and entirely fictional characters feel believable? Do you relate to their predicaments?

3. How do ideas about perfume and gardens weave through both story lines?

4. What surprised or shocked you in the story? Did you know about the events of the Spanish Civil War before reading *The Perfume Garden*? What do you think now about the role women played?

5. Why do you think so many ordinary men and women from all over the world joined the International Brigades to fight fascism in Spain?

6. Why do you think people in Spain are still reluctant to talk about the war? Do you think the past should remain buried?

St. Martin's
Griffin